What people are saying about …

THE RELUCTANT PROPHET

"I love this book! Hop on and ride with this 'reluctant prophet'—
but hold on tight, because the call of God not only takes Allison
the Tour Guide out of her comfort zone, but the reader as well. An
important novel about the awesome, quirky, breathtaking adventure
of obeying God's Nudge."

Neta Jackson, author of *The Yada
Yada Prayer Group* novels and The
Yada Yada House of Hope series

"In Allison Chamberlain, Nancy Rue has created a fresh and
unique protagonist to challenge all who follow Christ. How will we
change the world? By being willing to leave our comfortable pews
and habitual routines to truly *listen* to the voice of the Spirit …
and show the world that Jesus called us to love. Not to take care of
ourselves, but to take risks in loving others. *The Reluctant Prophet* is
a wonderful book with the power to changes hearts and lives."

Angela Hunt, author of *The Debt*

"In her latest novel, *The Reluctant Prophet*, Nancy Rue asks this
question: What can God do with broken people? The answer Rue
comes up with is humorous, hopeful, and challenging. A story to
remind us that God is involved in the everyday, and in love with

everyone. You'll cheer this motley band of people who decide love is more important than living a safe, easy life."

Bonnie Grove, award-winning
author of *Talking to the Dead*

"If you believe following Jesus can be an exciting adventure that is baffling at times and even a little messy, with zero tolerance for self-righteous complacency, then *The Reluctant Prophet* is a book for you."

Bill Myers, author of *The God Hater*

"*The Reluctant Prophet* is a bold, wonderful novel. If you have ever felt a Nudge and thought it might be God trying to get your attention, read this book. It might just give you the courage to follow that Nudge and see where it leads. Nancy Rue writes about the tough issues of life and faith with grace, love, and daring. I am so glad God Nudged Nancy to write and so glad that she followed, Harley and all!"

Joyce Magnin, author of *The Prayers of Agnes
Sparrow* and *Charlotte Figg Takes Over Paradise*

THE RELUCTANT PROPHET

OTHER FICTION BY NANCY RUE

For Adults

Pascal's Wager

Antonia's Choice

Tristan's Gap

For Adults, with Stephen Arterburn

Healing Stones

Healing Waters

Healing Sands

For Tweens

The Christian Heritage Series

The Lily Series

The Sophie Series

The Lucy Novels

For Teens

Row This Boat Ashore

The Janis Project

Home By Another Way

The Raise the Flag Series

The 'Nama Beach High Series

The RL (Real Life) Novels

THE RELUCTANT PROPHET

A NOVEL

NANCY RUE

David C Cook

transforming lives together

THE RELUCTANT PROPHET
Published by David C Cook
4050 Lee Vance View
Colorado Springs, CO 80918 U.S.A.

David C Cook Distribution Canada
55 Woodslee Avenue, Paris, Ontario, Canada N3L 3E5

David C Cook U.K., Kingsway Communications
Eastbourne, East Sussex BN23 6NT, England

David C Cook and the graphic circle C logo
are registered trademarks of Cook Communications Ministries.

The website addresses recommended throughout this book are offered as a
resource to you. These websites are not intended in any way to be or imply an
endorsement on the part of David C Cook, nor do we vouch for their content.

This story is a work of fiction. All characters and events are the product of the author's
imagination. Any resemblance to any person, living or dead, is coincidental.

The Scripture quotation on page 11 is taken from the *Holy Bible, New
International Version® NIV®* Copyright © 1973, 1978, 1984 International
Bible Society. The Scripture quotation on page 493 is taken from *THE
MESSAGE*. Copyright © by Eugene H. Peterson 1993, 1994, 1995, 1996,
2000, 2001, 2002. Used by permission of NavPress Publishing Group.

LCCN 2010932713
ISBN 978-1-4347-6496-6
eISBN 978-0-7814-0574-4

© 2010 Nancy Rue
Published in association with the literary agency of Alive Communications,
Inc., 7680 Goddard St., Suite 200, Colorado Springs, CO 80920.

The Team: Don Pape, Jamie Chavez, Amy Kiechlin,
Melody Bryce, Erin Prater, Karen Athen
Cover Design: DogEared Design, Kirk DouPonce
Cover Photo: iStockphoto, royalty-free

Printed in the United States of America
First edition 2010

1 2 3 4 5 6 7 8 9 10

080510

*For the sisters of Magdalene in Nashville, Tennessee,
who shared their stories and themselves and
humbled me with their courage and faith*

Acknowledgments

There are two kinds of readers—those who skip the acknowledgments and those who see them as peeks at what breathed real life into a book. If you fall into the latter category, enjoy a glimpse at the people I counted on unashamedly.

- **Rob Seiner and Rich Petrina,** Rider's Edge teachers who tried, in vain, to get me going on a motorcycle. My complete failure was due in no way to their teaching skills!

- **Clark Vitulli, Allen Good, and Shannon Ashley,** Harley-Davidson of St. Augustine, Florida, who opened their store to me and answered at least one thousand (clueless) questions.

- **All the women riders** associated with Bumpus Harley-Davidson of Murfreesboro, Tennessee, whose encouragement and stories and all-out living filled this sometimes somber story—and me—with fun.

- **Angel,** my St. Augustine carriage driver who taught me everything I needed to know about being a horse-drivin' tour guide—and took me on one unforgettable ride.

- **Jeremiah McElwain**—sunglasses expert! Bonner has him to thank for the right shades.

- **Megan Lee** of Cumberland University in Lebanon, Tennessee, and **Pamela Talley** of Washington University in St. Louis, Missouri, whose work as my intern/research assistants added an accuracy I couldn't have pulled off on my own.

◻ **Jackie Colburn,** who graciously shared her prophetic gift with me.

◻ **Lee Hough,** my literary agent, who helped me hone the story; **Don Pape,** who believed in it; and **Ingrid Beck, Jamie Chavez,** and **Erin Prater,** my editors who caught my mistakes. If you find any, they're all mine.

◻ **The women of Magdalene** in Nashville, Tennessee—especially **Valerie, Gladys, and Tracy**—who shared their stories, their hearts, their faith, themselves. They are living statements of the God-infused power of the human spirit.

◻ **The Reverend Becca Stevens** of St. Augustine's Chapel at Vanderbilt University in Nashville, Tennessee, founder of Magdalene, who inspired *The Reluctant Prophet* with her tireless work of respecting the dignity of every woman who wants to change her life in Christ. Every woman.

◻ **My husband, Jim Rue,** who takes me anywhere I want to go on his Harley—one ride at a time.

What I am commanding you today is not too difficult for
you or beyond your reach.... No, the word is very near you;
it is in your mouth and in your heart so you may obey it.
—Deuteronomy 30:11–14

Life is a church
These are the sacraments
This is the altar
Love is the spirit
Making the blue planet turn.
—Marcus Hummon

CHAPTER ONE

I found Jesus seven years ago, but until that Sunday morning, I didn't know what to do with him.

It wasn't for lack of asking. Nor was I above whining. I'd even taken to begging.

That day, in my usual third-row-from-the-back pew in Flagler Community Church, I started into what I called Allison Chamberlain's Pathetic Pleading Prayer: "Come on—I get it already. But what am I supposed to be *doing* about it?"

I had the usual undeniable sense that God was listening, probably leaning over to Jesus and saying, "There she goes with the badgering, Son." What I couldn't sense was his adding, "What do you say we throw her a bone?"

I'd have taken anything and run with it.

I recrossed my legs and tugged my uniform jacket over my hips and noticed that it didn't quite shimmy down like it used to. Too much time spent sitting in a carriage waiting for a fare. I folded my hands, angelically prayerlike in my lap, and refixed my gaze on the Reverend J. Garrett Howard, who was holding forth from the center aisle. This was his first Sunday not preaching from the cantilevered pulpit that hovered above us like Care Flight from Heaven. He said at the beginning of the service that he wanted to be closer to us as he brought forth the Word.

Very avant-garde, the Reverend Howard.

"What do you do when you're stricken by the slings and arrows of outrageous fortune?" he said now.

Also very literary.

"You take it to the foot of the cross."

Joshie McElhinney's towhead bobbed into my line of vision, blocking out Rev. Garry and giving me full view of his seven-year-old self. He appeared to be doing a 360-degree survey of the congregation, finger inserted into left nostril. Was he looking for the foot of the cross? For a second I thought he was about to raise his hand and ask for coordinates. The seven-year-old in me wanted to ask the same thing.

I followed his gaze until his mother put her hand on top of his head and twisted it forward like she was turning a jar lid. Once again I tried to focus on the Reverend Garry, but my glance snagged on Frank Parker, a fellow small-group member, who wore a puckered expression. Was he looking for the cross too? Or was that just acid reflux? Probably not the latter. Frank was far too much the Southern gentleman for indigestion.

I felt a little queasy myself, though. What was wrong with me? I adjusted my jacket yet again and telescoped my gaze toward the sermon. Except that across the aisle, Mary Alice Moss said, "Amen," and I had to look at my watch. Bless Mary Alice's heart. If she was true to form, we'd be hearing another one of those about …

"Amen."

… now. Thirty-two seconds on the nose. Garry must be into his third point at this juncture. Another thirty-two and …

"Amen."

My wonderful, multichinned Mary Alice must know exactly how to get to the foot of the cross. Or was it that the Reverend Garrett Howard was really that precisely inspiring?

Then why wasn't I inspired right now?

I mean, I always checked out India Morehead's outfit when she slipped into her pew because the woman could definitely put one together. I always watched Frank execute his ushering duties as if every service were a formal wedding. I always caught Bonner Bailey checking me out over the top of his hymnal. But until that day none of it had kept me from at least catching a thread of the sermon. I needed those threads to hold me together. I was a veritable tapestry woven from seven years' worth of them. Okay, maybe not something so elegant as a tapestry. Burlap feedbag, maybe.

Okay—*what* was going *on* with me? I snapped the jacket down so hard I felt the seam pop. And then I felt something else. A Nudge, like someone had given me a healthy shove with a beefy elbow. It was palpable—even though nobody was sitting on either side of me.

"Let us pray," the Reverend Howard said.

Heads bowed in unanimous reverence. I stared over the tops of ponytails and buzz cuts and tinted-blue perms, waiting for someone to poke me again while all the other eyes were closed. Nothing moved but Garry Howard's mustached lips as he poured out his prayer. No one else spoke, except a clear voice in my head.

Allison, it said. *Go out and buy a Harley.*

I whipped my head around, sharply enough to pull Bonner Bailey's eyes up from his lap and cock his head at me. I was obviously acting as weirded out as I felt. And I was obviously the only one who had heard it. Which meant it was probably my imagination.

Or maybe *I* was the one with acid reflux.

Bonner got to me before I could even slide my hymnal back into its
rack after the final song. Not that I'd uttered a note. Buy a Harley?
I was undoubtedly nuts, and I was afraid if I opened my mouth I'd
start reciting the preamble to the constitution or something.

"You okay, Allison?" Bonner said, with the usual touch-retract at
my elbow. He definitely wasn't the one who'd Nudged me. "Did I see
you having neck issues?"

"Thanks for asking," I said. I turned my head and let C1 and
C2 pop. He sympathetically readjusted his own inside the just-ironed
Oxford button-down collar.

"All better," I said.

"Is that from driving a horse all day?"

No. It was from having God tell me to purchase a motorcycle.
Only, as the seconds passed with Bonner smoothing the pockets of
his pressed Dockers, getting ready to ask me to brunch the way he did
absolutely every Sunday, the possibility that God had actually spoken
those words to me became less likely. A little Nexium and I'd be fine.

"Miss Allison."

Frank Parker was the only person who called me that, and thank
heaven for him at that moment. I wasn't in the mood for Bonner and
a Belgian waffle. Hallucination or not, I had to get to work.

Frank sidled up to the pew Bonner and I were conversing over
and settled his hands into prayer position at his lapels. "Miss Allison,
I don't mean to fuss at you, but—"

"Is it Bernard?" I said.

Bonner smothered a smirk with his hand. Frank nodded as if he
were in pain.

"Out front—he just …"

"I'm sorry, Frank," I said. "He must have busted another radiator hose. I've got to get that fixed."

"How are you going to do that?" Bonner said, straight-faced. "Dehydrate him?"

"We just can't have that, Miss Allison. Pastor is on the front steps greeting people, and in that heat, all you can smell is ..."

Frank looked from me to Bonner and back again, watered-down, blue eyes beseeching. When neither of us filled in the blank for him, he whispered, "Horse urine."

Bonner choked, and I took pity on poor Frank.

"I'll take care of it," I said. I gave his suit sleeve an affectionate tug.

"I just wish you wouldn't ... park it ... him ... there. Next thing you know, he'll be ..."

"Pooping, Frank?" Bonner said.

His eyes were practically streaming—he was working that hard to hold it in. I gave him a nudge and slipped my arm through Frank's.

"I don't usually work Sundays," I told him as I steered him toward the vestibule. "But business is so slow right now, I have to grab all the fares I can. I wouldn't have time to go all the way to the stables after church, so—"

"I understand, Missy." Frank slid into his soothing-daddy voice and patted my hand. At sixty-four, he actually was old enough to be my father, but at forty-two, I hardly felt like I needed one. "You go on to work and I'll see that ... things ... get cleaned up."

Bonner stood in the doorway ahead of us, shaking his head toward Valencia Street in mock solemnity. "Looks like your worst fears have been realized, Frank. You're going to need a fire hose."

Frank composed his face and, with a departing pat on my arm, hurried out and down the steps.

"You are evil in your soul," I said to Bonner.

"What? What did I say?"

"Allison," a voice purred behind me, "*nice* haircut, Honey."

India Morehead ran what I knew to be a perfectly manicured hand along the ends of my hair before brushing her lips against my cheek. She pecked Bonner's, too. India took to heart the admonition about greeting one another with a holy kiss. I didn't tell Bonner she'd left a Marvelous Mauve imprint just above his jawline.

She sailed the ends of a gray spun silk scarf behind her and surveyed me through slightly squinted dark eyes. I always wondered if India could actually *close* them with that much mascara clotting her lashes. "Shoulder length is a good start," she said. "If you go a little shorter, some highlights would be good, just to accentuate your natural blond." She dipped into sotto voce. "And cover any gray. Not that you have much. Just a little shorter, though, I think. Don't you?"

That question was for Bonner, who rested his chin on one hand and nodded.

India's gaze swept my uniform. "I hate that they dress you in beige. It washes you out. Something in a nice teal would bring out your eyes."

"Definitely," Bonner said.

"I'd love to stay for the makeover," I said, "but I've got to get to work."

"We'll see you Wednesday?" India said.

"Always."

I wiggled my fingers in a wave over my shoulder and tried to jockey my way out past the handshaking line.

The Reverend Garrett Howard, however, was quick for an old guy.

"You're not leaving without a hug, Allison."

He had his arms outstretched, the sleeves of his vestment spread like wings. It was hard not to compare them to the white waves of still-thick hair that unfurled from his forehead. He'd only recently taken to embracing members of his flock, having previously been a rather staid clasper of fingers. The last couple of ministerial retreats had convinced him he needed to enter the age of up-close-and-personal, which he saw as rather new and daring. I had to give him credit for trying at age seventy-something, though. India had told me he'd even recently acquired a Bluetooth.

I let him pull me into a this-is-a-hug-isn't-it side-armed thing and smiled. I expected the weekly query about my health followed by, "How are things in the datil pepper business?" I'd stopped reminding him the datil pepper shop had closed a year ago and that I was now giving horse-drawn carriage tours. When I'd first come to Flagler Church, it had taken the dear man two years to remember that my name wasn't Alice.

But today he surprised me with: "Now—you heard in the sermon that I'm giving the small groups a new charge."

"Ah," I said. So that was what we were taking to the foot of the cross.

"I want you to head up this one in your group. I think it's about time you took on a leadership role."

He patted both of my shoulders simultaneously. There was a lot of stroking and prodding of me going on today. This one made even less sense than the Nudge that told me to go get myself a Hog.

"You make sure she knows she's ready for this," he said over my shoulder.

"Done." Bonner motioned with his head toward the steps. "Over brunch."

"I told you I have to work."

"Oh—right."

He glanced at Garry Howard, but the reverend was disappearing into the shelter of the cool church. A dark splotch of perspiration had already filled the space on his robe between his shoulder blades.

"Okay," I said to Bonner, "you want to talk? Ride with me to the Bay Front."

It was a sly move. Bonner would have no part of animals, especially Bernard, who—unlike most of the carriage horses that weighed in at about eight hundred pounds—tipped the scales at two thousand, and had once overrun a Fourth of July parade when some kid in the crowd set off a firecracker. Bonner was a sure thing for a rain check.

"All right," he said. "I can walk back and get my car. It's a nice day."

"It's already eighty-five degrees! The humidity alone will probably kill you."

"Are you inviting me or not?"

"I'm just saying." I headed toward Bernard, who left off scraping his chin on the carriage shaft and pricked up his ears at me. His big Belgian head tossed, sending the dark mane dancing.

"Hey, buddy," I said. "We've got a passenger. You okay with that?"

Bonner raised an eyebrow at me as he climbed up onto the carriage's tuck-and-roll driver's seat, which was only wide enough for me and half of another person. "Why wouldn't he be okay with it? That's all he *does* is haul passengers around."

"Yeah," I said, "but he doesn't usually like a man in the seat with me."

"Are you serious?"

"As a heart attack." I pulled my sunglasses out of my bag and popped them on. "But we'll see how it goes."

Bonner slit his eyes at me, the look he always took on when he wasn't sure whether to believe me. In truth, he could always believe me. I never did have the knack for pulling off a lie. Bernard gave his chestnut head another toss—not necessarily a friendly one—and I told him to cool it before I signaled him forward. He ambled out onto Valencia and clopped toward Cordova Street, black tail flipping toward the lines on purpose. Eventually I'd have to stop and untangle him.

Bonner kept his eyes glued to Bernard's flanks as he put on his Ray-Ban Aviators. They hung from black Croakies dipping alongside his ears and resting on his already-dampening collar. The thing made him look like an entrepreneurial librarian.

"Welcome to Camelot Carriage Service," I said, "St. Augustine's first and most reputable guide to the nation's oldest city."

"Allison—"

"Sit back and relax in old-world style as you discover all the secrets of this ancient town—"

"Allison!"

I lowered my voice to a hoarse whisper. "Keep in mind that this is not your basic tacky Orange and Green Sightseeing Trolley—but you already know that, being a discerning lover of history." I winked at Bonner. "Not just another tourist."

"I don't need the tour. I could probably give it myself."

"But *I* am a licensed guide. I had to pass a test for this job, you know."

"Congratulations," he said drily. "You're dodging the issue."

I guided Bernard right onto Cordova and listened as his hooves settled into their rhythm on the brick pavement. Bonner was soft spoken, even when he was annoyed with me, which meant Bernard would probably behave.

Rats.

"Fifty-five years before the Mayflower landed at Plymouth Rock," I said. "Forty-two years before the Jamestown settlement, *La Florida* was established here at St. Augustine."

"As the oldest continuously occupied European settlement in the United States—blah, blah, blah. Realtors have to pass that test too."

"No kidding?"

"Garry's serious—he wants you to head up this new group thing."

I took Bernard right on Artillery Lane, one of the narrower of the labyrinth of streets that mazed through the historic district. He usually got jittery in the tiny alleys with the walled gardens snuggled up to the edge of the road and the wrought-iron balconies dripping pink petunias onto the top of his head. I was counting on one of the locals' cars to come roaring through so Bernard would buck and we'd avoid this topic altogether.

"You didn't even hear what Pastor wants us to do," Bonner said.

"How did you know?"

"Because you looked like you were in Neverland during the sermon."

I slanted a look out of the side of my glasses. "It was that obvious?"

"To me it was."

He shrugged, and a small red smear appeared at the top of each cheekbone. I cut him slack and said something unnecessary to Bernard. Bonner knew that I knew that he was always "aware" of me, although we never talked about it. I didn't want to have to tell him that he was "a nice guy, but ..."

"The discovery of Florida is credited to Don Juan Ponce de Leon," I said instead.

"Stop it."

"I like to say it. Don *Juan* Ponce de Leon—"

"What is your deal with not wanting to take a turn as leader?"

I grunted and let Bernard pick up a little speed. He could smell fishy Matanzas Bay ahead—who couldn't?—which meant soon he'd get to stop. Not the most ambitious horse on the Camelot team, Bernard.

"You've read the gospels at least fifty times," Bonner said.

"Well, yeah. I had to. That stuff is so freakin' good."

"You're in church every time the doors open."

"I have a lot of heathen-time to make up for."

"People respect you."

I let out a snort at the corner of Artillery and Charlotte.

"They do," Bonner said.

"Why? Because I can manhandle a horse? Step up, Bernard."

Bonner slid his sunglasses down his nose and peered at me. "You told me before that you *don't* manhandle the big horses, which is why they like you. That's why people respect you—because you don't bully them either."

"You're reaching. For openers, as far as I can tell, leadership in the church means you have to get all involved with the money and pleasing the cranky old people who *give* the money so they won't *stop* giving the money even though they have too *much* money in the first place—"

"This isn't even about that. We're talking spiritual leadership."

"Oh. Well, for that, I am *eminently* qualified."

I had Bernard take a left out onto busy Avenida Menendez and glanced around for cars with the potential to backfire. Bernard had been known to do some serious kicking-up-of-hooves under those conditions.

"Look, Bonner—faith-wise, I feel like it's going to take me the rest of my life to catch up to where everybody else is, much less lead anybody any further. I'm still trying to figure out what I want to be when I grow up."

"So who says this isn't part of that?"

"What—leading the Wednesday Night Watchdogs up some spiritual San Juan Hill?"

Bonner took his glasses completely off, and his eyes took on a mischievous green glow.

Oops.

"What did you call us? 'The Wednesday Night Watchdogs'?"

"Yes, and if you tell any of them, I'll cut your heart out. I love those people and you know it."

"*Watchdogs?*"

"In a good way. You all sniff out anything that's … amiss … and alert the Mack Daddy."

"The Mack *Daddy?*"

"Well, it's not like Garry's 'one of us.' He's the one who gives us the 'charges'—which is great—I mean, we grow through that. He's there for the open-heart surgeries and the premarital counseling. Look how great he was with Sylvia. I'd want him with me if *I* were dying. But we're not, like, his buddies. Maybe he just loves us in some kind of … corporate … way." I shrugged, because I had ceased to be coherent.

"Are you scared to be in charge of something?" Bonner said.

"No. Lazy, maybe."

The carriage swerved, lurching Bonner against me. I tightened the line on Bernard. Beside us at the stoplight just before the under-construction Bridge of Lions, a rottweiler thrust his head out the passenger window of a van and chopped at the air with his fangs, snarling like a junkyard sentry. The horse did a sidestep that would have put Fred Astaire to shame and came within inches of an excavator parked on the Bay Side.

"Are they ever gonna finish working on this bridge?" I said between my teeth. "Hold on, Bonner. I'm taking him through this light."

"It's red."

"I know. That's why you should hold on."

While Bonner white-knuckled the side of the carriage, I soothed Bernard and rolled us straight into the intersection. Cars stopped on all sides, some of them with tire squeals that wouldn't have been necessary if the drivers had been doing the speed limit. The jerks. I nodded my thanks to the Lincoln Navigator, only because the driver looked the most indignant of any of them, and coaxed Bernard out of a sidestep and on to the other side of Cathedral Place.

"Good boy," I said.

"You talking to me or him?" Bonner said.

"Did you wet your pants?"

"No!"

I grinned at him. "Then you're a good boy too. Bernard, you're home free, Pal."

Bernard took the last four blocks to the Bay Front where the carriages lined up as if he'd had back-to-back fares all day and was headed for the barn. If he had that much energy when he was actually working, he probably wouldn't weigh a ton. When we pulled up behind Caroline Cutty's rose-colored vis-à-vis, I climbed down to get him the bucket of water he didn't really need.

Bonner hopped down too and brushed off the seat of his Dockers—despite the fact that I kept an impeccable carriage.

"We're not done with this conversation," he said.

"I have to be for now." I swept an arm over the wide walkway bordering the Bay all the way to the old fort. "They're not exactly lined up waiting for tours, so I'm going to have to go hustle some."

"You guys get hit by the recession?" Bonner said.

"That, plus it's always slow all through September and into October. So if I'm going to make a living …"

I shrugged and took the bucket to the hose. When I came back, Bonner was standing with his arms folded, hands in opposite armpits, gazing over the Bay.

"The dolphins will be in to feed in about fifteen minutes," I said. "In case you want to wait around."

He shook his head, eyes leveled at some point between me and the horizon. He did that whenever he was about to tell me something he thought I didn't know about myself.

I groaned within. It wasn't that I didn't like Bonner. He was attractive enough if you were into clean-cut as an art form. No, that wasn't fair. He did have a nice reddish tint to his hair and a certain energy in his eyes, as if he were always searching for the positive. And unlike half the men I'd ever met, he was at least as tall as my five foot nine.

So, yeah, he was fine as somebody to drift through the St. John's Flea Market with on a Saturday afternoon or call up to meet for quesadillas just because it was Tuesday. But I rarely even did that much. He'd been a widower for five years, and it seemed somehow logical to him that because we were the only two single people our age at Flagler Community, by default we should be a couple. If I said, "Hey, come over for burgers," he'd turn it into a promise that next weekend I'd meet his parents.

Been there, done that a long time ago. A run of serial relationships after that had pretty much convinced me I was unmarried for a reason. I wouldn't be breaking my no-date-in-the-last-twelve-years record with Bonner.

The problem was getting him to grasp that without feeling like a complete heel while I was doing it. I never handled well those situations that called for finesse.

"Watch this," I said as I set the bucket in front of Bernard.

Bonner dabbed at his perspiring forehead with a monogrammed hanky, the kind I didn't think guys even carried anymore. "I've seen horses drink before."

"Have you seen one *not* drink? Watch."

True to form, Bernard sniffed disdainfully at the bucket, took a mincing step back, and neatly kicked the thing over, sending a small river of water down the gutter toward Hypolita Street. Just like he did every single time.

"Why did he do that?" Bonner said.

"Because he's ornery. We're a good match, he and I."

Bonner folded the hanky over and tucked it out of sight into his back pocket. "You're not as ornery as you pretend to be. And that isn't going to get you out of this group thing. Maybe we *need* somebody ornery."

"But you don't need somebody nuts."

It was out before I knew I was going to use it on him. I got the hoped-for cocked eyebrow, and nodded him toward the Bay.

"Sit with me for a minute," I said.

I left Bernard nosing at the now empty bucket and led Bonner to the wide seawall. I sat cross-legged on its coquina top, now warm with absorbed Florida sunshine, and faced him. For once he didn't examine the surface he was about to perch on.

"Look, something strange happened to me in church," I said. "It was probably my imagination … maybe last night's tacos. Who knows, but it was weird, and I need to sort it out before I take on any—"

"What happened?"

"Promise you won't think I've lost it," I said even though that was exactly the conclusion I wanted him to arrive at.

"What *happened?*"

"Did you ever feel like God was, I don't know—nudging you?"

Bonner rubbed his index finger under his nose. "Not physically elbowing me in the ribs, if that's what you mean. But, yeah, I've felt moved to do things and I pretty much knew God was behind it." His eyes went soft. "That's not crazy, Allison."

"Even if it felt like I was actually being pushed? Even if there was a voice attached to it?"

"What did it say?"

"It said, 'Allison, go buy a Harley.'"

"No it didn't!"

"Okay, then, you see—I *am* nuts."

"No—it's just—that doesn't sound like … God."

Bonner was looking at me exactly as if I'd just confided that I was having my tongue pierced. Two minutes ago I'd wanted that expression to appear on his face. Now that it was there, it marched up the back of my neck.

"How do you know what God sounds like to me?" I said.

"I don't. But, come on, Allison, a *Harley*? Isn't that more like wishful thinking?"

"Maybe—if I'd ever wanted a motorcycle for one second in my life, which I haven't."

I unfolded myself from the wall and stood to shake the hip-crease wrinkles out of my impractical linen pants. I suddenly felt as ridiculous and shapeless as they were.

"Y'know what? Forget it," I said. "I was just trying to prove a point, which is that I'm not ready to lead us in some charge when evidently I don't know God's voice from schizophrenia."

Bonner rolled his eyes. "That's not what I'm saying."

"Whatever. I've got to get to work."

I headed for Bernard, who looked up guiltily from the back wheel of the rosy vis-à-vis he was nudging to get a rise out of the high-strung mare harnessed to it. I could feel Bonner following me, but I didn't turn around.

"Did I tick you off?" he said.

"Nope. You set me straight—which obviously I still need people to do. So how about if *you* 'lead the charge'? You know I'll be there to follow. Whatever you need."

I glanced at him then and caught him with his eyes closed, apparently cursing himself. I was okay with that. And I would be even more okay if he'd go … sell some houses.

"See you Wednesday, then?" he asked.

"Yep."

"Okay, so …"

I smiled at him before I hoisted myself back up into the carriage and started Bernard toward the fort and around the bend in Castillo Drive. I really did hope Bonner didn't develop heatstroke before he made it to the church, but I didn't watch to make sure.

The walking traffic was just starting to pick up as Bernard and I approached the top of St. George Street. St. Augustine is a city of strollers, people in no hurry to get anywhere who simply happen upon the next enchanting little café or the next Oldest Something. I let Bernard linger beside the City Gates—which were impressive but were no longer attached to a wall—and scanned the street for tourists who showed signs that meandering through the Spanish Quarter was getting old. I always looked for paunchy men with palm trees on their shirts and sweat gleaming on their bald spots. They'd usually climb into my carriage in a heartbeat to give their ankles a chance to un-swell.

"Hawaiian shirt at two o'clock," I said to Bernard. "He's just about ready." I watched Shirt's round little wife bustle ahead of him into the City Gate Gallery, pulled by the lure of all things Thomas

Kinkade. "She isn't." I glanced at the sun blazing straight down on us. "Give it another five degrees."

I couldn't take the carriage down this part of St. George. It was restricted to foot traffic, which saved the Old World feel that people came in droves to experience—from serious seekers of history to collectors of refrigerator magnets. Having grown up here, I tended to look at something like Castillo de San Marcos and gaze right through it, which was hard to do, seeing how the fort dominated the Bay Front, as if at any moment we were going to be attacked by Frenchmen bent on stealing our Spanish charm. Even when I paused with a carriage full to pontificate on its checkered past, I often wondered if it actually made any difference to anybody.

So go buy a Harley, Allison.

Bernard reared his head up, mane flying, and for an instant I thought he'd felt the Nudge too. Until I realized I had a stranglehold on the lines.

"You for hire?"

I jerked to look down at Hawaiian Shirt. Saddlebags of sweat were darkening his palm trees. The round little wife wilted beside him, laden with plastic shopping bags.

"I want to go to the Fountain of Youth," she said.

"Well, who doesn't?" I said. "Climb aboard and we'll get your toes over there so you can dip them in it."

The man gave her rump a push and heaved himself up behind her. "I need to dunk my whole body in."

Bernard did his Fred Astaire, and the wife bobbed against her husband with a squeal. This was probably the most they'd touched each other in years.

"Welcome to Camelot Carriage Service," I said. "We are St. Augustine's first and most reputable guide to the nation's oldest city."

"As long as I can sit down and get out of this sauna," hubby said.

"You just relax," I said. "And I'll tell you all the secrets. You already know this is the oldest continuous European settlement in the United States, but you probably *don't* know—"

Blah, blah, blah.

The doleful saxophone of a street busker sobbed behind us as we clopped away from St. George Street. It had to be my imagination that it said, "Buy a Harley, Allison. I'm telling you, go buy one."

CHAPTER TWO

Hawaiian Shirt and Round Wife were from Michigan and ate up every off-the-wall morsel I tossed into the back of the carriage. The hubby showed his appreciation with a generous tip.

The rest of the day's fares, however, decreased steadily in quality—and gratuities—from there. The last group was so drunk that one of them threw up right in front of the former Ponce de Leon Hotel—still über-elegant as Flagler College. Henry Flagler had built his veritable castle for invited guests only; he would be banging his cane on the inside of his coffin right now if he saw this lush hurling in full view of his luxurious dream for St. Augustine. When I dropped the party off at Scarlett O'Hara's tavern at five p.m., I had to wait for ten minutes while two females in kitten-heeled sandals hauled out the guy who was passed out on the backseat, presumably so he could go inside and drink some more. I made a mental note to wipe the drool off the tuck-and-roll when I got back to the stables, and pointed Bernard down Cordova. He knew there was food in his future; he didn't need much urging.

"Who pays big bucks for a carriage tour and then stands up and screams through the whole thing?" I said to him. "Nice work trying to get that one idiot to fall out. If he'd gone over, I would have left him in the gutter for the homeless guys to pick clean later."

At least I'd accomplished one thing in the course of the afternoon. When it had become obvious that group and the one before it weren't interested in a thing I had to offer about Menendez or Henry Flagler, I'd had time to mull over the voice that said I was supposed to purchase a Harley. I'd come to the conclusion that it couldn't be real.

In the first place, Bonner was probably right: God didn't give instructions like that one. Did he? If he was going to push you to something outrageous, wasn't it more likely to be: "Sell everything you have and open a soup kitchen?"

"Go buy a Harley" *was* more like some twenty-five-year-old punk's wishful thinking. But if I were going to wish for something, it would be for a job that didn't involve looking at a horse's behind all day while I tried to make the absurdities of history sound noble to a carriage full of kids, all with their MP3s plugged in so they couldn't hear their parents saying, "Isn't that *interesting*, Justin?"

A car horn blared, and both Bernard and I started. I didn't know how long I'd been sitting at the sleepy intersection of Cordova and Treasury Streets, but for Pete's sake, you didn't honk at a horse unless you were delivering a kidney. Moron.

I waved for the driver to go around me on the left, but he—or apparently a she in a BMW with stuff to do—leaned on the horn again. Normally at that point I would have inched forward and stopped in front of every house on the street, just to get her shorts in a wad, but Bernard was freaking out. He tried to rear his head back, careening the carriage sideways.

"Whoa, Big Guy," I said, easing on the line to keep him from turning the whole thing over. That only gave him permission to try again. He kicked the shaft and lifted the left wheels off the pavement. Behind me the driver gave three obnoxious honks that set Bernard writhing like a snake on a stick. Either I had to get him out of there or we were both going down in the middle of Cordova, where we'd undoubtedly be run over by the Beemer and left for dead.

I took a firmer hold on the lines and pulled his head to the left to turn onto King Street. The driver chose that moment to wrench the car out from behind me and squeal into the left turn lane. I veered Bernard right with the carriage still teetering.

After a litany of whoa-buddy-whoa-it's-okays—as well as some general hoping under my breath that the wench in the BMW would arrive at her destination with serious horse poo on her tires—I was finally able to coax Bernard to a stop and get my bearings. Uneasiness crept up my spine.

"Great part of town you wound us up in," I said, though Bernard didn't seem to mind that we'd just landed in front of a boarded-up storefront with the remains of yellow crime scene tape dangling from its eaves. As long as he was away from sports cars with horns, he was momentarily happy.

There weren't too many vehicles of any kind on West King Street—the notoriously "bad" end of the otherwise elegant avenue—and there wouldn't be until dark, at least as far as I knew. I wasn't in the habit of hanging out down here, nor was anybody else unless they were interested in a good drug deal or a hookup with a prostitute.

In the still-stark light of late afternoon, it looked like a neighborhood everyone had abruptly abandoned and left to decay. The few remaining businesses—several bars with smoke-filmed glass doors, a dubious auto-repair shop, a tattoo parlor that practically screamed, "Get your Hepatitis C here!"—were in various stages of dissipation. They matched the man and mutt who slept in the shade of a Dumpster.

But by all reports, once darkness fell, it took on an entirely different tone. More violent crimes were committed on these few blocks than in the rest of the old city put together. Now and then my boss, Lonnie, would hire guys from down here to clean the stables, but they never lasted long. Some overdosed. One had been the perpetrator of one of those violent crimes, another the victim. But most just sort of gave up on the idea of working in a dead-end job. They didn't have to leave home to find a dead end.

"This isn't on our tour route, Big Guy," I said, although I had to admit it would be an interesting addition to my sightseeing spiel. "West King Street, gateway to the Lincolnville District of our fair city, where you can get you some crack cocaine, a little heroine, some hooker action ..."

I squirmed on the seat. It wouldn't be my best material. We were only two blocks from Henry Flagler's dream. Eight blocks from the house I grew up in, where I still lived, oblivious to the slow death going on down here. I couldn't make it funny.

The mongrel dog by the Dumpster began to stir from his coma, making this a good time to move on. Not so much with Bernard and canines. I picked up the lines, a U-turn in mind, but the man rolled over and stretched out his arm. The dog stopped eyeing Bernard and turned around three times before settling into the crook of his elbow. The man gave a contented groan, and they both sank back into sleep.

"It's not dead," I said to Bernard.

He shook his head.

"I'm serious." Somewhere beneath the death pall, something else was trying to get its breath. Something I couldn't name; I could only feel it, and it Nudged me—with a capital N—straight down West King Street.

I went with it.

The Camelot stables were on the corner of Ribiera and LaQuinta, not street names a tourist would find on the sightseeing map. It wouldn't do to mix the smell of horse manure with the scent of fine cuisine. There was only one way to get there from our tour routes, and the other side of the San Sebastian River wasn't it.

That fact wasn't lost on Lonnie, whose skinny form stood at the fence like a stick figure as I trotted up with Bernard and carriage. Not that he would have missed our arrival even if he'd been in the back of the barn. Bernard had an exhausting day for a horse that was normally content to amble one fare around the fort and call it good, and he wasn't wasting any time getting to the feed trough.

"Where were you?" Lonnie said—in lieu of "Hey, how'd it go today?"

He pushed back the rim of the inevitable cowboy hat to look up at me and shifted the equally as inevitable toothpick from one side of his mouth to the other.

"Had to take a detour," I said.

I jumped down from the seat and loosened Bernard's girth.

"Anything I want to know about?" he said.

"I don't think so."

"Anything I'm gonna hear about later?"

"You mean from a dissatisfied customer? No. Some of them were so wasted they won't even remember they *took* a carriage ride."

"That's all I need to know," Lonnie said.

I gave him a grunt. As long as the company owners didn't get ticked-off phone calls from customers, Lonnie's job was secure, and

so was mine. He reminded me regularly that horse poop always runs
down hill.

I got the trace free and led Bernard out from between the shafts
and nuzzled my nose against his. He dodged like a six-year-old boy
looking around to make sure none of his friends could see his mom
kissing him. In Bernard's case it was oats he was looking for.

"Water first, Big Guy," I said, "or you'll puke your guts."

"I'll get you a bucket." Lonnie turned to grab one from the stack,
revealing his somewhat comical profile. Skinny as he was, his blos-
soming beer belly gave him the appearance of a teenage girl who was
six months pregnant. You had to wonder how he'd developed a gut
like that at only thirty years old.

He stopped in front of us, empty pail in hand. Bernard poked at
it with his nose. "Seriously—how come you came from that direction? No matter what you run into, that's not on the approved route.
Ever."

"Gotcha," I said. "You want to give me that bucket or are we
going to let this animal dehydrate? I still have to bathe him—"

"I'd hate to have to terminate you. The owners would make me
do it if they heard you were prancin' this horse down West King.
Not to mention PETA—those bleeding hearts would be *all* up in our
business."

"Lonnie, you're killin' me here," I said. "Either fill that thing or
I'll do it myself."

"Just tellin' ya," he said as he headed for the spigot.

"Just hearin,'" I said.

I guessed I should have been anxious about that. Lonnie chastised
me about something I could be "terminated" for at least once a week,

but this was one he really might have to follow up on if it happened again. That was the thing. I couldn't guarantee I wouldn't be Nudged to go up West King Street—or do anything else weird for that matter. I knew it like I knew that Bernard was going to kick over his water bucket.

And the instant Lonnie set it down, he did.

All right. I could at least go look at Harleys.

After all, when had the approved routes ever taken me anywhere anyway?

It was Tuesday afternoon before I could get to the Harley dealership. Since it was located out by Interstate 95, way west of the historic district, I had to take my van, which started after only four or five cranks. It didn't get used that much because most of where I normally needed to go was within walking distance of my house. The Harley-Davidson store didn't qualify as "normally."

Once you get beyond US 1, St. Augustine looks like just about every other town in the continental US—a Chili's, a McDonald's, a Mapco station. Its only distinguishing feature at that intersection was what its owners claimed to be the Largest Adult Store in the State of Florida. Who knew—maybe it was the Oldest, too. It was, in fact, right next door to St. Augustine Harley-Davidson, and needless to say I'd never been in either one of them.

The Harley place was a lot classier than I'd expected. I was almost bowled over by the smell of leather when I walked through the door—that and the gleam of chrome. Bonner would've been going for his Ray-Bans.

Ignoring the cowhide bustiers on display—because if God told me to buy one of *those* we were going to have an issue—I threaded my way back to the actual showroom. And then I stopped before a sea of tailpipes and handlebars and studded seats and got an immediate case of dry mouth. It was like entering a classroom to take a final I hadn't studied for—hadn't even attended the class for. It had definitely been a long time since I'd had *that* feeling.

Okay. How hard could this be? Just check them out one at a time. I was only there to look anyway.

The bikes in the first row were almost as big as compact cars, with backseats and trunks and full sound systems. "Electra Glide," some tags said. "Ultra Glide," said those on larger ones. I'd seen men older than the Reverend Howard on bikes like these, tooling across the Bridge of Lions in post-midlife crisis. "Geezer Glides," I muttered.

I moved on to the next row, somewhat smaller but still intimidating with their wide, bright hips, and three-eyed stares. I liked the names better, though. Road King. Street Glide. Road Glide. Street Bob.

I turned over one tag and snorted. No way I was sitting on a bike called Fat Boy.

"You gon' let him buy one, huh?"

I looked up into a pair of grinning blue eyes, fixed into the forty-ish face of a guy with "Stan" embroidered on his polo shirt. Sandy hair brushed the top of his collar.

"Him?" I said.

"Husband? Boyfriend?"

The little chauvinist.

"I'm looking for myself," I said.

The covering of surprise was, I have to say, professionally done.

"Well, *there* you go," he said. "We get a lot of women buyers in here. What are you ridin' now?"

"Excuse me?"

"What kind of bike do you have?"

"Oh," I said, vaguely. "It's been a while."

That was true. In California, between the surf shop job and the gig at the nail polish boutique, I dated a guy with a rice rocket who seemed intent on killing us both every time I got on it with him. I hadn't gone near a motorcycle since.

"Your first Harley. All *right!*" Stan rubbed his hands together. "So—did you have one in mind?"

Yeah, I really should have studied.

"There's sure a lot to choose from," I said.

"Well, to begin with—what's your name?"

"Allison—Allison Chamberlain."

"Chamberlain as in Enterprises?"

I could almost hear his mind whirring like a calculator.

"I'm not associated with them," I said. "And I don't really need anything too fancy."

"It doesn't matter what you ride as long as you ride, right?"

"Uh-huh."

"So, Allison, anything trip your trigger so far?"

"Why don't you pitch something to me?" I said.

He went into salesman mode, which gave me fewer opportunities to reveal that I had no idea what I was looking at.

"You want one that's gon' be a good fit," he said, leading me past the Geezer Glides and Road Kings and, thankfully, Fat Boys and Bobs. "You get a good fit and then you can make it your own personal ride." He grinned with his eyes again. "You put the Screaming Eagle package on and ride up on that—people gon' be rollin' up their windows right quick and lockin' their doors."

"Yeah," I said. "That would be so me."

"You're familiar with the five families of Harleys," he said. "You've got your touring bikes, your Softails, your Sportsters, and the V-Rods." He looked at my legs and nodded. "I'm thinking maybe an FXDL—for you. That's in the Dyna line."

"Who is she?" I said.

"Who?"

"Dinah."

Stan couldn't quite maintain his professional cover this time. "You really don't know a thing about Harleys, do you?"

"Nada," I said.

"It's D-Y-N-A—"

"What about this one?"

Out of the crowd of chrome, a red bike with a glint of gold beckoned to me. It was the only one that didn't look like it was going to turn on me. It had a simple grace to it, from its gleaming chrome shafts all the way back to the leather bags hanging on either side of the back wheel like classy purses.

"The Heritage Softail Classic," Stan said. "Well, now, that could be a good choice for you. Nice lines, a little feminine but not too girly. Not that you aren't—"

"Shut up, Stan," I said.

"Right."

I ran my hand along what had to be the red gas tank just in front of the seat, almost as if I expected to feel a heartbeat.

"You want to sit on her?" Stan said.

Want was probably not the right word. *Have to* came closer.

"Sure," I said—and then stood there stupidly.

Stan cleared his throat. "This your first time on the driver's seat?"

"Yep," I said.

"Just a few pointers, then—"

"I need more than a few pointers, Stan. I need you to tell me exactly what to do so I don't fall on my butt."

"Got it. All right, just hold onto the handlebars—there you go—and then swing that left leg over—that's it. Now turn the wheel and stand her up."

I did, until I was straddling a machine that, from that angle, was as daunting as Bernard himself.

"What do I do now?" I said.

"I'll brace you so you can sit," Stan said, and put both hands on the handlebars and his feet on either side of the front wheel.

"You're not serious," I said.

"Trust me."

"Try again."

"I never lost anybody in the showroom yet," he said.

"Yeah, well, just don't let me be first."

Gingerly I lowered myself to the seat.

"Put your feet right on the pegs there," Stan said. "And just relax."

I didn't take my eyes off of him as I placed one foot and then the other on the narrow foot rests on either side of the wheel. The position slanted me back, arms extended straight from the handlebars.

"Dang, girl," Stan said. "You make this thing look good."

"I'm sure," I said.

"Hey, like I said, it's all about the way the bike fits. You can sit on it flat-footed and reach the handlebars. You can balance it and accept the weight of it. Handle the engine size—you've got 69 bhp, so you're good there. If your bike fits your skill level, you gon' be one with it, and that is pure beauty."

"What skill level, Stan?" I said.

"No worries. We've got the Rider's Edge class. In a weekend we'll have you out there drivin' it like you stole it."

I nodded, not because I believed a word of it, but because as I sat astride the Classic Softail Whatever It Was, I had the uncanny sense that I was supposed to be there. That in spite of my lack of any skill level whatsoever, this bike wanted to take me somewhere.

And right now I didn't have anyplace else to go.

"How much?" I said.

Stan, who was still holding me up by the handlebars, nodded at the tag. I flipped it over and tried not to gasp. I wasn't as successful at keeping the words, "Are you *serious?*" from escaping my lips.

"Eighteen thousand is actually a great price with all it's got on it," Stan said. "Our finance people can help you. We'll get you on the road." He nodded for me to stand up, and he let me turn the wheel and lean the bike back on its stand. "Let me introduce you to Kim in the loan office. I've seen her work magic."

"That's okay," I said. "I'll be back with the money."

"I can't promise this one will still be here. You want to put down a deposit?"

God hadn't said anything about a deposit. He hadn't, in fact, said anything at all about how I was going to pay for this command of his.

Clearly I was either going to have to wait for another Nudge or find the money myself. If neither came to be, I'd know it was time for the psychiatrist.

"Thanks for your time, Stan," I said and extended my hand.

"It's been my pleasure. You take care now."

As I once again picked my way among Road Kings and Fat Boys, I imagined him chalking the last fifteen minutes up as time he could have better spent playing solitaire on his computer. *We'll see, Stan. We'll just see.*

Wednesday was one of those days we have often in North Florida, where heavy black clouds threaten to break open from nine a.m. on, but never give up a drop. The tourists eyed the skies and headed for the museums, and Lonnie called me on my cell and cut me loose at ten thirty. I gave Bernard a cursory brushing, pretended not to hear Lonnie's hint that I could do a little touch-up painting on the carriage, and headed for home.

I needed to hack at something while I thought through this money thing, and the shrubs in my front yard were in dire need of hacking. I'd seen both of my neighbors take disapproving pauses as they passed. I could almost hear Owen Schatz preparing his lecture: "We run a tight ship here on Palm Row, Ally. Nobody expects you to keep your place manicured like Sylvia did, but you know, it's like polishing your silver. If you don't keep up with it, you have to use twice the elbow grease when you do get to it." Owen, a bachelor in his early seventies, had three hobbies: playing golf, keeping Palm Row pristine, and mixing his metaphors.

I sat on the front steps and slathered on sunscreen. Forty-plus years of Florida tans had left my skin just short of an Aigner handbag, but better late than never to give it some attention. I wasn't sure I could say the same about the azalea bushes that were now half covering the windows.

As I went after them with the clippers, I admitted that Owen had a point. Palm Row only ran for one block between lower St. George and Cordova Streets, with just the four houses on one side of the narrow road and their respective garages on the other. It was little more than a lovely alley, really, bordered with tall coconut palms—hence the name. If one of us let our yard go to seed, the whole street seemed shabby.

"One of us" was always me. Next door on the St. George side, my other neighbor, eighty-year-old Miz Vernell, made the White House Rose Garden look like a vacant lot. Although the empty house at the opposite end had been on the market for six months, a landscaper showed up weekly, effectively putting me to shame.

It was okay, because as I uncovered the bottom row of windowpanes and started a pile of chopped-off twigs by the screen porch, I had a chance to think about where in the Sam Hill I was going to get $18,000.

It wasn't like I could get a loan. Banks—and finance magicians—didn't lend money to people with my career history. Last time I counted while trying to fall asleep, I'd gotten to ten jobs before I dozed off.

My only asset was the house, and trying to get a mortgage on it was pointless for the same reason. Besides, that would have Sylvia rising from her grave to pinch my head off. She'd made me promise to keep what she left me, and that included the bank account for paying the taxes, insurance, and upkeep. A white wooden house in this climate meant painting every other year, and even now the gray shutters were peeling like a Yankee with a sunburn. Food and utilities were up to me, and what I made driving a carriage barely covered that.

I snipped a handful of gone-wild branches and added them to the pile. There *was* my van, the '01 Chevy Astro given to me by Scott, who'd owned the all-things-datil-pepper shop at the beach where I used to work. He signed the Astro over to me as the back pay he owed me when the business became a casualty of the economic downturn in '08. The Astro's starter was almost gone, and if I didn't replace the exhaust system soon, the EPA was going to be on my back. And then of course there was the fact that "You're Not Hot Till You See Scott" was still painted on the side. The datil pepper, he informed me more than once, scored one hundred thousand to two hundred thousand units on the Scoville scale; Tabasco sauce, he'd say proudly, was a mere twenty-five hundred. So, no, I wouldn't get enough for the van to buy myself a helmet.

I sat back on my heels and shoved my hair off of my seeping forehead so I could look across the lane at my garage. My only option was to sell the Jaguar—the one indulgence Sylvia allowed herself when she inherited her mini-fortune.

"I always wanted an XK," she told me. "I wanted to drive around Manhattan and show all them"—which came out "dem" off Sylvia's New York tongue—"people."

"What people?" I asked her.

"Just 'dem,'" she said. "We all got a 'dem.'"

Frankly, growing up with her nannying, I never saw her care what any of 'dem' said or did, including my parents who employed her. By the time she got her British-racing green Jaguar XK at age eighty-two, she apparently realized that too. I never saw her drive it more than a few times, even after she was too sick to get behind the wheel and had me drive her to doctors' appointments in it. To tell you the truth, I think she got more joy from beating me at gin rummy.

When she left everything to me in her will, I drove the Jag in her honor until I (a) decided I couldn't afford to pay the insurance *and* eat, and (b) discovered that a car like that required more attention than a high-maintenance boyfriend. I couldn't afford that, either. It had been parked in the garage ever since, with only two hundred miles on it. It was so not me.

But neither was a Harley. Until now.

I took another swab at my dripping forehead with the back of my hand and closed my eyes. I could hear the guide on the Orange and Green out on St. George, announcing the same history into his microphone that he did probably twenty times a day. Above it, the bells on Trinity Episcopal chimed the hour into the heavy air.

What's it going to be, Allison? Find a way and see where it leads you? Or mark your own hours tour by tour until you get 'terminated'?

"It isn't going to get done that way, Ally."

I jumped, nearly stabbing myself with the business end of the clippers. I hadn't heard Owen ease his black Lexus SUV in from St. George Street, the only end you could drive in from.

"You caught me daydreaming, Owen," I said.

He grinned, and I once again marveled at what a great job that dentist had done with his dentures. Although Owen had foregone the sunscreen altogether for his seven decades, so the new teeth were a little incongruent with his leathered face. And scalp.

"Owen, we've talked about you wearing a hat when you're out on the golf course," I said. "We don't want you getting skin cancer."

"You think you'd miss me?" He grinned even wider. Man, those teeth were great, all the way back to the molars.

"Who would guilt me into cleaning up my yard?" I said.

"Yeah, there's that. Listen, I heard we might be getting a new neighbor."

"They finally sell that house?"

"That's what Bonner Bailey told me. We played nine holes today."

"Ah—well, Bonner'll make a nice commission on that."

Owen winked. "That could be good news for you, yeah?"

"How do you figure?"

"Your name comes up every once in a while. I've seen him here a couple of times. Thought maybe you and him …" He winked again. "You two could do wonders with this place. You seen what he's done with his? Oh—of course you have."

He winked yet *again*.

"Did you get contact lenses too?" I said.

"Sorry. Didn't mean to put my spoon into your stew and start stirring. I just like to keep my ducks in a row, y'know?"

"Yeah, Owen," I said. "I know."

When he finally pulled the Lexus on into his garage, I left the clippers on the porch steps and crossed the brick road to my own. Inside, the Jag slumbered under its cover.

"Get ready to show your stuff, girlfriend," I said. "You're going on the auction block."

I wasn't quite sure where to start advertising, but I knew some of my Watchdogs would have ideas, especially Bonner, and Frank, an accountant, and India, who owned a clothing boutique on Aviles Street and was in the know about handling big-ticket items. The only articles I owned from "Secrets of India" were the scarves she gave me every year for Christmas. I wore a teal one, woven with silver threads, to the meeting that night, just to make her happy.

The instant I appeared in the doorway of the bride's lounge, she said, "You *see?* That color is *so* good on you."

"I knew you'd squeal over it," I said.

I sank onto the blue and cream brocade couch next to her, where I always sat on Wednesday nights so I could smell her signature Giorgio Armani, and thought my usual prayer: *Thank you, God, that we meet in here instead of one of those classrooms with the metal chairs that give everybody hemorrhoids.* Frank had claimed the lounge for us five years ago when small groups were first formed. He said ladies should have a comfortable place to sit, and probably would have pulled our chairs out for us when we arrived if they hadn't been constructed from solid oak and contained twenty pounds of upholstery. As it was, he stood up when any of us entered the room.

He was still standing now, looking awkward in his short-sleeved sport shirt, rubbing his age-spotted hands together. Frank always reminded me of a wrinkled thirteen-year-old boy when he wore anything but a suit. "Frank, I'm sorry about Bernard on Sunday," I said.

"It was fine, Missy. I got it taken care of."

"Still—I felt bad."

India snickered. "What happened? Did your horse poop in front of the church again?"

"Honestly!"

That came from Mary Alice, who was arranging coffee cups on a tray at the buffet. She put her hand, white and plump as a biscuit, over her little bow of a mouth, which made India snicker again.

"You're lucky, Mary Alice," she said. "I would have called it something worse before I was a believer."

India was forever reminding us what a heinous person she was in her pre Christian days. The woman was fifty-two and had been baptized at age twenty-one, but she still seemed to feel the need to recall her dark youth. Frankly I hadn't heard anything half as bad as some of the stuff I pulled in my own personal history, but if it reassured her that she was now safe from her former self, so be it.

Mary Alice let her hand slide down to her stack of chins, which she always seemed to be checking as if she were worried they'd somehow slipped away. She was only sixty, but she'd been protecting those chins ever since I'd known her, which was ten years now. She came to see Sylvia twice a week for the three years she was sick, every day toward the end. When I was catatonic with grief after Sylvia died and I couldn't leave the screen porch, Mary Alice came and sat and crocheted and murmured that this too would pass. But it was the checking of the chins that soothed both Sylvia and me as we groped to find our own handle-holds in the abyss of loss. Every time Mary Alice tucked her ivory fingers into those silken folds, I was reassured that at least some things remained the same. Mary Alice had subsequently shown me that God was one of those things. She and the rest of the Watchdogs.

"Sorry I'm late."

Bonner breezed in, still pulling the Croakies over his head to remove his sunglasses, which had left fresh sunburn lines across his temples. Probably from his afternoon on the golf course with Owen.

"Hey, big deals take time," I said. "Heard you signed one today."

"Well, do tell," India said.

She patted the couch on her other side, but Bonner took the gold chair opposite us and gave me the eyebrow.

I gave him one back. That's what he got for dropping my name like we were—what did Owen call it? An item?

"House on Palm Row and Cordova," he said. "It's a decent deal, yes."

"Thanks be to God, son," Frank said, hand out for the shake. The Reverend Howard's influence on Frank hadn't quite stretched to hugging men yet.

"I'm glad I brought this pie, then," Mary Alice said. "We need to celebrate."

India gave a ladylike groan. "Tell me it's not pecan."

"It is."

"So much for Jenny Craig."

"You're not serious, India," I said. "You're a stick. Eat two pieces. Three."

She waved me off with a set of white-tipped nails, which reminded me that mine were still grimy from my attack on the killer azaleas. Oh well.

Bonner took the cup and saucer Mary Alice handed him—who else served coffee with a saucer anymore?—and said to me, "So—we ready to get started?"

India leaned into me. "I think 'we' means 'you.'"

I gave Bonner a look. He looked back.

"All right, so we all heard Pastor Garry's sermon Sunday," he said, eyes still on me.

You are dog chow, I said to him with mine.

Mary Alice, God love her, gave her nervous bubble-laugh and said, "I didn't really understand it. I mean, no offense to Pastor, but I was confused."

"Give us a review, if you don't mind, Bonner," Frank said.

"Yeah," I said. "Lay it on us, Bonner."

The eyebrow said that I, too, was dog chow.

"Okay, Pastor has read, I don't know, several studies that say Buddhist books are more popular than Christian books with the general public—"

"We're talking the unsaved, then," India said.

I felt my teeth grit. Loved India, hated that word. And it was one of her favorites. That and *nonbeliever* and *unchurched*. For me they brought up visions of the fat girls with pimples longing to be at the popular table in the cafeteria.

"He just said the general population," Bonner said. "He didn't specify."

"Well, I would think—"

"Anyway," I said, pressing India's arm.

"Anyway, the reason, according to the studies, is that Buddhism presents itself as a way of life, while Christianity presents itself as a system of beliefs."

Mary Alice's hand fluttered over the chins as if she needed them more than ever. "That's what I don't understand. If you believe in Jesus, you do what he says. Don't you?"

"I think that's right," Frank said. "You ask, 'What would Jesus do?' and then that's what you do. It's Jesus first, last, and always, now isn't that right?"

I waited for "God is good all the time, all the time God is good." Frank seemed to live by those three adages and get along just fine. I always figured that must work in the black-and-white world of accounting.

Beside me India re-situated herself against the cushions. "I think it might be a *little* bit more complicated than that, Frank, honey," she said. "From my work with the girls, I know they've got to sort through a number of options before they know 'what Jesus would do.'" She snapped her fingers into a fold on her lap and I knew what was coming. "I learned that myself with Michael Morehead."

India always referred to her ex-husband as "Michael Morehead," and in a knife-blade tone. That was another thing she constantly reminded us of: that Michael Morehead was a womanizer and that was the only reason she divorced him, as Jesus said she was within her rights to do. The divorce had been ugly and public, but it had led her to minister to young women in the congregation who found themselves in the throes of relationship crisis. From what I'd seen, she was great with the acute-care approach. I'd often wondered if her counselees were able to move on as wonderfully well as she had. One thing she couldn't fault Michael Morehead for: his alimony paid for that boutique.

"But in the end you search your conscience and you do right," Frank said, pitch rising.

Mary Alice nodded. "And it's all in God's hands."

I could feel the gleam in my eyes as I looked at Bonner. "Well, there you go then."

He closed his eyes briefly, which meant he was about to calm Mary Alice's chins and Frank's pitch and India's shifting on the couch. Me, of course, he considered a lost cause.

"All Garry means is that he'd like to see us *live* our beliefs in a more obvious way, rather than just talking about them."

"He doesn't think we're behaving properly?" Mary Alice said.

"I doubt that, Mary Alice," I said. "If any of you behaved anymore properly, you'd be in the Wax Museum."

"Do you remember what he talked about in the sermon?" Bonner said quickly. "He doesn't want us to just be Ten Commandment people. He wants us to be spiritual-formation people."

India leaned into me again. "Oh that clears it up."

"If Pastor asks us to do something, I think we should do it," Mary Alice said.

"Amen," Frank said.

Mary Alice blinked her very-blue eyes rapidly. "But I just don't understand what he wants us to do."

"I think that's what he wants us to figure out," Bonner said. "We're supposed to sort through our beliefs and make sure we're living them."

"Which means we also have to look at how we're *not* living them."

All four gazes locked on me. *Did I just say that?*

"We all know we're sinners," Frank said. "At least I do."

"Amen, brother," India said. "Could I have a piece of that pie now, Mary Alice?"

She laughed the India-lightening-it-up-before-it-gets-too-intense laugh. Well-off Southern women do that so well.

"I wasn't speaking for all of you," I said—although until I said it, I wasn't aware that I had anything to say at all. "You're angels in my eyes, and you know it. Mary Alice saved me from suffocating in my own grief after Sylvia died. She and India brought me to this church every Sunday until I could breathe without having to be reminded to."

They exchanged misty looks.

"I ate up Frank's Bible studies like I'd just been released from a refugee camp, and I know I was a leech on all of you, sucking in all the stuff I never even knew was there." I swept them all in with a glance. "And every one of you was always willing to open a vein for me. When Garry started small groups—"

"You remember how proud he was of his sweet self?" India said. "You'd have thought he invented the concept."

"Yeah, he's always a few steps behind, but he gets there—"

"The point is—" Bonner said.

"The point is, when you invited me to be in this one with all of you—"

"The older singles," India put in, with an eye roll.

"You started the beginning stages of me-the-Christian. You aren't just angels—you're saints."

India laughed and accepted the healthy wedge of pie Mary Alice offered on a china plate. "Then it looks like we already have it figured out."

"Pie, darlin'?" Mary Alice said to me.

I shook my head. I was suddenly feeling a little wobbly, the way you do when you've just told somebody off. I hadn't, obviously, or they wouldn't all be looking at me like I'd canonized them.

Bonner took my slice from Mary Alice, but he left the fork resting on the plate. "So I'm going to tell Garry what? That we've decided we're all good God-fearing people and we don't need to go any further?"

Everyone blinked at him.

"Way to end the party, Bonner, honey," India said.

"We can all learn and grow," Frank said. "I pray every day, 'Lord, grow me.'"

Mary Alice frowned at the wedge she'd just cut for herself. "I think I might be big enough."

"Maybe it isn't just about us, then," I said—once again hearing the words launch from my mouth without a flight plan.

"What do you mean?" Bonner said.

"Maybe we're in such a great place that we ought to be, what— taking it outside the group. I don't know...."

I didn't. Well, I did, in a way, because the Harley message was once more whispering in my head, although why *now* was beyond me. That had nothing whatsoever to do with what we were talking about.

"You all right, Miss Allison?" Frank said.

"I'm sorry?"

India peered at me through the eyelash squint. "You looked a little intense there for a minute."

"There's something you can help me with," I said. I'd actually intended to bring it up more casually, but since words were pretty much acting on their own anyway ...

"You know Sylvia's Jaguar has been sitting in my garage all this time, and I think it's time to sell it."

"Oh, honey, that's all I need to do is buy a Jag," India said. "Michael Morehead would have me in front of the judge so fast, saying if I could afford a luxury car, I sure didn't need his alimony checks."

"I'm not expecting any of you to buy it," I said. "I just thought maybe you'd know somebody who'd be interested." I looked at Frank. "I know you have some wealthy clients."

"My clients need tax write-offs, Miss Allison," he said. "A Jaguar doesn't usually qualify."

Mary Alice motioned at me with the last slice of pie. "I have to say I'm glad you're getting rid of it and buying something practical."

Practical. I took the pie and dug into it, just to keep myself from blurting out what I was selling it for.

"How much do you want for it?" India said. "Just in case I run into somebody that looks like Jaguar material." She pressed her shoulder to mine. "I do get a lot of *cougars* in my shop."

"Nice," I said.

"Was I supposed to understand that?" Mary Alice said.

"No, Mary Alice," Bonner said. "You're fine."

He'd been uncharacteristically quiet for the last few minutes, and when I looked at him to exchange grins, I found him looking at me like he knew exactly what was going on.

Do not say it out loud, I telegraphed to him. *Or I will strike you dead.*

He got the message. But I wasn't surprised when, as the meeting was breaking up and everyone was promising to look at the non-Christian behaviors in their lives for next time, he touched my elbow and said, "I'm walking you home."

I didn't argue. This would be a good chance for me to swear him to secrecy about my word from God.

Good-byes said to the others, we stepped from the church into the humidity and started down Valencia. It was a little like walking through the middle of a down pillow, even at eight thirty at night. Ah, the beauty of pre-autumn in Florida.

"Thanks for not outing me," I said.

"You're going to buy a Harley. That's why you're selling the car."

He was taking the corner onto Cordova at an annoyed clip and I had to practically do the two-step to keep up.

"I know you think I'm out of my mind," I said, "but—"

"Have you ever ridden one?"

"I'll take classes."

"You're going to kill yourself."

I stopped on the sidewalk, just out of earshot of a group on the porch of a tapas restaurant. Their laughter was suddenly jarring.

"I feel like I'm talking to my father, Bonner," I said between my teeth, "and trust me, that is not a good thing. Look, I've gotten more than just that one 'hint' in church. If you can hear about it without launching into a lecture, I'll tell you. Otherwise, g'night."

The chortling over the Asian duck quesadillas ceased abruptly. I shrugged at the curious faces of the diners on the porch and pitched myself on toward the light at King Street, arms swinging. I was surprised by my own anger.

Bonner was beside me before I got to the walk signal. "No lecture. Tell me."

I cast him a quick glance. He had his hands in his pockets, face intent on the stoplight.

"It won't leave me alone," I said.

"What won't?"

"This Nudging thing. I'll be giving a tour or clipping my toenails or shoveling horse poo and there it is, whispering me to … do this … buy a motorcycle—and I don't think it's just about me being born to be wild. There's something else attached to it."

"What?"

"I have no idea, but that's not the only unplanned thing that's been coming out of me lately." I let a cab crawl past us and stepped off the curb. "Tonight when we were all congratulating ourselves on what wonderful Christians we are, and I said maybe it was time to take it outside the group?"

"Yeah."

"I didn't think that up. I didn't even want to say it. I'm *fine* with the group. The group is the only stable thing in my life."

"What you said, though—*that* I would believe was God."

"It was the same voice, Bonner. Do I get to pick when I obey it and when I don't?"

He didn't answer and I didn't prod him. We walked the last block in muggy silence. With each step I cared less whether he agreed with me or not, and that made my heart ache a little.

When we got to the house, I folded my arms and shrugged my shoulders up to my earlobes.

"You don't have to buy into this," I said. "But I'd appreciate it if you didn't ride me about it."

He nodded toward my garage. "Is the Jag in there?"

"Yeah," I said.

"Let me take a look at it."

I rolled my eyes. "Did you notice Miz Vernell and Owen sitting on his porch when we walked by just now? If I take you into my garage at this time of night, they're going to start planning our engagement party."

"I just want to see it."

"Why?"

"Because I might want to buy it."

I felt my jaw drop, chin slamming to chest.

"Are you serious?" I said.

"Aren't you?"

"Well, yeah, but ... why?"

I didn't finish, because I was sure we both knew what I was thinking. There were going to be strings attached to this.

"I've never heard you say you wanted a Jag." I said.

"I never heard you say you wanted a Harley." His gaze went to the garage roof. The effort to understand was all over his face.

"Okay, come on," I said. "I'll show her to you."

CHAPTER THREE

I'd been away from Chamberlain wealth long enough to forget how fast things can move when there are large amounts of cash involved. Bonner presented me with a check for $20,000, I waltzed into the Harley dealership with one for $18,000—trying not very hard to hide my smugness from Stan as we posed together for the obligatory photo by the bell they rang when I made my purchase—and came out with a Red Hot Sunglo Heritage Softail Classic. Which Stan then had to drive home for me while I followed in the van.

"You won't be riding it until after you pass your class," he told me when we had it safely tucked in the garage. "You'll learn on a little Buell on the range. But after that ..." The eyes grinned. "You can ride it like—"

"I know," I said. "Like I stole it."

That all happened in forty-eight hours. Friday night I took the classroom portion of Rider's Edge, during which Ulysses, a fortyish instructor with a curly dark bun of hair at the nape of his neck—a look India would have had a stroke over—basically told us which questions were going to be on the written test. Some, obviously, were not.

"Here's one," he said to the class of six—all of whom were men except me, and all of whom looked like they had spent most of their youth astride a Hog. "Why can't a motorcycle stand up by itself?"

Before any of us could give the obvious answer, he said, "Because it's two tired."

We groaned appreciatively, which only encouraged him to give everything he said a punch line. Except his parting words to us as we left for the evening.

"All joking aside, we're going to get serious tomorrow," he said. "Very serious. Because more than half of all motorcycle crashes occur on bikes ridden by the operator for less than six months."

Until then I'd thought, you know, how hard could it be? I had learned to ride a ten-speed, surf on a short board, drive a two-thousand-pound horse. I could do this.

After he said that, I barely slept all night.

But I showed up the next morning in the new jeans and boots and gloves and jacket and helmet I'd bought with some of the profit I'd made on the Jag. It was a sweltering steam bath of a day, but the sweat that poured like a brook down the hollow of my chest wasn't just from all that required clothing I was wearing.

I was scared spitless.

The six silver-gray Buells were lined up, ready to serve as our training bikes. They were made by Harley-Davidson for the less affluent rider. In other words it wouldn't cost the dealership as much if one of them crashed, which did nothing to relieve my fears.

"The body of a Buell is a naked minimalist," Ulysses said as he led us to them. "Nothing fancy to distract you. Just a nice simple machine."

Uh-*huh*. When I threw my leg over and stood the bike up, I did not get the I-belong-here feeling I'd gotten on my Classic both times I'd mounted it. This one clearly said, "You want to lay bets on how long you can stay upright on me?" The insides of my thighs flooded with terrified perspiration.

Ulysses gave instructions for starting our bikes using the terms we learned the night before for all the switches and doohickeys. None of them looked like they did on the diagram in the workbook. By the time I actually got mine started, I was ready to throw up. All the other bikes were growling and snarling. I rolled the throttle like Ulysses told me to, and the sound actually brought some reflux up my throat. It was like being on the back of a bear. A starving bear—a just-out-of-hibernation bear.

Ulysses had us all stop our engines so he could describe the first exercise. I swallowed my breakfast again.

"You're going to power-walk it until you get up to ten miles an hour. Then you can put your feet on the pedals and give it a little gas. Stop when you get to the orange cones down there."

I peered at the cones. They had to be a half mile away. When did the parking lot get that long?

"All right—you know what to do," Ulysses said. "Put it in neutral, start your engine, and then put it in first and start walkin'."

Engines fired up around me and brought my entire stomach into my throat. Frantically I searched for neutral with my left foot. That was my first issue with this whole riding thing. I'd read in the book that the gear shift was by your foot and the clutch by your hand, but twenty-six years of driving stick-shift cars made that counterintuitive, not to mention impossible to remember. By the time I finally located neutral, with some personal coaching from Ulysses, the rest of the class was already at the other end of the range, bikes turned around, facing me.

I got mine started, nearly blowing Ulysses aside when I rolled too hard on the throttle with my right hand and tried to walk it forward.

"You're not going anywhere in neutral," he said over my engine's screaming complaint. "Engage the clutch and put it in gear."

I did, though it wasn't easy with my hands shaking as if palsy had set in.

"Okay, let out easy on the clutch and give it some gas."

I did that, too, and shot across the parking lot, legs flailing out to the sides. Oh my *gosh,* where the Sam Hill was the brake?

I groped for it with my foot, but I couldn't find it with the wheel turning in a direction I never told it to go. Oh wait—the brake was in my hand. I let go of something and grabbed and squeezed something else and the thing lurched to a stop with a squeal matched only by my own as I went over, onto the blacktop, with the machine on top of me. Mercifully it shut off, so there was only the fear that I'd broken every bone in my body to contend with, rather than the terror that the engine was going to eat me alive.

Somebody pulled it off of me. Somebody else—I thought it was the twenty-five-year-old kid who'd sat next to me in class—got me to my feet. Ulysses stood there nodding, for no apparent reason.

"Okay," he said as his assistant—Darrell or something—wheeled the bike away. "What did you do wrong?"

"I don't have the slightest idea."

"What did she do wrong?" he asked the rest of the class who had managed to keep themselves vertical. They were more than willing to attest to the fact that I had clutched when I should have given it gas, and turned the wheel when I applied the brake. No one seemed to consider that I might have road rash sizzling up my leg, and I wasn't about to point that out.

"You ever ridden a horse?" Ulysses said to me.

"Yes."

"Then you know the best thing to do now is to get right back on."

No, the best thing to do would be to go home and forget this whole thing. God had just better not whisper something to me right then, or I would lose my religion. Literally.

The five guys rode back to the starting cones, and Darrell returned the Buell to me, reset and ready to go. With my heart throbbing in my throat, I got back on. I could do this. It couldn't be rocket science. The other students barely had a set of teeth among them, right? Okay, that wasn't entirely true, but I had to tell myself something so I could think clearly enough to find the ignition button and rediscover neutral and force myself to get the bike to the cones. Maybe I *did* want God to speak to me now—and tell me which one was the clutch again….

I stalled twice before I made it back to the starting line. I never did get up to ten miles an hour, but since my classmates were ready for Exercise 2, I nodded that I was up for it, too, and tried to listen to Ulysses.

He might as well have been explaining the principles of nuclear fission.

"All right. Let's try it," he said, engines roaring to life. Mine sputtered and stalled but finally began to move me forward, but by then I'd forgotten what we were supposed to be doing. I couldn't have done whatever it was anyway, because my hands shook so hard that I couldn't hold the brake or the clutch in. Which was probably why the bike and I leaped forward and screamed across the range. Ulysses yelled something, which, of course, I couldn't hear because my engine was winding up like a frantic psychopath. I had no thoughts at all— God's or otherwise—as I bounced off the pavement and onto the grass. Sheer panic has no mind—it is only slapping branches and screaming engine and barbed wire coursing through your veins. There wasn't a single thought involved at all, until I flew from the bike into a creek and lay there with green algae soaking through my jeans. Then my only thought was: *Bonner was right.*

I was going to kill myself.

It would be better than suffering this humiliation.

"You okay?" Ulysses said above me.

"I'm swell," I said.

He crouched and nodded. "Good thing you landed in a creek bed. You sure nothing's broken?"

"Only my pride."

"Nah. Your crash train's just a little longer than most people's, that's all. Now tell me what you did wrong."

I lifted the visor on my helmet and stared at him.

"You sure she didn't bust her skull open?" Darrel said behind him.

Ulysses shook his head at me. "You're just thinking too much. That's the problem. You just have to go with—"

"It's not a matter of thinking too *much*," I said. "It's a matter of thinking the wrong *thing*." I took off my helmet and showered us all with sweat, including my fellow trainees who had gathered for the wake. "Not to worry, guys," I told them. "I'm counseling myself out."

I didn't sleep much that night either, although some of it could be attributed to my sitting on my Classic, in my garage, for hours, talking out loud to God. Was there a punch line to all this? Or was it just a lesson in knowing my limits? That couldn't be it. I never stretched farther than the next day. Which was why this was so disappointing. I'd thought that at last I was being led in a direction.

I dragged myself into bed around three a.m., but when I did fall asleep until nine, I woke up feeling like I'd ...

Oh yeah—been in a motorcycle crash.

I counted the bruises in the bathtub. Eleven on one leg, thirteen on the other, and a long, run-together one down each arm. I decided it was a good thing I couldn't see my backside.

The soak didn't help the pain. In fact, I could hardly hobble down to the kitchen to make coffee. When I leaned over to the freezer drawer to pull out a bag of French-roast beans I'd been saving for the next time was in a funk, it took me a good thirty seconds to stand up again.

I wasn't going to church, that was for sure—a decision confirmed when I made the mistake of peeking in the mirror in the downstairs powder room. The deep circles under my eyes made me look like I'd been on a three-day drinking binge. No, I would've looked better if that had been the case.

I also determined that coffee was too much of an effort, and that escaping to my favorite red chair-and-a-half in the living room would make me imagine Sylvia there, saying, "*What* were you thinking, Allison?"

So at about eleven I put on shorts, prepared an ice bag and a glass of sweet tea, and shuffled my way to the open porch on the side of the house facing Miz Vernell's. On the way the phone rang, and I stopped to listen to the answering machine.

It was Bonner. He'd missed me at church. Was I all right? How did the lessons go? Oh that's right, they were scheduled to go all day Sunday, too. He'd forgotten.

Yeah. Right now I was supposed to be learning to stop on wet surfaces or something. The rest of the class would be taking their test in a few hours and posing for the group graduation photo. Why did I feel like I'd just been dishonorably discharged from the armed forces?

I closed the kitchen door behind me and ignored Bonner's request that I call him when I had a chance. I didn't feel like eating crow right now. I could barely get my ice tea down.

The air was warm, in the eighties, but not heavy. I propped my legs up on the porch railing, draped the ice bag over them, and leaned back into the slouchy navy blue canvas chair where I liked to pray.

Except that today, even the Pathetic Pleading Prayer gave me no peace. "Okay, so I heard you wrong. Maybe you meant, 'Go buy barley.' Do you want me to open a bakery?" My only answer came from the goldfinches in the live oak tree, who I could have sworn were mocking me from behind their curtains of Spanish moss. I was definitely getting it wrong—as each throb from some new part of my body reminded me.

"What happened to *you?*"

I stifled a groan and didn't open my eyes. "Hi, Owen," I said.

I heard him take the steps in his Top-Siders. Next the porch swing creaked under his weight. He was staying a while.

"Your horse do that?" he said.

"Nope."

"It wasn't your date, was it? I'll break his neck. Who is the—"

I put up a hand before he could turn the air blue.

"I fell off a motorcycle," I said.

"You what?"

"Long story," I said. "But I just took a handful of ibuprofen, so I'll probably drop off here any minute."

"I won't keep you. But we do have a situation."

I opened one eye. Owen's bushy gray eyebrows were hanging over his eyes like hoods, he was frowning that hard.

"What's going on?"

"That guy that bought the house on the corner, next to Miz Vernell's?"

"Yeah?"

"The son of a gun's going to turn it into a bed-and-breakfast."

"Oh," I said without enthusiasm. "Just what we need around here is another B&B, huh?"

"Not on Palm Row! You know what kind of traffic that's going to mean. People parking in the road, blocking our driveways."

"We don't really have driveways, Owen."

"Exactly my point."

Was it me, or was he making no sense? I couldn't trust myself to tell the difference.

"People partying at all hours," he went on. "They'll turn this place into the Las Vegas strip. It's going to be Mardi Gras on Bourbon Street. We might as well be living right in the middle of Broadway."

My head was spinning, geographically speaking. "The kind of people who stay at a bed-and-breakfast don't party. They have the Early Bird Special down at Barnacle Bill's and turn out the lights at ten. Trust me—they end up in my carriage the next day, telling me how great the soft-shell crab was."

"It would change things, Ally, and you know it. We just don't want that here."

"We."

"You, me, Miz Vernell—and the Jablonskis behind me—and the Fisks behind Miz Vernell."

"What are we supposed to do about it?" My body hurt more with each word. Whatever it took to get Owen to shut up and get off the porch, I'd do it.

"I'm putting together a letter for all of us to sign."

"Great. Let me see it."

"I'll bring it around when I've got a final draft. I just wanted to make sure you were in."

"Why wouldn't I be?"

"Because it could make a difference in whether the sale goes through."

"You don't *want* it to go through."

"But Bonner Bailey does. I know you—"

"Owen." I came up on my elbows and felt my whole back wince. "You don't 'know' anything about Bonner and me because there's nothing to know. Just bring me the letter and I'll sign it."

He gave me the dentured smile. "I knew I could count on you."

"Good," I said. "Now go away and let me suffer in peace."

"You need something stronger than that," he said, nodding at my glass. "Let me bring you some single malt scotch. That'll fix you up."

"I don't drink, Owen."

"I know, and it's a shame at times like this." To my utter relief he stood up. "You call me if you need anything."

"I need peace and quiet," I said. "Good luck with your campaign."

He was already down the steps, on a mission to get around the corner to the Jablonskis before the neighborhood went up in smoke, down the tubes, and around the bend.

I had barely closed my eyes again so I could try once more to get connected with the God who had obviously *not* sent me the last message I'd thought I'd heard—when an unmistakable sound, and a recently familiar anxiety, roared right up my spine. There was no other sound like the thundering rumble of a Harley-Davidson.

I did some deep breathing and waited for it to roar on past the palm trees, realize it couldn't get out the other end of the alley, and turn around. If the driver had passed his Rider's Edge class he could do it without—

The engine muttered to a stop. Every muscle hollered, "What are you doing?" as I sat up and craned to see over the porch railing. A silver blue—what was that, a Sportster?—was being parked on the short stretch of concrete in front of my garage, by a short, chunky woman in a blue bandana do-rag and a denim jacket that strained across her ample bosom. I watched as she hung her rose-crested white helmet on her handlebars and dropped her gloves inside it as if it were a pocketbook. Her every confident move around that bike made me feel more inadequate by the second.

She walked toward the house and gave me a stubby wave. "Hey," she said. "You Allison Chamberlain?"

"Who wants to know?" I said. "Little Auggie from Detroit?"

Her square face broke into a grin. "No. Little Hank from Harley-Davidson."

I pulled my legs from the porch railing and looked around for a place to hide them. With my bruises in full view, I wouldn't be able to convince her I was not guilty of crashing one of her Buells, not once but twice.

"You got a minute?" she said from the steps.

She had a voice that made me think of gravel and Harvard Yard. She clearly wasn't the type you avoided.

"Why not?" I said. "Come on up."

She took the steps with surprisingly light feet and crossed to my chair. "Don't get up," she said. Her dark eyes widened at my shins.

"Not that you could anyway. They didn't tell me you were hurt this badly. Have you seen a doctor?"

"It looks worse than it is," I said. "You should see the other guy."

"I did."

Which was exactly why she was here. I'd thought about that too while I was sitting on my bike half the night. How was I going to pay for the damages to the training bike? The no-brainer, of course, was to sell my Harley.

The woman nodded toward the porch swing. "Mind if I—"

"Of course. Sit. I'm sorry," I said. "Can I get you some sweet tea?"

"No, you can't. Literally. I'm surprised you were able to get your-self any. I'm Hank D'Angelo."

"Hank?'" I said. "Great name."

"It's short for Henrietta, but don't call me that or I'll have to deck you. You're in enough pain already."

"Duly noted. Look … Hank … I'm sorry about the Buell. Just tell me how much I owe and I'll write you a check."

She scanned the porch, the side yard, the entrance to the kitchen. Probably assessing how much the place was worth. Good grief, were they going to *sue?*

"The bike's fine," she said, bringing her gaze back to me. "That stuff happens all the time. That's why we don't have students ride their own bikes when they're learning." She settled back against the red, white, and blue stripes, appearing to be as comfortable in my swing as she was in her own skin. "I heard you bought a nice one."

I grunted. "Probably a mistake, seeing how I'll never be able to ride it."

"Why not?"

I looked from her to my battered appendages and stopped short of saying, "Du-uh."

"There are two kinds of Harley riders," she said. "Those who *have* dumped a bike, and those who *will*. You've established which kind you are."

She smiled. I didn't.

"Look, I don't mean to be rude," I said, "but if you're not here about the bike I crashed ..."

"I'm the director of the Rider's Edge program for this area," she said. "We don't like for anybody to have a bad experience in one of our classes, so when I heard what happened yesterday, I thought I'd stop by and see how we can help you get back on a bike."

"You have quotas to maintain?"

She shook her head. A fringe of blunt-cut black hair at the base of the bandana shook with it. "Was Ulysses a jerk to you?"

I'm sure my surprised showed. "No. His jokes leave something to be desired, but—I just knew I couldn't do it, so I counseled myself out."

She scratched absently at her cheek. "We're not always our own best counsel."

"Now, you do have a point there," I said. "I shouldn't have listened when I told myself to buy an $18,000 motorcycle without even knowing how to start it up—"

My breath caught. Hank slid to the edge of the seat.

"You okay?" she said.

I didn't know how to answer. It wasn't my own counsel I'd listened to. But if it wasn't God's, whose was it? The not-knowing suddenly bordered on anger.

"I don't know what I am," I said to this perfect stranger.

"Who does? But let me ask you this."

"What?"

"Why did you buy a bike?"

"You really want to know?"

"Wouldn't have asked if I didn't."

I gave it one more beat, one more glance at my battered body, and then blurted out, "I felt like God was telling me to do it. More than once."

Everything was quiet for a moment. Even the birds seemed to stop laughing in the tree, and I watched Hank sink back into the swing, her feet sticking out several inches off the porch floor. Her face was impassive, but I was sure I could see the thoughts lining up in formation behind her eyes. It almost didn't matter what they were. What else *could* they be except, "Wow, you really are a nut bar, aren't you?"

It was okay, though. It had sounded awkward and halting coming out of my mouth—but, at last, very right.

"So," she said, "was it an audible voice?"

"No," I said. "It was much louder than that."

Hank shrugged her stocky shoulders. "Then I don't see how you can stay off the thing, Al. I think we have work to do."

CHAPTER FOUR

Work wasn't quite the right word for what Hank put me through on a Buell over the next four days. Not to put too fine a point on it, but she wore my fanny down to the bones.

"Don't let my domicile fool you," I told her Monday when we met on the now-empty range at the dealership after I got off work. "I've looked at my finances, and I can't afford private lessons."

"Who mentioned anything about paying me?" she said. "We've got God down our backs, so fuh-get-about-it."

I did, because the only thing I could think about during our four-hour sessions—besides how weird this was even for God—was exactly what she was telling me, in increments so tiny a four-year-old could get it. Or a panicked woman whose antiperspirant continued to fail her.

We spent the first two hours getting me in control of clutch-brakes-throttle.

"It's a smooth operation," Hank told me. "Kind of like wringing out a towel."

She got me up to speed fairly quickly because, as she put it, "Under ten miles an hour, it's like riding a huge bicycle. As we know, balance isn't your strong suit."

The first time I made it all the way across the range without falling or stalling or heading for the creek bed, I was so thrilled I took off my helmet and waved it in the air.

"There you go, Al," she said. "Each smooth start and smooth stop you make will build your confidence."

"Was that smooth?"

"Not at all. But you'll get there."

My confidence resisted, but after another two hours I started to get it, even though I continued to drift every time I looked down at the controls to make sure I was braking, not throttling. Hank still said I was the most freaked-out student she'd ever had, though not the most hopeless.

"Thanks for that," I said.

"At least you *know* that you don't know it." She gave her mouth the funny twist I was coming to enjoy. "I'll take you over an eighteen-year-old boy any day. They want to pop wheelies in the second hour."

"I have to learn to pop wheelies?" I said.

"That's not covered in this course. But …" She shrugged. "You never know what God's got in mind, yeah?"

I looked at her closely to make sure she wasn't mocking me.

She wasn't.

By the end of the first hour Tuesday, I could keep the thing upright, shift all the way to third gear—where everything was less jerky—and take a slight curve without dumping it. From there we moved on to steering, since, as Hank pointed out drily, I wasn't always going to be moving in a straight line.

"Build up speed in the straightaways, and then slow down for the turns. The faster you go, the less wobbly you are…."

"You have to maintain momentum in order to remain upright," I chanted. "Slowing down is not always the answer."

As I learned when I nearly toppled it on a turn because I put on the brakes.

It was, however, getting easier to stay on and keep practicing until the critiques at the ends of exercises were less along the lines of, "You're killin' me here, Al," and more like, "It's slow, look, press, and *roll*—not slow, look, press, and *maintain*."

It occurred to me sometime Wednesday, as I finally heard her cheer when I made a clean sweep all the way around the range, that the reason it was so hard for me to speed up and stay there was that it went against my very nature. Or maybe just against my experience.

Then I decided it was a good thing I didn't have time to ponder that too much.

Just when I got the hang of maintaining speed, on Day Three, it was time to work on braking.

"Constant and steady," Hank said. "Squeeze that hand brake like it's a Florida orange."

We did so many starts and stops and had so many critique sessions that I knew very well how to squeeze the brake—by imagining myself squeezing Hank's neck. She was a relentless teacher, exacting and whip-cracking—all Ivy League vocabulary delivered like a Boston street thug. Yet never once did I think about quitting.

"What am I learning today?" I asked her Thursday when we met at the range for our three o'clock lesson.

"You know it all intellectually," Hank said. "Now you have to practice until it comes naturally to you."

"When's that going to happen? Sometime this decade, I hope."

She ignored me. "Just practice whatever you're struggling with, and I'll interject."

"I still feel like a klutz on it about half the time. I wish I could just practice with nobody watching."

"Yeah," Hank said. "Too bad life doesn't work like that."

Friday morning dawned as a "spit day"—one of those we had now and then in the fall in St. A when it didn't exactly rain. It was more like having a conversation with someone who occasionally sprays you with fine saliva, but it's so brief and astonishing that you're not quite sure you actually felt it. Once again the early-September tourists made tracks to the Lightner Museum, and Lonnie didn't see any reason for me to hang out at the Bay Front waiting for fares that weren't going to show up.

"You've been cutting out early all week anyway," he told me when he called at eight a.m. "So I don't figure you need the money that bad."

"I've worked five hours a day, Lonnie," I said, and then turned on my coffee bean grinder so I wouldn't hear most of what he said next.

"—got a wedding coming up and the bride's parents have requested you, but I don't know—"

"I'll do it," I said. "After tomorrow I'll be back to putting in sixes and sevens, okay?"

He sighed. I rolled my eyes and poured the grounds into the filter basket. He was waxing dramatic.

"Just so you know," he said, "Bernard gets restless when you don't work him regular."

"You're a lying sack of cow manure, Lonnie. He's the laziest horse in that stable. Feed him some extra oats and I'll see you Saturday."

"Morning."

"Afternoon."

"Why?"

"Personal business. See ya."

I hung up before he could pry further. I wasn't about to tell him I had to take my motorcycle test Saturday morning. Him or anybody else. Although I hadn't been successful in keeping it from Bonner when he'd called Wednesday afternoon to see if I was coming to Watchdogs and I had to tell him no.

"I don't mean to be nosy," he said after a concerned pause, "but is anything wrong? You never miss."

I toyed with the idea of pretending I was losing service on my cell phone, but I knew if I did that he'd book right over to the house and call 911 on the way.

"I have a motorcycle lesson," I said. "From four till eight."

Another pause. A long man-sigh.

"What do you want me to tell everybody?" he said finally.

"Tell them I have a motorcycle lesson."

He actually laughed. "You sure you want to miss the expressions on their faces when they get *that* news? Nah—I don't want to deprive you."

"You're chicken," I said.

"Bok-bok," he said. "I'll tell them you have some personal business to take care of."

Which was where I got the line for Lonnie.

With the day free Friday, I could practice with Hank all morning and get my final instructions for the test, which I would take with a few other Chopper-challenged trainees who were coming in for a redo. We ran through the course several times until she was convinced I wouldn't score more than twenty-five points. Every time I made a mistake, she explained, the tester would add points, depending on how bad the error was. You couldn't make over thirty.

"Does anybody ever get a perfect score?" I asked her as we walked to our cars, the Buell put away and probably thanking its lucky tires it was almost done with me.

"Not even the instructors when they take a refresher," she said.

"How reassuring," I said.

"It kind of is, actually." Hank put her hands on the hips that lined up solidly with her waist and shoulders. "If nobody's perfect, then nobody has to drive themselves nuts because they aren't."

I laughed. "Trying to be perfect has never been my MO. Anybody who knows me will tell you that."

"I'd like to know you," she said. "You want to go for coffee?"

The woman had a way of making me feel like somebody had just changed the channel when I wasn't looking—because she knew where the good programs were.

"Sure," I said.

We met at the Spanish Galleon, a struggling little café in the Lyon Building, across the street from the Episcopal Church just south of King. It was a long, narrow hole-in-the-wall I'd never been in, but Hank was apparently a regular, because the hippie-esque woman behind the counter had a double-shot mocha with extra whipped cream ready for her before the bell stopped tinkling on the door.

"You're an angel from heaven, Patrice," Hank said to her.

"You want your waffle?"

"You have fresh blueberries today?"

"Of course."

"Then let's do it." Hank looked at me. "You want something? The Belgian waffles are to die for."

Patrice shook her impressive head of lion-mane hair. "I have her pegged for the Walk the Plank omelet."

Hank nodded, eyes closed. "Mushrooms, peppers, onions, spinach, tomatoes, ham, and aged cheddar. Fabulous."

"I'll just have coffee," I said. "Black."

When Patrice returned, visibly deflated, to the kitchen, Hank said, "Are you fasting?"

"No," I said. "I'm just freaked out about tomorrow. I figure the less I have to eat between now and then, the less I'll have to throw up before the test. Or during."

I waited—hopefully—for Hank to tell me I had nothing to worry about. Instead she placed her compact hands in a neat fold on the table and looked pretty much into my soul. It was startling enough to make me knock over the saltshaker I wasn't even using.

"So tell me," she said, "why *is* this so important to you?"

I pulled the hair-tie off my ponytail, checked my cell phone for messages I didn't care about, took a frenetic survey of the room crowded with reproduction sea trunks and large Jack Sparrow figurines.

"Wonder where they got all this funky nautical stuff," I said.

"You don't want to answer the question."

"No."

"I'm okay with that."

"But I think I have to."

"I'm okay with that too."

I raked my hand through my hair, which I was sure now looked like I'd been through a shipwreck. "I've got to be able to ride that motorcycle so I'll get another Nudge from God," I said. Then I added, "I didn't even know that I knew that until it just came out of my mouth. That happens all the time lately—at *the* most inopportune moments."

"I wouldn't call this one 'inopportune.'" Hank's gravelly voice had smoothed to something more like marvelous, luscious mud. "I'd like to hear about it."

I nodded, as once again she looked into me.

"It's weird," I said. "And yet when I think about it, it isn't—at least not for me."

"Always been weird, have you?" she said, mouth twitching.

"You could say that."

"I can relate. Go on."

"It's like with my conversion—to Christianity."

"From?"

"From … nothing."

"Everybody believes something."

"I believed everything my parents didn't believe," I said. "They drank, so I didn't. They exploited their workers, so I picketed with the strikers. They prided themselves on their vehicles, so I went everywhere on a bicycle."

"A bicycle?" Her lips twitched again. "You could've fooled me."

"It was a long time ago."

"How long?"

"I was about fourteen. I broke with Chamberlain tradition and insisted on going to public high school—where I found out that the rules are different for the rich, of which I was one—which ticks off the poor and makes them cynical and bitter and rebellious, and, in my opinion, a whole lot more interesting. I decided I wanted to be one of them."

The food arrived, and I watched in amazement, tinged with nausea, as Patrice set down a platter groaning under two Belgian waffles, a pint of blueberries, a cumulus cloud of whipped cream, and a generous sprinkling of powdered sugar. The whole buffet swam in a pool of melted butter.

"Patrice, you are an artiste," Hank said, face reverent.

"It's nice to be appreciated," Patrice said.

She looked at me from beneath the mane.

"Okay," I said, "I'll have a bagel."

"Oh for Pete's sake, at least bring her a carrot-raisin muffin." Hank leveled her eyes at me as Patrice went off, happier this time. "So if this is part of your vow of poverty, I'm treating."

"You've already treated me to twenty hours of free instruction. I should be treating you."

"You already are. This is the most stimulating conversation I've had in months."

"You don't get out much, do you?"

"I get out plenty." She tapped her forehead. "I don't get *in* much. So, about your conversion." She picked up her fork. "You talk, I'll eat."

I watched for a moment to check out her approach to the feast before her. She cut daintily into the corner of the waffle, scooped up the tiny morsel and swept it through the whipped cream, and placed the tidbit into her mouth with such savor I found myself drooling. She nodded at me before she uncovered a pecan, smiled at it, and tucked it between her lips.

"I went to the 'right' church growing up," I said. "The one where it was important to be seen. When I realized everybody was looking at us and not actually seeing a doggone thing that was really there, I refused to go anymore."

Hank was relishing each bite. "How old were you?"

"Sixteen. My mother would've forced me, but Sylvia told her that would only seal my fate as a complete heathen, so I slept in on Sundays."

"And did you become a complete heathen?" She stopped with half a forkful midway to her mouth. "You sure you don't want some of this?"

I shook my head to both questions. "Like I said, I didn't party, because that would make me too much like them. Didn't sleep around or hang out with the 'wrong crowd,' although I did love to bring home friends who were sure to send my mother running for the Valium."

"For you or for her?" Hank said.

"For my father, so he wouldn't blow a gasket. That was pretty much her job description in our household. Sylvia told her that if she didn't leave her body print on the ceiling every time I brought in a kid with a pierced ear, I would probably stop doing it."

"I love it." Hank tapped my plate with her fork tines. "Eat that muffin while it's still warm. Who's Sylvia, by the way?"

"My nanny, from the time I was born basically until she died when I was thirty-five. There were some years in there—eighteen to twenty-five, I guess, when I was out in California, trying to 'find myself'—where we didn't talk that much, but she was always in my head. I'd wonder if she was still praying for me." I wiggled my hand. "I'd vacillate between hoping she was and wanting to call her up and tell her she was wasting her time. Anyway, any spiritual influence I got in my youth was hers."

"I take it that was a good thing. At least taste a couple of these blueberries. I don't know what Patrice does with them but they're dee-vine."

I relented and scooped a few onto a spoon. She was right, of course.

"Nectar of the gods?" Hank said.

"Pretty close," I said. "And, yeah, now that I look back on it, it was a good thing. When I was twelve and I'd come home all ready for a fight because some little Miss Thing was putting me down at school, she'd say, 'You let God handle it, Allison. He's got a special place in hell for people like that.'"

Hank's eyes widened over her coffee cup.

"I know," I said. "The theology's questionable, but I didn't realize until I had my own relationship with God that she was telling me He loved me, in a way that, at that time, nobody but she did. Anyway— when she got sick, about ten years ago, I was renting a room from her and working for a restoration company, so I quit that job and took care of her until she passed away in '03."

Hank put her fork down. "You were her caregiver for three years?"

"Don't be impressed," I said. "It was the best job I ever had. I bumped into Jesus so many times at her bedside, I finally said, 'All right, what's the deal?'"

"And did he tell you?"

"Sylvia did, because I asked her." I smiled into the memory. "She said, 'Now's a fine time to ask—I'm dyin' here.' I just told her to hit me with the high points, which took a year. During that whole period the doctors kept telling me she had three months max, no more than a few weeks, wouldn't last through the night. She just kept talking to me, telling me, 'Forget all this Jesus-is-my-boyfriend nonsense. He's not gonna give you everything you want because you swoon over him.'" I glanced at Hank, who was grinning. "Yeah, like I ever 'swooned' in my life. Although—that one day—I'll never forget it … she was bedridden by then, but she wanted to go down to the living room and sit in her favorite chair. I carried her in there—she was nothing but tissue and soul at that point—and put her in this red chair-and-a-half she bought when she first inherited the house from my parents—another story. She looked so tiny in it that day, the way I must have looked to her when I was a little girl and she was carrying *me* around. I thought, 'She's going to die right now.' But her eyes were so alive, and I watched her take in every inch of that room. 'I made it ours,' she said. 'Yours and mine. We finally got a real home.'"

I pushed the remainder of the muffin away, because my throat was closing up. I hadn't talked about this in so long. Maybe even never—not like this. I tried to grin at Hank.

"What are you doin' to me here?" I said. "I was going to give you the *Reader's Digest* version."

"I hate those. I always wonder what I'm missing." She pushed aside her own plate, now miraculously empty. "I'm a little confused about the house."

"It was my parents' house. I grew up in it, and then when they were—when they died, they left it to Sylvia, who left it to me."

She didn't ask the obvious question. She just said, "Got it," and I went on.

"Sylvia sat there for the longest time that day, just looking at everything she'd done to make the place her own, and she'd done a lot. Took out the brocade draperies, ripped off the matching wallpaper. She'd said she always thought my mother's décor was like Early Whorehouse."

Hank spit out a laugh.

"The gold carpeting came up, and she had the wood floors refinished. She sold all my mother's 'antiques,' most of which were reproductions anyway because my mother could never get the idea out of her head that a real antique was still 'secondhand.' Sylvia replaced it all with bright colors and curtains that let in the sunshine and cushiony furniture you could actually sit on without being afraid you were going to leave an imprint in the velveteen. It was like she let the house breathe again, and she just curled up there in her comfort-chair that day and let *it* breathe for *her* until she fell asleep."

"Did she pass then?" Hank said.

"No. She just slept like I hadn't seen her do since she got the diagnosis. It was like she'd done everything she was put here by God to do and now she could rest some. And y'know, as I tried to look at the room and see it like she did, it hit me that it wasn't just the furniture and the pictures on the walls that she'd changed. Her spirit had driven out their shallowness. She'd knocked down the façade I'd lived with all my life. Nobody could ever be false in that house again. Including me." I looked up from my muffin plate at Hank, who was giving me her steady gaze. "I think that's why I finally saw Christ there, at that moment, and I just said, 'Why fight it? You're real and I believe in you.'"

"Did you tell Sylvia?"

"Yeah, the next morning."

"How did she respond?"

"She died. With a big ol' sigh of relief."

"Dear God, I love that," Hank said.

She obviously really did. Her eyes were as bright as a child's.

"So are you a nun or something?" I said. "I mean, you're really into this."

"I'm a far cry from a nun! If you're talking about my 'professional' Christianity, I was an Army chaplain until four years ago. I was up at Bethesda; counseled soldiers just back from Iraq and Afghanistan."

"Of course you did. You could probably get anybody to spill their guts."

She glanced at the check Patrice slipped on the table and turned it over. The hands folded on top of it. "I get the sense that you don't 'spill your guts' until you're ready, no matter who's asking the questions."

"True."

"So you've spent the last seven years learning how to be a good Christian…."

"I think mostly what I've learned is what *not* to do anymore because I'm a Christian. I guess I was fine with that until recently, and then I started getting this restless feeling, like there's got to be more to it than just being good. I'm not the most ambitious person in society, so the urge to be more than I am seems significant somehow."

"I don't think you can ignore it," Hank said.

"So you don't think this Nudgy, kind of almost-a-voice thing is my imagination? I mean, is that how people know God's talking to them?"

"In my experience, it doesn't matter *how* you know. It only matters *that* you know. And I've gotta tell you, Al, people buy motorcycles they can't handle all the time, and most of them wind up selling them within three months of purchase. I've never seen any of them work as hard as you have to get control of the thing. If you're as devoid of ambition as you claim you are, then this sure seems like God to me." She shrugged. "What have you got to lose by giving it a go?"

"Do you seriously think I'll pass tomorrow?" I said. "I want you to be honest."

She did the little mouth twist. "If you can keep your cool, you'll more than pass. Pray, of course, and remember what I've told you."

"Which thing?"

"They can tell what your head is doing by what your motorcycle is doing." She gave the table a sound pat and picked up the check. "I'm going to go take care of this."

I nodded and watched her stride her stocky self up to the counter and realized she was talking about far more than a motorcycle test.

Hank was right. I did pass, with a score of twenty and a minimum of profuse sweating. There was no vomiting.

Ulysses was there, and Darrell, and Stan, among others from the dealership who whistled and cheered when I received my certificate as if I were accepting the Stanley Cup. I'd actually expected some eye-rolling, some indication that the sport of motorcycling was now going downhill if they'd give *me* a license.

Hank passed around sparkling cider—and told Stan to bag it when he complained that it wasn't champagne. She gave me the mouth twitch when she handed me my glass.

Ulysses pounded me on the back, which was still aching from my bout with his class. "Now you can join HOG."

"Can I please?" I said drily.

"It stands for Harley Owners Group," Stan said. "We have a meeting tomorrow at noon." He wiggled his eyebrows. "We all want to see you on your own ride, girl."

"She's going to go home and practice on that right now," Hank said. "And no harassing her tomorrow or you'll all be in a hurt locker, every one of you."

I had no idea what a hurt locker was, but it looked like nobody wanted to be in one, especially if Hank was going to put them there.

"Don't worry about it," she said to me later when we pulled my Classic out of the garage to admire it together. "They'll tease you about initiating you, but it's all talk. We're all about safety and everybody having a good time." She nodded at my bike. "Now get on that thing and ride it to the end of the block here. I want to take a picture."

I fired her up—that sleek, Hot Sunglo machine. And for the first time since I sat on her in the showroom, she seemed one with me again—her and her shine and her chrome and her eighty-one-point-three cubic inches of engine.

I belonged with her—and I was going wherever she took me. Even if it killed me.

CHAPTER FIVE

I decided the next day that the Classic wasn't taking me to church. After a Saturday morning of testing and celebrating, and an afternoon of particularly obnoxious groups of tourists—one of which spoke not a word of English and glared at me for the entire hour because I didn't know Croatian—I was too worn out to face the Watchdogs and the Reverend Howard from the back of a Harley.

Their accosting me en masse on the church steps after the service was exhausting enough.

"We missed you Wednesday, Miss Allison," Frank said.

"Everything all right?" Mary Alice said.

India was less subtle. "So—what personal business was more important than us?"

I caught Bonner smirking behind her.

"Bonner can fill you in," I said. "I really have to run."

And then I did, literally, straight into Pastor Garry's open wings.

"A good Sunday morning to you, Allison!" he sang out, and then he held me at arm's length. I wanted to squirm like a puppy. "How's your group coming along?"

"I'll touch base with you this week," I said. "I really have to get going." I glanced over my shoulder, where Bonner was now smoldering at me. "If you need to know right this minute, Bonner's your man."

I wriggled away and took the steps two at a time. I was probably home before Bonner finished the conversation.

After I showered off the sweat, I put on my jeans and my boots and the leather jacket and chaps I'd treated myself to when I passed the test and went out to the garage. Where I sat—broiling—on my bike and had an attack of nerves.

"I can do this," I said to her. "*We* can do this. Milestone by milestone, just like MOM says."

"MOM" was the Motorcycle Owner's Manual. "If you want to know anything just ask your MOM," Ulysses told us that first night in class. It was an unfortunate acronym as far as I was concerned. My mother had been something less than maternally helpful.

But I'd still read the guide cover to cover the night before, and I had the Milestones memorized.

"Milestone Number One," I said out loud as I brought the engine to life. "Riding your own bike for the first time alone." Why did that sound like I was about to commit a crime?

I eased out of the garage and realized I was going to have to make a slow left turn to get headed toward St. George Street. Neither left turns nor slow ones of any kind were my top skills, but I fixed Hank's voice in my head and managed to get onto Palm Row. Still, I had to get up some speed or I was going to dump it, right in front of Miz Vernell's house—where she was currently standing in her pastel paisley muumuu, pulling beetles off of her roses.

Out of the corner of my eye, I saw her gape, but I had to imagine the rest—the eyes popping behind the magnifying glasses that already made her look like a pug dog, the garden-gloved hand going to her little dried lips. If I'd actually looked, I would have driven right up onto her lawn (I could hear Hank saying, "The bike's going to go where your head goes"), and the bewildered little woman would have suffered cardiac arrest. Just seeing me on a motorcycle probably had her halfway there already.

Part of me, however, couldn't resist sitting at the corner for a moment, rolling the throttle. I was starting to love the fact that I had the power to make that sound. And I was still trying to decide whether to head for the HOG meeting. I'd gone approximately fifty yards by myself, so that was Milestone Number One. If I hung one left onto St. George and went up to Artillery Lane, I could keep making right turns after that and take care of Milestone Number Two: "riding around your own neighborhood."

Once I got onto Artillery, I realized that I hadn't counted on the engine's rumble being so ominous on the narrow street crammed with two-story buildings. By the time I got to Aviles, I'd freaked out a Yorkie on a balcony and made a man in a bathrobe jump back from the newspaper in his driveway. Left turn or not, I decided I'd better take the next street, Charlotte, to King, which, though busier, was more wide open. People were used to Harleys roaring through there.

I just wasn't used to being the one doing the roaring. I had to focus hard, both feet down at the same time at the stoplight, keeping my distance from the truck spewing fumes in my face—smooth, smooth, smooth, everything smooth.

Even at that I was aware of the stares, the heads turning to the deep growl that could only come from a Hog. I didn't let myself wonder whether they were cursing or envying as I cruised between Flagler College and the old Alcazar Hotel building like a rolling anachronism. I just kept going—*it's okay, you can pass this guy looking for a parking place, keep your speed up, slow down in front of the police station, they love to pull bikers over*—until nobody was staring anymore because the crowd had thinned.

And then I saw why. I was crossing Ponce de Leon Boulevard. US One.

I was on West King Street.

I knew better than to slow down too much or I'd start to wobble, and this definitely wasn't a place where you wanted to look like you didn't have control. Although it was as vacant-looking as it had been two weeks before when Bernard and I had found ourselves here, this time I felt like eyes were watching me from the cracks in the boards on the windows and the doors half hung on their hinges and the dank alleys I'd never noticed before. I was even more vulnerable on a motorcycle than I'd been in a carriage—and a whole lot louder. West King was wide, but my engine's roar reverberated off of the concrete-everything like the woofers on a gang kid's car stereo.

Yeah, this met the requirements of Milestone Number Three: "riding outside my neighborhood."

I was almost to I-95 by then, with the hidden eyes of West King closing again behind me and the Harley dealership beckoning ahead. I forgot what Milestone Number Four was, but I knew Number Five, and I headed straight for it.

"Becoming a HOG member." Every woman's dream. I'd refused to even sit on a bike that was called a Fat Boy, and now I was going to sign up to be something that inspired even more visions of obesity.

I had the urge to snort—until I pulled into the parking lot and found myself in an ocean of chrome and handlebars and studded leather saddlebags. There must have been two hundred bikes, and half again as many people in a rainbow of do-rags. It felt like Day One on the training range all over again.

I managed to nose my own bike between a Road King and a Street Glide without knocking either of them down, and then saw that every one of the motorcycles there had been backed into their spaces. Headlights taunted me as I walked away from them while my Classic remained with her backside facing the world. She and I were becoming more alike by the minute.

The eyes of the other Harleys weren't the only ones on me as I strode across the parking lot and tried to look like I should be there. Despite the leather jacket and chaps, I knew I still looked about as much like a biker chick as Jacqueline Kennedy.

"Hey," a male voice said. "Nice chassis."

I turned around, tongue already in half-lash, but the voice's owner was pointing to my bike.

"Brand new?" he said.

"Yeah," I said. I didn't think I needed to add that this was my first time riding it.

"Good-lookin' ride," he said.

I started to ask him where I had to go to sign up, but someone else said, "Dude, that thing is slammed to the ground!"

I twisted the other way, expecting to catch somebody's Harley under a truck. All I saw was a small masculine crowd around a bike that looked like everything on it had been lowered and stretched. Except for the handlebars, which would have extended over my head if I'd been sitting on the thing.

"I'll never understand ape hangers," a woman near me muttered.

She was even taller than I and a little older and, in spite of the past-its-prime show of cleavage that was spilling out of her tank top, she looked pretty safe.

"What are ape hangers?" I said.

"Those handlebars," she said. "They make you look like an ape when you're riding." She demonstrated, arms chimpanzee-like in the air.

"So slammed to the ground means ..."

"A bike that's been modified so your butt's practically on the street." She looked at me a little more closely. "First time with us?"

"Could you tell?"

"Don't worry about it. Everybody's great. Let me get you a packet."

She disappeared into the crowd. I looked around and quickly came to the conclusion that to be a HOG of the male variety, you either had to have a shaved head or hair down to your rear. I couldn't tell about the women because they were all wearing bandanas that equalized everyone. I was wondering if they called female members SOWs when a short, soft-looking man came up to me, put his hand out, and said, "I'm Rex. I'm the chapter president."

I almost said, "Are you serious?" Although his graying temples and mushy paunch put him at middle age, he had the face of an over-sized toddler. He didn't look like officer material, but I was beginning to figure out that, when they donned helmet and leather, nobody looked like who they probably really were.

"Allison," I said, returning his chubby handshake. "This is— wow—a big turnout."

He looked around as if he'd just noticed the crowd. "Not as big as most," he said with a whisper of a French accent. "Usually we have three, four hundred bike for a group ride."

I was trying to determine whether "bike" was the plural form when you were talking about a herd of motorcycles when the woman returned with the HOG packet and introduced herself as Leighanne.

"She's our secretary," Rex said to me.

Before I could ask what they needed a secretary for, someone else whistled through his fingers, and the attention shifted to instructions for The Ride—with a capital R, obviously, because people immediately began donning helmets and putting on fingerless gloves—what was the point in those?—and revving up engines until the concrete under us vibrated. When I was pretty much the only one still standing there, it came to me that a chapter meeting meant everybody got on their bikes and rode someplace. All at once. In a herd.

I went cold all over.

"You like your bike so far?"

Despite the thunder of departing Harleys, the low voice beside me made me practically jump out of my chaps. I looked up—and up a little more—at a man with a gray ponytail down to his broad shoulders. Snappish brown eyes looked back at me from either side of a striking nose. It was like meeting an eagle at close range.

He pointed at my Classic.

"Yes, sir," I said.

"You weren't planning to take it on this ride, were you?"

My urge to pay him Harley-homage faded, and I lowered my sunglasses. "The way you asked that, I guess my answer is supposed to be no?"

He hitched his big shoulders slightly, as if a full shrug was too much effort. "You could do it, but you'd probably kill yourself."

"How would you *know* that?"

"Because I saw you ride in."

The sweat-matted hair on the back of my neck tried to bristle. "I passed my test."

"Yesterday?"

"Yeah."

"Then the answer is supposed to be no."

I looked for a smile somewhere on the raptor face, but I couldn't tell if there was one. He seemed like the kind of guy who only had one expression: slightly ticked off.

"How do you propose I get experience if I don't ride?" I said.

"You want some experience? Ride with me."

Only because it didn't sound like a line did I ask, "Where would we go?"

"Back streets—some nice curves. You looked pretty steady, but you aren't ready for a group ride."

"So, what do I—"

"Follow me, and just look at every situation out there in traffic as a possible ambush situation. You'll be fine."

He turned and took long-legged strides toward a black and chrome Road King. For no reason I could fathom, I trotted after him.

"On your bike, Classic," he said over his shoulder.

"I knew that," I called to him. And added "chauvinist" under my breath.

I scurried to my bike, appalled that I was actually doing this, and wrestled her out of the parking space. No wonder everybody else backed in. When I pulled up behind the Road King, the guy nodded, ponytail trailing from his helmet, and glided out of the lot. I considered taking a left when he signaled a right onto Pelicer, but I really, really didn't like left turns. And there was something about the way he leaned so easily and flowed so smoothly into the traffic that almost gave me no choice but to follow him. Nobody *else* was leading me right now.

God didn't seem to realize I was referring to him.

My guide sailed onto Old Moultrie, which seemed to me an odd route for a nice bike ride. Aside from the old oaks that hung their Spanish moss heads romantically amid the strip malls and gas stations, it wasn't particularly scenic. I was supposed to be paying attention to my driving—that had to be the reason for this choice.

I stayed a car length back and changed lanes every time he did— and realized something two stoplights down when he pulled up in the lane beside me.

"What's your name?" I yelled.

"Chief," he called back.

"I'm Allison."

"I know."

Sheesh. Evidently being a HOG was like living in a small town. Did they have dossiers on every piglet?

I fell in behind him again, and he immediately signaled a left turn into a parking lot. It happened so fast I didn't see the gaping pothole in the asphalt until it was staring me in the face and I was staring back. I jerked to get around and missed it, but when I hit the brake, I slid crazily on a patch of gravel. There was no reason that I didn't dump it, except maybe the grace of God.

It was about time he showed up. I was floundering.

"You okay?" Chief was already off his bike, hanging his helmet on the handlebar.

"Oh yeah. I've done worse."

"A little word of advice?"

"Sure," I said, fumbling for my kickstand. "Why not?"

"Don't look at what you don't want to run over. You had a little target fixation going on there. Other than that, you're doing okay."

"Did I miss the part where I signed you on as my personal trainer?"

"No," he said. "Hank was busy today, so she told me to watch out for you."

"Remind me to thank her," I mumbled. I tilted my head back to pull off my helmet, and my gaze snagged on the sign on the block building we'd pulled up to. Resurrection Convalescent Center, it read.

"I *did* miss the part where you said we were going to a nursing home," I said.

"I come here every Sunday—give some of the old guys rides."

"On your *Harley*?" I said.

"I take a couple of the ladies when I bring my sidecar."

He peeled off his gloves and denim jacket, revealing fit biceps that didn't match the gray hair on his forearms.

"You're serious," I said.

"Some riders do Toys for Tots. I do Toys for …"

"Old dots," I said.

"Something like that."

He started toward the front door. I was still in my helmet.

"Wait," I said. "I'm not ready to be carrying anybody yet."

"You won't be," he said without looking back as he continued to the entrance. "I just need to check on someone."

I didn't have time to hook my helmet over the handlebars, so I tucked it under my arm and once again trailed after him with no idea why. He held the door open for me, and as I slid past him, he said, "This won't take long."

Quite frankly, I didn't want it to take any time at all. I'd managed to avoid convalescent homes all my life. My Grandfather Chamberlain had suffered a dignified massive heart attack at his carved mahogany desk and died right there like the proud man he was. My parents had died too young and too suddenly to need one. And I'd sworn Sylvia would never spend a day in such a place. The very name was a misnomer to me, since I'd never heard of anybody convalescing and going home once they'd been admitted.

But as we stepped into the lobby and were greeted by potted ficus trees and piped-in Frank Sinatra, it was obvious this one didn't match any of the horror stories I'd heard. There were no confused and raving old people strapped to wheelchairs in the lobby or, as Lonnie had told me about his great-grandmother, pawing at visitors in the hall, begging them to rescue them. The faint scent of urine covered by Pine-Sol and baby powder wasn't even that disconcerting.

I tried to keep up with Chief as he strode down a tiled hallway lined with paint-by-number oils of pastoral scenes. I made a vow that when I was set aside to convalesce, I'd have a nice, racy Picasso to look at.

We were about to enter a room across from the nurses' station when a caramel-colored woman in scrubs with a deep worry line between her eyebrows hurried out from behind the desk, tennis shoes squealing on the white linoleum. Chief leaned his head down to her, his own face suddenly all concern. So he did have more than one expression.

"What's up, Willie?" he said.

"Your boy's not so good," she said.

"Define 'not so good.'"

"We can't get his sugar reg-a-lated. He just about went into a coma last night."

"What does his doc say?"

Willie's voice pitched upward with her eyebrows. "It's Sunday. He ain't comin' in on a *Sun*day, you know that."

"What's his number?" Chief pawed a cell phone out of his back pocket. "I'll call the—"

"Chief." Willie put her hand on his arm. "I told you this was comin'."

They were apparently talking about some relative of his, and it felt inappropriate for me to be privy to this obviously aching moment. I didn't even know "Chief's" real name.

"I'm going to go ahead and go," I whispered, already taking a step backward.

Willie looked at me as if I'd just materialized, and her gaze fell on the helmet I still had under my arm.

"Old Ed won't be doin' any ridin' today," she said softly.

"No, I wasn't planning—"

"Can we see him?" Chief said.

"'Course you can. Y'all go on in—he'll love that."

I started to stammer that this really ought to be a private moment, but Chief was already holding the door open for me, big shoulders caving toward his chest. It didn't look like this was a thing he could do alone, and Willie was on her way down the hall. I crept past him into the room.

There was barely a lump in the covers, and at first I thought the bed was empty. Chief crossed directly to the window and opened the blinds, shafting sunlight on a dark, wizened face that was sunken into the pillow. An almost sickeningly sweet smell rose from him, and the hands that rested on top of the sheets were bloated as water balloons. For a man as sick as he looked, there were surprisingly few tubes running in and out of his body. When Sylvia was in the hospital for the last time, before I took her home to be cared for by hospice and me, she'd resembled a hydra.

The man's eyes stuttered open and lit up like tiny birthday candles when Chief sat on the edge of the bed. I leaned against the wall and watched as they groped for each other's hands.

"How's it goin', Ed?" Chief said.

"It's not, Chief," the man said.

His voice was weak, but it didn't sound as old as I'd expected. His head was only slightly dusted in gray, though I knew a lot of African-Americans naturally kept their dark hair into their eighties.

"Yeah, you're not up for a ride today, Buddy," Chief said. "But next week—"

"I don't think so. I think my ridin' days is over."

Ed patted Chief's hand, an effort that set him wheezing. Chief looked around wildly for something—anything—but the coughing subsided and the old guy stroked Chief's hand again, as if Chief were the one in need of comforting. I'd known Ed for five minutes and I wanted to take him home.

Sylvia had always needed an ice chip when her throat dried out like that. I fished one from Ed's plastic pitcher with a spoon and handed it to Chief.

"This'll help," I said.

He took it without hesitation and offered it to Ed, who accepted it gratefully on his tongue. It was like watching somebody take communion.

"I bet you need your feet raised," I said. If they looked anything like his hands, they needed to be elevated. I found the button on the bed and held it down until the furrows in Ed's forehead smoothed.

"Who this angel?" Ed said.

"This is Allison," Chief said.

"One of your biker friends?"

"Yes."

Ed attempted a smile in my direction. "She reminds me of Geneveve—before she got on the drugs." His lower lip trembled and he turned fitfully to Chief. "I think she's usin' again. She ain't been in to see me in weeks."

He raised a hand and let it drop, and I suspected it had probably been more than weeks since the elusive Geneveve had darkened the doors of the Resurrection Nursing Home.

"Maybe she came when you were sleeping," Chief said.

Ed shook his head. "I'd know she was here. I can tell without even openin' my eyes." He closed them now, just as moisture was beginning to form. "She workin' the street, Chief. I know it."

His voice broke, and Chief took the old man's face in both of his hands. He said nothing until Ed drifted off. It appeared there was nothing *to* say.

Chief nodded me toward the door, and I followed him out and down the hall in silence. By the time we got outside, his face had worked itself back in control.

"Can I ask who Geneveve is?" I said.

"His daughter."

"Is she—"

"She's a hooker," he said. "Down on West King Street."

For a moment I thought he was going to spit. Instead, he shook his head and started toward the bikes.

"You still wanna go for a ride?" he said.

"No."

He stopped and turned. I was still standing under the Resurrection overhang.

"Thanks," I said, "but I have something else I have to do."

"Suit yourself," he said. "Just be careful out there."

"I'm going to have to be where I'm going," I murmured as I watched him take off on the Road King. The Nudge was so strong and so clear, I couldn't talk or think or snort it away this time.

Find her, Allison, it said. *Find Geneveve.*

CHAPTER SIX

My first thought was to head for West King right then, but it occurred to me that I hadn't seen anyone down there when I passed through, much less a prostitute working the street. The reasonable thing to do was to go home and wait for nightfall.

Okay, so maybe *reasonable* was too strong a word.

It was only about three p.m. when I returned to Palm Row, which, with Daylight Savings Time still in effect, gave me about four and a half hours to obsess. I went from the red chair to the kitchen counter where I'd always liked to sit and swing my legs while Sylvia cooked, to the window seat in her old room where I'd listened to her talk about "Our Lord," as she always called him. I avoided either of the porches. I wasn't up for Miz Vernell or Owen's input on my new acquisition.

But as much as I tried to pick up on Sylvia's lingering wisdom, it was my father who kept preempting my thoughts. I had no trouble imagining what he would say, on the million-to-one chance that I would have told him. He would at this very moment be trying to shut me down. Give him another hour with me saying I was doing it anyway and he'd have his lawyer working on my commitment papers. I could almost see his eyes drilling a hole into me while we waited for the guys with the straightjacket. *Do you recall what I said the last time I saw you, Allison? I said the only thing Chamberlain you have in you is the DNA. Well, I'm retracting that now. The only way to account for this is that your mother brought the wrong kid home from the hospital. I have somebody else's mess on my hands.*

I tried to shut him out by digging into my stash of Oreos, but after I licked a few middles, I abandoned the effort. Oreos were for

guilt, and I had no guilt about my father. What I had right now was
an unexplained dull ache, right in the middle of my chest.

Sitting on the bottom step of the staircase, I stared at my out-
line in the dark wood floor that I still kept shiny in Sylvia's honor.
I was blurry to myself—so out of focus I couldn't determine what
about this whole thing was making me hurt. I didn't even know Ed
Whatever-His-Name-Was, or his wayward daughter, and yet it was as
if I did, as if I *were* them in some way that wasn't any clearer to me
than my face on the floor.

Only the Nudge was clear. So when Miz Vernell's porch light
turned on automatically and I could no longer see the tops of the
palms, I put on my gear again and drove the Classic out of the garage.
Owen's light went on—manually, I knew. He'd have a list of questions
for me tomorrow. Tonight I didn't have any answers.

It was disturbing how little time it took to get from my house
to West King. It was only eight blocks; I marked them as I went.
Somehow I'd always thought I lived a world away.

Once I got there, I certainly *felt* like a foreigner, cruising as slowly
as I dared without falling over, looking for something I wasn't sure
I'd recognize when I found it. What I'd heard turned out to be true.
There was life here—of sorts—after sundown.

I counted four bars on my first pass along the three-block stretch.
None of them appeared to have air-conditioning because their doors
were propped open and figures lounged in the doorways, bottles in
hand, sweat gleaming in the light of the bare bulbs screwed in above
their heads. Although I could hear raspy female laughter mingled
with the battering music from within, by the time I was almost to
I-95, I hadn't seen any women on the sidewalks.

What was I expecting? Pretty women stopping cars? Where did prostitutes advertise their—how did they pick up a trick? Find a john?

I rolled my eyes inside my helmet. I didn't even know the language. How was I supposed to talk to this woman if I did find her? Maybe I would have been better off dressing up like a potential male client. Except I didn't know how it worked from that side of it either.

As I made my second pass, this time heading east, I realized that not all of the action was in the bars. People were gathered in dark clumps on the corners and in the doorway of a closed diner. I'd thought West King was scary in the daytime with its vacuous eyes spying on me, but it had a distinctly more sinister feel at night when those eyes were out in the open, coldly sizing up the Classic and me.

Strangely, though, I didn't feel as vulnerable as I had in the carriage. There was a sort of implied respect for the Harley in the way they watched—and didn't hurl beer bottles or epithets. At least that I could hear, anyway.

But by the time I'd nearly reached Malaga Street and the "good" side of King, I was losing hope of locating a lady of the night. If I cruised those three blocks too many more times, I was bound to stir up suspicion. Either that or somebody would stop me and try to make a drug deal. They had to assume I was either selling or buying. What else would somebody on a $20,000 motorcycle be doing down here?

I was just about to make a left down one of the side streets when I did see a woman. I pulled hopefully over to the curb, but she was walking with purpose and carrying a piled-high laundry basket. She took the outside stairs up the side of the auto repair building—C.A.R.S.

it was called, as indicated by the plastic letters gone crooked on the marquee.

I didn't imagine a hooker would be doing her laundry during prime time. But—wow—did that mean somebody actually lived here? I was completely mystified that anyone would call this place home.

As I watched a screen door slap closed behind her, I wondered if she'd ever thought the same thing.

I decided to take that side street after all and checked over my shoulder before pulling back out onto the road—not that I was exactly looking at rush hour. That was when I saw a pair of women across from me, leaning against the vacant storefront next to the tattoo parlor. I'd never actually seen a prostitute—that I was aware of—but when I spotted them now, there was no mistaking it.

It wasn't their clothes, necessarily. Half the young women I saw around town wore what India referred to as "hooker wear." And these two weren't wearing any less clothing than anybody on Crescent Beach, including the middle-aged men in Speedos. It was the *way* they were wearing them. Tops cut desperately to their navels. Sleeves dragged savagely over bare, bony shoulders. Pants so punishingly tight they were obviously cutting off all flow of life. There was definitely none making it to their faces.

The questions I'd practiced at home wouldn't even come up on my radar as I drove the Harley across the street and shut off the engine at the curb in front of them. They watched stonily as I lifted my visor and smiled.

"Hello, ladies," I said.

Aw, man, did that sound sarcastic?

"How's it going?"

Oh—bad question.

"Do you have a minute?"

Allison. Just ask.

"Have y'all seen Geneveve?"

The bigger one of the pair jerked her chin. "Geneveve who?"

I had no idea. "You have more than one Geneveve around here?" I said.

The smaller girl grunted. It sounded like it may have been a laugh at one time, when she remembered how. She closed off when the other woman cut her with a look. To me, the bigger woman said, "Who wants to know?"

"Someone with a message for her," I said. At least I remembered one of the lines I'd practiced. Even though at close range both of them looked like a healthy breeze would knock them over, my heart was slamming in my chest.

The woman pointed a finger toward the next block. I could almost see the bones in it trembling beneath the brittle skin. "She down there. In 'at bar."

I followed her point. "The Magic Moment?" I said.

"Mmm-hmmm. She in trouble?"

I was surprised by the question, for some reason. Of course, all of this was a surprise to me. Like the birthday party you didn't want.

"No," I said. "I just have some information for her."

"She down there." This time she didn't seem to be able to point. How did these women come up with the energy to do what they did when they had to do it? Old Ed was in better shape than they were.

The woman poked her smaller friend and the two drifted toward the tattoo place. I started up my bike, then just sat there.

If Geneveve was inside the bar, that would necessitate my going in too. Maybe I could bribe somebody to go in and fetch her for me. Everybody I saw looked like they had their price.

With that as my only plan, I drove down the block and across the street and parked in front of the Magic Moment. The only thing magical about it was that it was still standing. Duct tape held one whole corner of the front window together, and the doorsill sagged like a fat man's belt. There weren't as many customers hanging out in the doorway as at the other bars, although I couldn't understand how anybody lasted long inside. Even from the curb I could smell the saturation of stale beer and cigarettes.

Someone tapped my shoulder. I gasped and waited to die.

"She ain't gon' come out anytime soon," a barely audible voice rasped just outside my helmet.

I turned to see the bigger of the two woman sidling herself onto the rear fender of my Harley.

"How long do you think it'll be?" I said, as if it had even occurred to me to just wait for Geneveve out here.

"Depends."

"On what?"

"On how much it worth to you."

So I'd been right. I dug into the pocket of my jacket and pulled out a roll of bills—a twenty disguising a dozen ones. I'd seen that done on *Burn Notice.*

She reached for it, but I stuffed it inside my jacket, near my now soon-to-be-imploding heart. "When you bring her out," I said.

She didn't have to be told twice but inserted herself unnoticed between two inebriated bookends at the door and disappeared inside.

I refused to think about what she was going to do with the $32. Did that even buy enough dope for a fix anymore? I'd lost touch with the drug world after I quit working at the rehab center in Orange County in '91. Back then the fifty bucks our graduates were given when they left the place was plenty to get them right back in before the week was out.

"You got you a Haawwwg, Mama?"

I jerked my head away from the doorway. A group had arranged themselves in front of me on the street. There were only four guys, but it might as well have been a mob. They would have blended with the inky blackness of the place if not for the paltry neon Coors Light sign in the Magic Moment's window and the gold teeth every one of them seemed to possess. I should have such a dental plan.

The one who'd spoken—the only one who appeared coherent enough—approached me, leading with his pelvis.

"You come down here to give me a ride, Mama? Pretty *Ma*-ma?"

"Sorry," I said. "I don't take passengers."

How lame was that? It was the best I could come up with under extreme distress. The only thing keeping me there was the fact that I was frozen to the seat. With sweat gushing down the back of my neck.

"Come on, now. Every other mama down here for hire. But ain't one of 'em got what you got."

He stroked his hand across the fender, and I was close to throwing up on him when the now familiar female voice said, "Go on now—she ain't got nothin' for you."

My woman shooed them off with her hand, to which they responded with comments that rapidly escalated in crudeness. I zeroed in on the figure behind her and gasped before I could stop myself.

She was little more than a fragile collection of bones clothed in sallow-brown flesh. Her eyes would have engulfed her tiny face if they hadn't been sunken into her skull. How could she be a prostitute? If anyone touched her, she would surely crush like onionskin between their fingertips.

Please, God, tell me this isn't her.

"You got my money?"

The other woman, who now looked hearty in comparison, was close enough for her sour smell to nearly knock me over. She talked tightly between her few teeth that meth hadn't eaten away, her back to the gold-toothed crew who were now watching from the corner with feigned disinterest.

I put my hand over my jacket pocket and nodded at the tiny figure behind her.

"What's your name?" I said.

"Geneveve," she said, in a whisper that wouldn't have blown out a match.

"What's your daddy's name?"

"Edwin Sanborn."

"You gon' give me my money, or do I got to turn them dudes on you?"

I pulled out the wad and slipped it to the other woman without taking my eyes off Geneveve. The woman skittered away like a rabid squirrel, leaving me alone on West King Street with old Ed's daughter.

"My daddy sick?" she said.

I was surprised she'd been able to figure that much out, but I just nodded. "He wants to see you."

"I can't," she said.

"He's dying," I said. "And he asked for you."

I expected her to ask who *I* was, but she seemed to be accustomed to strangers bringing her bad news. Either that, or she was too strung out to care.

"Why can't you?" I said.

"I got no way to get there."

"I'll take you," I said.

Dear God, had I just said, "I'll take you?" Or was that God himself talking?

She shook her head, but the sunken eyes were swimming. "I can't let him see me like this."

"He doesn't have to. I'll get you cleaned up."

There was no use fighting it. It was just coming out of my mouth. And the Gold Tooth Crew was once again sauntering across the street toward us.

"Get on," I said. "We have to hurry."

It took another frantic nod of my helmet to get her to climb onto the seat behind me. What Milestone was this, "carrying a passenger"? Hank would pull my certificate. Bonner would have a seizure.

It couldn't matter, because I barely got the bike in first before the Gold Teeth were in range. I took the corner of Davis and West King at a hard lean and hauled us away from them. This wouldn't count as carrying a passenger anyway. I wouldn't have known the wisp of a woman was even behind me if not for the arms wrapped around my waist, clinging like a koala bear. Both of us were shaking.

Prayers were never prayed so hard as those that came out of me before we got to Palm Row. I didn't drive the Classic like I stole her. I drove her like I had ten Nazis and a pack of dogs chasing me. I gave

God the credit for getting us there, where I half-carried Geneveve into the house. She probably had no idea that I was barely remaining vertical myself.

Inside, under the kitchen lights, I decided "I'll clean you up" was going to entail more than a toothbrush and a change of clothes. Her eyes were caked with something hard and crusty, and her hair hung in locks that were more than dreadful. I got her upstairs and ran a bath and suggested she get in while I rifled through my closet for something that wouldn't swallow her. I located a knit tunic I'd bought in a moment of optimism several diets ago and knocked on the bathroom door.

"I'll hang this on the doorknob out here for when you're ready," I said. "I'm going down to make you some food."

Silence.

"Geneveve?"

When there was still no answer, I clawed past a vision of her drowned in three inches of water, threw open the door, and found her curled up on the rug, half-naked and shivering.

"I couldn't get in," she said.

"Okay."

I toyed with the idea of a quick sponge bath, but it wouldn't make a dent in the odor that oozed from her. I'd smelled swamps I could tolerate better.

"All right," I said. "I'll just lift you in, clothes and all. Those are going in the wash anyway."

On second thought they were going in the trash, but first things first. I picked her up and set her in the water, which seemed to perk her up enough to peel off the tank top and the dental floss she was calling underwear. I didn't let her see me holding them with thumb and index finger as I carried them away.

When I returned, she was holding onto the side of the tub, lips trembling.

"I can't sit up," she said.

If she didn't sit up, she *was* going to drown. I could do nothing else but hold her with one hand and bathe her with the other, all the while praying that the van would start, because there was no way I was putting her back on my motorcycle. Naked, her emaciation was even more shocking. I should be taking her to a hospital.

Once she was dressed—looking like a child playing dress-up in her mother's clothes—I brought a turkey sandwich and hot cup of coffee with cream upstairs to her. The little she ate of it was enough to enable her to stand up. And to start crying, in hard, tearless sobs.

"What?" I said. "We'll get there in time. I think he'll wait for you."

Her eyes bulged only slightly from their sunken sockets. "I'm scared."

"Scared?" I said. "Geneveve, you were just in a bar where people get stabbed monthly. *That* is scary. This—is your father."

"He so disappointed in the way I turned out. I let him down so many times."

"You've got one more chance not to," I said. "And this is the most important one of all." I spoke with more conviction than I felt.

She let me guide her back to the garage, but she was still shaking her head when I hoisted her into the van.

"I know about dads and disappointment," I said.

She looked at me hopefully, but I couldn't say anything more to reassure her. Her father wanted a reason to believe in her. *That* I didn't know about fathers.

Although the front door of the convalescent center was still unlocked when we got there, it was long past visiting hours and the hall lights had been dimmed. Fortunately there was no one at the nurses' station, so I smuggled Geneveve into her father's room and closed the door behind us. Her lips were so dry with terror that I could hear them sticking together. I had to push her to the bed, afraid at every step that I'd break one of her brittle bones.

Ed appeared to be in a twilight sleep. His eyelids were thin as tissue under the ghostly recessed light above his bed, and I could almost see his life ebbing away beneath them. The monitor was still beeping, though, faintly but steadily. I didn't realize until then that I'd basically been holding my breath ever since I picked Geneveve up from the street.

She leaned into me and quivered, every breath she took rattling in her throat. I took her hand and placed it over Ed's swollen one. His eyes fluttered open.

"Geneveve?" he said. "Genny Girl—that you?"

"I'm here, Daddy," she said.

He turned his head toward her, and his eyes glowed back from the edge of wherever he'd been headed.

"I knew you'd be comin'." he said.

"'Course, Daddy."

She talked so low that if he could hear her, I'd be surprised. But, then, he didn't seem to need to. As he pulled her hand to his face and sighed into it, I faded to the wall.

"You all right, Baby?" he said.

"I'm so good, Daddy."

"You ain't usin'?"

I held my breath, but she said the right words.

"No, I'm clean."

"And?" He garbled a name.

"Yeah, him, too. It's okay, Daddy."

"All right then. All right."

His eyes closed.

"Daddy?" Geneveve clawed at the bedclothes. "*Daddy?*"

"He's still with us, Geneveve," I said. "See—the monitor? He's just sleeping."

The door flew open, and a wide man with a mullet filled the room.

"Excuse me—what's the deal here?" he said.

"She needed to see her father," I said.

"You can't just come in here without—"

"Okay, okay," I said. "We're going."

Geneveve was already on the verge of coming completely apart, and I knew a sharp word from him at this point could cut her right open. I uncurled her fingers from the sheet and tugged her toward the door.

"He's stable right now," the nurse said, in a gentler voice. "Bring her back in the morning, and she can stay with him as long as she wants."

Although it irritated me, I couldn't blame him for talking about Geneveve like she wasn't in the room. She was so eerily quiet now, she was almost invisible.

She stayed that way until I started up the van.

"Where can I take you?" I said.

"It don't matter," she said. "Just back to the—"

"Y'know what?" I said. "You've just had a pretty rough couple of hours. Maybe you need some—time off."

My foot was once again halfway down my throat, but she just stared straight through the windshield as if everything she was able to feel had just been spent.

"Let me take you home," I said.

She shook her head. Another faux pas on my part. She probably didn't want me to see where she lived.

"All right, let's do this. I'll pay for a night at a hotel—just so you can get some rest. Tomorrow could be a rough day. You need someplace quiet—I know I do when I'm stressed out."

I let that peter out as she continued to shake her head. When she didn't stop, I realized it wasn't me she was saying no to.

There were several fairly inexpensive motels on Route 1 that never showed up in the crime news. I pulled into a Knight's Inn and turned to her.

"This look okay to you?"

She nodded, but I was sure she wasn't even seeing it.

When I'd seen her into a room on the second floor, away from the noise of the highway, I stood with my hand on the door knob while she perched like a frightened bird on the edge of the bed.

"Get some sleep," I said. "They've got a free breakfast here, so have something to eat in the morning … okay?"

She nodded again.

"Good night, then," I said. "I'll be praying for you and your dad."

She didn't answer. Her silence followed me all the way home, where I perched on the edge of my own bed and wondered if any of it had made any difference at all.

CHAPTER SEVEN

I didn't turn my cell phone back on until seven the next morning, when I'd finally given up trying to sleep. I'd been awake since three, reliving my Sunday from The Twilight Zone. When I did check my calls, there was one from Bonner, which I skipped, and one from Lonnie telling me I had a group of fifth graders at ten o'clock—from "SBA." That was Lonnie-code for Spoiled Brat Academy. I was grateful for the distraction. Spoiled Brats I could do. Visions of Geneveve and Ed and the Gold Tooth Crew—not so much.

As I was going out the kitchen door, I noticed the light blinking on the answering machine, which I forgot to check most of the time; *I should probably get rid of the landline anyway.*

I poked the button and was greeted with a cobweb of a voice.

"Allison? This is Miz Vernell. Your next-door neighbor."

Yes. For the last forty years.

"I don't like to complain...."

What was she talking about? That was her career.

"But that ... motorbike you're driving ... it's too loud. Surely you can find a way to quiet it down when you drive it here on our street."

There was a pause as if she'd forgotten she was talking to a recording and expected me to answer.

"Thank you for taking care of that," she said. Another expectant pause. "Well ... good-bye."

I pushed the delete button. Yeah, I definitely needed to get rid of the landline.

The morning I stepped out into was Florida September at its finest. No wind. Minimal humidity. Sun softly dissolving the fog and leaving a sky of seamless blue. It was perfect for a bike ride, but since I didn't know where the mute button was, I opted for the van. Normally I would have walked on such a day, but I had a detour I wanted to make before I went to the stables.

Because despite my leaning toward forgetting yesterday and everything in it, my brain wouldn't leave it alone. Maybe if I just went by the Knight's Inn and made sure Geneveve had made it through the night, I could put it all out of my mind. Ed had gotten to see her. That was plenty on my part, right?

When I pulled around to the back of the hotel, the door to Geneveve's room was wide open, and the maid's cart was parked outside. Geneveve must be having breakfast while her room was being made up. Odd, though, that they'd clean it before she checked out.

I knew what that meant before I even got up the steps.

"Is she—is this guest gone?" I said to the woman coming out of the room with an armful of sheets.

She nodded. I took the steps back down and headed for the breakfast room only half-hoping I'd find her there with a bowl of cereal. I wasn't one to waste hope.

No Geneveve enjoying a cup of joe. As I hurried back to the van with only thirty minutes to get Bernard hitched up and out to the Bay Front, I couldn't even conjure up an image of that wasted waif of a woman doing something as normal as sipping morning coffee and checking her email.

Nor could I come up with a vision of me being able to make so much as a dent in the trouble she was in. God wasn't giving me any new directions, and one thing was clear: Without them, I had absolutely no idea what to do.

I apparently wasn't much better at the "normal" stuff either. The fifth-grade boys were far more fascinated with grossing the girls out over Bernard's bodily functions than with my stuff about Osceola in the dungeon, so I just let them snort and squeal about horse poop through the last half of the tour. Back at the stables at the end of my shift at three, my van wouldn't start until Lonnie gave me a jump, informing me needlessly from beneath his cowboy hat that the thing was a piece of junk. And when I took out my cell phone to call the nursing home, I saw that Bonner had left me another message.

"Think we could have supper together tonight?" it said. "I swear—no lecture. Call me."

I tapped the phone against my forehead. Supper with Bonner. Same table. Same menu. Same conversation. Mundane. Predictable.

Safe.

I looked at the phone, rather stupidly, I supposed. Did anything I was being Nudged to do say I couldn't have some security in the midst of it? Something that didn't have a clutch where a gearshift ought to be? Something that didn't fray me at the edges?

Maybe this really was about me appreciating what I had and doing something with it. Maybe that was it.

Several seconds passed. Long enough. I poked in Bonner's number.

Yet even after I promised to meet him at six at the Athena Café—rather than our usual greasy taco place—I couldn't shake the thought of Ed, eyes glowing with hope in that bed. I had no idea if Geneveve went back to see him, but *I* had to—even if it was just to tie up the tattered ends of everything that had flapped against me the day before.

The minute I turned the corner and headed for the nurses'

station, I knew I might have missed my chance. Willie stalked out of his room, phone in hand, worry line cutting an abyss between her eyes.

"No disrespect, *Doctor*," she said in a voice she didn't need a phone for, "but I have seen a patient in renal failure before, and that is what is happening here…. Yes, he has a DNR order, but that does not mean we can't make the man comfortable. *Yes,* I want Haldol for him, and I want to up his morphine, too…. You would know that if you'd *seen* him in the last *week*."

At that point she saw me and waved me to Ed's room. I tiptoed in, though there was no need. The room was a cacophony of beeps and blips and the rattle of Ed's own breathing. I had to pick my way through torn-open plastic bags and discarded parts of things that had been unsuccessfully tried. A gray-permed nurse with red-rimmed eyes was changing the bag on his IV pole and muttering much the same thing Willie was lambasting the doctor with.

"I don't know if he'll be able to talk to you," she said to me. "He's in a lot of pain." She shook her head and headed for the door with the empty bag. "Nobody should have to die like this."

Ed's face was contorting, although not a sound escaped from him. I was afraid to touch his hand for fear it would burst open—or that I would feel the agony coursing under his skin. To my surprise he touched *my* hand and struggled to bring me into focus.

"It's Allison, Ed," I said. "I don't know if you remember me from yesterday, and it's okay if you don't—"

"You're the angel."

"Well, all I did was—"

"You brought my Genny Girl."

"Yeah," I said.

He nodded and tried to lick his lips, although there was no moisture to do it with. All of the fluids in his body were filling his lungs and drowning him.

"She in trouble again," he said. "She tried to tell me she weren't—but I know."

I wanted to lie and let the poor man pass with some peace. It was obvious he hadn't had much while he was alive.

"I couldn't take care of her—her and Dehmun."

There was that other name again. *Dear God—I don't even know this man's family. Why am I the one about to watch him die?*

"You."

The sudden strength in his voice startled me. His eyes were bright, and as he opened his face in a smile, he looked like a sixty-year-old ready for a promised new lease on life.

"You'll take care of them," he said.

"You mean Geneveve?"

"Both of them. I know you will." He clenched my hand with the grip of a man who wouldn't go until he got his promise. "Say you will, Angel. Please."

"I'll do what I can, Ed," I said.

He searched my eyes. I saw in his that it wasn't good enough. And I felt it in the Nudge that made me put my lips close to his ear.

"Okay," I said. "I'll take the best care of them that I can. I will, Ed."

"You will," he said.

His engorged fingers opened, and his eyes sank back into their oldness.

"Ed?" I said.

"Is he gone?"

I jerked my head to see Chief standing behind me. He nodded at the tears on my face that I was only now aware of myself.

"I know," he said. His voice was thick. "They get to you when you figure out you're just like them."

"What?" I said.

But his eyes moved to the monitor, at the same moment I realized the blips and beeps were now humming a straight line. Willie and the other nurse pushed open the door and stopped when Chief put his hand up.

"Let him be," he said. "He deserves to rest."

I left the room so Chief could be alone with his friend, but I couldn't leave the building yet. The nurse with the perm—Janice, her nametag said—brought me a cup of water and offered me a chair. Willie was busy coldly informing the doctor on the phone that *her* patient didn't need that Haldol after all. When she hung up, she patted me on the shoulder.

"He's gone on to a better place now," she said.

I looked up to answer, but the words had been meant for Chief, who was closing Ed's door as if he didn't want to disturb his newfound sleep. Chief looked at Willie, but he didn't appear convinced about the better place.

"There's no number here to notify somebody," Janice said from the counter. She flipped through the pages of a file and glanced, wet-eyed, at Willie.

"I know," Willie said. "He told me this morning that an angel brought his daughter to see him last night." She grunted. "Ain't no angel gonna touch that girl."

"At least he died thinking she'd been here." I got up and put the cup on the counter. "I need to go."

It was no surprise that Chief followed me outside to my van. Nor did I have to guess how much he'd heard of what I said to Ed. It was all there in his eagle gaze.

I stopped at the van door, and looked back at him. "Just so we're clear, I'm not an angel."

"Don't believe in them. How bad off is the daughter?"

"She's beyond what I can do for her, that's for sure." I dug in my bag for my keys.

"So why'd you promise to take care of her and her kid?"

I stopped digging. "Kid? What kid?"

"Ed said she had a son. I never saw him myself."

"FIP probably has him. One would hope anyway."

I gave up on the bag and patted the pockets of my uniform pants. Chief continued to watch me until the sick feeling in the pit of my chest turned to irritation.

"What?" I said.

"I'm just wondering what you're planning to do."

"Okay, I promised the old man I'd do what I could—"

"And that is?"

"What are you, the promise police?"

"No. Whatever it is, I'll help."

I stopped patting myself down for my car keys and stared.

"Oh," I said. "Okay."

He waited, eyes still. His intensity was riveting.

"I guess I'll start by finding Geneveve again and tell her he's passed. The *first* thing I need to do is find my keys."

"Try the ignition."

I followed his gaze through the driver's side window, where I could see the wooden cross keychain dangling like a lure.

"Bummer," I said. "I keep leaving them there, hoping somebody'll steal this thing and take it off my hands."

"I don't see that happening," Chief said. He was surveying Scott's paint job, but he didn't ask.

"I'll notify her," I said again. "I don't know what to do after that."

"Here's my number, in case you think of anything." He pressed a card into my hand and strode away. "I'll make some calls," he said over his shoulder.

To whom? I wondered.

But he was already striding toward his Road King, and I didn't call after him. It was annoying the way he made me think I should do things I wouldn't have considered doing ten minutes before.

Or was he the one putting that idea in my head?

No matter. I knew where to find Geneveve. When I told her the old man had died, it might be incentive for her to clean up her act, and she could take care of her*self.*

And her son.

I stuffed the card in my pocket and started the van in two tries. I could only focus on one catastrophe at a time.

I was all the way to West King Street before I remembered I was supposed to meet Bonner for supper. What state of mind had I been in when I'd agreed to that? Obviously not the same one that had me cruising the bars at dusk, looking for my favorite prostitute.

The only one I found was the woman I'd bribed the night before. She was at what must have been her usual spot in front of Titus Tattoos, smoking a cigarette that should have been put out seven puffs ago. Her lips moved soundlessly as she gazed at the lettering on the side of the van. When I leaned out the driver's side window, her eyes flitted hopefully to me, and then died again.

"Hi," I said. "Remember me? From last night?"

She pulled in her chin.

"I paid you to find Geneveve for me."

Hope sprung anew, and she came toward me with a decided lean to her gait. I looked around for spare change—since I'd literally spent my whole wad on her the night before. I just remembered my emergency $10 stash in the ashtray when she reached the window.

"You need me to fin' her again?" she said.

"Yes—well, no." I looked at my watch. It was almost six, and Bonner at least deserved an explanation.

I folded the ten-dollar bill in her full view. "I need you to give her a message for me."

She nodded, eyeing it hungrily.

"You need to tell her—"

"Uh-huh."

This wasn't going to work. She was fixated on the cash, and probably what it could bring her. From the way her hand shook as she reached for it, she needed whatever it was soon.

"What's your name?" I said.

Her eyes left the money and went into suspicious slits. "You a cop?"

"Are you serious?" I said. "I'm just a friend of Geneveve's. You obviously are too. What's your name?"

"Mercedes. What you want me to tell her?"

I sighed and stuck the bill out the window. "Her daddy passed away today."

"Got it," she said, and snatched the money from my hand. She was gone before I could put the van in drive. That was the biggest waste of ten bucks on record.

The Athena Café was on Cathedral Place, only two and a half blocks from my house, so I parked the van in my garage, exchanged my uniform for crop pants and a tee, and put my hair in a bun while I walked up St. George Street—praying all the way that I wouldn't run into India. She'd tell me I could have at least added some earrings.

I so did not need to send Bonner the wrong message by dressing up for him. I was wary enough because he'd chosen a restaurant several levels pricier than our usual haunts. That meant he wasn't planning for us to go dutch, which meant he considered this a date.

I finished arranging the bun by the time I got to the Episcopal church. Her two-trim spires were already silhouettes, and the faux gas lamps were winking on around the Plaza de la Constitucion, the long rectangular park between Cathedral Place and King Street to the north and south, Charlotte and St. George to the east and west. Across the street the dauntless Roman Catholic cathedral fronted the plaza in Spanish dignity.

The day had lost its afternoon mugginess, and the early diners who had discriminating taste were making their way to the cafés and bistros on the cathedral side, where the dinner menus offered dishes the main crowd couldn't pronounce. *They* would be on their way to

Harry's Seafood Bar and Grille, right after they finished up at Ripley's Believe It or Not Museum and checked it off their to-see list.

As I crossed King and cut a diagonal across the park, I made my customary conscious effort not to let my gaze touch the First National Bank of St. Augustine building on the corner. I had nothing against the bank—at least, not anymore than I did any other financial institution. It was the offices that occupied the rest of the 1928 edifice that I took issue with. The less often I had to read the gold letters "Chamberlain Enterprises," the less often I found myself feeling mean as a snake.

I tried to focus instead on the park itself, reciting part of my tour spiel to myself. The plaza has been the gathering place for St. Augustine's citizens since the city's founding in 1565 ... although these days not many people gathered there.

Probably, I thought, *because none of the benches had backs on them.* Tourists would sit just long enough to unfold their maps and get their bearings before they ambled on. The only comfortable places to sit were in the gazebo in the center of the park, and those were usually occupied by the homeless. Even now, while one man slept curled up on said bench, another man parked a bike laden with what looked like everything he owned, dug a ball out of his belongings, and stood on the steps of the gazebo to throw it for his dog.

I knew that dog. He was the same one I saw sleeping by the Dumpster on West King. I'd always wondered why men without roofs over their heads always had dogs when they could barely feed themselves. Remembering that scene, I understood, and it ached in me.

That must have shown on my face when I walked into the Athena and blinked through the semidarkness for Bonner, because his own was fixed with concern when he waved me to a table by the window.

"You okay?" he said as I dropped into the chair across from him.

"Yeah, just … weird day."

"Seems like they've all been a little weird for you lately."

"Don't start with me, Bonner," I said.

"Not starting. Just saying. You eaten here before?"

I let him get away with that none-too-subtle change of subject and looked around at the decor, made up largely of arrangements of grapes and exotic olive oil bottles. "I don't think so. Funny how you can live in a town all your life and never see half the things in it." I sniffed the air, which was thick with garlic and oregano. "It's nothing if not authentic."

"Yeah, the proprietor's been yelling at somebody in the kitchen in Greek ever since I got here." Bonner grinned. "But never let it be forgotten that you are in the South. They serve grits with everything."

I looked at the menu, just to humor him. I actually couldn't imagine myself eating. The list of kebabs was so accusing, in fact, that I folded the paper and said, "Recommend something I can pronounce. I'm not that hungry."

"The spinach pie is stupid-good. Fresh feta in a puffed pastry."

"Sure."

Outside the window a duo of Harleys grumbled up and backed into side-by-side parking places just across from us along the edge of the plaza. I stretched my neck to check out the homeless guy in the gazebo, who snoozed on. How could he sleep with that rumble? And really, had there always been this many motorcycles in town? It was like I was seeing my city with somebody else's eyes.

"Allison?"

I jerked back to Bonner.

"Sorry," I said. "I got distracted."

"Harleys."

I shrugged.

"That's okay," he said. "The last girl I went out with texted on her cell phone all the way through dinner."

I relaxed into a smile. "You went on a date, Bonner? Talk to me."

"A couple of them, actually. It didn't turn into anything."

Rats.

"So—client? Somebody you met at a realtors' conference?"

"A girl you went to high school with, as a matter of fact."

"No kidding. Who?" Not that I would remember. That was twenty-five years ago, and I'd worked hard to forget anything associated with that period. Even now, I squirmed slightly in the seat.

"You too cold here?" Bonner said. "The air-conditioning vent is right over your head—"

"Bonner," I said. "Your date?"

"Elizabeth Doyle. Used to be Fenwick. She said she knew who you were." He gave me half a grin. "I bet you were pretty hard to miss. She said you were always cool with the underdogs."

"Was she one?"

"She says so. She told me the story about the time you—"

"Bonner."

"What?"

"If you discussed me the whole time, no wonder it didn't turn into anything. Women like to talk about themselves—hadn't you noticed?"

I wanted to bite my tongue completely off before the words even left it. The food I didn't realize he'd ordered arrived, and I used that time to try to figure out a way to get out of the trap I'd just created for myself. I came up with zilch by the time the server dashed off to get Bonner more tzatziki sauce for his pita bread.

"Okay," he said. "I'll pray, and then let's talk about you."

While Bonner thanked God for the food, I begged him for appendicitis. I did *not* want to go where Bonner was going to try to take me.

The amen was barely out of his mouth before he started in. The topic, however, caught me off guard.

"The Watchdogs, as you call them, are worried about you. I am too."

I was only relieved for a half a second. This wasn't a subject I was crazy about either.

"Why?" I said. "Because I missed one meeting?"

"No."

"Then it's the *reason* I missed. You told them about the Harley lessons, I take it."

"That's only part of it—"

"Do tell me what that has to do with the group."

"I will," he said. "If you'll just hush up a minute."

"Sorry," I said. I snapped the cloth napkin into my lap. "Go on."

"Just hear me out before you jump in."

I stuffed a forkful of spinach pie into my mouth and chewed. It tasted like cardboard, which I was sure wasn't the chef's fault.

"It's you dodging this new thing Garry has us looking at," Bonner said. "*Not* that you won't be in charge of it. I'm happy to do that. Again."

I kept chewing.

"It's about you not seeing the point."

"What *is* the point?"

"It's what it always is. Salvation."

"As in where you gonna go when you die."

He frowned. "You know I don't think it's as simple as that. It's about having a relationship with Jesus Christ that will last into eternity."

"For us. You, me, and the Watchdogs."

"See?" Bonner pointed his fork at me, and then put it down when I scowled at it. "That's it, though. We talked about it at the meeting. Once we all thought about it, it was like you were telling us we're being selfish with our faith."

My neck bristled, and I put my own fork down. "When did I say that?"

"You didn't exactly say it. We just felt like that was what you were thinking."

"Since when did I not just come right out and say what I was thinking? What I *said* was what I meant: We've got this live-a-moral-life thing down; maybe it's time to get out there and do something with that."

"You don't think we all witness? Frank alone has probably brought more people to Christ than Garry himself."

"Which means what?" I said, although I had no idea *why* I said it.

"Their souls are saved," he said simply.

"And what about everything between now and death?"

Bonner tilted his head.

"We're all so caught up in the afterlife, we have no idea what's going on in *this* life. I've seen things in the last twenty-four hours that tell me I don't know a dad-gum thing about God's world. And neither do you or Frank, or anybody else in our church as far as I can see."

He blinked as if I'd slapped him. Maybe I would have, if I didn't have anymore control over my hand than I did my mouth. Where was all this stuff coming from?

Yet even as I watched Bonner poke at his lamb kebab for a moment and then push his plate to the edge of the table, I didn't want to take the words back. They might not have been mine, but they were true. Still, I hated that I'd put those two red smears at the tops of Bonner's cheeks.

"Y'know what?" I said. "I think we need a change of topic—and a change of scene. You want to come see my Harley?"

"I don't know what to do with this, Allison."

"I don't either," I said. "Let's just drop it till we figure it out, huh?"

He agreed, which meant we rode in silence in the Jag down to Palm Row. When we pulled in, I automatically looked to see if Owen or Miz Vernell were on their porches, waiting up for me.

They were, along with a police officer on my front walkway, leaning over two shadowy figures on my steps.

"What in the *world*?" Bonner said.

The red-and-blues on the police cruiser flashed alarmingly on the faces of the two on the steps. One was a wisp of a woman, hugging her knees to her chest and rocking back and forth.

It was Geneveve. And next to her sprawled a preadolescent boy.

CHAPTER EIGHT

I was out of the car before Bonner had it completely stopped.

"Allison, wait!" he hissed after me. "You don't know what you're walking into!"

I ignored both him and Miz Vernell, whose cobweb voice tried to thread its way to me from her side porch. Owen was standing at the other edge of my yard, rubbernecking like he was at the site of a train wreck. I ignored him, too. I had eyes only for Geneveve, who was clearly unraveling right there on my steps.

"Is there a problem, officer?"

He turned his red head toward me, hand up as if that were going to stop me from marching across my own property.

"I'm Allison Chamberlain," I said. "This is my house."

His look was so doubtful I went for my ID. At which point his hand went to his gun.

"Oh for Pete's sake, don't go all *Law & Order* on me. I'm just trying to show you my driver's license."

"It's okay, Kent," Bonner said behind me. "She's for real."

The ruddy-faced officer, to his credit, looked relieved, as well he should. He couldn't have been more than twenty-one years old. I would hate to have to smack his little freckled face.

"What's going on?" I said.

He let me approach, and I went straight to the step next to Geneveve.

"So you know these folks?" Kent said.

"I know this lady," I said. "What's the problem?"

I was asking Geneveve, who only continued to rock and retch out a guttural moan. On the other side of her, the kid was flipping something from one hand to the other and seemed completely unconcerned that a police officer was shining a flashlight in his face.

"We got a call from a neighbor reporting a possible break-in," Kent said.

"Were you trying to break into my house, Geneveve?"

Bonner let out a disgusted sigh. Geneveve shook her head and mumbled something unintelligible. Beside her the kid had moved on to Olympic-level stunts with whatever it was he was playing with.

Another, bulkier officer coming from my house passed us down the steps and shook his head at Kent, who looked at me.

"We have no reason to arrest her unless you want to press trespassing charges."

"She was waiting for me on my steps," I said. "Since when is that trespassing?"

"When you say it is," the other officer said—in a Florida cracker accent you could have scooped up like a spoonful of grits.

"I don't," I said.

Kent once again looked relieved and nodded to his partner.

"Thanks for coming by," Bonner said to them, hand out for the grateful handshake. *Him* I really did want to smack.

I turned to Geneveve, who had stopped rocking and was simply staring as if she could no longer remember how to move. Her scrawny kid, on the other hand, couldn't seem to *stop* moving. Apparently oblivious to the cruiser lights still bruising his face, he was now standing up on the middle step, flipping the whatever-it-was behind his back and attempting to catch it with his tongue. He missed, and the toy pinged onto the walkway just beyond my foot.

Only it wasn't a toy. It was the house key I kept under one of the terra-cotta pots on the front porch.

He dove for it, but I covered it with my foot and almost took his hand out. By then, Bonner had already seen Kent and Company to the cruiser as if they'd been attending a friendly barbecue in my backyard.

"You just cheated death, kid," I said. I pocketed the key. "I think you better have a seat."

"Hey, it's all good," he said, in a voice still some distance from manhood. And then he stunned me with a smile. For all his skinny, swaggering arrogance, he was a downright cute kid.

With skin like rubbed sage and cinnamon-colored, out-of-control hair, he was obviously mulatto, though there was no denying he was Geneveve's child. His enormous brown eyes took up the entire upper half of his face, and if she still knew how to smile, I imagined her grin would have matched his—wide and toothy and completely charming. His build, however, had come from someone else's DNA. He was already a head and a half taller than Geneveve, even if you didn't count the four inches of stand-up hair. In fact most of his body weight was probably in that 'do as well. A closer look, and I retracted that thought. His huge feet were as out of proportion as a puppy's.

He sat on the step like I'd told him to, back curved as if he wasn't yet proud of his height.

"So what's your name?" I said.

"What makes you think I have one?" he said.

"Okay, I'll just make one up for you. I'm going to call you Clarence."

"Say what?"

"Clarence. I think it fits."

He spewed out an expletive. "My name Desmond," he informed me.

I didn't see how that was a whole lot better than "Clarence," but I nodded. Beside me Geneveve nodded as well, the first sign of coherence I'd seen since I arrived.

"This your boy?" I asked.

Another nod.

"How old is he?"

"Fifteen," Desmond said.

"Did I ask you?"

"I'm just sayin'."

"No, you're just lyin'. You can't be over ten years old."

"Ex-*cuse* me?"

He dropped another word-bomb that would have gotten my teeth knocked from my head at that age. By Sylvia. Which was the main reason I didn't swear to this day.

"He twelve," Geneveve whispered.

I did a double take, not only because she'd spoken, but because she must have been all of about fifteen when she gave birth to him. Even through her dope-ravaged skin I could tell she wasn't much more than twenty-seven.

"Everything's cool, Allison." Bonner was standing at the edge of the lane where the cruiser had finally pulled away. "I'm going to go talk to Owen, let him know."

"Yeah, Owen'll be better off if you tell him." I stood up, hand on Geneveve's elbow so she had to rise with me. "Listen, thanks for keeping Barney Fife from drawing on me."

"They were just doing their job."

With one hand on Geneveve and the other on the back of Desmond's T-shirt, I moved toward the house. "Can we take a rain check on the bike showing?"

Bonner's eyebrows rose. "What are you doing, Allison?"

"I'm taking my guests inside. I'll call you."

I didn't wait for another protest before I used the key I'd taken from Desmond to open the front door and escorted him and his mother into the foyer. Geneveve went straight to the old church pew against the wall and all but disappeared into the array of throw pillows. Desmond stood gazing around with an awe he forgot to hide.

I took in the view with him—the yellow and white walls, the splotches of red in the pillows and rugs, the wainscoting that gleamed like a happy gaze. As Sylvia-filled and honest as my home was, it suddenly seemed pretentious again.

"Nice digs," Desmond said. "You rich?"

He'd successfully covered his awe with a half-smirk he must have practiced in front of a mirror. No prepubescent male just naturally looked that on top of it. I swallowed a snicker.

"Why do you ask?" I said.

"I just like to know what I'm workin' with."

"Get over yourself, kid. You already dodged a police bullet once tonight. Don't push it."

He gave me The Smile and put out his fist for what I assumed was some kind of brothers-in-the-hood exchange. I just looked at him.

"It's all good...." He tilted his chin up. "So what's your name—or do I get to make one up?"

This kid was just too cute for his own good.

"Allison," I said.

"Naw—you don't look like no Allison to me. You look more like a ..." He rubbed his chin. "A Tiffany. I'ma call you that."

"Call me anything you want, Clarence."

His barely there eyebrows knit together over his finely chiseled nose—the one thing that indicated he was going to be more than just cute someday. If he lived that long.

"What you say your name was?"

"Allison."

He shook his head solemnly. "That's not workin' for me. What about if I call you 'Big Al'? You still gon' call me Clarence if I do that?"

"I'll think about it," I said.

I turned to Geneveve, who was on her way to a fetal position on the pew.

"Come on, girlfriend," I said. "Let's get some food into you."

I wrangled her to her feet and half carried her through the dining room and into the kitchen. Desmond trailed us in there. I could only assume he was casing the place for the family silver. Good thing Sylvia and I had sold it years ago and spent the money on a trip to Tahiti.

"What are we havin' for dinner, Big Al?" he said. "You gon' cook us some T-bone steaks?"

I watched Geneveve as I deposited her in one of the chairs at the bistro table and hoped she didn't slither off onto the floor. She was either completely unaware of the mouth her kid had on him or she didn't care. In either case, no wonder he was such a little wise guy.

"You missed the dinner hour, dude," I said. "It's mac and cheese or nothing. Take your pick."

He pondered that before saying, "I ain't had no mac and cheese in a long time. You got a TV?"

Why hadn't I thought of that?

I handed him a Granny Smith to hold him over—which he looked at and said, "How come this apple green?"—and set him up in the small den just off the kitchen.

"Have at it," I said, and handed him the remote as he slouched into the green leather recliner.

"You got cable?" he said.

Before I could even answer, he was devouring the screen with his eyes. I left him to it and went back to Geneveve.

She'd managed to stay in the chair, but her head was facedown in her arms on the tabletop. Her shoulders shook, but no sound escaped her lips. She reminded me of her father who refused to give his pain a voice, and I got that ache in my chest again.

"All right," I said. "I'm going to feed you and the pipsqueak in there, and then we'll talk showers for both of you. Once we get him down for the night, we can discuss why you came here. I mean, I'm glad you did, but it caught me a little off guard. I didn't have time to notify the neighbors. Like I should have to, right?"

She didn't answer, and I didn't expect her to. I was babbling more for myself than for her anyway. Beneath it was the subtext: *Is this what you want me to do, God? Because once again, I'm driving off a cliff here. Right on the back of that Harley you told me to buy.*

I kept up the chatter as I prepared some absolutely-no-nutritional-value macaroni and cheese from a box and put it on plates with baby carrots. When I delivered Desmond's, he never moved his eyes from the TV screen.

Which meant I practically had to handcuff him to get him into the bathroom to take a shower. His charm failed him at that point, and he made an attempt at being menacing by pulling his entire face into a pout. I laughed out loud.

"What?" he said. "That ain't funny!"

"Actually, no, Desmond, the way you smell goes way beyond funny. Five minutes in the shower—you'll be a new man."

"I ain't takin' no shower!"

"Fine. Then it's outside with the hose. Your choice."

He slammed the bathroom door, and I could hear him fumbling with the knob.

"Give it up," I said from the hallway. "It doesn't lock."

Fortunately the window in there was nailed shut. Resistance was futile. Thirty seconds later I heard water running. Another minute and he was performing a rap song under the spray. Obscene lyrics aside, at least it was better than a screaming fit. I got the impression that wasn't his style anyway.

Meanwhile I had Geneveve soaking in the tub in my bathroom, which gave me a few minutes to determine what the next step should be. I wasn't even sure why I'd done as much as I had already. Why hadn't I just found out what Geneveve wanted, given them a free meal, and driven them home?

Because they don't have a home.

"I knew that, God," I said. "I did."

But it wasn't what I wanted to hear. Neither that nor Ed's last words to me: "You'll take care of them. I know you will."

Desmond was easier after his shower—in which he used up all the hot water—and a cup of warm milk with cinnamon, Sylvia's

prescription for hyper kids at bedtime. I had gallons of it in my childhood, and just as I always had, Desmond conked out. His fingers
were still curled loosely around the remote in his lap in the recliner
when I covered him with a blanket.

Finally I could talk to Geneveve alone. By the time she was
propped in the cushions of the red chair in the living room, swallowed up in one of my nightgowns and two of Sylvia's crocheted
afghans, she was in less of a stupor. I actually would have preferred
the semicoma to the fretful plucking at the fibers I was seeing now,
but I had to get some information out of her.

I sat on my feet at the end of the plaid couch with a glass of
ice water wondering how Geneveve could have all those covers on
her and still be shivering—and went into the paragraph I'd prepared
while she was in the tub.

"Don't get me wrong. I'm glad you felt like you could come
here." I didn't add that I was flabbergasted that she'd found the
house again in the condition she was in. "And if it was just for a
place to be while you grieve for your father, that's perfectly fine. I
just need to know—"

"He said you was an angel."

I blinked. Had Ed said that when she was there? If he had, I was
amazed that she'd even heard it, much less recalled it. That was at once
reassuring and enough to curdle the spinach pie in my stomach.

"I'm not an angel by any means," I said.

Geneveve shook her head. "If my daddy said it, it was so. He was
right about everything. Only I never listened."

Her face collapsed and once again she wept without sound, without tears.

"None of us listened to our parents," I said. "We probably spend most of our adult lives trying to sort out what we should have paid attention to and what we were better off without." I stopped short of mentioning that I'd been through that process and had come out with about two sentences I was glad I'd heard from my father—even fewer from my mother.

"I disappointed him his whole life," Geneveve said. "I don't want to be disappointin' him in his death, too."

That made so much sense I put my glass down and motioned for her to go on.

"He shoudna died by hisself in that place. I shoulda took care of him."

I couldn't argue with her there.

"He took care of me and Desmond till he got so sick he couldn't do it no more, and then I left him with nobody to look after him. My sister, she done left before that and went to Africa 'cause I told her I'd be there for him." She pushed out the last sentence between the cracks of her sobs. "I ain't never kept a promise in my life."

I let her cry while I fought back the pain in my chest. Her pain. It was big enough for both of us.

When she seemed to have nothing left but raw-edged sighs, I unfolded myself from the couch.

"I'll get us some tea," I said.

I was halfway to the kitchen when I heard, "You ask me why I come here."

"Yeah." I crossed my arms and rubbed my shoulders. I was shivering now too. "Why did you?'

"I want a funeral for my daddy," she said. "But I don't know how to do it."

I didn't either, but I didn't tell her that. I just nodded and said, "Okay, Geneveve. We'll get on it first thing in the morning."

She closed her eyes and nodded back. By the time I returned with the tea, she was sleeping the sleep of a soothed little girl.

I sat down and watched her.

Planning a funeral for a virtually destitute man was no easy matter.

My first call Tuesday morning was to Willie at the nursing home, who told me the same thing she said she'd told Chief: Ed's body had been turned over to the county coroner. A weary-sounding woman in that office said "the deceased" would be held for two days and buried in the San Lorenzo Cemetery on Highway 1. Unless someone claimed his remains. I said I'd like to do that.

"You a relative?" she said.

"I'm representing his daughter," I said.

That seemed to satisfy her, though it terrified me.

The next dilemma was where to have old Ed delivered for embalming, and how to pay for it. I called Willie back.

"Who do I talk to about Ed's finances?" I said. "I'm trying to put a funeral together and—"

"You and Chief need to work on your communication skills," she said.

"I'm sorry?"

"I told him when he called—the business office has all that. You have Chief's number, don't you?"

As a matter of fact I did. When we hung up, I located the card that was still in my jacket. And then I sat staring at it. Crisp black letters on professional cream-colored stock read: *John J. Ellington, Attorney at Law.*

"You have *got* to be *kid*din' *me*," I said out loud.

"What?"

I looked up at Desmond, who had finally hauled himself out of the chair in the den and was standing in the kitchen doorway, hair even more reminiscent of a giant wad of steel wool than it had been the night before. Evidently the boy woke up the same way he went to sleep: running his mouth.

"Trouble with yer man, Big Al?" he said. He scratched his armpit, which had to be difficult to find in my old black T-shirt. He was wearing the same jeans he'd had on when he arrived, though I'd put them in the dryer with some Dryel while he was in the shower to remove the faint but unmistakable scent of marijuana.

"You want some breakfast, Clarence?" I said.

"Yeah." He grinned widely as he went for the other armpit. "You gonna make me some of them Eggs Dominic?"

"Are you talking about Eggs Benedict?" I said.

"Yeah."

I was having trouble keeping the laughter out of my voice. "Do you even know what they are?"

"I just know rich people eat 'em."

"I'm not rich, dude. What's it going to be, a frozen waffle or a bowl of Raisin Bran?"

"*Raisin* Bran?" He swore his way into his next sentence. "That is *old* people's cereal. My granddaddy used to eat that."

I was about to address the language issue, but I switched gears at the mention of his grandfather. I pulled a waffle out of the freezer and popped it into the toaster first, then poured him a glass of orange juice and waved him to the bistro table.

"You talking about your Granddaddy Ed—your mom's father?"

"I ain't got no other granddaddy." He chugged the juice and set the glass on the table like he was down at the Magic Moment. "Hit me again, will ya, Big Al?"

I narrowed my eyes. He smiled.

"Please?"

I filled his glass. "You had breakfast with him from time to time, did you?"

"Me and him lived together till he had him a stoke."

A *stoke?*

"I ain't seen him in a while."

The waffle popped up, and I supplied Desmond with plate, syrup, and butter.

"Have at it," I said, heading for the doorway. "I have to make a few phone calls."

"'Bout what?"

"You like to get in my business, don't you? I'm trying to make arrangements for your grandfather's funeral."

"He dead?"

I wished *I* were when I turned around. His face was stricken.

"Desmond, you didn't know?" I said. "I am so sorry."

I started toward him, but he slid out of the chair and dodged me like a pinball as he headed for the den. I let the door slam without comment. My next impulse was to wake Geneveve up and wring her neck.

Instead I dialed the cell phone number Chief had written on his card. He answered on the first ring with "Jack Ellington."

"You didn't tell me you were a lawyer," I said.

"Do you need one?"

"I might. This is Allison Chamberlain."

"I was hoping you'd call."

His tone was professional, though not what I would call lawyerly. The image of his ponytail flying out of his Harley helmet still made that hard to fathom. If anything, his manner was calming, and heaven knew I needed that at the moment.

"I'm trying to organize a funeral for Ed," I said. "You've talked to the people at the nursing home?"

"Yeah. He had enough set aside for the basics, which, incidentally, his daughter tried to withdraw at one point, but it's their policy that at least enough to cover funeral expenses has to remain in the account. I called the county morgue, and they said—"

"Yeah, I claimed his body for Geneveve. They just need to know where to send it." I swallowed a rising lump. "I hate that we're talking about him like he's a package nobody knows what to do with."

"I hear that," Chief said. "Resurrection recommended Bates and Hockley. You want me to take care of that end?"

"I would owe you big time."

"You can't afford to owe me. You already made a promise that's probably going to cost you more than you bargained for."

"You don't need to tell *me*." I slipped out the kitchen door to the shady heat of the side porch and lowered my voice. "I've got Geneveve *and* her son here—and let me tell you, this kid is a piece of work. Little con artist. Plus she didn't even tell him his grandfather died. Here I am, casually tossing it into the conversation and he doesn't even know."

I peeked through the den window. Desmond was concave in the chair, remote pointed at the television. I'd have bet the farm he had no idea what he was watching.

"Geneveve wants a funeral, which is fine, but who's going to come? She said her sister was in Africa—I don't even know what that's about—"

"I'll get some people there," Chief said. "You take care of the rest."

"That's my next phone call," I said. "Listen, Chief—thanks, okay? I'm freaking out here, and I really appreciate the help."

"This is you freaking out?" he said. "You want to come work for me?"

I laughed—for what seemed like the first time in days.

Okay, maybe this wasn't going to be so hard. At least I could count on Pastor Garry. Weddings, baptisms, even funerals—he shone when it came to administering the sacraments. Bonner told me Garry's handling of his wife's funeral was the reason he started coming to Flagler Community. And Mary Alice's husband's memorial service was one of the most beautiful sacraments I'd ever been a part of. It had made me want to go to meet the Lord right then, yet at the same time embrace the rest of my life.

The Reverend Howard was predictably glad to hear from me. I closed my eyes for a moment and savored his ecclesiastical jollyness. I really had to get me some of that.

I told him why I was calling, including the part where the daughter of the departed was a drug addict living on the street with her son. With every word I felt a little more unburdened. This must be what it felt like to make a confession to a priest. When I was finally empty, Garry paused and I breathed into it. Yeah, I should do this more often.

"How well did you know this man, Allison?" he said.

"Not very," I said.

"Do you know anything about where he was with the Lord?"

There was an unexpected sternness in his voice that made me switch the phone to my other ear, as if he'd sound different from that side. "Do you mean, was he a Christian? I don't know. Does that matter?"

"Does being a Christian *matter*?"

"That's not what I mean. Are you saying you can't do his funeral if he wasn't?" I was already shaking my head.

"I'm not saying that at all."

"Okay, so …"

"It just makes a difference in how I conduct the service."

I switched ears again. I could *not* be hearing this.

"Is it because he's not a member of our church?" I said.

"No—"

"Look, this was a good man. And his daughter needs this. So does his grandson. There's money to pay you, if that's what you're concerned about."

"Allison. You know better than that."

Five minutes ago I thought I did. That was when I was talking to someone who didn't go all patriarchal on me.

I could hear him flipping pages. "When do you want to do it?"

"I'll have to get back to you after I know when Bates and Hockley is going to have him ready."

"I have tomorrow afternoon free, but that's about it."

"Pencil me in," I said between gritted teeth.

"I'm not trying to dance around this, my dear—"

"Really?" I said. "Because it seems like you're doing a pretty effective foxtrot right now. I'll call you back."

"Do," he said. "We need to talk in more depth."

I hung up knowing I didn't want to dig any deeper. I already didn't like what I'd just uncovered.

The funeral was finally set for the next afternoon, Wednesday, at three p.m. By the time that was established, I had twenty-four hours left to keep Geneveve clean and sober, and myself from flushing her kid down the toilet. The latter was harder by a long shot.

Geneveve slept, except for the two hours we spent at the Premium Outlets just outside town buying them something to wear to the funeral that didn't make them look like refugees. Which, I realized with a start, they were.

When we arrived, Desmond emerged from mourning with the speed of someone who is terrified of his own grief. At least that was my take on it as he sprang from the car like a greyhound at the starting gate and sprinted across the parking lot. When we reached him, he had his face pressed to the window at the Nike store.

"Those right there," he said, smearing the glass with his finger. "That's what I'm talkin' about."

"We won't be adding that pair to your wardrobe today," I said. I'd noted when he arrived at my house that he was wearing a pricey-looking pair of Adidas. I didn't even want to know how he'd acquired those.

With a grin he said, "It's all good," and headed toward American Eagle.

"Your mom gets to be first," I said, and corralled him into Coldwater Creek.

Where Genevieve sat shivering in the dressing room while I scraped hangers across the racks and wished India were there. I wasn't even that good at picking out clothes for *myself*. I just grabbed everything black I could find in extra small and sort of shoved it all at her, and then went after Desmond, who was scoping out the jewelry display. I patted him down and found two pairs of gold hoop earrings in his pocket.

"I was hopin' you was gonna buy these for me," he said.

I studied his earlobes. "You don't even have pierced ears. Try again."

"I was just seein' if you was payin' attention." He gave me the magical grin again. I was less charmed by it all the time.

Genevieve couldn't quite choose an outfit, and the sales clerk did little more than guard the cash register as if we were in there to stage a heist. I snatched up a skirt, tank, and jacket and a pair of leather sling-backs and slid them across the counter at her.

There was no, "Will that be all for you?" or "Did you find everything you were looking for today?" or "We have some cute necklaces that would give this a little color." The woman seemed bent on getting us out of the store as fast as she could—which was good, because Genevieve and I emerged just in time for me to keep Desmond from jimmying open the gumball machine outside the door.

"Come on," I said. "We're going to Old Navy."

"No Abercrumble and Finch?"

"Aber—in your dreams, Clarence. Come on, move it."

We had to, because his mother was beginning to splinter again. She crept behind Desmond and me with her arms crossed tightly enough to cut off her heartbeat, and her knees buckled about every five steps. Her eyes were the only part of her that seemed fully operational as they cut from side to side like fugitives ducking down alleys. It was hard to tell whether she was on the lookout for cops, a john, or a score. It was probably all three, but in any case, it was disturbing—and not only to me but apparently to the other shoppers as well. One mother pushed her two kids completely off the sidewalk to avoid contact with us. A pair of middle-aged women in capris stepped into the doorway of Gap to let us pass. If somebody didn't call security before we left, I'd be surprised.

Some of that was understandable. Desmond was, after all, cavorting several yards in front of me, leaving his fingerprints on every object within pawing distance and making remarks laced with profanity that could probably be heard out on the interstate. As for Genevieve, she looked as if I'd plucked her out of a brothel for a field trip.

Actually I kind of had.

Old Navy was a nightmare even before we walked in there—sale items piled in heaps where rabid shoppers had already picked through and left the dregs, and rock music blaring so loud I thought our next stop was going to have to be the hearing-aid center.

Nix that. I was never taking Desmond, alias Fingers Sanborn, into a store again after this. I had to frisk him twice before we got to the checkout line with black jeans, three already faded-looking collared shirts that he insisted on having in two sizes too big for him, and a package of socks. I relieved him of the wallet and man necklace he'd slipped into his pockets and handed them to the cashier.

"We won't be needing these after all," I said.

Desmond muttered his favorite epithet under his breath. He seemed to be able to use that word for everything but a coordinating conjunction.

I had the undeniable sense that I was going down in quicksand.

Geneveve headed for bed the minute we got to my house, but I knew it wouldn't be long before she'd need another dose of whatever she was on. It was either going to get ugly, or she would simply disappear and leave me with her little reincarnation of Al Capone.

Just to be proactive, I made sure the lock on her bedroom was secure. I could barely move the thing myself, so she definitely wouldn't be able to. I checked the medicine cabinet in the guest bath; the only thing in there was a container of Tylenol, which I pocketed, and an aging tube of Crest. I hadn't had an overnight guest since Sylvia died.

I tried to be quiet as I tiptoed out and crossed the guest room to the door, but Geneveve came up on her elbows. Whatever she had to say, she better make it quick, because her neck could barely support her head.

"Thank you, Miss Angel," she said.

"You're going to look beautiful at your daddy's service," I said.

"No." She closed her eyes as if to puzzle something out. "I mean thank you for not treatin' me like a ho. I know I am one, but thank you."

She let the elbows slide her back onto the pillow. In an instant she was halfway to someplace else.

"You're welcome," I said anyway.

I watched her, the way I had for a long time the night before. Clearly she was an addict, but there was something sweet about her that went deeper than the drugs and the child neglect and the bad sex she'd been guilty of. It was something that whispered with every sleeping breath, "I don't want to be this way."

I just had no idea how to help her be anything else.

For which there was no reason to be guilty, but I made tracks for the Oreos anyway. I owed it to myself.

MTV was screaming from the den, and Desmond was in a shoulder stand twirling a throw pillow on the soles of his Adidas.

"Look at this, Big Al," he said as I passed.

"I could do that too if I had feet the size of surfboards," I said.

In the kitchen I opened the snack drawer—and it was all *I* could do not to scream obscenities.

I could handle the channel-flipping, the attempted shoplifting, the gutter talk. But when I saw that empty package, crumb-less, with the plastic literally licked clean and stuffed back in between the pretzels and the granola bars, I lost it. Defiled wrapper in hand, I marched from the kitchen to the den, stood over the kid, and waved the thing in his face.

"You ate my Oreos," I said. "Nobody eats my Oreos and lives to tell about it."

I was pulling out all the stops—demon voice, flaring nostrils—which apparently called for him to bring out his best stuff as well. Desmond lowered his feet, sat up, and raised his hands in surrender.

"I didn't know that was your drug a choice, Big Al," he said, smile engaged to the fullest extent of its charm. "Otherwise I'd a stopped with them M&M's."

"No way you ate my M&Ms, too," I growled.

"Not yet."

He reached under the cushion on the loveseat and pulled out the bag I'd been hoarding—in the drawer of my bedside table upstairs.

"That's it," I said. "Give me the bag."

He tossed it to me as if it were his idea.

"Come on, we're going." I grabbed my purse from the hook by the kitchen door and shook it at him. "There better not be anything missing from here, or our first stop is going to be juvenile hall." I gave him a slight shove onto the porch. "Although you've probably been there already."

"Nah. Ain't nobody ever caught me before."

"Is everybody in your neighborhood blind?" I gave him another push down the steps.

"Nah," he said again. "They just stupid."

"Yeah, well, I'm not. Keep going—we're headed for that garage, straight ahead."

I kept my fingers curled around his T-shirt sleeve, just in case he decided to shoot off behind Owen Schatz's house and lose himself in the shadows like the Artful Dodger in *Oliver Twist.* Though if he did, I wasn't sure I'd stop him.

"What are we doin'?" he said.

"We're going for a ride."

"Where? Juvie?"

There was only a hint of apprehension in the question, but I capitalized on it.

"If you're not careful, yeah. For openers we're just going for a ride in my van."

"Why?"

"Because there's nothing in there you can destroy, steal, or use as a weapon."

"Huh," he said.

Great. I'd just challenged him.

"You like horses?" I said.

"No."

"Too bad, because we're going to go see one." And my boss, who would only believe my reason for taking two days off if I brought him the living proof.

"Can I drive?" Desmond said as I opened the garage door.

"Do I have a death wish? You are unbe—"

I stopped, because *he* had—three reverent steps in front of my Harley. He breathed his favorite word out long and awe-filled, but beyond that he didn't seem able to speak at all.

"You like?" I said.

He nodded and began a slow circle around the bike, all wide eyes and open mouth, as if he were in the presence of royalty. If I'd known it would render him speechless, I would have brought him out here twenty-four hours ago.

"This your old man's?" he managed to say.

"No," I said. "I don't have an old man. It's mine."

"No way." Desmond looked at me with only half the awe he was bestowing on the bike, but I could see my coolness factor rising in his eyes.

"Can I ride it?" he said, predictably.

"What do you think?"

"Can you *take* me for a ride?"

"I don't have a helmet for you or I would," I said. Before I could stop them, more words tumbled out. "But you can sit on it if you want to."

For the first time since I'd laid eyes on the boy, he looked like he'd come up against something he couldn't fake his way through. I knew the feeling.

"I'll show you," I said, and I gave him the same instructions Stan had given me in the showroom. Desmond's feet didn't quite touch the ground, but when I held the bike up so he could put them on the pegs, he leaned back in the seat and extended his arms from the handlebars and looked at me with a pure delight that doubled the ache in my chest.

I knew what was stirring in him as he sat astride the bike that seemed to have a soul—I could see it in the awed innocence that shone in his enormous eyes. He looked like any other young boy now—young enough and wise enough to know what he couldn't do and what he so wanted to do. I meant it this time—if I had an extra helmet I would take him for a ride right now, out into the labyrinth of streets and …

And where? Where could we go that would lead us anywhere but right back here, where neither of us knew the first thing about what to do?

Desmond rolled the silent throttle and made his own rumbling Harley noise.

I guessed we would just fake it till we made it.

Or until God showed up again.

CHAPTER NINE

Mid-September usually meant the beginning of a soft autumn for St. Augustine, with a sweet, salty breeze blowing in off the bay and sunshine turning the coquina to gold. But the morning of the funeral dawned iron gray and windy, the effects of some hurricane in the Caribbean, the weather man said—when I could get the remote away from Desmond long enough to check.

Rain came in periodic dumps, filling the gutters with murky brown water and rendering even the indomitable cathedral drab and despondent. It was so appropriately dismal, even if Chief had paid people to come to the service, they would probably cancel rather than come out and add more misery to the day.

But there were a handful of cars in front of Bates and Hockley when Geneveve, Desmond, and I arrived in my van. The "basic" funeral didn't include a limo for the family, which was fine with me. Desmond would probably have had the whole thing dismantled before we could pull out of Palm Row.

Chief met us at the door in a well-cut gray suit, which he somehow made work with the ponytail. While Mr. Hockley took Desmond and Geneveve to see Ed, Chief ushered me to the back of the chapel for a peek. Five people took up one row; I recognized Willie, Janice, and the male night nurse with the mullet among them. On the other side of the aisle, a short dark-haired woman sat, head bowed.

"Is that Hank?" I whispered.

"Yeah. She's good to have at things like this."

I could see that. I also thought I could see a trace of tenderness in Chief's eyes. Owen would have them pegged as an item. Made sense.

A long wail rose from the viewing room and Desmond appeared in the doorway as if the sound had thrust him into the lobby. He crossed to me, visibly shaking off fear as he came, so that by the time he reached my side, he was again swaggering like he was about to sell us a used car. Behind him his mother's grief continued to permeate the air, right along with the oppressive scent of roses. They had to be piping that aroma in with the organ music, because I saw only two flower arrangements at the front of the chapel, and there wasn't a rose in the bunch.

"Chief," I said, "this is Desmond Sanborn, Ed's grandson."

"I'm sorry for your loss, son," Chief said.

Desmond grinned at him. "I ain't never met my daddy that I know of, but I'm pretty sure he ain't you."

"What are you *talking* about?" I said.

"He callin' me 'son,' like he my daddy or somethin'."

"Not guilty," Chief said. I could barely keep a straight face, but Chief was, as usual, unfazed.

Desmond peered into the chapel, and his grin shrank. "I got to sit in a church?"

"It won't kill you," I said. "I'll probably take care of that first."

"Big Al got it in for me," Desmond said to Chief, grin reappearing. "Dude—here come the Preacher Man."

He punctuated the announcement with a curse, though it was at least under his breath. The Reverend Howard didn't appear to hear it as he swept down the aisle of the chapel still zipping his robe, something I'd never seen him do before.

"Big Al?" Chief whispered to me.

"At least it's not something obscene," I whispered back.

I put my hand out to Garry to avert a hug, although he didn't look like he was in an affectionate mood. He nodded politely to Chief and Desmond—with a second glance for Desmond because he had his eyes closed and his hands pressed in mock prayer at his chest—and said to me, "It's time to get started."

Simultaneously Mr. Hockley and a younger man in an obviously borrowed suit rolled the closed casket through a side door at the front of the chapel, and the six people in the pews stood up.

I put Desmond in Chief's care, retrieved a once-again rocking Geneveve from the floor of the viewing room, and joined them on the front row. I looked twice to make sure the figure standing in the aisle was the Reverend Garry Howard. His face was sketched with hard lines, as if he were steeled for a fight rather than a funeral. A sweaty uneasiness seeped into my palms.

"We've come together," he said, "to pay our respects to …" He consulted the full sheet of paper in his hand. "Edwin Sanborn. And to share the grief of …" Back to the notes. "Desmond and Guinevere."

I heard Desmond mutter something, and saw Chief's big hand come down on the kid's leg. Geneveve seemed oblivious to the mistake that went up my spine like barbed wire.

From there Garry opened his Bible to, as he put it, "perhaps bring some meaning to this sad occasion." The lines in his face relaxed a little, and so did I. He hadn't had a lot of time to prepare. Maybe he was thrown off by that. Maybe now we'd get a glimpse of the Garry Howard who could put not only the deceased but the mourners to rest in their souls.

But he chose for his text the story of Lazarus and the rich man, and there was no doubt that he saw Edwin as the one crying out for water from the fires of hell.

"The death of an unsaved person calls up a deeper sadness in us," he said as he closed his Bible on the obtrusive sheet of paper, "for the one who has not passed into the loving arms of Jesus Christ and for those left to mourn not just the loss of a loved one but his eternal fate."

I could taste the metallic tinge of blood as I bit down on my lip. Only the fact that Geneveve was obviously not absorbing any of it kept me from bolting from my seat and screaming, "Stop this!"

"But we can still take comfort in this cautionary tale that Jesus has shared with us," Garry went on. "He is telling us that all we have to do is believe in Him, give our lives to Him, so that those who lay us to *our* final rest will be able to rejoice that we are at last at home with Him. Amen."

A voice or two answered with faint amens. Mine wasn't one of them.

"Let's take a moment for silent prayer."

He held out his winged arms briefly and bowed his head, while "Amazing Grace" swelled through the pipeline. I stared at him. He couldn't even offer a prayer for Edwin or Geneveve or Desmond? I'd always had a list of happily irreverent adjectives for the Reverend Garry Howard, but the word *cruel* had never been among them.

The "prayer" lasted all of fifteen seconds, after which Mr. Hockley and his hired hand wheeled the casket down the aisle as if there were two more waiting in the wings for their turn. They had it in the hearse before we could get Geneveve out of the chapel. She'd slipped so far into shock that she couldn't walk. Chief finally lifted her into his arms and carried her to the door, where Garry Howard was peeling off his robe. I collected all the self-control I had and went over to him.

"The internment is at San Lorenzo," I said.

His brow furrowed. "You didn't say anything about a graveside service."

"I thought it was part of the package."

He draped his vestment over his arm and looked warily at the pitifully small knot of mourners who were standing near the front door not even attempting to look like they weren't listening. He leaned close to me, hand on my elbow. "I'm sorry for the misunderstanding, Allison. I think you and I have more than one of those to work out, don't we?" He gave my arm a squeeze and let go. "But right now I have another commitment."

"Who does half a funeral?" I wanted to shout at him. He did, obviously, because that was what Ed had just gotten. If that much.

He looked into my eyes as if he expected agreement. I gave him none, but turned to look for Chief. With Geneveve still shivering in his arms, he stood outside under the dripping awning, whistling through his fingers at the hearse as it pulled away.

"Where's it going?" I said.

"To the cemetery," Hank said. She was already putting on her riding gloves. "We're going to have to book to catch up."

I gaped at the empty driveway. "They're going to go dump the coffin in the hole and leave?"

"Not if I can help it." Hank jerked her head toward the door. "You and the family follow Chief and me in your van. I know a shortcut."

Her voice was so solid that I would have followed her to the gallows right then. It had to be more sacred than this unholy place.

"We're right behind you," Willie said to her. "Lord, I never saw such a funeral."

Chief deposited Geneveve in my front seat, where she held onto herself as if she were afraid she would shake apart. Desmond knelt on the floor between her and me, giving a running commentary on the coolness of following a pair of Harleys down the back roads of St. John's County.

"This is *sweet*," he said more than once. "I have got to get me one of those."

I had one, and I was sure I didn't look as "sweet" and sure as Chief and Hank did, their bikes leaning in perfect synch like a pair of figure skaters. They had a command of the road, and yet there was a flow, an ease to their riding as they led us wherever we were going. Following them was the only thing that had seemed at all right about this funeral.

"Lookit!" Desmond cried out. He jabbed his index finger at the hearse, which we caught up to at the cemetery gate. "Us and them choppers, dude, we kicked us some serious—"

"Tail," I finished for him.

I wasn't sure how we'd managed to cut the hearse off at the proverbial pass. The kid at the wheel took the cemetery's curves so fast I expected the coffin to be upside down by now.

The rain was slanting sideways in sheets as the driver and another guy, who hadn't even bothered with a suit, skidded the hearse to a stop on the wide gravel path near an open grave and yanked the coffin out onto the bier. While we huddled without a traditional canopy, sharing umbrellas and dashboard shields and whatever else we could find to cover our heads, they positioned the casket over the hole, lowered it in with the respect due a dead hamster, and took off, spewing gravel in their wake.

"Are you serious?" I said.

"Godspeed," Hank said drily. She visibly rearranged her thoughts and looked up at Chief. "You want to say a few words?"

He nodded and, with rainwater dripping from his eyebrows, began to speak. The wind caught many of his phrases and carried them off, but I captured a few.

"Faithful husband to his beloved Coreen until she passed ...

"As a father and grandfather ... sacrificed everything for Geneveve and Priscilla and Desmond ...

"Told me stories about his work as a landscaper for the city ... he said very few people noticed when his work was done well, but let a hedge have a twig out of place and someone was always ready to point that out to him ...

"... said that's how he grew as a person, when somebody trimmed him back." Chief closed his eyes. I could see him swallowing his way to his next words. "We can say he would have lived longer if he'd had better care ... our refusal to accept that a man barely sixty should die. But I think Edwin Sanborn was perfectly shaped when he passed from us. The work was done. Now ours begins."

I felt movement at my shoulder and looked down to see Geneveve bobbing her head. At last someone was talking about her daddy.

Chief stepped back, and Hank turned to us, her motley, soggy congregation. She had spoken several sentences before I realized she was using not her own words but our Lord's.

"Oh, my friends, blessed are the poor in spirit, for theirs is the kingdom of heaven. Blessed are those who mourn for they will be comforted, yes?"

There were amens I had no urge to time. I said one myself.

"Blessed are the meek—Geneveve and Desmond—for they will inherit the earth. Blessed are those who hunger and thirst for righteousness—such as Allison, and the merciful—Chief and Willie and Janie and Bud. Blessed are the pure in heart like our Edwin. For they will see God."

"Amen," we said again. "Amen." Only Chief remained silent, as if he'd used all the words he had. Desmond mumbled something, which clearly wasn't amen, but for once didn't include ghetto vocabulary. The word *Grandaddy* was tangled in there somewhere. As for Geneveve, the earth seemed to give way beneath her. She collapsed into the mud piled beside the grave and sobbed until my own heart broke.

"Chief," Hank said, "maybe you should—"

"I'll do it," I said.

I knelt beside her, saturated soil seeping through my pants, and dispensed with the plastic bag from Old Navy I'd been using as an umbrella for the two of us. The relentless rain plastered my hair to my skull.

Only when I put my arm around Geneveve and tried to stand her up did I realize that half of her sobs were words. There was no frenzied rocking now, no paralyzing shock. She was weeping from her gut, speaking her pain, as any grief-stricken daughter would.

"I don't know what to do," she said. "I need help."

"I'll get you some help," I said. "Come on, let's get out of this rain."

"No, Miss Angel. I need *you*."

She looked up at me, really looked at me, and for the first time since I'd scraped her out of West King Street, she seemed truly human. I wasn't surprised to feel the Nudge.

Hank crouched beside us and held a yellow umbrella over us. Both Geneveve and I were beyond rescue from being soaked to the skin, but the gesture was like a bath and a warm blanket.

"The sacrament of burial is never complete without comfort food," Hank said.

I nodded. "We can go to my place."

"I'll ride with you, Mr. Chief," I heard Desmond say. "You and me can pick us up a six-pack."

I didn't hear Chief's response, but Desmond wound up in the van with me, muttering about how these people did not know how to party.

A sentiment shared by Hank when she opened my pantry, scowled, and reported that she was going to the grocery store. Evidently my idea of comfort food and hers were worlds apart.

The nurses from Resurrection didn't join us, though Willie asked Hank and Chief before she took off if she could call them to do funerals in the future. While Hank was at the market, I left Chief in charge of Desmond and ran a bath for Geneveve and a shower for myself. She headed for the bed still wrapped in a towel.

"I'm too tired, Miss Angel," she said. "But I know it's gon' be all right now."

Her faith in that juiced the anxiety down to my fingertips, but I said, "Okay, Geneveve."

In sweats and a wet ponytail, I went downstairs to see how Chief and Desmond were faring. I expected to see the kid tied to a kitchen chair being advised of his rights. Wait, it was the police who did that. Chief was a lawyer. I grunted to myself. Desmond would undoubtedly need one someday. Soon.

But I found them on the couch in the living room, each holding a soda can as if they were indeed sharing a six pack, feet propped on the steamer trunk I used as a coffee table. Desmond's were almost as big as Chief's.

"I'm glad y'all made yourselves at home," I said.

Chief started to pull his from the trunk but I shook my head at him. Desmond, of course, slouched in deeper and crossed his ankles.

"We just doin' a little male bonding, Big Al," he said. "We don't really need nothing right now, thanks."

"Who said I was offering anything?" I said. "You pretty much help yourself anyway."

"Oh yeah, huh?" Here came the grin. "You think that Hankenstein lady gonna get some more Oreos? We out."

"You so did not just say that to me."

Desmond looked at Chief. "I told you she got it in for me."

"I don't blame her," Chief said.

His voice, his face—both remained unmoved. He would handle this kid so much better than I could, he and Hank. I'd seen Chief's whispered, heads-touching conversation with her by the door before she left. It had the intimate look of people who finished each other's sentences and had whole discussions across rooms without uttering a word. I could always detect it in couples, even though I'd never experienced it myself.

"A person could starve hisself waitin' on women," Desmond was saying to Chief. "I'ma hit the kitchen. You want anything? Light beer?"

"I don't have any beer," I said.

"Chips? Wings? We got some of them hot wings in the freezer."

THE RELUCTANT PROPHET   171

"I'm good," Chief said.

"Okay, just thought I'd ask."

Desmond untangled his legs and strutted across the room to the beat of some inner, slightly off drum.

"He reminds me of a Q-tip," Chief said as he watched Desmond disappear into my kitchen.

"He reminds me of possible suicide. Who knew promising to take care of his mother was going to mean dealing with the next John Dillinger?"

I brushed off the cushion Desmond had just vacated and dropped onto it. As I tucked one foot under me, I caught Chief observing.

"What?" I said.

"I've actually been thinking about that."

"Thinking like a lawyer?"

"No. Just thinking. You'll know when I'm thinking like a lawyer."

"So ..."

"You made a promise to a man who's now dead. It's all very noble to think you have to keep it, but there's really nothing holding you to it."

"Yeah there is."

"You mean Geneveve."

"I mean God."

His blankness became blanker.

"So," I said. "I take it you don't—you're not—"

Sheesh, how could I say this without sounding like India?

"I don't believe a thing that came out of that minister's mouth today, if that's where you're going," Chief said.

"What about what Hank said?"

"Let's just say she and I have agreed to disagree."

Part of me wanted to ask how *that* worked in a relationship. The other part was glad he changed the subject.

"You live here alone?"

"Just me and the cockroaches. It's the curse of an old house in Florida."

"Nice place. Did you buy it like this, or did you do all this restoration?"

"Neither. I inherited it."

"Grandparents?"

"Parents."

Faint surprise finally stirred his face. "They must have died young."

"They did. Are you this good in the courtroom?"

"Sorry?"

"I'm answering all these questions like I'm under oath. How do you do that?" I grunted. "I usually tell people to mind their own business after about two."

He spread his big palms. "I got nothing up my sleeves. Just interested. Am I prying?"

"No. Besides, you could look it up on the Internet and find out more than you really wanted to know. My mother and father were murdered."

I wasn't sure if it was the statement or the cavalier way I delivered it that widened his eyes. It had been a while since I'd had to reveal that family tragedy to anyone, because most people in St. A. had lived through the horror of it themselves. I'd forgotten how it could affect somebody who hadn't.

"You don't have to talk about it," Chief said.

"It's fine. It was a long time ago—1998."

"Both of them—at the same time?"

"Yeah. Car bomb."

"*Car* bomb? Here?"

"Right in the driveway of their home in Grand Haven."

"Did you ever find out who did it?"

I nodded and untucked my legs and tucked them in again. Sweat was forming behind my knees. This was the only part of the story I'd ever had trouble talking about, even right after it happened.

"It was a guy who was employed by their corporation—Chamberlain Enterprises—for twenty-nine years and six months. He was about to retire and receive his pension and—whataya know, he was 'terminated.' So he left a note and planted a bomb and 'terminated' my parents. Then he killed himself."

Chief was slowly shaking his head. "I am so sorry."

"Well, thank you. Like I said, it was twelve years ago, and yeah, I mean, it shook me up, but the strange thing is, I felt almost as sorry for the guy as I did for them. That probably doesn't make any sense to you. It doesn't to most people."

"I'm usually not most people," he said.

His voice was husky. It almost made me blurt out what I thought on the rare occasion when this subject came up: "They were cold, heartless people, and they brought it on themselves." It also made me want to explain my attitude.

"Murder's always wrong," I said. "The guy could've sued CE or used his severance package to start a new life—whatever. But the thing is, the way my parents died was like that." I snapped my fingers. "The coroner said they never even felt it. But they'd made that man *suffer,* and for no reason except that it would improve their profit margin."

"That a shock for you, finding that out?"

I shook my head. "It only confirmed what I'd known about them since I was about twelve years old."

"If you don't mind me asking—"

"No—go ahead."

"How did you deal with that?"

"There wasn't much to deal with. They'd cut me out of the will when I was eighteen and out of their lives two weeks before they were killed. I was thirty."

"So the house …"

"They left this house to my nanny, and she later left it to me. Nice irony, huh?"

Chief turned his head a mere fraction of an inch. "Is it?" he said.

"Man, you are good." I stretched out my legs and picked up his empty soda can. "I might even answer that, if I knew. Another drink?"

Once again I split into halves—one hoping he'd push it just a little further, the other ready to kiss Hank's feet when she breezed in with enough food for three funeral receptions. That was the half that catapulted me to the kitchen.

"Observe, Al," Hank said as she unloaded pita bread, hummus, imported olives, and a half-pound of prosciutto onto the counter. "*This* is food. What you have in your refrigerator is—I don't know what it is—it's inedible." She turned to Desmond, who was sniffing from the den doorway. "Hey, Desi, how are you at chopping?"

"You are so not going to give him a *knife!*" I said.

"It's all good," Desmond said for about the five hundredth time in the forty-eight hours I'd known him. "I am strickly nonviolent." He smiled half of his smile. "I got other ways."

Ya think?

But I watched as he turned down Hank's offer to let him slice and made a fruitless survey of the snack drawer, giving up too easily when Chief denied his fifth request to let him take his Road King for a spin. The bright-eyed edge was gone from his routine, and I realized the kid was exhausted by his own charm.

"You can go veg in front of the TV if you want," I said. "I'll bring you a plate."

"No, Big Al, it's—"

"I know it's all good. I just thought you might want to kick back."

He delivered a cheerful reply that on the radio would have been one long bleep. I was pretty sure he *had* just used his favorite curse as a coordinating conjunction.

"Hey, buddy."

We all turned to Chief as if he'd called us to attention. The eagle eyes were honed in on Desmond.

"Let's lighten up on the language," he said.

"'Scuse me?"

"Enough with the swearing."

Neither Chief's tone nor his face was anymore commanding than usual, but an order had been given. If I were a twelve-year-old kid, I'd be saluting at this point. Desmond clearly didn't have that reflex. He took a begrudging step backward, eyes never leaving Chief's, and it dawned on me that he was waiting for Chief's next move.

When Chief didn't deliver whatever it was he expected, Desmond applied the smile and offered a palm-down fist. Unlike me, Chief knew what to do with that, and Desmond turned toward the den.

"I'ma chill," he said.

"Good idea," I said.

I made sure the den door was closed, and even then I beckoned Hank and Chief into the dining room and spoke in a hoarse whisper.

"I can't do what you just did."

"Of course you can't," Hank said. "You're not a six-foot-three male with eyes like the business end of a .357 Magnum."

"I'm serious," I said. "I've got to have help with this, or I'm going to end up doing what everybody else has obviously done with that kid. And his mother."

Chief hitched his shoulders. "Like I told you, you don't have to."

"And like I told you, yes I do."

"What do you need?" Hank said.

"Will you just stay with him for about an hour? Maybe less. I think I know where I can get some support."

"You've got it." Hank leaned against Chief. "He'll help me. As long as I feed him, he's putty in my hands."

"Okay. Good. Thanks," I said. And then I just stood there.

"Was there something else?" Hank said.

"Yeah," I said. "Just—pray for me."

Hank nodded. Chief didn't.

I didn't have time to sort that out.

CHAPTER TEN

The rain had given up and gone away, so I rode my bike to the church. India pulled in at the same time I did, and to say that her mascara-laden eyes popped from her head was an understatement.

"I didn't think Bonner was serious when he told us you'd done this," she said before she got all the way out of her Miata.

"He was," I said. "But do you dig the jacket? I thought of you when I bought it."

She ignored my leather and stared at my Harley. "Do I even want to know what possessed you to do such a thing?"

"You probably do," I said. "I bought it because God told me to."

Before that night I would have enjoyed watching her try to keep her eyes from completely dropping out onto the church parking lot. But I didn't say it for shock value. If I was going to go through with what I'd come for, I couldn't cut any corners getting there.

"Let's go inside before you pass out," I said.

"Oh I'm fine. I just want to see what Mary Alice does when she sees you on that thing."

Mary Alice had already seen, which was obvious when we walked into the bride's lounge and she and Frank were still bending the blinds to peer through the window. Bonner greeted me from the couch with, "You had to bring it, didn't you?"

"I'm not hiding it," I said. "Matter of fact I'm not hiding anything."

The Harley, the coffee, the pound cake were abandoned as if I'd just announced I was pregnant. Mary Alice was already checking her chins as she sank onto the couch next to Bonner. "All right," India said. "*What* is going on with you, girl?"

"This is going to sound strange to you, I know—"

"Is it stranger than you buying a motorcycle?" Mary Alice said.

"Forget the Harley," India said. "I'm talking about what you just said to me outside—about *God* telling you to buy it."

Frank audibly gasped. Bonner dropped his elbows to his knees and covered his face with both hands. Mary Alice couldn't even *find* her chins.

"Please, y'all," I said. "Just let me tell you what's happened in the last four days, and then I think you'll get it. Please?"

"I already get that your icing has slipped off your cupcakes," India said. She dropped herself into the chair.

"You wanted me to take some leadership. I'm offering it."

Bonner pulled his hands from his face. "Let her go for it."

"Just let me tell you what's happened," I said, "and then you can tell me what we need to do—because I know you'll know."

Frank motioned for me to sit so that he could, but I shook my head. This had to be done standing up. I started the story from the day in church, seventeen days ago, when I'd first felt the Nudge, and I stopped at the graveside where Geneveve looked up from the mire and begged me to help her.

"Garry gave this pathetic little homily about Lazarus and the rich man that I thought was—well, never mind—the point is, we can be the Rich Man and give Lazarus some help *before* he dies."

"That's a salvation story, Miss Allison." Frank's voice had a patronizing tone I'd never heard before.

"Fine. But just because we don't have to do anything about our salvation, that doesn't mean there's nothing important for us to do." The words had a slippery quality as they slid out. They kept sliding.

"We have so much. Our faith is solid. This is our chance to use it to make a difference for somebody besides just us."

"I get that," India said. "But Allison, honey, we need to be so careful. You remember that woman that showed up in Kathleen McElhinney's group and told everybody she had pancreatic cancer? They raised all kinds of money for her medical bills and then she took off with the cash and they never saw her again. Turns out she'd pulled the same scam in three other churches. The woman never even had cancer."

Frank inched to the edge of his chair, already shaping what he was going to say with his hands. "I don't doubt that this woman and her son are in real trouble, but there are free rehabilitation programs."

"That boy ought to be in foster care," Mary Alice said. "They have people with experience handling children like that."

"Are you serious?" I said. "Do you know how many kids who grow up in foster care end up in prison?"

"It sounds like this kid is halfway there already." India put up her hand before I could protest. "So we give money for her to have decent rehab. What are the odds she won't come out and start using again? These people have deep-seated problems, darlin'. I just think you're being naive to think we can save them."

"I hear they go right back to where they were living before and start all over," Mary Alice said.

Bonner leaned forward on the couch. "Where *are* they living now?"

I pulled in a long breath through my nose. "They're staying with me."

"Lord have mercy," someone said. It could have been any of them.

"Look, I haven't said a word about giving Geneveve and her boy money. All I want is your help. Desmond needs male role models. Geneveve needs the kind of support I got from you all when I was lost—"

"Honey, that was *completely* different!" India tossed her head back. "You weren't doing drugs and selling your body down on West King Street."

"Allison."

They all turned to Bonner, desperation on their faces.

"We're concerned about your safety in this," he said. "The Harley's bad enough. Every day I think I'm going to get a call that the paramedics have had to scrape you up off of US 1."

"Thanks for that," I said.

"But taking in strangers you don't really know anything about, except that one's a drug addict and the other one's a juvenile klep-tomaniac, that's just—irresponsible. You're going to wake up one morning with everything you own gone, your identity stolen." He closed his eyes. "And your heart broken."

"I have to agree with that, Missy," Frank said. "I surely do. I think we all do."

I stared from one face to the next and didn't see one that was familiar. It was as if each of them were masquerading as someone else. Or was it that they'd just now removed the masks I'd always thought were the genuinely compassionate countenances of Mary Alice Moss and India Morehead and Frank Parker and Bonner Bailey? I had no idea what to do. I didn't have a disguise to put on or take off. I could only stand there with my disbelief hanging out and let them work me over like a panel of strangers.

Until the Nudge became a Shove, pushing me naked out of the middle-school locker room and into the hall, where all I could do was blurt out what I didn't know was in me.

"So that's what we're about then," I said. "Staying safe in our gated-community faith, where we make room for God. Well, you know what? That's a fantasy and a lie."

"Allison!" Mary Alice said.

"We're about saving souls," Frank said.

"No, we're about numbers. We're about how many people— 'decent' people, mind you—can be saved and put on the rolls and expected to tithe."

"That's not fair," Bonner said.

"We give them the fire insurance salvation pitch, and they buy into it, and then we protect them in here so that none of us has to see what's going on outside the gates. We're in here worshiping a Jesus we've made up, while most of the souls out there, *right* out there, are crying out for the Jesus that really exists. I didn't realize until I wound up down there on West King that I don't know a thing about the real Jesus. Not a *thing*. And you just showed me that you don't either."

I could see it as I stood there heaving for air that I was as bumbling and obnoxious as that naked middle-school kid, but I didn't try to tell them the words hadn't been mine. That they'd come from a place I didn't know about until I found myself there. As shocked and hurt as my friends now looked, I didn't want to take a single syllable back.

"We're family," Bonner said. "You don't go after family that way."

"If you can't tell your own family how you feel, then what's the point in having one?" I shook my head. "I've been here before with 'family.' I just thought this one was different."

I didn't need a Nudge to tell me it was time to leave. There was no hurry. I knew nobody would try to stop me, and I wasn't running away anyway. I just had to go before the sadness sank in.

My bike was waiting for me, silent and ready, as if she knew all along I wouldn't come out happy. I sat on it for a minute in a yellow circle of light from the faux gas street lamp.

In my teens, whenever I had a meltdown in front of my father and told him what a greedy, narrow-minded impostor he was, I always came away feeling smug and self-righteous and satisfied with my adolescent self. I felt none of that now. I'd seen in the unmasked faces of my Watchdogs that I had come off that way, but I had no sense of a job well done—no urge to brush my hands together and say, "They know what time it is now." This job was just beginning, a job I still had no idea how to do. All I knew was that I was going to have to do it without them.

It was overwhelmingly sad. No one should have to attend two funerals in one day.

Maybe it was the sadness that distracted me from paying attention to what I was doing. Or maybe Bonner was right that I would inevitably crash someday and have to be peeled from the pavement with a spatula. Whatever it was, I careened too fast around the corner into Palm Row and overcorrected myself straight toward a coconut palm. Somehow I managed to remain upright and avoid it, but not before Chief saw it all from the side porch.

I took off my helmet and glared at him. "If you say, 'What did you do wrong?' so help me I'll run you over."

"Not saying a word," Chief said.

He got up from the swing and moved easily down the steps. The moment I realized I was *enjoying* the way he moved, I hastened the Classic into the garage, parked her, and came out with my helmet and a clearer head. Chief was astride the Road King, his own helmet fastened in place.

"Get on," he said. "Let's go for a ride."

"Chief, really, it's been a rough evening—"

"I can see that. That's why you need a ride."

As I climbed on behind him, I told myself I just didn't have the energy to argue. Then I told myself the truth, which was that the man had an intensity that was hard to resist. No wonder Hank was—

"Where is she?" I said over the slow idle of the engine.

"Who?"

"Hank."

"She had to go."

"I can't leave that kid alone."

"Trust me. He's down for the count. Hank said to give you this."

He held up a folded note between two gloved fingers.

"Sorry I couldn't wait," she'd written. "Meet me at the Galleon on Friday morning if you want to talk."

"Hang on," Chief said.

The bike rolled quietly to the corner, but I knew we were about to take off in Chief's no-messing-around-let's-get-this-done style. I fumbled around with where to put my hands, until he reached back and pulled them to his waist.

"That's holding on," he said.

If I'd ever known him to actually smile, I would imagine something on the amused side curving his lips.

I didn't ask where we were going because it felt good to have somebody else choosing the direction. What Chief chose was an easy cruise up St. George Street to King and a smooth sweep over the temporary Bridge of Lions that wouldn't have been possible at high traffic times. Reconstruction of the aging 1920s structure, guarded by its famous pair of kingly concrete beasts, made crossing it a teeth-gnashing experience during the day. With the sun sunken beyond the city and her inhabitants settled into their brews at Scarlett O'Hara's or their lobsters at O. C. White's, we floated over the Matanzas Bay with the freedom of the seagulls that now slept on the sea wall. I'd never crossed it on a bike, and the unfettered feel of it was at once frightening and exhilarating—the first time. The second time, after a U-turn on Anastasia Boulevard, I tilted my head and closed my eyes and wished it would never end.

Chief pulled the bike to the curb on Avenida Menendez and took off his helmet.

"I like to sit on the wall," he said. "You?"

"How'd you know?"

"Lucky guess."

I actually did like to come here on evenings like this, when a warm wind was blowing the stars around. It was especially delicious to me after a dreary day when stars weren't expected and came out as a treat for those who were paying attention.

At this end the wall was lined with short, thick posts called bollards, all connected by nautical-size chain designed to separate people on the walkway from the marina below, with moderate success. More than one drunk had sat on the decorative chains and found

himself—or herself—thrashing among the mackerel in the Matanzas.
I stepped over one and lowered myself to the wall to let my legs hang
over the side. Below, the anchored sailboats rocked themselves to
sleep and the fish leaped from the water, some of them as high as four
feet above its surface as if they knew they were safe from the fishermen
soaking up suds at the bar at the Santa Maria out on the pier.

When Chief eased down beside me, I said, "You really have a
passion for riding, don't you?"

"Don't you?"

"Why is it that every time I ask you something about yourself, we
wind up talking about me?"

"Occupational habit," he said. "What do you want to know?"

"What it's like to really love doing something so much you can't
not do it."

"Feels like freedom," he said. "Like the possibilities are endless."
He looked at me sideways. "You never had that?"

I shook my head. "I thought I did when I was about seventeen.
We—I wanted to just take off and go until I found something that
needed doing and do it and move on to the next place. But it was
just an old dream that didn't work out." I laughed. "Do I sound like a
heroine in a romance novel?"

"Never read a romance novel."

"Come to think of it, I never have either."

"Didn't think you were the type. So—rough time at the church."

He said it as if he'd predicted it. I wondered if he and Hank had
laid bets on it.

"Yeah," I said. "I expected support and I didn't get it, which
leaves me pretty much where I started." I stopped bouncing my

heels against the wall. "I have to see this through with Geneveve and the kid—I know that. I guess I'll just take baby steps and see what happens."

"If you go too slow, it's hard to keep your balance."

I grunted. "I've heard that before."

"Something every biker has to remember." Chief pressed his hands on either side of him on the wall. "I'll be reminding you of that, among other things."

"I'm sorry?"

"You need a Riding Guide—it's like a mentor until you get some miles on you." It was his turn to grunt. "Otherwise you're going to kill yourself or somebody else."

"You're the second person to tell me that tonight," I said. "Only you I actually believe. Are you saying you're going to be this guide person for me?"

"If it works for you."

"I guess it does," I said.

"I'm going to start by showing you how to get your bike out of your street without revving the engine all the way up." I thought I saw his lip twitch. "I had a visit from your next-door neighbor while you were gone."

"Which one?"

"Lady with—"

"Miz Vernell."

"She was actually leaving a note on the door when I opened it. Almost gave her a coronary."

"Let me guess: She said my bike was too loud and I was disturb-ing the serenity of Palm Row."

"No, she said she was calling the police the next time she couldn't hear *Wheel of Fortune* because you were starting up that awful machine."

I blinked at him. "What did you do, take notes? I know that's exactly what she said." I raked a hand through my hair. "I'll have to go over there tomorrow and try to appease her somehow."

"Or you can just let me show you how to drive it out without drowning out Pat Sajak. I promised her I would."

"You did." I rolled my eyes. That was going to be her main topic of conversation over coffee cake with Owen tomorrow. "Thanks. Otherwise I'm looking at jail time."

"They don't put you in jail for violating a noise ordinance."

"You're not going to charge me for that piece of advice, are you?"

"Nah. This is strictly pro bono."

I felt myself smile. "And the help with the Harley?"

"I'm doing that so you don't give the rest of us a bad name. Next piece of advice."

"Yeah?"

He looked me straight in the eyes, once more the eagle with wisdom borne from the heights. "Take it one ride at a time."

"Am I to also take it that you're not just talking about the Harley?"

"Take it however it fits, Classic," he said. "However it fits."

CHAPTER ELEVEN

I got up the next morning with my first "ride" planned: I had to enroll Desmond in school. My motive was not entirely his welfare. Not only had he already missed the first month, but if he hung around at my house one more day, one of us was going down.

My announcement was met with the resistance I expected, although I had to give the kid credit for being consistent. He used every charm-filled ploy in his repertoire to get me to change my mind, including telling me how much he would miss me. It didn't occur to me until Geneveve and I left him in the office at the middle school that by now all the who's-cool-and-who's-not lines had already been drawn. For once I hoped his technique worked for him, because from what I saw in that place, he was going to need *something* to survive. The lineup of kids in the office all looked like they'd done time or were about to. And half of them were girls.

Geneveve seemed only slightly more aware of him that day than previously. It was me he said good-bye to, me he told he'd have this place under control before lunch. His mother just looked at him as if she wondered where he'd come from.

That was understandable, considering the condition she was still in. I watched her nervously, waiting for the DT's or some other ugly sign of withdrawal to kick in. Early Friday morning she finally seemed to have slept herself out and came down to the kitchen before I had to drag her from the bed. I put a cup of coffee in her hand and laid things out for her across the bistro table.

"How are you doing this, Geneveve? You were so doped up when

I found you, you've got to be craving by now. I'm not going to throw you out if somehow you're using, but I have to know."

She stared into the coffee as if she were waiting for the answer to float to the top. "I'm clean right now. I done this before—got myself not using for sometime a week, maybe two. And then I go right back."

"Well, yeah. You're an addict. That's how it works."

"I don't want it to work that way no more. I wanna stop this time, for good." Her eyes did a frenetic search of the room and came to rest on me, brimming fear. "I want my boy to know his real mama. 'Cept—Miss Angel—I don't even know her—and she's *me*."

"That's all I wanted to hear," I said. "I'll look into some programs today—"

"Ain't gonna work."

I hadn't heard that kind of firmness in her voice before and it made me set my cup on the table.

"I been in so many programs. My daddy spent all his money on trying to get me clean. My sister use all kinda candles and crystals and she done give up on me cause she said I didn't wanna change. But I do now, Miss Angel. And I know you can change me."

I was still shaking my head when she came off the bistro chair and flew into my arms. Once again I was caught off guard by the brittle weightless form that was her body. I knew if I told her now that I couldn't change her, that I didn't even know how to help her, she would crush to powder in my hands.

I decided one thing for sure when I'd dropped Desmond off for his second day at school and was headed for the Spanish Galleon for a quick cup with Hank before I went to work. I wasn't going to try any of the things Geneveve had already attempted. It was pointless to tell her what a mess she'd made of her life; that was as apparent to her as it was to everybody else. And I wasn't going to make her a prisoner in my house. I'd never understood that approach when I worked teaching arts and crafts to patients in the rehab facility. They were locked up so they couldn't get their hands on any of the substances that had put them there, but it was obvious that most of them were going to be released, clean and sober, and go right back to the old neighborhood—where nobody made decoupage or macramé—and pick up where they left off because they didn't know how to do anything else. Just like India said.

So I knew what I wasn't going to do. I just didn't know what to put in its place.

I didn't start off with that with Hank because we got into my experience at the Watchdogs meeting. She nodded when I wound up with a recap of my outburst.

"You certainly have a way with people, Al," she said.

"A lot of them do find me hard to take. I know I can give off a vibe."

"A 'vibe.'"

"When I was working as a waitress at a truck stop in Palatka, this driver called me over to his table and told me I should smile more because when I was serious I looked like I was about to hold up a liquor store." I shrugged. "I try to keep that in mind."

"I was thinking more of that way you have of looking at somebody like you're reading their mind."

"I get that a lot too. Some people ask me straight out what I'm looking at. I notice people checking their noses, I guess to find out if I'm staring at a booger hanging or something. I don't know."

"So are you?"

"What—looking at boogers?"

"No. Reading our minds."

"No. I guess I'm usually just waiting to see if somebody has something to say. I've never been that good at small talk—you know, party chatter, conversations with strangers in checkout lines."

"Which is what I like about you," Hank said. "However, unlike me, most people aren't ready to jump into in-depth conversations after five minutes of being introduced to you."

"Or after five *years*, evidently." I felt the sadness drain me again. "It was different with my group. But last night it was like they changed right there before my eyes."

Hank chewed thoughtfully on a mouthful of the Walk the Plank omelet she'd tried again to talk me into. I'd gotten away with just a café au lait. "Have you considered that maybe you're the one who changed?"

"Yeah, well, there's that, only I don't know where it's all coming from."

Hank held up two fingers on the hand she wasn't eating with. "One, yes you do, and two, that isn't the point."

"You going to tell me what the point is?"

"No. You're going to tell me." She turned to Patrice. "Hon, would it offend you if I asked for just a drop more of Tabasco sauce?"

While hippie-haired Patrice assured her that the only thing that offended her was people turning down her food, I got no closer to the point. I shook my head at Hank as she sprinkled hot sauce on the remains of her eggs.

"All right," she said, "we've established that God is behind all this, yes?"

"Yes."

"It hasn't been my experience that God gives an assignment and then leaves you to figure out how to carry it out by yourself."

"He's not saying anything."

"Maybe he doesn't have to. Maybe you already know."

"I already know how to take care of somebody who's basically dying."

She was nodding before the words settled between us. "Yeah, Al, you do."

It was worth a shot, and it made even more sense when the longer Geneveve went without using, the sicker she seemed. She showed no awareness of what was night and what was day. She never remembered to eat on her own. And she clearly saw no point in brushing her teeth or bathing or doing much of anything but wander restlessly around the house, touching everything and feeling nothing. She showed every mental symptom of a dying patient letting go of her spirit. I had to turn my house back into a hospice.

I set up a routine for her of rising and going to bed, taking regular naps, soaking in Celtic salt baths, just as I'd done for Sylvia. I set out the toothbrush with the paste already on it—curled her fingers around a glass of water every time she licked her lips—sat across from her at the bistro table and fed her apple slices and almonds until she figured out how to pick them up and put them into her own mouth.

By Saturday afternoon she started to thank me, with long, embarrassing hugs and lengthy paragraphs about how I was saving her life and how she was never going to use drugs again. She always ended with tears, and, "You *are* an angel."

Any chance I had of actually believing that was dashed on a regular basis by Desmond. Two days of middle school had evidently exhausted his witty repartee and wiped out the energy he normally used to work me. He had moved on to finding all my buttons and mashing them. Over and over.

He emptied the snack drawer, and, I suspected, flushed some of the contents down the john, judging from the backup I had to deal with Saturday morning. The TV, the CD player, and the radio were all going at full volume, simultaneously, every time I left the first floor. I found him wearing my yellow Harley T-shirt, with the neck and sleeves cut out, caught him sifting through my jewelry box and mumbling about my bling not being worth a thing, and discovered him looking at porn on the computer in the den. Within a twenty-four-hour period I could have had him arrested for theft, destruction of property, and attempted crazy-making. I was glad I now knew a good attorney, because I was going to need one to defend me when I committed homicide. Mary Alice was the one who was right about this one: I did not know how to handle this kid.

The one thing I found interesting—rather than just stupefying—was that he never tried to run away. He could have split any of a number of times when I was occupied with Geneveve, and the way I was cramping his style, he had to want to. But every time I thought—and, admittedly, hoped—he'd slipped out the side door or taken off out the front, I would come downstairs to find him eating the bag of mini-marshmallows I was saving for hot chocolate or trying to order from the Harley catalog over the phone. I just kept locking things in cabinets and hiding them in closets, and took to keeping my debit card and cell phone on my person at all times. But the one thing I didn't keep a close enough eye on was the key to my Harley.

Late Saturday afternoon, when Geneveve was napping and Desmond had at last fallen into a stupor in front of VH1, and I was sure everything valuable was nailed down, I decided that clumsy as I still was, I had to go for a bike ride or I was seriously going to lose it. When I reached for the key on the brass hook by the kitchen door and it wasn't there, I did. Loud and long and livid.

"*Desmond,* get in here! *Now!*"

I was answered with a mild expletive and, "Big Al, you ever considered switchin' to some decaf?" At which point I catapulted myself into the den and yanked him out of the chair by the front of my yellow Harley T-shirt.

"In there *now*," I said.

"You don't got to get all up in my dental work about it." He shook out the shirt as if he'd just spent an hour ironing it and sauntered into the kitchen. I cut him off halfway across.

"Where is the key to my Harley?" I said. "And don't waste my time telling me you didn't take it because you've had your hands on everything else I own. Give it to me. Now."

Desmond shoved his hands into the pockets of his baggy shorts and for an insane moment I thought he was simply going to hand it over. But his head went back, and challenge gleamed in his big eyes. He was no longer a cute kid. And I was no longer his understanding keeper.

"I'm not playing with you, Desmond," I said.

"C'mon, Big Al, we always playin'. I'll give you a hint—"

"You'll give me the key."

"And if I don't?"

"You don't even want to know."

He tried to laugh, but he didn't get far. I curled my fingers around his left ear and pulled him sideways toward the ground. With his hands in his pockets, he had no place to go but down, which he did while I grabbed his right wrist and pulled out his hand. It was still fisted around the key.

"Make a choice," I said. "You can give up your ear or you can give up my key."

His fingers opened and the key clattered to the floor, but not before I saw surprise, anger, and fear flip through his eyes like cards in a Rolodex. There was no satisfaction in it for me, not only because I felt like a playground bully, but because it had been so easy to do. Too easy. For a kid who'd grown up on West King Street, he had no moves, no strength, no toughness quotient whatsoever. How he'd survived this long I had no idea, but I did know one thing: He wouldn't have made it out there much longer.

I stood up and put a hand down to him. He didn't seem to notice that it was shaking as he glared at it.

"Game over," I said.

If he knew I was giving him a chance to save face, he wasn't having it. He pulled the shirt off, revealing ribs that climbed his chest like rickety ladders, and tossed it to me.

"You can have that back," he said, and took himself to the den, visibly trying to keep his tail from disappearing between his legs.

I looked away, ashamed for both of us.

Desmond didn't speak for the rest of the night, and the silence was unnerving. Somewhere in the midst of it, I decided there was no way I was taking those two to church the next day—and even less of a way I was leaving them in the house by themselves. What was it going to accomplish for me to go anyway? More grief from my community of believers? More discouragement expressed as concern for my safety? Another invitation from Garry Howard for us to sit down and discuss our "misunderstandings"? I was surprised he hadn't already called me to dismantle my word from God; surely Frank or Mary Alice had informed him of that by now. And seeing Bonner would just send me running for the Oreos—if I'd had any left.

I dipped into my hidden stash of cocoa instead and took it, minus marshmallows, to the side porch in my bare feet and pajamas. Almost October. Miz Vernell had a pot of fiery-colored mums on both ends of every step to her house and a wreath of autumnal leaves on each door. If you wanted a gold-and-red fall in Florida, you had to import it. I usually headed up the pumpkin-carving with the kids at church....

The cocoa wasn't doing it for me. It was going to take more than guilt-assuaging chocolate to make hunkering down on my porch on a Sunday morning okay. I'd rarely missed a service in seven years. If I did, I never missed checking in with Mary Alice or India to tell them why I wouldn't be there. The emptiness was as new and raw as fresh grief.

When the phone rang, I was sure I'd see Bonner's number on the screen, but it was Chief. As usual he dispensed with the pleasantries.

"You coming to the HOG meeting?"

"No. I'm being held prisoner."

"Say again?"

"I can't leave Desmond here unsupervised."

"Bring him with."

"Seriously? I have a life-size picture of him—"

"Let him wear your helmet and you can pick up another one for him here."

"I love how you're spending my money."

"Starts at noon," Chief said. "Meet you there."

"Riding Guide" apparently meant, "I get to tell you what to do with your day—not to mention your bank account." But I was only slightly irritated when I hung up. This had to be better than trying to fill the emptiness with a cup of cold cocoa.

Fortunately Desmond didn't drag himself out of his den until noon, and he didn't break his vow of silence over Rice Krispies or my directive that he put on jeans and his one long-sleeved shirt. He only spoke when I opened the garage and handed him my helmet.

"We're going for a ride," I said.

As I recited the rules for being a passenger on a motorcycle that I'd just memorized from MOM, it was hard to tell whether he was listening. A shimmer of sheer reverence lit his face.

"You sayin' we *both* goin' for a ride. Me and you?"

"That's what I'm sayin'. And just so you know—I'm driving."

"Sweet," he whispered. It could have passed for a prayer.

I was a little shaky as we pulled onto Palm Row, enough to forget to keep the bike in low gear until I was ready to turn on St. George. The only rider I'd carried was Geneveve, and the one I was hauling now was likely to try to grab light poles or stand up on the pegs, despite my litany of rules. Chief wouldn't have suggested it if he didn't think it was safe. But he hadn't watched Desmond turn into Clyde Barrow over the past two days.

"Remember," I called over my shoulder, "no messing around."

But the Desmond I'd been ready to bind and gag an hour before became a different child within the first quarter mile. I could feel the excitement racing through the hands that gripped the sides of my jacket and the amazement in the wiry body that leaned with every curve like he was born to it. I could have forgotten there was even anyone sitting behind me if I hadn't heard the laughter winding out of his helmet. The kid was giggling. I was sure I'd never giggled in my life, but I felt delight bubbling up into my throat now, and I laughed with him. It didn't occur to me until I was parked, tailpipe first, in a parking slot at the dealership that it was the best riding I'd done so far.

As promised, Chief met us inside at the helmet display. By then Desmond had recovered from temporary normal boyhood and took to inspecting the key chains that dangled from their hooks practically shouting, "Steal me! Steal me!" I told him to put his hands in his pockets and leave them there.

"This is what they have in your size," Chief said to him.

"What do they have in my price?" I asked.

Desmond went immediately for a shiny black one engulfed in orange flames. "Now *that* is what I am *talkin' about*."

"Try it on," Chief said.

He took care of adjusting the strap while I snuck a peek at the price tag. Another week of macaroni and cheese. But if it meant the kid could have a few minutes to forget he was supposed to act like a gangsta....

"Check it out, Big Al," Desmond said, voice muffled by the gray-tinted visor.

I stifled a guffaw, because the thing made him look a cross between Darth Vader and a cartoon cockroach. It obviously made him *feel* like Somebody, though, because he stood still and tall and, thank the good Lord, quiet.

"You make it look good," I said, although I registered a mental note to have his hair cut. It was puffing out the bottom like tufts of sofa stuffing. "All right, let's take it to checkout."

Desmond wore it across the store and leaned over so the clerk could run the scanner over the tag still hanging from the strap. She, too, hid the laughter that danced in her eyes.

"You gonna sleep in it?" she said.

"You'll need these, too," Chief said. He dumped an armload of items on the counter beside me. "Reflective clothing for both of you. It pays to get noticed."

My cheeks burned. "Have you *seen* my bank balance?" I hissed to him.

"I'm buying."

"I can't let you do that."

He gave me a fatherly look. Not *my* father's fatherly. More like Bill Cosby's fatherly. It was beyond my experience, which was why I just nodded.

"Free food out front," Chief said when he'd put away his wallet.

"Let me treat y'all to that." Desmond grinned through his visor.

I lifted the visor to the top of his helmet. "Your generosity is overwhelming. Keep this thing up so I can see your eyes."

"Why you got to see my eyes?"

"So I can tell what you're going to do next," I said.

"Next" involved piling a paper plate full of runny baked beans and hot dogs on Styrofoam buns as if it were Hank's gourmet fare. The way the kid ate, I'd expect him to have gained ten pounds since I started feeding him, but if anything he looked scrawnier than ever. Might have been the helmet.

"Where's Hank?" I said to Chief as we settled into one of the long tables set up on the parking lot.

He paused, I thought, to make sure he wasn't imagining the conglomeration of condiments Desmond had piled on his dogs. I tried not to look, myself. It was nauseating.

"Why do you ask?" Chief said.

"Just curious. Desmond, aren't you even going to take your helmet off to eat?"

"Nah. The boy's a real biker. Eats with his gear on."

I looked down the table to see Ulysses grinning at me. Leighanne, whom I'd met before, sat next to him. I recognized her by the spillage from her tank top.

"Sign him up," she said.

"That all I got to do?" Desmond said, spewing pickle relish from his helmet. "Just sign somethin'?"

"*You* tell him," I said to Rex, who sat on the other side of Leighanne. "Sounds like a presidential duty to me." I turned back to Chief.

"Hank's still at church," he said. "Interferes too much with her biking life if you ask me."

"I don't have to ask," I said. "You've made your opinion about organized religion pretty clear."

"Have I?"

"Yeah, and right now it's about the same as mine."

"Which is?"

"I'm fed up with the whole hypocritical, judgmental, afterlife -obsessed thing."

"Preach it sister," Ulysses said.

"Uh, what's-your-face—"

Leighanne was snapping her fingers at me. The Hispanic woman on the other side of her rose from her chair and looked like she was about to go over the table.

"Isn't that your bike that kid is—"

Even as I whipped around I heard my Harley start up. So, apparently, did everyone else, because heads turned—and mouths formed horrified O's.

Desmond sat astride the Classic, and I watched, paralyzed, as his left foot pawed at the gears. Even while I tried to shout "No!" the way you do in a delirious dream, the bike shifted into second and lurched—off the kickstand and over onto its side like a wounded horse. Its landing shook the parking lot at five on the Richter scale.

I shoved four HOGs aside, my heart slamming its way up my throat, my arms stretched out as if I could stop Desmond from going with it. I got to him at the same time Chief did, and it was myself I heard this time, screaming the kid's name as Ulysses and Rex pulled eight hundred pounds off of his leg.

His eyes bulged so far from their sockets that I thought they'd been pushed from his head by the impact. But the moment the bike was upright, he was up and twisting toward escape. Chief stopped him with one hand on the back of his shirt.

"Girl," Ulysses said to me, "you can't even keep your bike vertical when you aren't on it, can you?"

"I'd shut up if I were you," Leighanne said. I heard her add to the Hispanic woman, "She's going to kill that kid."

I might have, at least verbally, if Chief hadn't lifted him up by the scruff of the collar like a puppy so he could talk right into his half-frightened, half-thrilled face.

"You think you're all about risks, don't you, son?" He didn't wait for the answer Desmond was obviously too stunned to give. "You're gonna learn real fast that there's no risk that doesn't come with responsibility. You can't be a biker unless you learn responsibility first. We clear?"

I was sure Desmond didn't understand a word of that, that it was Chief's gut-grabbing intensity that made him nod his head.

"I don't believe I heard you."

"Yeah."

"That'll work for now."

Chief set the kid on the ground and turned his head halfway to me. "You better get him out of here, Classic."

Rex's presidential duties apparently included damage assessment. "Your kickstand is bent," he said. "He didn't hit any of the other motorcycles, so that is good."

"You have no idea how good," Ulysses muttered.

The group around us drifted back to their tables and hot dogs, and I grabbed my helmet from the handlebar.

"Let's go," I said to Desmond.

"You still gonna let me ride with you?"

"How else am I going to get you home?" I straddled the seat and started the engine. "Get on. And I'm adding a new rule: Don't talk to me until we get there."

He followed that order to the letter.

CHAPTER TWELVE

The day just kept getting better and better. Bonner was parked in my driveway when we pulled in. I could feel Desmond's back straighten when he saw the Jaguar.

"Forget about asking for a ride in it," I said as the Harley's engine grumbled to a sullen silence. "You and I have some business to take care of. Get off, please."

Desmond swung his long, lanky leg over the back of the bike and tried the grin on me. The ride had evidently wiped away the image of Chief dangling him in the air like a rag doll. Either that or he thought I couldn't hold a candle to the big guy.

Maybe I couldn't, but from now on I was going to try. It was no longer a matter of me threatening to do this kid bodily harm. It was about him doing it to himself, and now I knew that he was perfectly capable of making that happen—and that he didn't care if it did.

With Bonner looking on openly from the Jag, I said to Desmond, "Give me the helmet."

The grin vanished. "It's mine. The Chief bought me it."

"You can take that up with him next time you see him. Right now Big Al is taking it away from you. Give it."

I held out my hand until I thought my arm was going to break. He tried to outstare, outglare, and outwait me, but I didn't move until he finally undid the strap and pulled the helmet from his head. His hair was matted down like a wet doormat, which made the scene all the more wretched for him, I was sure. I could have predicted, though, that he would suddenly laugh and do some kind of Michael Jordan wannabe move with the thing before depositing it into my hand.

"When I'm gonna get it back?" he asked.

"When you do what the Chief said and show me some responsibility."

"What I gotta do?"

I shrugged. "I'll know it when I see it. And just so you know, Florida law says no one under eighteen can ride without a helmet, so your biking days are over until I see that you're ready to take the risk in a responsible way."

He couldn't cover his disappointment, not even with an "it's all good." When he opened his mouth, I said, "Every cuss word puts you further behind, Dude, so don't even start with me."

Lips pressed together, he tried to swagger to the house. Halfway there he broke into a run and disappeared through the front door. I sagged onto the seat of my Harley and listened to Bonner's car door open and close.

"Gee, that went well," he said.

"I'm not in the mood, Bonner."

"I can see that. Why don't you let me buy you lunch?"

I shrugged my jacket off and shook my head. "I can't leave him here. His mother's not ready to handle him yet."

"And you are?"

I scalded him with a look.

"Sorry." Bonner's voice softened. "Why don't I come in and make you some lunch while you put your feet up. You look like you've been caught in a stampede."

"Boy, you're just full of encouragement today, aren't you?"

He looked stung, and I closed my eyes to it. The truth was, I didn't want him to come in the house. I couldn't imagine him sitting at my bistro table and not shattering Geneveve with a disapproving look he didn't even know he was giving.

"I don't get you, Allison. You say you want support, so I come over here to give you some and you slap it down. What is it that you're asking for?"

"You could start by accepting that this is a God-thing, and that I'm going to do it."

"Do what exactly?"

"Get this woman healed somehow so she can take care of her son."

It was his turn to close his eyes, in relief, it seemed.

"Okay, that sounds doable. I think you need to talk to Liz Doyle, then."

"Who's—oh, that woman you dated?"

"You said you knew her from high school."

"Vaguely. I don't get why—"

"I told you she works for the county Family Integrity Program—she's a social worker." He put up a hand. "I know you're determined to do this all yourself—"

"No, I'm not! I need all the help I can get."

"Then talk to her. She knows about services you can get for the kid, free counselors, all that stuff."

I slowly folded my arms. "You two sure had an in-depth conversation about her job description on your two dates."

"Okay—so I called her and told her what you had going, and she said you should come in tomorrow."

"Before you even mentioned it to me."

"Does it matter?" Bonner's voice went high. "Have you even

thought about what could happen if that kid gets hurt riding around with you on this thing?"

I patted the seat on either side of me. "'This thing' is the only leverage I have with him."

"Which means you're in way over your head. Go talk to Liz, okay?"

"If I need to," I said. It was the only way I could think of to get him to go away.

He pulled a card out of his shirt pocket. "Here's the reminder. Ten o'clock."

I took it and tried my hardest to smile. "I appreciate your trying to help, I really do."

But as he drove off, I wondered why his kind of help made me feel less competent than I did before he offered.

Lonnie called me at eight a.m. Monday to tell me I had a special group tour at ten. "The kind you're good at," he said.

"What kind is that?" I said.

"The uppity kind. Five syllables in every word. That crowd." I imagined him switching the toothpick from one side of his mouth to the other. "Probably tip good, which you need since you took so much time off last week."

"Uh-huh," I said. I tucked the phone in my neck so I could get the half-and-half out of the refrigerator. The carton was empty. That kid was never getting that helmet back at this rate.

"We'll have a lot more tours now that the school groups are back on St. George Street in droves," Lonnie was saying. "The rich tourists don't want to deal with them hangin' out of the trolleys. You spend more time on the Bay Front, you'll get you some nice fares."

"Point taken."

"Huh?"

"That means I get it already. I'll be there till three."

"Why three?"

"Because that's when I have to pick up my—I just need to leave then."

Lonnie snickered through the toothpick. "Don't tell me you found a guy that's willing to put up with you."

"Something like that," I said.

As I hung up, I considered the fact that, despite my unwillingness to invest in a me-and-a-male relationship ever again, it might be easier than the "guy" I was investing in right now.

I wrote out a plan for the day for Geneveve and went over it with her while I packed a lunch for Desmond, who still wasn't speaking to me. When I got him out the door and into the van we were already late, but I had no choice but to stop for the police cruiser who blocked my driveway when I was backing out.

"What now?" I said into the rearview mirror.

Desmond looked back and his eyes widened. I looked at him straight on.

"Before he gets here, I need to know if you did anything I should know about. Just so I don't look like an idiot in front of this guy."

"I didn't do nothin'—I swear."

"Lie to me and you'll never ride a Harley again."

I looked at him long and hard, but he didn't give. By then the freckled officer—what was his name? Kent?—was at my window. I was still giving Desmond one last chance as I lowered it.

"Morning, Miz Chamberlain," he said. "Sorry to hold you up."

I could feel Desmond opening his mouth and I stuck my hand over it. "What's up?" I said.

"I have to issue you a warning."

"For what?"

"For violating the city noise ordinance. According to your neighbors you haven't been cooperative in muffling your motorcycle." He cleared his throat, and I realized he was trying not to laugh. "If you don't mind my asking, what kind of bike do you have that would make the kind of noise they're—"

"It's a Harley Heritage Softail Classic," I said.

"Oh."

I removed my hand from Desmond's mouth and gave him a warning look. He turned on the innocence. To Officer Kent, I said, "I promised I'd keep it in low until I got out onto St. George, but I got in a hurry yesterday and I forgot. It won't happen again."

"I still have to issue a warning. If you'll just sign here to indicate that you've received it."

I sighed and took the pen from him. "Does this go on my record or anything?"

He shook his head and watched me write my name. "It just means if they complain again, they can press charges."

"I won't give them a reason to," I said. "Is that it?"

"Yes, ma'am," he said.

But he didn't move. I lifted my shoulders.

"I'm sorry," he said. "I just have to ask—do you really drive a Harley?"

"Yes," I said between my teeth. "I'd take you for a spin, but I really have to get going."

"Right. Sorry. You have a nice day."

I barely had the window up before Desmond let out a hoot. "You are smooth, Big Al. You show him who the real Mack Daddy is now."

"I did not," I said. "I was polite, I took care of business, and then I— told him to get lost."

"That's what I'm sayin'. I'ma have to try that next time I get busted."

"I thought you said you'd never been busted."

"I ain't. I'm just sayin' if I do."

"If you do, I'm selling your helmet."

"You ain't never gonna have to do that." He twisted in the seat so he could look at me, so earnestly I almost laughed out loud. "I'ma get me some responsibility—you're gonna see that. You ain't never seen the kind I'ma get."

"Glad to hear it," I said.

"First thing I'ma do is apologize."

"To who?"

"You. For all actin' the fool, takin' your bike. You shoulda throwed me out right then."

"Desmond," I said.

"Yes, ma'am?"

"Give it up. I'm not feelin' it."

"Man," he said. "That's cold."

The October day was already sticky hot by the time I got Bernard hitched up and down to the Bay Front. He was so lethargic I calculated that today's fifty-minute tour was going to take an hour and a half.

When the "uppity" party pulled up in a white limo, Caroline turned in the driver's seat of her vis-à-vis and shook her head at me. "You catch all the breaks," she said.

"Oh yeah," I said. "That's me."

Five people dressed in business suits climbed into the carriage. One of the women clearly had stock in Mary Kay and told me how charming this all was. The other one seemed to think stress was a trend she had set, and proceeded to fit her earpiece beneath her sleek brunette bob and into her ear. The three men gave me grudging smiles. I couldn't imagine whose idea this had been.

"Welcome," I said, my own smile just as grudging. "What brings y'all to St. Augustine?"

"Business," the tallest man said.

"Most of us are investors," Mary Kay Lady said. "We're told some exciting new developments are happening in the city."

"Well, we won't be talking about new developments today." I picked up the lines, and Bernard rolled the carriage forward. "We'll be all about the old."

The shortest man stopped mopping his magenta face with a Kleenex. "I'd like to be all about a Long Island iced tea."

"Can't help you there." This was going to be an endless gig. I urged Bernard to step up, but he, too, was grudging.

They listened politely to my spiel about the City Gates and the Spanish Quarter and the Huguenot Cemetery filled with victims of the 1821 yellow fever epidemic. That took all of fifteen minutes. By the time we reached Spanish Street, they were chatting among themselves. I could have launched into the Sermon on the Mount and they wouldn't have known the difference.

"The beautiful yellow building material that you see is coquina," I said, "which is our native shell stone."

"He says the properties will all go for under a hundred thousand," Kleenex Man said. "Which means they're piles of junk."

"Blah, blah, blah," I said.

"I'm still not clear why Chamberlain is interested in that," said the Mary Kay consultant.

Chamberlain. Of course. I should have known.

I glanced back to see the second woman cease texting and pull out her earpiece to sweep them all with a hurried gaze. "Because Troy sees the potential," she said. "That's where his genius lies."

I picked up the lines and Bernard took the left onto Cordova at a virtual trot. Both women made conservative squealing noises. I was sure one of the men swore.

"Sorry," I said over my shoulder. "Bernard hears the name 'Chamberlain' and he gets a little crazy. Now we're coming up on the famous Love Tree—"

The tall man looked through me and turned back to Stress Woman. "I still want to see some strong projections—"

"You will. I've seen some of what he's going to show us this afternoon."

"You're pretty cozy with Irwin. Troy this and Troy that—"

"—and the Catholic Tolomato Cemetery," I said, "where the first bishop of St. Augustine was laid to rest and where I personally would like to see Troy Irwin buried, and the sooner the better. He isn't Catholic, but I'm sure he could pay somebody off."

"Did she just say—"

"The lovely Grace Church here on your left was funded in part by the infamous Henry Flagler, of whom you are undoubtedly aware if you've spent more than seven seconds with the equally infamous Mr. Irwin."

"What in the *world?*"

"And here we are at Scarlett O'Hara's, where good food and drunkenness are served nightly to a packed crowd of tourists and students from Flagler College and other real people, which means you won't be dining there as long as Chamberlain Enterprises is footing the bill."

There was complete silence in the carriage.

"We're now turning onto King Street, the original site of the golden age of Flagler St. Augustine. They say, by the way, that the town was discovered twice—first by Menendez and then by Henry Flagler. Normally I would stop here and regale you with tales of the robber baron who founded Standard Oil and then came here to save St. Augustine from oblivion. But instead …"

By then we'd crossed Ponce de Leon Boulevard, where I could just hear the gasps above the traffic noise as I slowed Bernard in front of Titus Tattoo. West King and Davis Street to our left both yawned at us as he made a mincing stop. I turned all the way around in the seat.

"So you folks are being wooed by Chamberlain Enterprises," I said.

The tall man was glowering. "You want to tell us what's going on?"

"What's next on the agenda? Lunch at the Café Alcazar? A cruise on the Intercoastal in the company yacht? Cracked stone crab claws?"

Mary Kay blinked at me. "They're not in season, are they?"

"No crustacean stands a chance with Troy Irwin. He'll convince them it's in their best interest to make an exception. Now"—I picked up the lines and Bernard edged nervously forward—"around 1738, African slaves fled from the Carolinas and found refuge in St. Augustine. We're now entering the section where their descendants still reside. On your right you'll see the city's oldest crack house, and just beyond that a Dumpster that is popular with the homeless. Fortunately one of the state's oldest police stations is just one block back—that lovely white building with the columns upholding justice. Although that doesn't seem to make a whole lot of difference, due to law enforcement's focus on the areas that Troy Irwin, CEO, wants them to focus on. Money talks almost as loud as history in St. Augustine. Anyone interested in seeing some of the back streets? Things you won't see on the regular tour?"

"All right, we've heard enough." Stress Lady waved her phone at the others. "I've called for the limo to meet us."

Mary Kay clutched at her necklace. "Not in this neighborhood!"

"I'm happy to take you back to the First American Bank building, where you'll undoubtedly be more at home," I said.

The limo met us at King and Sevilla, and the party couldn't break up fast enough. As they disembarked and retreated into the insulated safety of the long white car, no one had a word of complaint for me. In fact I didn't get so much as a glance. The whole experience was probably forgotten before they purred away from the curb.

"What does that tell you, Bernard?" My voice, so cocky and caustic five minutes before, splintered around the edges, and I wanted to get someplace where I could wash my mouth out, preferably with lye soap. I hadn't spoken the name Troy Irwin in at least seven years, but saying it still tasted like a curse. And as always, it made me wonder if every woman had the same reaction to the rediscovered flavor of her first love.

My cell phone rang. "That was fast," I said to Bernard. "We're busted, Buddy."

But it wasn't Lonnie with my termination. "Muldoon Middle School" appeared on the screen.

I was on my way to the stables as I answered it.

CHAPTER THIRTEEN

The woman from the school didn't tell me much more than that Desmond had been in a fight. While I was conjuring up broken noses and ruptured spleens, she went on to her bigger concern.

"You're on the sheet as an emergency contact," she said as I trotted Bernard and carriage up to the stable gate and threw the lines to the kid who was mucking manure. "But we do like to have a parent in these situations, and I couldn't reach his mother at the number I have. The legalities—"

"I'll be there in five minutes," I said, and fishtailed out with Lonnie in my rearview mirror, chewing on his toothpick.

It took me ten. I got behind a pickup truck doing twenty in a thirty-five, and all I could do was stew in its exhaust fumes and picture Desmond handcuffed to a police cruiser. Who knew what he'd said to a cop by now? Probably enough to land him in juvie with his jaw wired shut. I arrived at the school without a plan, which would have done me no good anyway because I found not a sheriff's car but an ambulance parked in front.

"DearGoddearGoddearGod," was all I could say as I left the van door hanging open and tore toward the flashing lights. I plowed through a line of gawking kids and brushed aside a woman with a clipboard until I got to the back of the ambulance. Desmond sat on its floor, wrapped in a blanket in the smothering heat, huge feet hanging almost to the ground like a marionette's. A female paramedic was in the process of wrapping gauze around his head and was barely staying ahead of the blood that wept through. His upper lip was as swollen as a banana slug.

"Desmond!" I said.

The paramedic shook her head at me. "Ma'am, if you'll just hold on for about two more minutes, you can have at him."

I took a step back and onto the toe of a female eighth-grader disguised as a twenty-year-old.

"Just so you know," she said to me, slick lips speaking emphatically, "three boys attacked him. He didn't do *nothin'*."

I didn't find that hard to believe. I'd had the boy down on the kitchen floor myself.

"He was just messin' with their heads like he always does," another girl said, bringing out her scarlet talons to enhance the story. "And they just, like, went ballistic on him." Her eyes were aghast as she added, "He didn't even have a chance to fight back."

I looked at Desmond, ready for the comeback, the retort that would inform them it was all good. I saw only pure humiliation curve his back as he stared at his knees, and I knew it was more painful than the gash on his forehead.

"Okay, he's all yours," the paramedic said to me. "He didn't suffer a concussion and it doesn't look like he needs stitches, so I don't think we need to take him to the emergency room. You can if you want to make sure—"

"I don't want to go to no hospital," Desmond said. His voice was muffled by the swelling and the shame.

"I'll take it from here," I said.

"So they didn't crack his head open?" one of the girls complained.

The woman with the clipboard waved it at the group. "All right, people, it's over. Let's get to class."

A palpable wave of disappointment rolled over the crowd as they dispersed.

"We've got your back, Desmond," a female voice called out.

Three different adults were suddenly at me with release forms and reassurances that the full power of the administration would be brought to bear on the three perpetrators. The question, "Where is his mother?" was asked repeatedly.

"She's unavailable at the moment," I kept saying. I signed until there were no more forms, wondering with each signature how legal it was, and finally nodded Desmond toward the van.

"What do you say we go home and sort this out?"

He muttered, "Ain't nothin' to sort," but he followed me, bandage wrapped around his bush of hair so that he looked more like a child refugee than ever.

When we were in the van, I checked to make sure there were no Gossip Girls lingering on the school steps before I dug out a Hershey Kiss I'd been saving in my pocket and held it out to him. He shook his head, which was enough for me to head for the ER right there.

"Look," I said, "forget the part where they had you down before you even knew what hit you. You're not a fighter, and there's no sense in even going there."

He fixed his eyes on the windshield.

"You have a different skill set," I said, "which brings me to the real point. What did you say to those kids before they started swinging? I know you said something to set them off."

Desmond continued to stare for a moment before the puffy lip tried to curve. "This one kid—he got eyes go out all weird."

"Yeah."

"I told him he look like a frog on crack."

"That would do it," I said. "What did he say to you first?"

"Whatchoo mean?"

"You don't waste your best stuff on nothing. He said something to provoke you. What was it?"

Desmond's eyes shifted. "He said I wasn't nothin' but a son of a ho."

The word *jackal* was off my tongue almost before I thought it.

"Okay, look," I said, "I know about not being able to control your own mouth. I have that problem myself. But it has to be done or you're going to end up with worse than a busted lip and a scar on your face."

"You think I'ma have a scar?" he said, eyes brightening as he felt the bandage.

"If you do, I gotta tell you, that isn't going to make you tough. Just so you know."

I knew it was the wrong thing to say the moment it left my lips. Desmond curved back into himself, and we drove home in uncomfortable silence. I'd failed at more jobs in my life than most people even get hired for, but I'd never been as bad at anything as I was at this.

When we pulled into the garage, Desmond stared dismally at the Harley, and I did too until I felt something Nudge lightly at my spirit.

"Y'know," I said, "you did the responsible thing by not fighting back."

"I didn't fight back 'cause I knew I couldn't win!"

The eyes that turned on me were so full of adolescent agony, I winced.

"Then you're even smarter than I thought," I said. "Come on."

We climbed out of the van, and I opened the footlocker where I kept the motorcycle gear. I lifted the black helmet with the orange flames and handed it to him.

"You took the responsibility instead of the risk," I said. "You've earned this back."

Desmond stared from me to the helmet in what could only be described as pure shock. I was a little shocked myself. Had I actually just done the right thing with this kid? I must have, because he placed the helmet on his head with the awed dignity of a crown prince who'd never expected to take the throne.

Huh. Ten minutes before, I was sure I was going to have to notch another false start into my personal fuselage. Now I felt like the female version of Cliff Huxtable. I yanked Desmond's visor over his face and grinned at him.

He grinned back like a twelve-year-old boy.

Yeah, this child needed a mother. It was time to go to his and get her involved in his life. With Desmond still wearing his beloved helmet, we went into the house through the side door, but the minute we stepped into the kitchen, my breath caught. The air was different, as if something had been sucked out of it and left the rooms naked and vulnerable.

Or maybe something had merely been sucked out of my brain. I headed for the pantry. "You want some lunch, Desmond? I think we could both use some carbs after that little altercation—"

"Big Al, I swear to you I did not do it."

I stuck my head out of the pantry. Desmond stood in the den doorway, face pinched.

"What didn't you do?"

"I didn't rip off your DVD player. Or your laptop. But they gone."

I was already headed for the den and poking my finger at him. "Don't play with me, Desmond."

"I ain't playin'. They not there."

He was still defending his innocence when I stopped in the middle of the room and stared below the TV. The empty place in the cabinet where the DVD player should have been gaped back at me.

"Maybe your mom moved it upstairs so she could watch a movie," I said.

"She don't know nothin' 'bout hooking up no DVD—and she *sure* don't know nothin' 'bout no computer."

"I locked that in the desk," I said.

But before I even looked, I knew the keyhole had been jimmied.

"Now I *did* do that," Desmond said, "before I got responsibility. But I just wanted to use it—I didn't steal it out your house like she done."

"Who? Your mother?"

"Who else gonna do it?"

"Okay." I pressed my fingers to my temples and made tracks for the stairs. "There has to be an explanation for this."

"I give you ten to one odds she ain't here," Desmond said as he followed.

"I don't gamble." Although I had the sinking feeling I'd already bet the farm on a weak horse.

I did a thorough search with Desmond dogging me, telling me I was wasting my time. He turned out to be right, because Geneveve wasn't in her room, the bathroom, or the back of the closet, which I checked in desperation. Her few extra clothes still hung there, but they weren't talking. Other than that. she'd left only a sense of violation. I sat at the bottom of the stairs and rubbed the tops of my thighs with Desmond sprawled beside me, watching.

"You gonna call the cops, Big Al?" he said.

"Not yet." I glanced at my watch. "Chief's probably working. Hank. I'll call Hank."

"That little squatty Harley woman that makes the weird food?"

"I'm not calling her to order lunch," I said. I was calling her because I needed somebody sane who might know what God was doing. I sure didn't.

She arrived within the half hour, with Chief. Although they were both on their bikes, it was obvious they'd somehow discussed the situation, because they came in with the plan I hadn't been able to think of.

"I think the best thing is for us to go look for her," Chief said to me.

"I'll ride with you, Big Al," Desmond said. "We good together."

"You and I are staying here," Hank said. "I'll make lunch." Before Desmond could get too far into an incredulous look at me, Hank produced a thick book with a custom V-rod on the front cover. "We can look at this while we eat. It never hurts to dream."

He gave me one last look over his shoulder as he followed her into the kitchen. "Get that DVD player. I was planning to watch *Hellboy* tonight."

Chief was a stride ahead of me as we crossed the lane to the garage.

"We'll take the bikes," he said. "That way we can split up and cover more ground faster."

"Okay."

"If you find her in trouble, call me before you do anything—I've got my phone in my shirt pocket on vibrate. You do the same with yours."

"All right."

He watched me turn the Classic to face the driveway. "Don't try to handle this alone. I know it's broad daylight, but that won't matter if somebody's up against the wall. Okay?"

"Okay," I said again.

I reached for the ignition but he caught my hand. The intensity that always gave weight to his gaze was there in his palm as well.

"Think of the whole thing like riding your bike," he said. "Measure the risk and consider the consequences."

I nodded and fired up the engine. I could still feel his hand pressing it in.

Everything was surreal as I followed the Road King out onto St. George Street. The only thing I was sure of was my hand on the throttle. And the Nudge on the seat behind me that said, *For once in your life do what somebody tells you.*

When the sun faded beyond West King and left us in dismal darkness, we still hadn't found Geneveve. Although the denizens were beginning to emerge from wherever it was they hid themselves in the daylight hours, nobody was talking, not even the two prostitutes who'd helped me locate her before. Even when I offered them money in front of Titus Tattoo, they gazed longingly at it for only a moment before they shook their heads again. Both of them were visibly working to keep fear in check.

"I'm not trying to make trouble for her, ladies," I said. "I just want to help her. I've *been* helping her."

"That ain't the kinda help she needs," the smaller one mumbled through her fingers.

The taller woman jabbed her hard on the shoulder and shoved her back as she stepped toward me. Her eyes glittered through the film of drugs.

"You wanna help Geneveve right now? Then just leave her alone, or it's gon' go down bad for her. Real bad."

"See, I don't know what that means," I said.

"And you don't *wanna* know."

I held up the money again, all the cash I had on me, but the woman pulled her companion into the alley beside the tattoo shop and they dissolved into the shadows. A new layer of evil had descended on the neighborhood—a layer so heavy it even smothered the one thing that usually trumped all else. Something or somebody had more power than the next score.

The parking lot in front of C.A.R.S. was empty, so I pulled over to it and stopped in the fuzzy gleam of a Pennzoil light with half the letters broken out. I checked my cell phone, but I hadn't missed a call from Chief, which meant he wasn't having anymore luck than I was. Either that or he'd been offed. As much as I doubted that, I held my breath after I dialed him. When he answered with "Talk to me," I forgot to exhale. The little bit I'd gleaned from the ladies of the night came out like somebody was strangling me.

"That's more than I've gotten out of anybody," he said. "Something's definitely gone down. I can't even get anyone to try to talk me out of my Harley."

"What do we do?"

"Let's go back to the house and regroup. Hank could probably use some relief by now."

"You want me to meet you there?"

"No. Let's hook up on Davis and we'll make one more loop and then ride back together."

If I hadn't turned into a large gelatinous mass, I would have pointed out that "hook up" was a poor choice of words at the moment, but I just agreed and restarted the engine, startling myself as if I'd never heard the thing before. I was truly a complete mess.

And became more so when I felt something sharp dig into my back. My hand involuntarily rolled the throttle, and the motor's responding roar covered my scream. I fumbled to get it in gear and forgot to engage the clutch. The engine cut out in a stall so hard I lurched against the handlebars. When I felt the sharp poke again, the insane thought that this was definitely not God shot through my head.

"Okay—the money's in my left jacket pocket," I said. I'd intended for it to come out calm and soothing, but I sounded like the nearly hysterical woman I was. My voice hit the side of the building with an almost audible splat, and, crazily, I followed it with my eyes and caught the image of myself in the smeary window. Myself and the diminished little prostitute jabbing her finger into my ribs.

I only caved enough into relief to say, "Take the money." I probably could've taken *her*—she was smaller even than Geneveve or Desmond, who I *had* taken. But she had a different look in her eyes, a fever that might overpower my height and weight and muscle tone if it meant she could get the thing her body was screaming for. What was left of it.

She put her hand in my right pocket and clawed at its lining. A frantic whimper followed as she grabbed at nothing. It was as violating as a rape.

"Other side," I said. "You can have it all—I swear—just relax—"

It sounded so idiotic I shut up. Inside my jacket the phone vibrated against my chest but I didn't go for it. Ten seconds and this would be over and I could go screaming to Chief in person.

She found the pocket and the money, which she yanked out and stared at as if suddenly she didn't know what it was and why she was holding it.

"If you'll just step back, I'll get this thing out of your way and you can go—do—whatever."

Some small, good thing in me really wanted to snatch the cash back from her and drag her back to my house and—

Do what? I'd been so incredibly successful with Genevieve, why not think I could change this woman's life too?

She remained there, staring at the money, and shaking her head.

"Just take one step back," I said. I even started the engine, slow and soft. It brought her eyes to my face, but she was still. Only her expression moved, into something like sheer disgust. She swallowed and cringed and squeezed her eyes shut, and I somehow knew it was herself she was repulsed by. Or something beyond her that was making her do this.

"I'll show you where she is," she said.

I shut off the engine. "Who? Genevieve? Is that who you mean?"

She nodded, eyes still closed. "But we got to hurry."

"Can we get there on this?"

She was on the seat before I could even reach for my cell phone. With Chief's warning in my ear—call me before you do anything—I once more restarted the Harley, pulled her shrunken arms around me and said, "Where are we going?"

"Back there."

She jerked her head toward a potholed driveway that rambled off into darkness next to C.A.R.S. Praying wordlessly, I followed her frantic directions, down a veritable gulley that backed the row of empty stores, then sharply to the left into an alley that ran like a gutter between darkened buildings that, even through my visor, reeked of humanity at its lowest.

"Next driveway!" she said, voice cracking against my helmet.

I started to lean into the turn, but a massive body leaped from a doorway and made a lunge for the bike. My passenger yelped like a whipped dog, but I couldn't scream. She was squeezing off my breath as she jammed her bones into my torso.

An arm bounced off the windshield and was gone, and I felt more than saw the hulking mass skid on its back and into the wall. After that I was too panicked to look in my mirror. I gunned it to the end of the alley and managed to make the turn without slamming us to the ground. I started to slow down, but the woman pounded my shoulder with her fist.

"Don't stop! You can't stop!"

"I have to see if he's okay. I can't just leave—"

"He okay. He done run off! I seen him!"

I wanted to believe her and keep going, but what little sanity that remained forced me to make a U-turn in the middle of West King and return to the alley. My phone was vibrating like a pacemaker but I left it alone as I slowed as much as I dared and searched through the dankness.

"I tol' you. He done run off. That's what he always do—he just run off."

I lowered my feet and jerked my head toward her. "You knew who it was?"

"He the same one—you got to get to Geneveve *now*."

"Okay, okay." I dragged in a long breath and settled my hands on the controls. "Which way?"

She pointed to what at first appeared to be a recess in the wall. When I peered in, I saw that it was a long, impossibly narrow hallway that cut through the building and led to the next street. Halfway in, a metal garbage can lay on its side, its contents spewed into a reeking heap.

"There she is."

"Where?"

"Right there. On the ground. I got to go."

The woman virtually fell off the back of my bike and skittered away like a stray cat. I wanted to go after her, take her out of the picture that formed in my mind, of her turning the corner and being filleted by a man who thought he could wrestle a Harley. As perhaps Geneveve already had been.

I somehow got the bike propped on its stand and crept into the tight alley, eyes on the garbage can until they adjusted to the broken-necked beer bottles and the misshapen forms of produce so rotted they were no longer recognizable. That little wench I'd felt so sorry for had literally taken me for a ride, and almost gotten us both killed en route.

I glanced over my shoulder. If she'd been telling the truth—if Mr. Man had survived—he was probably ticked off enough to come back looking for me. It would definitely be best if all he found was a stenched-out load of last week's leftovers. Nearly gagging, I tried to turn around, but my foot slid on a trail of slime that had escaped along the ground. Both arms groped for balance and found only the walls, which were slick in the dampness and delivered me face forward into the foul heap.

Another face fell against mine.

Even as my scream reverberated down the alley, even as I shoved a blackened banana skin from its cheek, I knew the face was Geneveve's. Bile rose in my throat as I scraped through the oozing detritus and uncovered her lips, purple and swollen together, blood trailing into them from her nose. A gash forked across her forehead like a lightning bolt. It was a hideous kind of *déjà vu*.

I took her head in my hands, "Geneveve! Geneveve—can you hear me?"

When she groaned between my palms, I yanked her into my arms, where she went limp.

"Oh, dear God, don't let her die—okay, okay—Chief."

Somehow I retrieved my phone and poked at his name on the screen with one palsied hand while I held Geneveve with the other and rocked us both. Now I knew why she did that when she was panicked. It was the only way to make sure you were still alive.

It took several rings for Chief to answer. When he did, he didn't bother with hello. "Where are you?" was his greeting.

I could only whisper nonsensically, "I'm in some alley off of some other alley off of King—"

"I'll find you," he said.

I shoved the phone somewhere onto my person and cradled Geneveve with both arms. "Can you hear me?" I said. "Geneveve?"

Her eyes opened and rolled back, leaving only a white stare that shivered through me. I put my face close to her distended mouth and felt her breath wheeze against my cheek.

"Okay—thankyouGodthankyouGodthankyouGod." I kicked at the garbage and made a space. Still holding her in the crook of my arm, I struggled out of my jacket and spread it on the ground with my elbow.

"I'm going to stretch you out so you can breathe—just keep doing it—don't stop breathing—"

"She alive?"

I practically convulsed. I had myself thrown across her, yelling for the jackal to stay away from her, before I realized it was Chief's big hands that took hold of my shoulders and held on until I stopped freaking out.

"Easy, Classic," he said. "It's just me."

I put my hand over my mouth to keep from retching. "I didn't even hear you ride up."

"Didn't. I walked it." He crouched next to us, seemingly unaware that he was squatting in filth. "She's breathing. Pulse?"

"I didn't check, but she was conscious for a second." I was feeling a little more conscious myself, now that I was next to somebody sane.

He lifted one of her eyelids. "She still is. Yo, Geneveve." He patted her face and her eyes rolled open again. "Can you move?"

I ran my hands up and down her arms. "I don't think anything's broken."

Geneveve shuffled her feet on the ground and flopped her hands before she lolled her head to the side again.

"Okay—she heard you, right?" I said. "She's not brain-damaged."

I was sounding like a bad episode of *Grey's Anatomy,* but Chief nodded as if I were making sense.

"Her nose is probably broken."

"If that's as bad as it is, she's lucky, then."

"I don't think that's as bad as it is, Classic." Chief rubbed the sides of his thighs and shook his head. "This girl is loaded."

CHAPTER FOURTEEN

Chief formed a plan for getting Geneveve home, and I followed it without question, which was quickly—and strangely—becoming my new career. He waited with her while I drove my bike back to the house to pick up the van, and he promised in the meantime to determine whether we should take her to the hospital. There were going to be big questions if we did.

I had enough of my own. Not even considering the ones about why she ran off when she seemed to be doing better, what had happened on West King? Did she try to pawn my stuff and get robbed and beaten? That was the most logical explanation, if one iota of this was logical. But nobody needed to mess up a puny little thing like her that badly to get a DVD player away from her. And who was "Nobody"? The woman who'd led me to Geneveve seemed to know, and it didn't take a rocket scientist to see she thought it was the same clueless thug who'd tried to take down an eight-hundred-pound motorcycle at thirty miles an hour. My biggest question was why I didn't crash into a wall when it happened. That had to be the grace of God, because I didn't have the biking skills to avert that kind of wreck. But Mr. Man was still on the loose like the wasp you didn't get the first time you smacked at him with the flyswatter. Only because I was distracted enough already to be a danger on the bike did I not keep looking over my shoulder to see if that hulking shadow was coming after me.

Which was why I almost screamed when I opened the garage and Owen was there, sitting on the gear locker in his golf togs, solemn as a judge. As it was, I stayed astride the bike and shook for fifteen seconds before I shut it off and swallowed and breathed and did every other thing I could think of to keep myself from running him over with the thing. I'd had one freak-out too many, and there was still Geneveve and Chief to get back to with the van.

I whipped off my helmet. "Owen, what are you doing here?"

"We have to talk, Ally," he said.

Another long breath. "I know, I know—I'm sorry about the noise. I'll take care of it." I got off the bike and waved my hand at him. "I need to get in there, Owen—could you please move?"

He didn't, except to sniff the air and rub at his nose and visibly decide that what he'd come for was more important than the stench coming off of me. "I was against calling the police," he said. "That was Miz Vernell. She runs from confrontation like a scared rabbit. Now me, you know I'm more of a Mack truck in these situations. But now, Ally, you've got me between a rock and a hard place—"

"Owen, get up."

"You don't have five minutes for ten years of friendship?"

"Not this five minutes."

I all but stamped my foot. When he still didn't budge, I hung the helmet from the handlebars and dug my keys and cell phone out of my jacket pocket. I was drenched in sweat and smeared in blood and saturated with the nauseating odor of decayed life, but Owen merely shook his head and said, "You're leaving us no choice, then. I've got to—"

"You and Miz Vernell and whoever else, just do what you have to do. Right now, I've got things to do and …"

I threw it off with a head shake and jumped into the van, my cell phone already one with my ear. "Hank?" I said. "We'll be back in about ten minutes with Geneveve—I'll explain then. Just have Desmond sequestered somewhere, will you? He doesn't need to see this."

I left Owen open-mouthed in my garage and screamed the van out of Palm Row. Once on St. George, I got Chief on the phone and let his voice pull me back to West King, one cryptic word, one calming phrase at a time. By the time I arrived, I was together enough not to come apart again when I saw Geneveve's head dropped over his arm as he carried her to the van, her mouth agape and slick with fresh vomit.

"That's the drugs," he assured me. "She's just passed out."

"What a comfort," I said.

He looked at me over Geneveve's lolling head, and for an instant in the midst of the blood and the scum and the wretchedness, his eyes twinkled at me.

"There you go, Classic," he said. "Keep your sense of humor."

He eased Geneveve onto the backseat and propped her head up with the various articles of clothing that littered my van. For once I was grateful that, as Bonner always pointed out, I drove around in a closet.

"Take the turns easy or she'll end up on the floorboards," Chief said. "I'll be right behind you."

"Un-huh. I'm following you," I said.

And then I spent the entire drive to Number 2 Palm Row wondering what possessed me to say that. Okay, yes, I'd been happy for him to call the shots through the whole thing because I hadn't even known where to begin. But for Pete's sake, I knew my way home.

Didn't I?

It took some time to get Geneveve bathed and disinfected and iced, which Hank mostly took care of while I stood in the shower and washed away things that had never been on my body before. The only thing that wouldn't go down the drain were the mental pictures—the hardcore women twitchy with fear, the tiny one running like an alley cat, Geneveve left in the alley with the garbage. That was what I still saw when I joined Hank and Chief in the living room. That and Geneveve buried under blankets in the red chair, father back than the day I first wrapped her up and put her there.

I sank onto the couch and took whatever was in the mug Hank tucked into my hand. Its scent was enough to erase the odor lingering in my nostrils, but the house itself still felt as if its peace were being pressed down by something heavy.

"Is she passed out, unconscious, what?" I said.

"Geneveve," Chief said, in a voice at once low and yet commanding enough to force her eyes open. She seemed to have to bring herself back from a dead place, which she returned to in seconds, as if responding to us required too much effort.

"Has Desmond seen her?" I said.

Hank nodded.

"Was he freaked?"

"No, I got the feeling this was not a new experience for him—at least the blood and the bruises. He did say—how was it he put it?"

Chief looked up from his cell phone screen. "He said, 'I seen her wasted before, but never this bad. She gone.'"

I almost let go a laugh, but I knew if I did it would turn into something out-of-control that would require drugs for *me*.

"So much for 'I'll never use again,'" I said. "I am completely at a loss now. Any ideas? Anybody?"

Chief sat up straighter, stretching his back, and I noticed for the first time that he was still smeared with Geneveve's bodily fluids. And that this whole time he'd been in a dress shirt and slacks.

"Did you come straight from the office?" I said.

"I have one idea. It means somebody coming over here—and I don't even know if it'll pan out."

"You want to call the police?"

"Do you?"

"Should we?"

"Is somebody ever going to *answer* a question?" Hank said. "Or are we just going to keep asking them?"

"I'm just afraid if we bring in the police, they'll take Desmond."

They both raised their eyebrows. If I'd been them, I would have looked at me that way too. It was another one of those things I didn't know I thought until it came out of my mouth.

"He's driving me nuts, and I'm probably screwing the whole thing up," I said. "But it doesn't feel to me like anybody else is going to do any better right now."

"I agree," Chief said. "Not every foster home is a precursor to the penitentiary, but since this kid's halfway there already…."

"So what's your idea?"

"I know a couple people involved in NA. It's worked for them. I could make a call."

"NA?"

"Narcotics Anonymous."

"You're thinking of—yeah," Hank said. "Al, it's worth a try, in my view."

I couldn't picture Geneveve sitting in a circle of corporate cocaine users saying, "Hi, I'm Geneveve, and I'm an addict." I couldn't even imagine her sitting up, period, at this point. But I was fresh out of options, so for the umpteenth time that night, I looked at Chief and said, "Okay."

Up until then I hadn't said okay that many times to one person in my entire life.

Chief went out onto the screen porch with his phone, and Hank nodded at the mug I hadn't taken a sip from.

"Drink," she said.

"You're lucky," my mouth said. "No, I don't believe in luck. You're blessed."

"Why? Because I'm the only one in the room who doesn't smell like rotten eggs? I might take him out in the back and hose him down in a minute."

No. Because you can *be the one to take him out and hose him down.*

Fortunately it didn't come out of me this time. I'd have to figure out a way to purge it later, though, because it couldn't stay in there.

Hank let there be quiet for a while, which I appreciated. We were still resting in it when I heard a Harley rumble, two rumbles, rounding the corner and mumbling to a stop in front of the house.

"That should be them," Hank said.

"Who?"

But Hank was already at the front door waving. Chief came back in from the screen porch.

"Whoever it is came on bikes?" I said.

He passed me with, "We'll have to keep this confidential."

I gave up asking questions.

Hank led two women in from the foyer—one tall and statuesque, the other short and golden and beautifully Hispanic.

"I think you know Leighanne and Nita," Hank said.

I wouldn't have if she hadn't said their names. Leighanne hadn't packed herself into a tank top tonight, and her sleeveless apricot turtleneck was as classy as the bob of thick gray hair that was, for the first time, not poking out of a bandana. The Hispanic woman had to be Nita, though she, too, was a far cry from the woman I'd seen downing hot dogs with the best of them.

"We haven't actually met," she said, putting a hand out to me. Her voice was soft with an accent that whispered from south of the border, though she had undoubtedly learned English in the American South.

Leighanne pointed her chin toward the chair where Geneveve made a mere lump on the cushions. "Is that our friend?"

"Yeah. So you two are in—oh, wait, I'm not supposed to ask that—sorry—"

Leighanne gave a laugh reminiscent of a smoking habit somewhere in her past. "It's okay. We just came to help if she's willing."

Nita craned her neck toward Geneveve. "How many times have we seen this picture, huh?"

"I appreciate it," I said, "but I have to say—I don't know if she's going to go for it. She keeps saying she wants *me* to help her change, which, as you can see, I'm doing a bang-up job of."

"Forget that," Leighanne said. "You can't do it for her. And it doesn't sound like in-patient rehab's done much for her either."

"That's what she says."

Nita nodded, which I noticed she did every time she started a sentence, as if she were eager for me to agree. "We'd be willing to take her to an NA meeting if she wants to go."

"You really think she's going to sit in a circle with people and talk about her issues?" I said. "I mean, have you really looked at this woman? Come with me."

I led them across the living room and wafted an arm toward the shriveled curl that was Geneveve. I waited for the shock, but both of them just nodded.

"Been there," Leighanne said. "Twelve short years ago."

Nita raised a hand. "Fifteen. Except you would have found me in a jail cell. This woman's not even close to where I was."

I looked from Geneveve to the two of them with their clear eyes and their confident postures and their Harleys parked at my front curb. The distance between Geneveve and them gaped so wide I almost fell into it.

"She's going to have to wake up first, of course," Nita said. "When she does, give her the option and call us if she goes for it."

Hank touched my arm. "I have a feeling if you suggest it, she will."

"But after that it's up to her." Leighanne pulled a pamphlet out of her bag. "She'll probably be all contrite and think she can stay clean for a couple of days—"

"And probably will," Nita put in.

"This'll give you the signs that'll tell you she's using again, or is about to."

I looked lamely at the pamphlet while everyone watched as if they were waiting for me to say something profound. I was entirely out of words, my own or the ones that came out unbidden.

Hank clasped her hands tidily together. "Anybody up for prayer?"

"Sounds like the next right thing," Leighanne said.

She put her hands out for Hank and Nita to take hold, and Nita slipped a warm palm into mine. My other one hung next to Chief. I felt like the thirteen-year-old girl in square dance class that nobody wants to touch for fear of a cootie infestation. I stuck it in my pocket and closed my eyes.

"I don't bite."

My mouth came open but I clamped it shut and let Chief pull out my hand and smother it in his. The way it felt … it was best to say nothing at all. Except maybe "okay."

"The Lord be with you," Hank said.

"And also with you," the women answered.

"Let us pray."

And then she did, in words that went beyond words into the heart of the tangled mess I found myself in. Words that made me forget for the moment that my life had been snatched away and replaced with someone else's—some other Allison who took in prostitutes and fatherless boys with half-mothers and rode a Harley into the 'hood and let another woman's man make her palm sweat. I couldn't hold all her words. The ones that stayed simply tugged at the knots until a few came loose and I could breathe again. Until I could say thankyouGodthankyouGodthankyouGod.

When we raised our heads at the amen, I extricated my hand and made the excuse that I had to check on Desmond. I found him asleep, on his blanket on the floor with his head next to the door. Just as I'd done as a kid when I'd been sent off to bed during one of my parents' parties and I wanted to listen to the chatter. I hoped what he'd heard didn't sound as mindless to him as those long-ago conversations had to me.

I covered him up and returned to the living room, where Hank was seeing Leighanne and Nita out. Chief stood at the side window, arms folded as if he were done for the night. I felt compelled to do something to set myself straight—even if I blew it.

Hands in my pockets, I crossed the room and stood next to him.

"That was nice," I said.

He didn't answer.

"I know you don't buy into it, but as somebody who didn't believe it for most of her life either, I gotta tell ya, Hank is the real deal. If you ever do—"

"I won't," he said.

"O-kay."

"There something you're not telling me?"

I could feel my eyes bug. "I'm sorry?"

"About what went down tonight. How'd you find Geneveve?"

"One of the other 'girls' showed me. I practically have a sister-hood with two of them down there now."

My voice was coming out too upbeat, and from the way he cut his eyes at me, I knew he heard it too.

"She know anything about who did it?"

"I think she did," I said.

I was suddenly having a hard time getting anything to come out at all. It only made sense to tell him about the guy who tried to take us down. If I wanted to be told to stay completely out of this from now on.

"I guess it doesn't matter," he said. "The cops don't try that hard to pursue assault on a prostitute. Whole different set of rules down there."

"Yeah."

"Yeah? You knew that?"

"Somehow," I said. "I told a tour group that the other day, and I had no idea where it came from."

His eyes took on the same twinkle I saw in the alley, bright and unexpected and—dang it—pulse-quickening. "That's on the tour?"

"It was that day. It just seemed like that particular group needed to hear it. I'd keep it in my spiel but I'd probably get fired."

"We agreed you were going to call me right away."

"If I got fired? When did we agree to that?"

"No, if you ran into trouble. Tonight."

"You and Hank—I swear, you're like a man with a remote control, flipping the channels on me—"

"Classic."

"What?"

His eyes narrowed at me. They'd lost their twinkle. "Don't do that again." He turned abruptly and gathered his jacket and his riding gloves and gave me one last, searing look. "Okay?"

I didn't answer. I was done saying "okay." Because I couldn't promise I'd only do what I had to do on this journey with his consent.

He didn't wait long before he pressed his lips together and left. It was a good thing he wasn't a love interest, because that was the sexiest thing I'd ever seen a man do.

I didn't expect to see Chief again, but I did, every evening for the next week when he came by with items he collected from the HOG members.

"Just some stuff they might need," he said. There was no sign that anything had changed in his attitude toward me, and I'd managed to get mine sorted and folded and put away. So, as Desmond would say, it was all good.

While Chief's nightly haul-always included clothes and toiletries for Genevieve, the bulk of it was school supplies and apparel for Desmond, some of it with a decidedly Harley flavor. I let Desmond cut the sleeves and neck out of the two that wouldn't be allowed at school anyway and said he could wear those at home. The minute he was in the house in the afternoon, he'd put one on, with a bandana and the boots somebody (I suspected Chief) contributed so he'd be ready to ride when I was.

That became a daily ritual for us. I taught him how to do the pre-ride check, which he did with more flair than the average biker. Then we rode—not usually far because I couldn't leave Genevieve for long—just over the bridge and back, or along the Avenida, or down to the fort. It was the only time during the day that he didn't fight to stay ahead of what might come out of an alley and grab him. He didn't have a choice but to hang on and lean with me.

Genevieve was hanging on too, but her dependence on me was significantly more smothering than his. I could hardly step out of the shower without her assuring me that she hadn't touched a thing while my back was turned.

"I'm so sorry, Miss Angel," she said over and over, ad nauseam. "I let everybody down, but I never wanted to let you down. I never did."

I didn't ask her why she had, and she didn't offer an explanation. Chief, Hank, and I agreed over veal picatta in my dining room one evening that I should leave the issue of the DVD player and laptop alone until we got past the next step.

"She probably doesn't even remember who she sold them to anyway," Chief said.

"Are they insured?" Hank said.

"Yeah—"

"But if you make a claim, you have to have a police report." Chief looked at me.

"Not yet," I said. "I don't know when, but not yet."

The whole thing still didn't make sense to me, especially the obvious explanation that she needed the money to get high. I read the NA pamphlet three times, and none of the signs of drug use it listed had shown themselves in Geneveve in the days before she ran. Even Desmond had seemed surprised, and nothing surprised that kid except the steady flow of goods that daily made him look more like a normal kid living a normal life. He was still the main reason I didn't want to involve the police, and he was the same reason I avoided Bonner when he left a message asking why I hadn't kept my appointment with Liz Doyle. Now wasn't the time to bring in the authorities. I knew it like I knew the Nudges that more and more kept me from stepping off the path.

"Just keep telling me I'm not nuts to believe in it," I said to Hank when we met Friday morning at the Galleon.

"You're not nuts," she said. "A little strange maybe. Who comes in here and only has black coffee?" She folded her hands. "All kidding aside, Al, I see God all over this. Just keep doing what you're doing. You'll get there."

"I don't see how. I've tried to talk to Geneveve about NA twice, and she just starts crying and telling me it's going to be different this time."

"What do you say when she tells you that?"

"Not much. What am I supposed to say?"

"What any good Southern Christian woman would say to a friend who was deluding herself."

"What? 'You're a lying sack of cow manure, and you better get your tail to NA before I slap you silly'?"

"That's the one." Hank leaned into the table, her chest barely missing the pool of syrup on her plate. "She isn't going to shatter. If she were that delicate, she'd be dead by now. Show her some Jesus love. He did not, as you'll recall, pussyfoot around."

Neither did I that night when I sat Geneveve down and told her she was, in those exact words, a lying sack of cow manure.

The next morning, Saturday, Leighanne picked her up and took her to an NA meeting.

She said it was better that I didn't go, if Geneveve was going to make the necessary decision on her own, so Desmond and I watched from the side porch as they drove off on Leighanne's Sportster, Geneveve looking ridiculous but noble in my helmet. I felt the gelatinous relief you experience after you've just thrown up. That lasted until Desmond pointed to the sidewalk and said, "You 'bout to get busted, Big Al."

Owen was heading up the walkway to the porch, wearing a blue terry cloth bathrobe and a day's growth of whiskers. As he got closer, I realized he hadn't even put in his dentures yet. His mouth looked like a drawstring bag.

"Morning, Owen," I called to him. "Desmond, go in and pour Mr. Schatz a cup of coffee, would you?"

"I didn't come for coffee."

"Get it anyway," I whispered to Desmond.

He let the screen door close behind him just as Owen reached the porch.

"Why aren't you out on the golf course?" I said. "It's perfect weather for it."

"Because I haven't slept in three nights, that's why."

At least that was what I thought he said. Without his teeth the words mumbled around in his mouth like loose marbles.

"Are you sick?"

"Yes. Sick of the noise."

I sighed. "Ever since our last conversation about this topic that I'm getting really tired of, I have made sure I didn't rev up my engine when I drove out of here. I'm not making anymore noise than your Lexus."

"What about the rest of the Hell's Angels that are coming in and out of here at all hours of the day and night?"

"We got Hell's Angels comin' here?" Desmond said from the doorway, mug in hand.

"Go put some cream and sugar in that," I said.

Owen growled, "I don't want—"

"Go," I said to Desmond. "And toast him a bagel too."

Desmond grinned. "How he gonna eat a bagel? The man ain't got no teeth."

"Desmond."

"Goin'."

He disappeared into the kitchen again, and I got my lips under control before I turned back to Owen. I knew I wasn't as successful at keeping the laughter out of my eyes.

"I guess there has been more motorcycle traffic than usual," I said.

"We didn't used to have *any*. And there I was complaining about a bed-and-breakfast. That would be a sleeping potion compared to this."

"I know. I'll tell my friends to keep it down."

"How long is this going to go on?"

I opened my mouth, but I couldn't shoot a barb at a toothless man who was armed with nothing but his desperate love for a one-block street. He'd even left his dignity at home with his dentures.

"I'm sure it's only temporary," I said. "Just until my guests get back on their feet."

"They must be pretty far down if it takes a whole motorcycle gang to stand them up." He licked at his purse-strung lips. "In my day you pulled yourself up by your own bootstraps."

"I don't got no straps on my boots." Desmond backed out of the kitchen with a coffee mug and a charred bagel on a paper towel. The screen door banged behind him as he presented both to Owen. "I gotta see how you gon' eat that," he said.

"Desmond," I said.

But Owen waved me off and fished in his robe pocket until he produced his false teeth. Desmond and I watched in fascination as he fit them into his mouth and used his finger to make the final adjustment. I could feel an amazed expletive ready to come out of Desmond, and I gave him a look.

"I gotta get me some a them," he said instead.

"Pray you never have to, kid." Owen looked at me. "This one of your guests?"

"Oh, sorry. This is Desmond Sanborn," I said. "Desmond, this is Mr. Schatz."

"Shots," Desmond said. He dropped into the canvas chair next to mine and threw one leg over the side. "That like shots a tequila?"

Owen paused over the mug. "What would you know about that?"

"I know a lot about a lotta things."

"Such as?"

I hovered between sending Desmond back in the house for the next course and settling in to watch the show. I landed on the latter.

"I know a lot about Harleys," Desmond said, and then shifted his eyes to me. "Not everything, but enough to get by, you know what I'm sayin'?"

"Go on," Owen said. He dipped the bagel into the coffee. Good grief, he was actually going to eat it.

"I got some techniques with women. You know. How to talk all sweet to 'em till they melt like butter."

"How old are you?"

"Fourteen."

"Excuse me?" I said.

"I'll be fourteen. In two years."

"Don't wish your life away, kid," Owen said. "Enjoy every year like you're licking an ice-cream cone. You know, it's like an onion. Each layer you peel off as you grow up shows you something new, but you don't want to rush it. A life's like a good cheese: It has to be allowed to age very slowly."

Desmond had his chin pulled all the way into his chest. "So which one is it—a cheese or a onion or a ice-cream cone?"

I feigned a coughing spell. Owen barely batted an eyelash.

"So what else do you think you know?" he said. "Do you have any talents?"

"Oh yeah. I got lotsa talents."

I shifted in the chair. It might be time for me to wind this up before Desmond started giving a résumé of his recent larcenies.

"Best one, though, is I draw real good."

I blinked.

"How good is 'real good'?"

Desmond shrugged. "I could show you."

"I'd like to see your portfolio."

"I don't know 'bout that. I gotta a bunch of my drawings."

"Let's have a look."

While I watched, jaw unhinged, Desmond unwound himself from the chair and hurried into the house.

"He doesn't act like he needs a pack of motorcycles," Owen said. "Just some straight talk would do it."

"And evidently you're just the person to give it to him, Owen." I sat up straight in the chair. "Look, I'm really sorry about the bike noise and the traffic and all that. You don't need to bring the police in anymore. I'll take care of it."

"It's not just me you need to tell that to." He pointed east and lowered his voice to a whisper that couldn't be heard on Aviles Street, let alone on Miz Vernell's screen porch where she was undoubtedly listening. "She won't be satisfied until every Honda, Harley, and Yamaha is confiscated by the sheriff. I'm just trying to keep you out of court, Ally."

"I'll talk to her," I said.

His eyes went to the door where Desmond was emerging with a spiral notebook, part of one of Chief's recent deliveries.

"All right, let's see what you got, kid."

"I don't show this to most people, Mr. Shotzie. Only people I know got a eye for art."

"I'm no expert, but I know what I like."

Desmond nodded as if that were the qualifying answer and sat on the swing next to Owen. He opened the notebook to the page he had his finger in and gave a brief nod.

"This isn't my best," he said. "But itta give you a idea."

The idea was plain on Owen's face. The isn't-this-a-cute-kid look faded from his eyes as they scanned the page and looked up at me.

"Have you seen this?" he said.

I shook my head. Oh, man, had he drawn something obscene? Was Liz Doyle going to be hearing from Owen, too?

"I ain't showed her yet," Desmond said. "Now this one here, I was experimenting with a different technique."

"I see. Something along the lines of Picasso."

Desmond's eyebrows lowered. "You think it look like some kinda spaghetti?"

"You haven't studied the artist? Picasso?"

"I ain't studied nobody. I just draw."

Owen glared at me as if I alone were responsible for Desmond's lack of cultural education.

"We're going to have to remedy that," he said. "Let me see what else you've got."

The exchange of artistic ideas went on for another thirty minutes, during which I was allowed a brief peek at what had Owen's eyes gleaming and his mind forgetting what he'd come over for. The drawing depicted a Harley, mine but with the fenders and engine enlarged and enflamed, and the front wheel bowing the windshield gracefully to the ground. I knew without question this was our Classic—because Desmond had drawn her soul.

Owen went home whistling and Desmond sequestered himself in his den, announcing that he needed space to create. I simply sat in wonder on the side porch and waited for Geneveve to come home. Sylvia would like where this was going. My mother, on the other hand, would be way ahead of Miz Vernell and have me locked up by now.

I was foraging for lunch when Leighanne returned with Geneveve, who looked as if her emotions had been drained from her veins and she was, even now, being filled with a trickle of a new one. Eyes puffy from what had apparently been hours of weeping, she looked at me from a different place: a tentative, perhaps unfamiliar place, but a different one than she'd lived in before. Different was good at this point.

"They say I got a long ways to go," she said. "I don't know if I can do it."

I looked quizzically at Leighanne. She nodded at Geneveve.

"Maybe you should tell her the rest."

"I can only do it for today," Geneveve said. "Tomorrow, that's a whole other thing. I'ma think about that when it gets here. Right now I got to go lie down."

When she'd gone upstairs, I turned back to Leighanne, who was smiling a secret smile.

"What is that, the Scarlett O'Hara approach to recovery?" I said.

"It works. For today."

"And tomorrow?"

"Tomorrow is its own today."

I sat on the bottom step and tightened my ponytail. "Okay, so what does she need from me?"

Leighanne looked around. "Just make this the safest place you possibly can while she's taking these critical first steps. The rest is up to her."

"That's it?"

"That's it."

I, too, looked around—at the polished floor and the chairs cozied up to the dining-room table and the red chair-and-a-half waiting for the next person who needed to weep or wail or decide there. "Okay," I said. "I can do safe here."

Geneveve went to another meeting with Leighanne and Nita the next morning.

"The goal is ninety meetings in ninety days," Nita told me. "She can't do this alone, not even for twenty-four hours."

I had a small pity party for myself after they left because Geneveve had a group to go to on Sunday morning, and I no longer felt like I did. The bells ringing from the Episcopal church rang out taunts, telling me I was a loser for not being able to make my own people understand me or themselves or the God who was Nudging his way into my life. I was stark lonely, and I soon ran out of chocolate.

There was nothing to do then but beef up my safety plan for Geneveve. I started with a call to Lonnie's cell phone to leave a message that I was going to have to cut back my work hours for a while. Even though I'd worked all week, I'd managed to avoid him since the day I left Bernard and the carriage for him to clean up. I knew he wouldn't answer this early—

"Hey," he said after the second ring.

"Oh," I said, "it's you."

"Yeah, that's would make sense since you dialed my number. I'm surprised you remembered it."

"That's why I called." I tried to grab the upper hand by imagining him pulling his first toothpick of the day out of its box and sticking it between as yet unbrushed teeth. The hair was definitely sticking out in all directions like a sea urchin—

"I was gonna call you today anyways," he said. "Basically to tell you I won't be calling you. At all."

"Oh," I said. "So I'm finally being terminated."

I snickered and waited for our usual conversation to take place— the one where he hemmed and hawed and gnawed and ended up telling me I was his best guide and he'd keep me on even though I drove him nuts.

But he sighed into the phone. "Listen. I like you, Allison, but I have to cut back because of the economy, and lately, you've kinda made yourself the logical choice."

There was something odd in his voice, something not-Lonnie, as if he were reading from a card. I could no longer imagine the toothpick.

"That's it?" I said. "Seriously?"

"You can come by and say good-bye to Bernard. That horse works better for you than he has for anybody. I don't know who I'm gonna get to replace you who can—"

He stopped, caught in his own lie. I *could* imagine his face going red.

"You tell him for me, Lonnie," I said. "Thanks for everything."

When I hung up, I had one of those rare moments when I was tempted to wish I'd kowtowed to my parents just a smidge so I'd have a little cash to fall back on. But that passed with the sudden relief that shimmered through me. I had no clue how I was going to pay the utilities a few weeks from now, but I had a Nudge. Not a Nudge *toward*, but a Nudge away. I figured I'd know what it was I was leaving behind soon enough. The sacred foolishness of it made me laugh.

"Hey, Desmond," I said. "You wanna go for a ride or what?"

"We goin' in the rain?"

He joined me in the kitchen, where we both looked out the window at a deluge I hadn't seen coming. Even as we stood there a clap of thunder made him jump and very nearly push himself under my arm. Prepubescent pride saved him.

"Yeah, I guess we won't be going out in this." A flash lit up the window, and I covered my ears. "The next one's going to be huge, trust me."

"I ain't scared a that."

"Uh-huh."

The crash rattled the glass, sending us both howling across the room.

"Jackal!" he hollered.

"What?"

"You won't let me say my own cuss words, so I gotta say yours."

I covered my mouth so I wouldn't guffaw in the poor kid's face. His eyes suddenly widened, and he cocked his head.

"What?" I asked again.

"Somebody's at the door."

"How do you know?"

"I just know."

"It's probably your mom…." Although as I passed through the living room. I wondered why she wouldn't just come in. It wasn't locked. This was Desmond diverting me from seeing that he was freaked out over the thunder. I opened the front door anyway, just to have something to give him grief over.

The gutter was overflowed onto the front steps, shutting two forlorn female figures behind a curtain of rainwater, yet I knew immediately who they were. The savagely skimpy clothes, the last brittle attempts to hold their heads up. Away from West King Street, even the tall one looked diminished and terrified.

Although there was no way it could be, I said, "Are you ladies here to see Geneveve?"

"No," said the prostitute. "We here to see you."

CHAPTER FIFTEEN

Their names were Jasmine Woods and Mercedes Phillips. I didn't inquire whether those were their real names. I just brought them in out of the storm and went to find towels. When I returned to they foyer, they stood huddled together, eyes wild and terrified as they looked down at the puddle they made on the wood floor. They seemed more frightened in my entrance way than I'd ever seen them on West King Street.

"It's okay," I said. "That's why God made mops."

I watched them pat themselves haphazardly as if they'd never operated a bath towel before. They made little headway anyway, since their clothes were soaked through and stuck to their skin like shrink-wrap.

"Bathrobes," I said. "Would that work?"

They stared at me.

"You can put them on while I pop your clothes in the dryer. No sense sitting around feeling like a wet sponge. You can put your own stuff back on when you leave."

That seemed to mystify them even more. The tall one—Mercedes—ran her tongue over her very full lips like she was dragging it across sandpaper. All of her features were large and would have been voluptuous, even sensuous, if her life hadn't dissipated her into downright unloveliness.

"Geneveve," she said. "She gon' leave?"

"I hope not. She's just at a meeting right now."

Jasmine turned her head, as if she could only look at me through one eye. I was relieved to see that the man in the alley didn't seem to have found her. The emaciated face was still intact.

"What kinda meeting?" she said.

Mercedes knocked at her with the heel of her hand. "Don't matter. Is she stayin' here?"

"Yeah," I said slowly.

"Then we wanna stay here. She said you would help us like you done her."

As my dear Sylvia would have said, holy mackerel.

Jasmine was watching me in that sideways manner, large liquid eyes overpowering her other features, which had lost all definition.

"You don't want us?" she said.

"I didn't say that. Just give me a minute here. How 'bout I fix you something to eat?"

They both shook their heads, but I brought out two bathrobes that were in Chief's last delivery and had them change into them while I threw together grilled cheese sandwiches and tomato soup. They didn't eat much, but the robes seemed to comfort them. Whatever worked.

By then I had my first few paragraphs ready. They'd been Nudged into me, and since the women had initially left me with my tongue tied around my tonsils, I had to go with it.

"Whether I can help you depends on what kind of help you want," I told them when they'd curled themselves as tightly as was humanly possible into the corners of the couch. I sat facing them on the trunk table, trying not to look like I was making this up as I went along. "If you just want a place to crash until you're ready for your next fix, it's not happening here. Here you start by getting on a schedule: you eat, bathe, sleep, and wear clean clothes on a regular basis."

"Ain't got no clean clothes," Jasmine said.

Mercedes gave her a heavy glare. If she'd been close enough I knew by now she'd have bruised her with her fist.

Jasmine's voice dropped into timidity as if she had. "We *don't*. All I got's what I was wearin' when I come in here. I was runnin' for my life."

"I've got plenty of clothes," I said. "Okay—second thing—if you're going to stay here, you can't go back and forth to whatever you were running from. No drugs in my house. Matter of fact, you'll be encouraged to go to Narcotics Anonymous meetings."

It was coming out of me faster than I could grasp it. If even half of it was sinking into the women in front of me, we were doing good.

"How we gon' get there?" Mercedes said.

Jasmine was the one to glare this time, tentatively, as if it were a new thing. "Why you askin' so many questions? If Miss Angel gon' help us, then we gon' do it her way."

"To a point," I said. "You won't be prisoners here. You can leave anytime you want, but once you do, there's no coming back until I have reason to believe you really want to change. And that decision is entirely up to you."

Jasmine shook her head with a vehemence I wouldn't have given her credit for. "I ain't goin' nowhere, and that's it." Then she crumpled herself into a ball and silently wept.

Mercedes barely glanced at her.

"What about you?" I said. "You told me the other night Geneveve didn't need my kind of help, that it was going to go down bad for her if I didn't leave her alone. Now here you are."

She tried to level her eyes at me, but she couldn't quite get them to focus. Everything about her was almost there. She was almost keeping

up her proud front. She was almost maintaining her lead ahead of
Jasmine. She was almost convincing herself that she was indeed making a choice. But the evidence that she was out of options—that was
the one thing that was whole. She had something breathing down her
neck and it had blown her straight to me.

"Jasmine told me what happen to Geneveve," she said finally,
"and I seen there ain't no other way outta that happening to us."

"You mean getting beaten up."

She swatted that away. "I mean getting so loaded you can't even
take care of yourself no more. That ain't no life. She tol' Jasmine she
got a life here, and I want that. That's what I want."

I could almost believe her. Or maybe it was only that I wanted to.
I waited for clarity but the words had stopped, and I didn't feel even
the faintest of Nudges.

"Mer-say-*deez*!"

I swiveled on the trunk to see Desmond, who had apparently
gone into hiding under something in the den because his hair had
reached new heights of wildness. I really did need to put a haircut for
him at the top of my list.

"Whatchoo doin' here, girlfriend?" he said.

He loped across the room to Mercedes and put his puppy-paw
hand up for her to slap it. She gave it a weak try, and then she smiled
at him. Wan and cracked, it obviously took everything she had. Her
effort broke my heart in half.

"You behavin', boy?" she said.

"You *serious*?" Desmond's voice pitched up into the stratosphere.
"You *got* to act right if you gon' live in Big Al's house." He turned
suddenly to me. "They gon' move in with us, her and the Jazz-Man?"

I looked at Mercedes, whose long-lost beauty wobbled faintly in that smile she fought to keep for Desmond.

"Yes, they are," I said. "I think you better go run a bath for somebody."

"Who goin' first?" he said. "Jazz-Man, I think it better be you, 'cause I can smell you—wooh. These some sorry-lookin' women right here."

"You watch your mouth, boy," Mercedes said.

She was still smiling.

Over the next four days I felt as if I'd stepped into a different dimension, and all I knew to do was to try to make it a normal one. Not an easy task, seeing as how Jasmine and Mercedes were even less acquainted with normal than Geneveve had been. I was amazed to see how far she'd come as she modeled the simplest things, like putting oneself to sleep.

Mercedes was up every hour, churning around the house until she dropped again onto the nearest horizontal plane.

"I'm used to takin' me some power naps," she told me. "On the street you got to keep awake if you want to score, you know what I'm sayin'?"

I didn't, which was why I made going to NA meetings less a suggestion and more part of the routine. Jasmine took to it best and attached herself to Nita like a joey in a pouch.

"Is this okay with you?" I asked Nita one night when she dropped them off after a meeting. "She's got to be draining you."

"It's what we do," she said. "It won't be like this forever for her—you watch. She'll start to gain confidence, then *I'll* be trying to catch up with *her*."

I couldn't imagine it.

Nor could I picture Mercedes letting anyone tell her what her next step should be. But evidently Leighanne was the person for the job, because they spent hours on the phone and side-by-side in the canvas chairs on the side porch talking, sometimes until the sun crept up over the bay. Mercedes acted like she knew a lot when she knew a little, but Leighanne seemed to know how to handle it. From the kitchen I'd hear Mercedes's voice go shrill, and I'd wait for Leighanne to finally have it up to her helmet and take off on her Sportster. But phrases like *one day at a time* and *powerless over my addiction* and words like *unmanageable* and *surrender* would waft from the porch and I'd hear Mercedes's acquiescent silence. In my opinion Leighanne glowed in the dark.

Thursday evening of that week, I followed her out to her bike. "I'm going to start calling you 'St. Leighanne,'" I said.

She gave me the two-packs-a-day laugh. "Don't even go there. A saint I am *definitely* not." She stopped cramming all that hair into her bandana and grinned. "Although I guess I ought to take that seriously, coming from an angel. All three of them call you that now."

I grunted. "Talk about definitely not. I have moments when I want to take off my halo and start swinging it at them."

"Of course. But do you do it?"

"No. That would send them right back to West King."

"Then there you go." She picked up her helmet, but she didn't put it on.

"What?" I said.

"Whether you're an angel or a saint or whatever it is you are that makes you nutty enough to do this, there may come a time when one of them is going to turn on you because she blames you for having to face her demons."

I motioned for her to go on.

"Right now just not using makes them think they're making it. They have to get clean, of course, before they can make any progress. But what they have ahead of them is going to get ugly, and you being the most secure thing they've probably ever had in their lives—they're going to feel safe taking some of their frustration out on you." She pulled on her helmet. "I'd just hate to see you get burned out."

I leaned against one of the palms and watched her turn onto St. George Street—and longed to go with her. Just get on my Classic and cruise to the beach and beyond until I came to my senses and realized I was not equipped to take care of three addicted women and a juvenile delinquent. Even as I thought it, it sounded like the title of a bad cable show that was destined for cancellation after half a season. One I shouldn't be starring in because I was irresponsible and flakey and never saw anything through. Except Sylvia. That was my one claim to integrity.

Really? And I am, then, chopped liver?

The Nudge was so clear that I looked around to make sure a human voice hadn't spoken to me from behind the palm. But what human could say I'd committed to him?

"Okay," I whispered to the fishy breeze that blew from the bay. "I'm seeing you through."

As I crossed Palm Row to the house, I had a post-massage kind of peace—until I got to the side porch and heard all Hades opening up in the kitchen.

"You don't be tellin' me why I'm here. I know why I'm here." That was Mercedes's strident voice, going, as Desmond would say, straight up into someone's grill work. Jasmine's timid whine urged her to "hush up 'fore Miss Angel hear you." But it was the third voice that pressed me onto the porch swing to wait and hear.

"You better be sayin' the truth," Geneveve said. "'Cause if you here to spy on me and go runnin' back—"

"You think Sultan send me here?"

"Don't you ever speak that name to me! Don't you *ever*."

"And don't you never be accusin' me of bein' in with him, or I will—"

Her threat was cut off by Jasmine, whimpering, "She ain't messin' with you, Geneveve. We as scared of him as you are."

"Ain't no way. He ain't done to you what he done to me."

"But don't you think he won't," Mercedes said. "When he come back and found you left, who you think he come to for information? And you know he weren't askin' pretty please."

"That why you tol' Opus Behr where to find me?"

"I didn't tell him no such thing!"

"Then how did he know?"

"Why you askin' me? You the one knows how Sultan operate."

A hard silence fell. I held my breath and craned my neck toward the window in the door. Through the thin curtain I could see only shapes. Jasmine cowering on a bistro chair. Mercedes standing in the middle of the floor. And Geneveve backing her toward the sink.

"I'ma tell you one last time, Mercedes. Don't you ever say that name to me again."

"Whatchoo think you gon' do to me if I do?" Mercedes said.

Although she was forced to lean against the counter, her voice was like a switchblade. I stood up, the hair on my arms standing up with me. It would probably be better to break this up before it came to fingernails and teeth. Desmond was one thing. The two of them—

"It's not enough just me askin' you?" Geneveve said. "What we got left but this place and Miss Angel and each other? You tell me, what else we got?"

"We got nothin'," I heard Jasmine whisper.

I watched Geneveve's form disappear through the doorway, Jasmine after her, leaving only Mercedes in the kitchen. When I walked in, she was at the den door, ear pressed to the crack.

"I hate him hearin' that," she said without turning around.

"Then why did you have that conversation in the kitchen?" I said.

"Just where it happen." She looked at me, face hard, but eyes wary. "You hear all that?"

"Some of it. Who's Sultan?"

She started for the dining room.

"Mercedes."

When she stopped, midway through the room, she kept her back to me. "He what you would call her pimp. He think he own Geneveve, that's all. You don't need to get messed up in this."

"I do if he's going to come here and finish off the job he started on her—her and everybody else in here."

She turned her head, but she still wouldn't look at me. "That weren't Sultan messed her up. That ain't his style, and it ain't his style to come here, so you don't got to worry about that."

"Then what *do* I need to worry about?"

This time she did face me, with eyes I couldn't read. "He ain't gon' come lookin' for her. Sultan don't chase."

"So ..."

"You just got to keep her from goin' back there, Miss Angel." She slowly shook her head. "'Cause if she does, you ain't never gonna see her again."

I lay awake most of the night, tossing the scene in the kitchen and my conversation with Mercedes back and forth, turning Leighanne's warning and Sultan's looming existence over and over. Every time I started to doze off, Desmond's face would flash into the almost-sleep and I'd have to go down and check on him. I must have done that five times until four a.m., when he rolled open his eyes and said, "I done my homework, Big Al. Why you got to dog me?"

There was something so incredibly ordinary about that, I almost cried. I brewed coffee and went for the half-and-half and told myself he couldn't have heard the whole verbal catfight or he'd either be sitting in a self-imposed daze in front of the TV or trying to pick the lock I'd installed on the stereo cabinet or sketching in his notebook, curved backbone shielding it from the rest of the world.

"DearGoddearGoddearGod, let it be ordinary for him," I whispered into the refrigerator.

"Desmond's the one I'm worried about the most," I told Hank later that morning at the Galleon.

I'd dropped him off at school and the women at an NA breakfast meeting and barreled into the coffee shop with the Sultan story practically out before I got to the table. Hank had a pumpkin-carrot-raisin-zucchini muffin waiting at my place.

"Why Desmond?" she said.

"Because they made the choices that landed them where they are, and they can choose to either stay there or get out. He doesn't get to choose. He just has to go with what his mother decides for him." I poked at the muffin with my finger. "And that's the thing—she doesn't even seem to be thinking about him. At all. Mercedes is more concerned about the kid than Geneveve is."

"It's probably all Geneveve can do to keep her*self* together. She knows you've got him handled. She'll start being a mother when she figures out how to be a person." Hank smiled her twisty smile. "At least, that's my opinion."

"And it oughta be mine, right? As long as you're handing them out, do you think I should be worried about this Sultan person coming into my home and killing us all in cold blood? I know what Mercedes said, but her take on this could be skewed."

Hank stopped in mid chew. "It's a chilling thought. I'm just creeped out by how close the name 'Sultan' is to 'Satan.' I'm not one to talk about the Devil much but … hmm."

"What 'hmm'?"

"I'm just thinking."

"It must be pretty heavy. You're putting your fork down."

"Yeah—just hear me out while I try to say this because it's just now coming to me."

"Been there," I said.

"Whether Sultan is Satan or whoever he is, it seems to me we have to fight him the same way."

"Which is …"

"With the power of the Spirit. And how do we get that?"

"Prayer," I said. "Communion. Hanging out with people of faith. If you wait long enough, you get Nudges." I shrugged. "That's just been my experience."

"Then shouldn't it be theirs?"

"Tell me some more."

She did the tidy hand-fold. "You've given them a routine of normal activities. Why not give them sacred normalcy, too?"

"So, like, regular times for prayer? Bible study? That kind of thing?" I closed my eyes and shook my head. "I'm having a hard time picturing it."

Hank laughed. "Didn't you have a hard time picturing them sitting in an NA meeting? For that matter, when did you ever feature yourself opening a home for harlots? What about this whole *thing* has been easy to fathom, Al?"

"So you're saying make God part of their day just like everything else."

"He's already part of it. You're just going to give them a chance to notice."

I pulled out the now dog-eared notepad I'd taken to using to keep up with everything. *Haircut for Desmond* was scrawled at the top. "Okay," I said as I wrote, "prayer, Scripture, fellowship—I guess that's like meals at the table—" I groaned.

"What?"

"I'm trying to see Desmond in the dining room with his napkin in his lap."

"Enough with the mental pictures, already."

"Right. Okay—worship." I stopped, a bitterness already filming my mouth.

"Problem?"

"I'm not taking them to church, Hank. My own people won't even accept me helping these women. I know what's going to happen if I walk into a service with three hookers. That's one scene I *can* picture, and it isn't pretty."

Hank refolded her hands and said nothing.

"What does that mean?" I said.

"I think you're right about not taking them just yet, but what about you?"

"What about me?"

"You still need a community of fellow believers to worship with."

"There is so much of that that no longer applies to my church, I don't even know where to start. In fact, I don't want to start. Okay? Back to the women?"

"All right, erase, erase, erase," Hank wiped the air with her palm. "I'd like to make an offer, and if this doesn't work for you, I won't be offended."

"When have I ever turned down an offer from you?"

"You do it every time I try to treat you to breakfast. Here's what I'm thinking. Why don't I bring communion over once a week and celebrate it with you and the woman and Desmond? Whatever time works with all their meetings—"

"You would do that?" I said.

"Would I have offered otherwise? Think about it and, like I said, you can turn me down—"

"And like *I* said, when have I ever turned you down? Uh—Patrice?"

Her hair preceded her over the counter.

"Could you fix me one of those Throw Me Overboard omelets?"

"You mean 'Walk the Plank'?" she said.

"Yes. Please. Hank's treating." I looked across the table. "Do Wednesday mornings work for you?"

And so it began. I went deeper into the new dimension and took the women with me. Most of the time they came willingly.

Amid the trips to the clinic for full physicals and, at Chief's suggestion, testing for hepatitis and STDs and HIV and a whole alphabet soup of diseases I'd never even heard of, we gathered for morning and noon and evening prayer. I did most of the praying, so the day Geneveve whispered, "Thank you for Miss Angel, God," I expected God to send a dove or something.

In addition to seeing dentists about meth-destroyed teeth and NA sponsors about equally damaged thinking, we sat down twice a week and looked at Scripture. I researched every harlot in the Bible and read them their stories in small pieces to fit their attention spans. I could get Desmond to work on his homework longer than they could focus on Gomer and Rahab, and that was saying something. He claimed he was too stupid to learn fractions; I claimed he was just behind and I would help him catch up if he'd stop wasting all his energy thinking up excuses not to try. The women never claimed stupidity about the Bible. They didn't say anything, actually. They listened, gave the occasional mmm-hmm, and sometimes nodded off. I kept at it only because Hank said you never knew what was sinking in, and that nothing was going to if I didn't pour it out in the first place.

We ate nightly around the dining-room table. I'd been right in one prediction: Desmond did not see the point in a napkin when you had a sleeve, or a fork when you had fingers, or a chair when you could grab a pork chop and walk around the house with it so you wouldn't miss anything that might be happening elsewhere. It seemed to require all the focus Geneveve could muster to sit there herself. The first two suppers involved all of them twitching in their chairs, fumbling with their utensils, looking over their shoulders as if they were afraid somebody was going to come along and steal their mashed potatoes. I didn't have to wonder where those instincts came from.

Once they got that the plate wasn't going anywhere, and there was no score to run after or pimp to run *from*, dinner at the table seemed to be the part of the day they liked most. When on Tuesday I found Jasmine and Geneveve already at their places before I had the salad made, I knew we'd reached some kind of turning point.

"Well," I said, "you can either sit there and wait for it, or you can help and it'll get there faster."

Protesting that they knew nothing about cooking, Jasmine set a somewhat cockeyed table, Geneveve tossed lettuce with nervous precision, and Mercedes took the knife from me and whacked up a red bell pepper. I tried not to imagine who she was really decimating with that blade.

When we sat down to eat, Desmond flung his arm across the table and groped for the breadbasket.

"Boy," Mercedes said, "we got to pray first 'fore you start grabbin' that food."

"The Lord be with you," I said.

Raspy, crackled, life-weary voices answered, "And also witchoo."

It was the best meal I ever ate until the communion feast Hank spread for us the next morning at that same table. As she reenacted the Last Supper with the words, "Take, eat, this is my body which is given for you," I didn't have to question whether they were listening. Eyes bugged, and when she broke the round, golden loaf and offered Mercedes a piece, saying, "The body of Christ, the bread of heaven," Mercedes blurted out, "I ain't eatin' no man's body!"

"I'm sorry. I should've prepared them," I whispered to Hank.

She smiled and put the bread back on the table. "Nobody's prepared for the miracle of the body and blood," she said. "I think that was the perfect reaction."

So we stopped right there in the middle of the sacrament and Hank explained the symbolism, which led to incredulous questions, the same ones I'd asked the Watchdogs when I was first told that breaking the bread reminded us that Jesus' body was broken for us, so we could be whole. Mercedes and Jasmine and Geneveve's responses were somewhat more colorful than my, "*What? Are you serious?* What does that even *mean?*" were six and seven years ago, but Hank's answers were also more vivid than the ones I got.

"Al's feeding you food here in her house so you can get strong enough to go out there and make it on your own. Jesus is feeding you Himself so you know you *can't* make it unless you depend on him."

Jasmine still had to make sure it was indeed bread and not actual flesh she was biting into. To my relief the blood of Christ wasn't wine for this group, but I was sure it was the cup of salvation, as thirstily as their souls drank from it. At least that was the picture that came to me. I made a note to share that with Hank.

Despite Jasmine's nightmares and Mercedes's miniexplosions and Geneveve's moody retreats into her room when she returned from NA meetings, it was still Desmond who provided the greatest challenge. He fought the haircut as if I'd told him we were having his ears chopped off. I once again had to threaten to take away his helmet, and I let him choose the barber since he insisted that "ain't no white person can cut a black person's hair." I asked one of the African-American HOG members where he had his done, and he grinned sheepishly.

"I go to a little hole in the wall off West King Street," he said. "It's got bars on the windows and the owner packs heat while he's cutting your hair, but you don't walk out looking like RuPaul."

That appeased Desmond somewhat, especially when I told him we could drive there on the Harley. By the time we walked into Bo's Barber Shop, he was strutting it like Shaft. The proprietor indeed had an unconcealed weapon in a holster around his waist and cameras prominently installed in four places, and I stood nervously between Desmond and the door as if I could actually bring down an intruder in this neighborhood—without my motorcycle. But Desmond came out with a wonderful soft 'do shaped like a pharaoh's turban, and he preened in the shop window before he put his helmet on.

"I told you it wouldn't kill you," I said.

"It was all right." He looked wistfully at the Classic. "Where we goin' now? Home?"

"Home is not a good place to celebrate a new look," I said. "I'm thinking we should go for a ride out to—"

He didn't seem to care where we went. He was already on the bike.

I'd heard new mothers say that sometimes the only way they could calm a colicky baby was to take the child out in the car. Some claimed they drove around for hours just to keep their sanity. I felt that way when I had Desmond behind me and we cruised without purpose. All his wire uncoiled, and so, for that matter, did mine. I never came close to dumping it when he was with me.

That day we wound up at the Bay Front, far enough from the carriages so that I wouldn't have to see Bernard or answer Caroline's questions if either of them showed up. We were just in time for the dolphins.

They came into the Bay by the north seawall every day around noon to feed. Mullet was the most popular thing on their menu, and the mullet knew it.

"Have you ever seen this action?" I asked Desmond as we swung our feet over the wall. I'd have sworn his had doubled in size since I'd known him.

"What action you talkin' about?"

I pointed to the water, where the mullet were coming up in mobs and running across the surface of the bay to avoid being eaten. It was a scene that never failed to make me clap my hands and cheer them on. Desmond was on the side of the dolphins, who lazily rolled beneath us and occasionally opened their mouths to take in the unfortunate fish who couldn't quite get up to speed. A few feet below them a large turtle quietly treaded, waiting for the lunch rush to pass.

"I ain't never seen nothin' like this," Desmond said.

As he coaxed a small notebook and a piece of chalk out of his pocket, I didn't point out that he'd spent most of his life only twelve blocks away. I said instead, "Where did you get that stuff?"

"It's mine. I didn't take it from nobody."

"Did I say you did?"

"Mr. Shots give it to me. So I can work on my technique."

He sketched happily for a while, glancing up at the mullet leaping for their lives across the water, then down at the notebook that puffed with chalk dust. It wasn't even close to ordinary.

"What do you draw mostly?" I asked.

"Stuff I see. Stuff I think about."

"Have you ever drawn Sultan?"

His hand halted on the page, and if I could've sucked the question back, I'd have been on it like a Shop-Vac.

"You don't have to answer that," I said quickly. "It's none of my business."

"I don't draw nothin' that I hate," Desmond said.

He didn't have to draw it—it was there in his voice, in the mean edge that sharpened the softness we'd played in moments before.

"Why do you hate him?" I wanted to say. "What did this jackal do to you and your mother?"

I didn't. Because I wanted the cocky, gawky twelve-year-old to come back and chase away the hate nobody was old enough to feel.

"That's a good policy," I said. "It's always better not to dwell on it."

"Dwell on what?" he said. The grin was already loping across his face, once again hiding whatever was behind it.

As we drove home, I wondered if we'd ever get there.

CHAPTER SIXTEEN

The women went off to their meeting, and Chief came by with a few more items he'd collected, and an unexpected offer.

"Why don't I hang with Desmond for a couple hours?" he said. "Give you a night off."

"Do I look like I need one?"

"Everybody needs one."

"You must be one slick lawyer," I said, and I took him up on it.

To Desmond's utter delight—as in, he was speechless, and that *never* happened—Chief suggested they go for a ride on the Road King. I was sure he grew two inches walking to it.

I was just breathing in the silence as my phone rang. When I saw that it was India, I almost didn't answer it. But there was always the hope that she'd had a change of heart. If anybody in that group was going to, it would be her.

"Hey," I said.

"I miss you," Her voice was thick, and sounded nothing like the boutique owner saying you looked marvelous in that $300 outfit.

"I miss you too," I said.

"Have dinner with me? Tonight? It's still nice outside at O. C. White's. We won't have many more evenings like this."

I hesitated, but hope won out. "Do I have to put on lipstick?"

"I don't care if you come in a burlap sack. And don't you dare put one on just to spite me."

"None of my burlap sacks fit me anymore," I said. "I'll see you in ten."

O. C. White's, a seafood restaurant on the Avenida, was only three blocks from my house, and I walked there with a light heart. October was the perfect time to be in St. Augustine—the humidity had gone south for the winter, the summer storms had passed, and the brick streets were less crowded with tourists on the weekdays. I loved walking down them and remembering why I'd come back here. Even though so much of it looked different to me now, nothing could change the history that had fought so hard to make it safe and free. I had a fleeting glimpse of somehow doing my part to keep it that way.

I must have been smiling when India waved to me from a back table on the O. C. White patio, because when I got there and accepted her customary holy kiss, she said, "You look happy. What does that mean? New man in your life?"

For some reason unknown to myself, my face went hot.

"Ah, I know that look." She patted the chair. "Do tell."

"It's not what you think," I said. "Uh, and what is this?"

She pushed a frosty glass full of something orange toward me. "It's a virgin mango margarita. Closest I could get to something that looks like autumn. It's glorious out, isn't it?"

I agreed, but I snuck a closer look at her as I sipped what turned out to be a sickeningly sweet concoction. She was way too up, even for India. Between that and her eyes darting toward the entrance every thirty seconds, I knew this wasn't just about two girlfriends coming together to discuss their love lives.

"You a little on edge, India?" I said.

"Why?"

"Just a feeling."

I took another sip and hid a cringe. They must have put a cup of sugar in that thing.

"We didn't exactly part on the best of terms last time I saw you," she said. "I wasn't even sure you'd meet me."

"Why wouldn't I?" I said. "Unless you're going to start in on me about how naïve and irresponsible I am."

A server brought a plate of crab cakes. She waited for him to go. I waited for the prepared speech. It was there, all over her face, and I didn't know how I hadn't seen it from across the patio.

"I don't think you're either naive or irresponsible," she said. "I just think you're trying to be a good person—and Lord knows you're a better one than I am."

"But …"

"But there's being a good person, and there's taking it to the extreme, to where you're in danger."

"I've heard this from you before," I said.

"Not since you took in two *more* whores."

I spit a mouthful of my drink back into the glass, and I might have thrown it in her face if I hadn't felt a tentative touch on my shoulder. A touch I'd have known anywhere.

"What are you doing here, Bonner?" I said. "Let me guess— you've got Frank with you." I twisted around, almost touching Frank's vest with my nose. "You didn't bring Mary Alice?"

"Mary Alice didn't think she could handle it, Miss Allison," Frank said.

I didn't ask what it was we were handling. I didn't intend to stay long enough to find out. Glaring at India across the table, I tried to stand up. Bonner held me there.

"Let me go," I said.

"I think you better stay and hear this, Missy," Frank said.

He took the chair next to me, face grave.

"It's Allison, Frank," I said. "Not 'Missy,' not 'little Missy.' Just Allison, and Allison is not going to sit here and listen to the same—"

"Hear us out," India said, "and then if you still want to, you can go do whatever—"

"I'll do that anyway. Since when did I need your permission to behave like Jesus?"

"Is that what you're calling it?" she said.

It was now.

Bonner let go of my shoulders and sat down on the other side of me. I stared at him until he lowered his eyes to the table. Okay, so this wasn't his idea. He was clearly just there to make sure I didn't break any restaurant crockery over someone's head. So it was Frank I turned on.

"Is this some kind of intervention?"

"You can call it that if you want to."

"I want to call it a setup." I tried again to stand up and this time India grabbed my wrist. When I wrenched it away, I hit the plate of crab cakes and sent it sliding across the table and crashing onto the patio. Silence fell among the other diners, and Frank's face blazed in gentlemanly embarrassment. India's blazed in anger.

"That is *just* enough, Allison," she said between her teeth. "We're here to keep you from wrecking your life."

"Wrecking my—"

"You have not one, not two, but three drug-addicted prostitutes living in your house *and* an at-risk kid. You've had the police over there. You're driving up and down West King Street at all hours of the night on that death trap you bought. It's not going to end well,

Allison, and we wouldn't be your brothers and sisters in Christ if we didn't tell you that."

I turned from her to Bonner. "Well, well," I said. "I guess you've been playing a lot of golf with Owen Schatz."

"None of this came from him, or from me," he said.

"Well, let's see. Since I walked in here, I've been blindsided, ridiculed, and patronized, so why should I be surprised that I'm now being lied to?"

"I'm telling you the truth!"

"He is," Frank said. "I got that information myself."

I whirled to face him. "How? How did you do that, Frank?"

"I hired someone."

He drew himself up with all the dignity of a plantation patriarch, but it didn't keep me from shaking my head at him and saying, "How dare you!"

India leaned across the table. "The fact that someone has been watching you without you even knowing it proves you're in way over your head."

"Are you done?" I said. "Because I am."

"No." Frank reached inside his suit coat and drew out a manila envelope. "We've put together some materials for you. Why don't you look them over, and then I'll be glad to—"

"Materials," I said. "My commitment papers?"

"Names and phone numbers for the various social services that can take care of the boy. Brochure for the St. John's rehab center and a check made out to them to get your people in. And a check for you." He had the gall to pat my hand. "We know you lost your job over this, and we thought you might need some help getting back on your feet."

"We care about you, Allison," India said. She had tears in her eyes now, and all I could think of was that the mascara soon would be trailing down the sides of her face.

"Too bad your paid snitch didn't work his way into my house somehow," I said to Frank as I pushed the envelope back into his hand, "because then you would also know that in there, three times a day, we pray together. Once a week we have a worship service and communion. Twice a week we've got Bible study going on. And every day—every day—we practice telling the truth and treating each other with respect and supporting each other in our decisions. You ought to stop in—you could all use some work in those areas." I stood up and shook my head. "Oh, wait—you wouldn't come in my house now, because it's full of people who've made huge, ugly mistakes, and even though they're repentant and forgiven—gosh—you might catch something from them. Like, I don't know, humility. Courage. Yeah, that would be a whole lot harder than sitting in a pew saying 'amen' and spying on your sister. Forget my invitation. Pharisees aren't welcome in our house."

When I left the Watchdogs this time, stitching my way among the tables of people pretending not to look at the woman who had just unloaded in the back corner, I wasn't heartbroken. That part of my grief was over. It was time to fire it up and move on down the road.

Still, I wrestled with a hideous mood all the next day and was still doing battle with it when I made my way through the hundreds, maybe thousands, of Harley riders to the Galleon on Friday morning. They were gathering for the Florida State HOG Rally—"Rendezvous With History," they called it. I had my own rendezvous with Hank, who saw my face when I walked in and said, "Patrice, we're going to need another cup of black coffee right after she finishes this one."

"Is it that obvious?" I said.

"You are the most transparent person I have ever known, and that is a compliment."

"You sure you want to hear all this stuff?"

"Oh, knock it off, Al. We've already established how we are with each other, and making sure you aren't too much for me isn't part of that. Come on, dish.

I did. She didn't have much to say about it because what was there to say? Her gaze sort of drifted over my head, and then she leaned across the table, voice low.

"I think the guy in the doorway is looking for you."

"Is it a cop?"

"No."

"Does he look like a private investigator?"

"I don't know. Does a PI wear Ray-Bans on black Croakies and dress like the cover of *GQ*?"

I turned around. Bonner stood just inside the doorway, looking miserable as a whipped dog.

"Oh, for Pete's sake come over here," I said. I looked at Hank. "Do you mind if *Bonner* joins us?"

"Wouldn't miss it," she said.

Bonner hesitated at the edge of the table, but I told him to sit down and introduced him to Hank.

"She's a friend," I said. "Whatever you need to say, you can say it in front of her."

"Or I can leave," Hank said, not too convincingly.

Bonner shook his head at her. "Looks like she's already told you—whatever."

"Coffee?" she said. "Muffin?"

He started to shake his head again but I said, "Order something. She won't leave you alone until you do."

"Just coffee," he said. "Black."

Hank rolled her eyes. "I can see why you two are friends."

"Are we?" Bonner said to me. "Are we still?"

"Correct me if I'm wrong, but I think you were there last night purely to make sure things didn't get out of hand. Which by the way you completely blew, but I'm not going to hold that against you. I guess it needed to happen."

"I told them I didn't think they should do it that way, but they knew you wouldn't come otherwise."

"And what about the content?" I said. "Did you agree with that?"

"Not entirely. I have a suggestion for you."

"Another welfare check?"

"No, just a thought. Do you want to hear it or not?"

I sat back and folded my arms. "Go for it," I said.

"I think what you're doing is good, I really do. I just wonder if it wouldn't be better, considering all that you're up against with your neighbors and for the sake of your own safety, if you rented a house for the women to live in, instead of having them live with you on Palm Row."

I looked at Hank, who appeared to be listening intently to Bonner. She nodded at me, and I told him to go on.

"I can help you find something reasonable, probably get you a good deal."

"Bonner's a real estate broker," I said to Hank.

"Ah. Well, listen, I've got to get going—I have a private lesson this morning—Al, talk to you later? And Bonner, it's been a pleasure. Really."

Bonner let out a sigh when she was gone.

"Did you think she was going to bite you?" I said.

"No—I'm just glad you have somebody like that as a friend. You've got to feel like India and Mary Alice have betrayed you."

I was surprised, and I felt bad that I was surprised. Bonner was a good man, and I'd lost sight of that. But there was one thing I had to know.

"Why are you making this offer, Bonner?" I said. "Be honest."

"It's partly because I want to see you be able to do what you think is right, even if I don't totally understand it. I certainly don't think it's *wrong*."

"And the other part?"

The tops of his cheeks reddened. "Ever since the first woman moved in—"

"Her name is Genevieve."

"Ever since Genevieve moved in, I haven't felt comfortable coming over and hanging out like I used to. I miss you."

He then gulped down half a mug of coffee, which, knowing how Patrice made the stuff, had to scald his throat, not to mention his esophagus. But it was his heart I was concerned about. It had taken a lot for him to admit that, just as it had been a huge thing for him to break ranks with the Watchdogs and make me this offer. I could return at least offer that much decency.

"I'm going to think about it," I said. "And I mean that."

I didn't have to think long. I was just finishing up Bible study with
the women Monday morning when a St. John's County sheriff's car
pulled up out front. It was as if they smelled it coming. Geneveve
ran upstairs, and Jasmine whimpered in the corner of the red chair.
Although Mercedes held her ground, she couldn't keep the fear out
of her voice as she cussed all law enforcement under her breath.

"Everybody just needs to cool their jets," I said as I headed for the
door. "He could just be collecting for a charity."

"You believe *that*?" she said.

"Okay, no. But whichever one of you is in trouble, we'll handle it."

The one who was in trouble was me, as I found out when I opened
the summons handed to me by the deputy with mirrored sunglasses
and a shaved head.

"If you'll sign here just to show you've been served," he said.

"I wouldn't sign nothing, Miss Angel," Mercedes whispered across
the room.

The deputy tried to look in, but I handed the paper back to him,
signed, and told him to have a nice day. Mine was going down the
tubes fast, and I didn't want it to get any worse.

"Would you go tell Geneveve she can relax?" I said to Mercedes
and Jasmine. "This is for me."

They didn't ask what it was about, though I was sure they would
have laughed when I told them Maizie J. Vernell of Number 1 Palm
Row had filed a formal lawsuit against Allison Chamberlain of Number
2 Palm Row for disturbing the peace and violating a zone law. That
wouldn't even sound like breaking the law to them. It didn't to me either.

But I knew it was serious. Miz Vernell had lived in St. Augustine all her life, and although she may have looked like a bag lady in her housecoats and fuzzy slippers, she had the kind of money and influence to make some judge take a second look at this. And I knew all too well where the power of that influence could land me. I'd seen my father exert it more than once.

I needed a lawyer, and I knew where to find one.

Chief came right over from the office that evening, on his Road King but wearing a suit. Once he sat down at the dining-room table with me, however, he was every bit the professional.

"They've got a case," he said when he'd looked over the summons. "You received an official warning, promised to keep the noise down, didn't, et cetera, et cetera." His lips twitched. "Now, this part about you bringing questionable people into the neighborhood, I'm a little offended by that."

I had to laugh. "Nah, she's got to be talking about Nita and Leighanne and Hank, don't you think?"

"That's got to be it." He smeared his hand over his mouth. "I don't think she'll get far with that part, but this other—the noise ordinance—you could have a problem there."

"So what do I do?"

He looked at me squarely. "*We* figure out a way to get this dropped, and the only way to do that is to show this Vernell woman that she has nothing further to worry about. How you're going to do that is—"

"I know how I *could* do that."

"And that is?"

"A realtor friend of mine suggested I rent a place for the women.

I could do the same things there that I do here, only it wouldn't—be here. He said he'd show me some properties, help me get a good deal." I yanked on my ponytail. "It's going to have to be a spectacular deal. Just the first and last month's rent and a cleaning deposit is going to make a significant dent in my savings, and I'd have to find another job to pay rent and utilities after that, which would mean I can't do all the things that are making this work in the first place."

"Look what you're doing, Classic," he said.

"What am I doing? I'm being realistic and practical."

"And you're getting way ahead of yourself. It's one ride at a time. You go as far as you can, you stop and fill up, you set out again. But if you slow down—"

"You lose momentum and balance and you fall over."

"That's it."

"So you think I should go for it? Find a rental?"

"Does it matter what I think?"

"Yeah," I said. "It does."

I expected the fatherly look, or another piece of Harley wisdom. What I saw in his eyes was something like gratitude, from one friend to another. The urge to hug his neck came on me wistfully. I was horrible with relationships with men—I'd given them up long ago. And this man belonged to a woman I deeply respected.

But if I weren't and if he didn't, I would have hugged him. And I could definitely picture how that would feel.

"So—you going to call him?"

"Who?" I said.

"Your realtor friend."

"Oh. Yeah. I think I have to."

He folded the summons and tucked it inside his suit coat. "I'll start working on this."

I groaned. "How much is this going to cost me?"

"Pro bono."

"No, Chief, you can't keep doing this for me."

"So I'm doing it for Desmond. That make you feel better?"

"Oh, you are good."

"That's why you hired me. I'll be in touch."

I had to fight back the need to say, "I hope so."

He was no sooner out the door when all three women were at the table with a bowl of popcorn and a liter of Coke and a stack of glasses.

"What's this?" I said.

"This is support," Geneveve said. "You give it to us all the time, so we need to be giving you some."

"And we know 'bout bein' in trouble with the law," Jasmine said.

"It's going to be okay. Chief's working on it and—"

I cut myself off. Now didn't seem like the time to tell them I was going to have to move them. We were definitely talking one ride at a time here.

"He just a lawyer," Mercedes said. "He ain't got no rap sheet."

"Well, no, probably not," I said. Though it struck me that I knew zilch about Chief's past.

"You need some advice from some people who been there," she said.

Geneveve put up a finger, and I noticed she actually had nails now. "Number one: Don't volunteer nothin' you don't have to. They might promise that's gonna help you, but they lyin' when they say that."

Jasmine nodded solemnly. "Number two: If you got to do any jail time, just keep your head down and don't talk to nobody. You can't trust nobody in there."

"Ladies, I doubt I'll be doing time—"

"And number three: Don't never look the judge in the eye, 'cause he think you bein' arrogant," Mercedes said. "I know that thing, now—you just keep your eyes to the floor no matter how much you want to tell that man he fulla … stuff."

I sat back and looked at them, passing the popcorn and the Coke and the hard-won wisdom. My heart was bursting.

"Thanks," I said. "I hate that you know this stuff, that you've had to live it, but, really, thank you for sharing."

"Ain't nothin' I don't know about it," Mercedes said.

Geneveve rolled her eyes, but I motioned for Mercedes to continue.

"Before I was twenty years old, I got picked up for possession so many times, and I'd do my time and go back out there and pick right up. And then this one time I got me a young judge thought he was gon' save the world one addict at a time."

"I never got that judge," Jasmine said ruefully.

"Instead a sendin' me to jail, he sentence me to rehab. And you know, it wasn't that bad."

Geneveve gave her a soft grunt.

"It wasn't," Mercedes said, voice shooting into space on the "wasn't." "Once I got clean, I thought I was cool 'cause, you know, that was always what I be lookin' for, to be cool."

"Mmm-hmm," Jasmine said.

The conversation was developing a rhythm, and I found myself moving with it.

"And me bein' cool was gettin' in the face of every addict that come in there acting the fool, like they was gonna get clean and make everybody think they was rehabilitated and then go right back out there and start usin' again. I'd get all *up* in they business."

"I *know* you did that," Geneveve said.

"When I completed that program, they asked me to come on staff."

"No they didn't!" Jasmine said.

"I ain't lyin' to you, girl. And you know what—I put all my energy into helpin' other addicts and I never did do nothin' to change myself. I was clean, but I still had all the hate and the disrespect for other people. I was still a punk. It was all about me and bein' cool."

"So what happened?" I said.

Mercedes spread out her hand. "I was clean for five years. And I got me a husband and I had my baby."

I froze.

"And then my husband, he start beatin' on me, and I couldn't handle it, so I started usin' again. 'Fore I knew it, he took my baby son away and divorced me, and I was down so far I just give up and went back out on the street." She tossed a handful of popcorn back into the bowl. "I been there ever since, thinkin' that was the only thing I could do since I had done lost everything. And then Geneveve, she come back tellin' me I might could have another chance."

"And you're going to have it, Mercedes," I said. "No matter what it takes."

Geneveve tilted her head. "Now I thought we was comin' in here to support you, and here we are runnin' our mouth 'bout our own stuff."

"It's my stuff too," I said.

They had absolutely no idea.

CHAPTER SEVENTEEN

I had never seen Bonner in his element before we went out Saturday to look at properties. For once his navy blue blazer and his khaki slacks and his shiny loafers didn't make him look like he was going off to prep school, and a sort of gentle confidence kicked in as he led me through three different properties in various parts of St. Augustine.

"Now this one has an open living space with a lot of natural light," he said, "which you and the women could use for your Bible studies and such."

About another he pointed out, "It has three bedrooms, which, granted, are small, but they could each have their own space, and I would think they'd like that."

The third had a great kitchen, in which he envisioned them, "doing communal meals, getting a sense of family. That's where families always end up anyway, in the kitchen. The rest of the house can be a pit, but as long as the kitchen's good, you've got something."

I was so enchanted by his presentation, I would have rented any one of them. The rent was also reasonable and the neighborhoods were perfect. The landlords, however, were another matter. All three were bothered by the idea of renting to a "group" rather than an actual intact family, and I wouldn't let Bonner represent it any other way. The only one who didn't seem to mind owned the fourth place Bonner took me to. A three-bedroom bungalow three blocks from West King Street.

"Granted, it's a fixer-upper," Bonner said as we walked through it.

"Fixer-upper? Whoever lived here last trashed the place."

There were fist-sized holes in several of the walls—the bathroom looked like it hadn't been cleaned since the first Bush administration—and the kitchen bore the faint odor of something that had died under the sink at one time.

"The landlord's willing to make improvements," Bonner said, "and utilities are included in the rent, which should help you out a lot."

I peered into the oven and closed it again. "It's the location I'm worried about, Bonner. It's too close to West King Street to suit me."

"I get that, I really do, but the neighborhood has street lights, and the police station's—what?—two blocks down."

"That's been such a crime deterrent in the past." I pressed my temples. "I'm sorry—you're right. This is the best deal we've seen yet."

"It's really the only deal, Allison."

"How much is the landlord willing to put into fixing it up?"

"I can find out."

"Okay, do. And I want Geneveve and Jasmine and Mercedes to see it. I can't just stick them someplace where they're not going to feel at home or they'll end up back on West King." I shuddered involuntarily. "That can't happen."

Bonner inspected the stovetop and frowned. "Have you told them about the move?"

"Yeah," I said.

"And?"

"I was actually surprised. They were just dumbfounded that I would trust them to live on their own—I felt like I was launching three teenage girls into the world." I considered that. "I guess, in a way, I am. That's about the time they all started using, so that's where they stopped growing."

"I'm hearing a 'but' in there," Bonner said.

"Yeah," I said. "The only objection they had was that some other house wasn't going to look like mine inside. I was amazed that they even noticed things like curtains and throw pillows."

"So why can't they pick out their own curtains and throw pillows?" Bonner shrugged. "No reason they can't decide on the paint colors too. I doubt this landlord is going to care."

"Seriously?"

"It might not be what you or I would choose, but you want it to be their house, right?"

"That's all going to be included in the cost?" I said.

Bonner closed his folder and gave it a tap. "Let me just see what I can do."

What he did was perform a miracle—and miracles, I learned, beget more miracles.

When Bonner said the landlord's budget covered materials but not labor, Chief assembled a crew of HOGs that put *Extreme Makeover: Home Edition* to shame. Who knew Stan dabbled in finish carpentry on the side, or that Ulysses could plumb with the best of them? And Kyle, the African-American who turned me on to the barber? Master electrician. The work they did on that house in a week was right up there with the loaves and fishes.

But Bonner walked on water when it came to the women.

Early in the week he brought over paint colors and fabric swatches for them to review at the dining-room table. I evidently hovered too much, because fifteen minutes in, he sent me to the kitchen to make tea. By then I was following Bonner's orders with no problem.

When I returned, I stopped in the doorway from the kitchen, and the tray tilted in my hand. Sylvia's teacups jittered. The sugar bowl slid into the creamer. But no one seemed to notice, because their heads were all bent over the paint chips Bonner had fanned out on the table. Geneveve held an array of blues like a hand of cards and studied it with the intensity of a poker pro. Jasmine touched each shade of pink with the ragged edge of her index fingernail and moved her lips without sound. Mercedes watched as Bonner placed a pale lavender next to an olive green and raised a questioning eyebrow at her. They were no longer prostitutes from West King Steet. They were three women choosing the colors of their lives.

Friday was painting day, and Chief's crew showed up in full force, but he still suggested that the women help paint their own rooms.

"I ain't never painted nothin' in my life," Jasmine said, shrinking back from the roller Nita put in front of her.

"I never rode a Harley till the day I got on one," Nita said, in that marvelous, soft half–Penelope Cruz, half–Dolly Parton voice. "You never know what you can do until you try."

They quickly ran out of ladders, so I drove home in the van to pick one up. While I was there I stopped by the kitchen to grab some snacks for the paint crew—which was when a wave of homesickness swept over me.

Something was about to be removed from this house. The constant aroma of popcorn. The bickering and bantering of female voices. The sassy retorts of a young male. The concern, the confusion, the confession. It was all going to leave with them, and I was missing it already.

I got out of there before I could change my mind.

Back at the house Bonner had arrived in a getup that was, by his standards, grungy, and he was waiting to unload the ladder from my van. Something besides the clothes had changed, and I knew what it was when he said, "They're going to be so happy here, Allison." His focus had shifted from doing this for me, to doing it for them, and maybe even for him. It made me say what popped from my mouth.

"When we're done today, what do you say I take you for a ride on my bike?"

He laughed.

"I'm serious. You'd love it. And for once you're not dressed like the Fortune 500, so we could totally make it work."

"I don't think so," he said, though his eyes were glowing green. "Not my thing."

"You're scared, aren'tcha?"

"Yeah, just like you should be. Haven't we had this conversation about twelve times?"

"I'll get you on it yet," I said.

It wasn't until he carried the ladder into the house that I realized Chief was standing a few yards away, fiddling with the hose.

"I'm not trying to be a jerk," he said. "But I don't think that's such a good idea."

"What?"

"Carrying him as a passenger."

"And that would be because …"

"Because he's heavier than Desmond or Geneveve or any of the women, and I don't think he could just go with it like they do."

"Okay," I said. "You're my Riding Guide."

"I'm not trying to be a jerk," he said again.

"You're not."

He looked at me for a moment longer, as if to be sure we were clear on the jerkhood thing. I felt a major need to change the subject.

"Have you seen Desmond?" I said.

"He's sitting on my bike, drawing a picture."

"You're trusting."

"Am I? He knows the rules."

"Uh-huh, but lately he's been regressing. Started cussing under his breath again. Messing around at the dinner table."

"Sounds like he's twelve."

"This morning I caught him going through my purse—which he didn't stop doing when he heard me coming—which I know he did because he has the auditory acuity of a bat."

"He's got a big change coming up."

"Yeah—he's not going to have me in his face twenty-four-seven."

"Then there you go," Chief said, and went inside.

I noticed after he left that he hadn't done a single thing with the hose.

🏍️

Saturday and Sunday, everything kicked into high gear. Curtains went up. Rugs were rolled out. Dead bolts were installed on the doors. Furniture arrived in pickup trucks and vans, the fruits of our trips to the flea market and the radio station's free Swap 'n' Shop and the

HOGs cleaning out of their garages and attics. The kitchen was stocked with food, the bathrooms with toiletries, the linen closet with towels and sheets and blankets. I had no idea where it all came from, but somebody had cast out nets, and I could hardly handle the holiness.

Early Sunday afternoon, as we were putting on the finishing touches, Desmond found me organizing the spices in the kitchen.

"Somebody just pull up in a *nice* ve-hicle," he said.

I looked down from the stepladder. "It's not a Miata, is it?"

He shook his head. There was something strange in the hang of his shoulders, as if he were trying to avoid a wasp sting.

"What's going on, Clarence?" I said.

"I don't like her."

"Who?"

"That woman drivin' that Lexus."

"Is she wielding a weapon? Handing out citations? What's the deal?"

"She just act like she smell something bad. I don't like her."

I sighed and came down from the ladder. "Do you want me to go see what she wants? Is that what it is?"

He shrugged, but that was evidently exactly what he wanted. This was strange behavior, even for him.

The crew putting pine needles around the azaleas out front were also looking suspicious as I came out and shaded my eyes to get a view of the woman leaning against a white Lexus and curling her upper lip as if she were, indeed, smelling something rancid. I'd seen that disdainful look before, in the back of my carriage, the day I took the detour down West King Street. I'd have known that Stress Queen posture anywhere.

I marched down the steps and met her halfway across the yard. She replaced the sneer with a smile that was high-end plastic.

"Vivienne Harkness," she said. "You must be Allison Chamberlain."

"And you must be Troy Irwin's lackey," I said.

She blinked behind rectangular black-framed glasses she hadn't been wearing that day. These apparently went with her current outfit.

"We've met before," I said.

She still didn't appear to recognize me, so I moved on. "And to what do we owe the honor?"

"We were just curious what's going on. This is a lot of upgrade for this neighborhood."

"And you care about that because …"

She nodded as if my attitude came as no surprise to her. "Like I said, we're just curious."

"Who are 'we'?"

"Those of us associated with Chamberlain Enterprises."

She flipped out a business card from somewhere and held it out to me. I ignored it.

"You of all people should know we like to keep our finger on the pulse of what's going on in the community," she said.

"Don't be misled by my name," I said. "I know nothing about what Chamberlain does and does not have its fingers on, and I'd like to keep it that way."

Once again she seemed unsurprised. Which made me wonder: If she somehow knew what to expect when she came, why was she here? I wasn't buying Chamberlain's concern for the city's heartbeat. The only life Troy Irwin cared about was his own.

"So," she said. "What *is* happening here? I'm fascinated."

"We're helping some people out," I said. "I guess you *would* find that fascinating—if not somewhat odd, yes?"

That one did seem to be outside the expected responses. She downgraded the plastic smile and took a step backward.

"I'll just let you get back to it, Allison," she said. "Maybe we can chat another time."

"Yeah," I said. "Have your people call my people, so I can tell them where to go too."

She drove off with an unnecessary squeal of tires. I was still coming down when I felt Hank at my side.

"Well," she said. "Miss Giorgio Armani certainly brought out your fangs.'"

I looked around warily. "You don't think Desmond heard that, do you?"

"He wouldn't have understood it if he did."

"I still shouldn't have said it. I can almost hear Sylvia saying, 'Now—was that the Christian attitude?'"

"So you screw up now and then. You okay?"

I stared out at the now empty street. "I have a bad feeling. A really bad feeling."

"Can you shake it for the ceremony?" she said. "Everything's ready."

When I turned to look at the little house, I didn't have to shake Vivienne Harkness off of me. She and everything she stood for fell away as I marveled at our finished product.

Shiny blue shutters against a fresh coat of white paint. Ruffled curtains and flower-filled window boxes framing bright, clear windows. Pots of geraniums and sink-into chairs on a front porch that said "Welcome" every bit as much as mine did.

As I stood there with home welling up in my throat, the red front door opened, and people began to file out. Chief and the HOGs and the NA supporters. Bonner and the locksmith and paint-spattered people I barely knew. And behind them, Jasmine and Geneveve and Mercedes, tugging Desmond by his puppy-paw hand.

Hank faced the house and held out her arms to it, suddenly seeming tall.

"Peace be to this place and all who dwell in it," she said.

She nodded to me, and I pulled three keys from my pockets, each attached to an initialed key chain. Hank beckoned Jasmine and Mercedes and Geneveve to stand before her.

"You've unlocked the doors that have kept you imprisoned," she said. "Now you can unlock the doors that welcome you home."

I pressed a key into Jasmine's hands, and one into Mercedes's, whispering "welcome home" to each. When I got to Geneveve, my throat closed. She was half a person more than she was the first night Mercedes pulled her out of the Magic Moment. The flesh on her cheeks had rounded out, and her body had taken on a firm, healthy layer. Her black hair pulled back from her forehead revealed a heart-shaped face, sweet as a child's. Yet the shame remained in her eyes, guarded by the smile, kept at bay by the tilt of her chin, but still holding onto her spirit.

I moved closer until my lips almost brushed her ear. "The more you've sinned, the more you're forgiven," I whispered. "I know, Geneveve."

She closed her eyes and whispered back, "Amen."

I stepped back, and Hank went to each of them in turn, placing her palms on their heads and saying, "May God the Son who sanctified a home at Nazareth fill you with love. Amen.'" Then raising her face to the circle formed around us, she cried, "The peace of the Lord be always with you!"

"And also with you!" the women replied.

Their arms flew out and embraced bodies—their lips brushed cheeks—their thank-you's filled the air with their contagious rhythm. If any Harley rider or NA sponsor or recruited stranger minded, no one let on. They turned to each other and passed a peace I was sure was heard in heaven. We were a veritable *agape* feast—and my spiritual high couldn't have been higher.

Bonner was in the thick of it when he put his arms around my waist and lifted me off the ground. "I get it, Allison," he said into my ear. "God bless you." He knew just when to let me go and turn to the next celebrant who had a hug ready. Holy mackerel.

I was still reeling from that when Chief was suddenly next to me, his hands spaded into his back pockets.

"The peace of the Lord, Chief," I said.

"What's my next line?" His voice had no edge of sarcasm. It sounded like a genuine question.

"It's not written in stone," I said. "Whatever you're moved to say."

He gazed off somewhere between the roof and the tops of the mimosa trees. "I can't say I ever felt any peace from the Lord. No offense."

"None taken," I said.

"Chief," Hank said from the middle of a nearby group hug. "I need everybody's attention."

He put his fingers between his lips and let out one of those whistles I'd tried a hundred times to accomplish and never could. Heads turned, and he pointed to Hank.

"The ladies would like us to see their rooms," she said.

We re-gathered in the house, and the women shyly but proudly allowed us to peek at the lavender swags and pink pillowcases and olive and blue bath towels that made up their decor. Food came next, a banquet of lasagna and Caesar salad and crusty warm loaves of French bread. Impassioned sparkling cider toasts went on until dusk began to settle in and with it a cozy fog. By the time everyone but Hank and Chief, the women, Desmond, and myself had left, we had the kitchen cleaned up. There was no reason to stay, yet I couldn't seem to make my way to the front door.

"We been talkin'," Geneveve said from the only slightly worse-for-wear chair-and-a-half Rex had delighted her with. "And we was wonderin' if we could do communion."

"I know we been blessed and all that," Mercedes said, "but we need us some body of Christ."

The high that couldn't get higher, did.

Bread was found and blessed alongside the cider, and we *all* got us some body of Christ. "That's what I call a sacrament," Hank said when we'd ended in thanks.

"I wanna make that the name of the house."

We looked at Geneveve.

"The Sacrament House," she said.

I looked around. "What do the other residents think?" I said— and realized that Desmond wasn't with us.

I looked up at Chief, who pointed toward the room off the kitchen.

"No way he's doing his laundry," I said out of the side of my mouth.

"That's his bedroom," Chief said out the side of his.

I left Hank giving a lesson on sacraments and went to the doorway between the kitchen and the laundry room.

Somebody had shoved a cot between the washer and dryer, where the kid was going to have nightmares about his head being caught in the spin cycle. A mesh laundry bag hung from the ceiling in the middle of the cubicle-of-a-room with a few of Desmond's clothes stuffed into it. A sign saying KEEP OUT, drawn in his inimitable style, was taped to the door. But he was going to have less privacy here than he'd had at the last crack house he'd paused in with his mother.

Even as I stood there imagining his easy escape out the back door, a bottle of fabric softener tumbled from the shelf above the washer and landed in the middle of his pillow. I reached up and pulled the bag from the ceiling, and hoisting it over my shoulder, went to the back door. Desmond was slumped over on the stoop, his motorcycle helmet hugged to his chest.

"I've got bad news for you, Desmond," I said. I dropped down beside him.

"You takin' my helmet?" he said.

"Why would I do that? Have you done something I don't know about?"

He gave his head only half a shake, eyes still on the orange flames.

"You can't ride with me without it, and I don't see myself riding alone all the time."

"You gonna forget about me. Which—hey—it's all good—"

"You're pretty hard to forget when you're under my feet every minute. I told you I had bad news?"

"What?"

"You're coming home with me."

His head jerked up and the helmet took a precarious roll toward the ground before he caught it.

"To stay?" he said.

"For now—until your mom really gets on her feet." Something struck me and I backpedaled. "I have to ask her about this, of course—"

"She ain't gonna care."

I started to assure him that she actually did, but his eyes were sparkling as if her neglect of him was the best thing he had going for him.

"I'm going to ask her anyway," I said.

His eyes continued to glow, even as he pulled his eyebrows together and started a litany of reasons why continuing to live with me was going to cramp his style like milk of magnesia. I left him gathering his drawing supplies and went to find Geneveve in her room.

"I won't do it if you want him here with you," I told her.

The shame lost some of its guard. "I ain't ready to take care of him, Miss Angel. I can't hardly take care of myself yet. I don't even know am I ready to live in this house without you remindin' me to say my prayers and brush my teeth."

"I don't think any of us know whether we're ready for the next step until we take it," I said. "It's always a leap of faith. But, Gen, there are leaps of faith and there are just plain ridiculous jumps everybody knows aren't going to end well."

Her forehead worked to sort that out. "So me livin' here is a leap of faith. Me tryin' to take care of my son right now—that's a jump gonna land us both on our face."

"Yeah," I said.

As I left her crying softly in her new room, I wondered whether I myself was taking a faith leap or a suicide jump. Only Desmond standing in the middle of the tiny living room, announcing that he hated to leave these fine women but he needed way more space—only that made me take in a breath and say my good-byes and usher him out to the Harley.

"One ride at a time," I whispered as I fired up the engine. To Desmond, I said, "Okay, let's go home."

It was our best ride yet.

CHAPTER EIGHTEEN

I had obviously never been on a honeymoon, but there were moments during the next two weeks when I thought I knew what it must feel like. A little bliss. A little insight. A little escape from all that couldn't wait to say, "Okay, enough with the fairy tale. When are you going to see that this isn't going to work?"

There was the moment at the outlet mall where each of the women had forty dollars to spend however they wanted. While Jasmine and Mercedes plowed through the sale table at T.J. Maxx, Geneveve stood smiling like she knew a secret.

"Whatcha thinkin', Gen?" I said.

"I'm thinkin' I'm at Disneyland, Miss Angel."

"You're going to have to explain that one to me."

"Here I am, out here in public—and I don't got to worry is that security guard over there gonna arrest me for bein' here. If I hear a siren, I know it ain't comin' for me." She went back to the enigmatic smile. "I ain't never been free before, and I'm just enjoyin' it."

Another moment came when they posted the chore chart I helped them make, and Jasmine burst into tears.

"You cryin' again, girl?" Mercedes said. "I ain't never seen a person cry so much."

"Those are happy tears," Geneveve said.

Jasmine nodded.

"You happy about *chores*?" Mercedes said.

"I get to wash the windows."

I grunted. "Now *there's* something to celebrate."

Jasmine shook her head. "You don't understand. For the past five years since I started hookin' to score drugs, I been feelin' like I'm lookin' through a dirty windshield. I couldn't see nothin, and I had to let somebody else drive."

"You're a poet, Jasmine," I said.

"I don't know 'bout that. But I'ma keep these windows *clean* so we can always see."

"Five years is a long time not to be able to see," I said.

Jasmine cut her eyes away. "It's been way longer than that. I was five years old when my grandmama give me whiskey."

No one else looked as dumfounded as I was, which was probably why she went on.

"She took care of me and all my sisters and brothers and cousins, and she'd give us all booze so we'd take a nap and get outta her hair. I was the one everybody picked on, and when I'd come cryin' to her—"

"So you've always been cryin'," Mercedes said. She slapped the hand Geneveve held out to her.

"She give me a little nip of whatever she was drinkin' to make me feel better. I came up thinkin' relief was just a swallow away—and I couldn't handle nothin' without 'help.'"

"I hear that," Geneveve said.

Jasmine bit down on her lip. "I'm ashamed to talk about all my stupid stuff."

"You already done admitted in a roomful of people that you let addiction take over your whole life," Mercedes said. "It don't get no stupider than that, so what you got to lose?"

And I thought *I* was blunt.

Jasmine still waited for me to nod her on before she continued. "I got me a lotta 'help' in middle school when I discovered pot. I didn't actually start usin' meth till I left home when I was seventeen. If you could call it home."

"I know that too," Mercedes said.

"I had so many 'stepfathers'—my mama never did marry none of them—and some of them abused me, only I didn't even know it was abuse. I just knew I couldn't stand it, so I did the drugs to keep it from hurtin'."

I didn't want to look at Mercedes. I somehow knew she'd be nodding in empathy.

"Them drugs, they turned me into somebody else," Jasmine said. "And that person kept choosin' to use. And there wasn't no rehab or jail could stop me, 'specially when my relatives stopped bailin' me out. They was all drunks and users, but, like we learn in NA, *I* had the disease."

Jasmine caught her breath, as if this was the most she'd ever spoken at one time in her life. Or the most anyone had ever listened. I thought she was finished, but she looked at Mercedes and said, "You the first person ever looked out for me."

"I didn't give you nothin' you needed," Mercedes said, though she couldn't hide the pleasure-flush in her cheeks.

"You didn't do it all the time—you had your own problems."

"You know I did."

Jasmine turned to me. "But if I was gettin' in trouble, she be the one to hide me. There always be somethin' real in Mercedes."

"You lyin', girlfriend," Mercedes said. "You didn't trust me—you didn't trust nobody. None of us did."

Jasmine shook her head. "But sometimes I didn't know what else to do but follow you—even if you was headin' off a cliff. So—" her eyes filled again—"I followed her to your house, Miss Angel."

That moment alone could have carried me for a week, but it didn't have to. I had the day they all got ID cards and gazed at them as if at last they had proof they were people. The morning Hank asked them to prepare the elements for her to consecrate for communion and they handled the bread and juice like Old Testament priests. The afternoon they took a peek outside themselves and complimented me on my eyebrows.

"Yeah, I'm pretty faithful with the tweezers," I told them. "I figure it's the cheapest way to keep from looking like I live hand to mouth."

Yet when Desmond said to me later, "You used to be rich, didn't you, Big Al?" I said in all sincerity, "I've never been as rich as I am right now."

We all needed those moments to shore up the hours when Geneveve's blood tests came in from the free clinic—thanks for being on top of it, people—and she had to go on major antibiotics for chlamydia. When Mercedes pitched one of her signature fits because Geneveve didn't do her dishes and it escalated into a two-day offensive. When Jasmine had to call Nita in the middle of the night to talk her down from the crazy tree.

Those were the times I was reminded how close they still were to West King Street, literally and figuratively—and never more so than the Thursday afternoon I dropped by and found them with a male visitor in the kitchen hocking down a turkey sandwich like he hadn't eaten in days, which, going by the way his wrists bones stuck out and his eyes sunk in, he hadn't. A colorless woman sat next to him, arms flung across the table, facedown between them in a puddle of murky drool. I knew the look of passed out versus sleeping. She was the former.

Mercedes was immediately on the defensive. "This wasn't my idea. I told them, 'Don't you give him none of the food that people meant for us.'"

"They was starvin'," Jasmine said. "How many times did *you* go beggin' for your breakfast?"

"Sherry ain't starvin'—least not for food. We don't need that here."

Geneveve put herself between the two of them. "We didn't know what to do."

"*I* knew," Mercedes said, jaw set.

"Yeah, you knew," Jasmine said. "You knew nothin'."

"Okay, okay." I put my fingers to my temples as I found myself doing at least ten times a day. "We're going to have to sort this out. Let's start by giving your friends a to-go bag, all right?"

"Ain't no friends a mine," Mercedes muttered.

"Huh. Everybody was your friend when you needed a fix," Jasmine said. "Now you all particular when somebody need somethin' from *you*."

"Stop!" Even I was startled by the sternness in Geneveve's voice. "We got to figure this out together, now."

Mercedes snapped her arms into a fold. Jasmine choked back tears. I held up both hands and said, "I'm just here to moderate."

One more thing I'd never been very good at. One more thing I was Nudged to do.

I told Chief about it when he came by that evening to deliver a pair of riding gloves someone had donated for Desmond, and lingered at the side door until I offered him a Coke. As always, I asked him where

Hank was, and he told me she was "somewhere doing something," so I decided it was okay. And then I told myself I was ridiculous for even thinking about it.

"What'd they come up with?" he said.

Thank goodness one of us could stay focused for seven seconds. "Oh, about the homeless couple?" I put the iced soda in front of him on the bistro table. "There really wasn't a simple answer. I tell them it's the Jesus thing to do to feed the hungry, but then there's the question: Do you feed everybody or just the people you think are going to change if you do? And are you taking a chance by feeding people who might drag you back to where you came from?"

"No rule about it in the Bible, huh?"

Again I looked for cynicism, and again, I just found curiosity.

"It *sounds* like there is when you read the gospels. Everybody who came to Jesus hungry, he fed. Maybe 'came to Jesus' is the operative phrase. I don't think this guy today was coming for spiritual food— and yet Geneveve and them weren't really after that either when they came to me. At least not that they were aware of." I squinted at Chief. "Did I just talk myself around in a circle?"

"I wouldn't use that argument with a jury. How did these people find the place, anyway?"

"That's what I asked the women, and all three of them swore they haven't had any contact with anybody from the old neighborhood. The thing is—but I didn't say this to them—I'm afraid they're going to come back with half the homeless on West King, and we're going to have to open up a soup kitchen."

Chief took a long drag of his Coke. "I don't think it's wise to diversify too much at this point."

"I was just kidding."

"Were you?" Those eagle eyes looked past my laughter. "You didn't say, 'We're going to have to call the cops to keep them away from the house.' You went immediately for, 'How are we going to feed all these people?'" He picked up the glass again. "I think you just answered your own question."

"Okay, I have to do something, but it can't be at Sacrament House. So—what? Do I do it someplace else? I can hardly handle what I'm already dealing with."

"Get somebody else to do it. You're good at that."

"Have we *met*?" I said.

"Did you fix that house up by yourself? Invent Narcotics Anonymous? Deck Desmond out in a full wardrobe?"

"Okay—I get the point. So do I just walk up to somebody and say, 'You ought to start a homeless shelter. If I can take in prostitutes, surely you can put up a few bums in your guest room.'"

"The way you go after people, yeah, somebody would probably do it." I saw Chief's eyes twinkle before he pulled out his cell phone.

"Who are you calling?" I said.

"Nobody. I'm checking my calendar."

"For …"

"You got all those people working on the house how?"

"I don't know. We started doing it, and people just kind of showed up. I like to think they caught what the Holy Spirit was doing—which I know totally turns you off, but it's—"

"November twenty-seventh. A week from this Saturday."

"What's happening that day?"

"We'll be feeding the homeless in the plaza."

"We."

"You and I and whoever else jumps in."

"And what are we feeding them?"

"Whatever we can get donated. Bagels. Coffee. Some fruit."

"Is that, like, legal? I mean, how do we make sure we're not breaking some city ordinance, which I am apparently very good at."

"Classic."

"What? Oh—yeah—duh. Why do I keep forgetting you're an attorney? I think it's the ponytail."

"There are a couple of judges that don't like it that much either."

"I didn't say I didn't like it. It's—I don't know—it's classy, it's you...."

It's time to shut up.

I went to the junk drawer and grabbed pad and pen. When I came back to the bistro table, Chief was making notes on his phone.

"I'll take care of the permits," he said. "Hank'll probably help get donations. If it's about food, she's all over it. Woman never met a sauce she didn't like."

Hank. Yes. Keep remembering Hank.

"What do you want me to do?" I said.

"We need to get people there."

"So—I send out an email to the homeless?"

"Cute. Anybody who's hungry will find us. We want to get the word out to the people we want to pass this job onto."

"Fliers," I said. "How cool would it be to put one of Desmond's drawings on it?"

"Very cool."

"So the twenty-seventh. That gives us …" I looked at the calendar on the refrigerator and frowned. "Did you realize that's Thanksgiving weekend?"

"That's why I picked it. This place will be packed with people looking for ways to show how grateful they are for what they have. We need to get them before that dries up and they start Christmas shopping."

I did catch the cynicism this time, but I had to admit I shared it.

"I'm still not seeing exactly what this is going to look like," I said.

"It's going to look like what it looks like," Chief said. "Is it on?"

I stared at the hand he held out for me to shake, and I only wanted mine in it if he wouldn't let go. I had to do something about this or I was going to make a major fool out of myself, lose two friendships.… "

I could have gone on, because that wasn't the Nudge talking, that was me.

I tapped his hand lightly and put on the best daughter-sister-buddy grin I could muster.

"Oh, it's on," I said. "It's definitely on."

But what was on the next morning at the Galleon would have to be me confessing to my friend that I was attracted to her man. I needed her to know that I wasn't going to do anything about it so she knew there was no need for concern.

Ugh. If it was going to sound as lame to her as it did in my head, maybe I should just get over myself and not say anything at all. Yeah. That was a better idea.

And then I walked in the door, and Hank looked up from her whipped cream and said, "Now if that isn't a cat-that-ate the-canary expression, I've never seen one." She nodded at the empty chair. "Come on into the confessional, Al. What's up?"

"I really like Chief," I said.

For Pete's sake, I sounded like a thirteen-year-old in the middle-school girls' restroom.

"He's good people," Hank said. "Sit down. I ordered you a muffin."

"No, I *really* like him." I dropped to the edge of the chair. "But I just want you to know that I'll deal with it, and I don't want it to come between you and me because for one of the few times in my life I have a friend I respect and trust. I don't know where I'd be if you hadn't come to my door and told me I could ride a Harley. Okay—I'm getting off track. I'm not going to try to take him from you. And I know I'll get over it."

Hank was staring at me blankly. "You're really bad at this, did you know that?"

"I've never had to do it before."

"No. I mean you're really bad at knowing a romantic relationship when you see one—and you're not seeing one."

"That's what I'm trying to say. I'm not going to pursue Chief like that."

"Neither am I." Her blank expression cracked into the grin she could no longer contain. "Al, I'm married. To Joe D'Angelo— whom you've never seen because he wouldn't go near a Harley if it were the last mode of transportation out of here in an evacuation. Chief is my riding buddy. That's it. There's nothing else to it. Zilch.

Nada." She raised her naked left hand. "I don't wear a ring because I 'outgrew' it."

The layers of things I'd just exposed about myself dropped on me one by one, and I just sat there under them. Hank's eyes were shining.

"So—you have a thing for the Chief. He's not seeing anybody."

"Tell anyone and I'll cut your heart out. It wouldn't go anywhere anyway."

"Why not? He's kind of a hunk."

"He's an old hunk—the man's got to be, what?"

"Sixty-two."

"He's almost as old as my father would be. And I know he doesn't feel anything for me *except* some kind of fatherly thing, so I don't need to get all strung out over something that's never going to happen. And besides all that, I stink at relationships with men—swore off them years ago—and there's no reason to think I'd be any better at them now. I have way too much to do anyway, so I don't have time to invest in somebody … would you please say something?"

"I was just waiting for you to finish talking yourself out of something you obviously want."

"I don't even know that I want it. Maybe I want what some people have, I guess—but that doesn't mean I'm ever going to get it."

"You don't think people have good relationships with their partners?"

"You probably do. I'm *sure* you do. I've just never seen it at close range."

"You're talking about your parents."

I grunted. "Now *there* were some role models for romance. Not that I saw much of them."

"You didn't go on vacations with them, that kind of thing?"

"I was seen with them only when it was important for me to be seen with them—and that became less and less important the more I developed a smart mouth." I looked at Hank's drooping eyes. "Don't start feeling sorry for me. It wasn't like in the movies where the little rich girl longs to be with her glamorous mother. Frankly I didn't find her all that interesting. I had Sylvia." I shook myself out. "How did I get off on that?"

"We were talking about you wanting a relationship with Chief and convincing yourself you aren't capable of having one."

"I'm not, Hank." An unexpected lump rose in my throat. "I feel like an idiot even telling you now."

"It stops with me. And for what it's worth, I think you are far from an idiot."

"It's worth a lot," I said. "You have no idea."

Hank brushed the crumbs from her hands. "Then let's get to work on this plaza project."

"Chief already told you? And you wonder why I thought you were living with the man."

She grinned and twisted in the chair. "So—Patrice. We have a proposition for you."

Fifteen minutes later the Spanish Galleon had agreed to donate twelve dozen bagels and ten dozen muffins in exchange for advertising on the flier that the Galleon was just a block from the plaza. And I was feeling less like the middle-schooler with the hopeless crush. Now that this plaza thing was real, I had to put my focus there.

Desmond tried to hide the fact that he was delighted to be asked to apply his artwork to the flier, but he was transparent as a piece of cellophane. He went immediately to "Mr. Shots'" house and came back an hour and a half later with several drawings for me to choose from. I chose the one picturing myriad hands, scanned it, and with him hanging over my shoulder like a persnickety boss, added the text.

"Dude, that is pro*fessional*," Desmond said.

"Not yet—I forgot to have you sign the graphic. We have to scan it again."

"You want me to sign it?"

It was one of those rare instants when he sounded like the child he was. I held my breath so it wouldn't go away. Which, of course, it did, when he said, "I'ma sign it 'Desi.' That's what the women call me."

"What women?"

"My women. At school." He patted his palm. "I got 'em right there, Big Al. Right there."

I made a mental note to ask Chief to talk to "Desi" about "women." For now I said, "Just so you know, I won't be calling you that. I am not, nor will I ever be, 'right here.'"

I tapped my own palm, and he slapped it happily.

"Ain't nobody got you right there, Big Al. Not Barnum and Bailey. Not Mr. Chief—"

"Barnum and Bailey? Are you talking about Bonner?"

"Dude with the sunglasses?"

"Yeah. Desmond, you are a trip."

He grinned his grin—and we were safely away from his rendition of the men in my life.

For the next five days, while Hank got together enough food for a football team and Chief did his attorney thing and procured the permits, the women of Sacrament House tried their luck at making cookies to contribute to the cause. Jasmine insisted her grandmother had taught her how, and I didn't inquire whether this was the same grandmother who'd filled her with Jack Daniels before she tucked her in. That became obvious anyway after the first few batches—which would have made excellent hockey pucks—but they continued to try.

Meanwhile Desmond and I went out on the Harley every day and distributed fliers. They went up in the windows of dry cleaners and T-shirt shops and bakeries in parts of the city Desmond said he'd never been to before. Like San Marco Avenue north of the historic district, where we stopped for a cupcake, and the southern strip of Avenida Menendez by the bay, where he feigned disinterest in the kids fishing off the wall, but couldn't take his eyes off of them. It never failed to sadden me that none of those places was more than a mile from where he grew up.

On Wednesday I looked at the map and saw that the only area we hadn't covered was the West King Street neighborhood. Chief said the hungry would smell the food and find it, but it still made sense to me to alert those whose noses might not be that keen, for various reasons. I thought about doing it before Desmond got home from school, but I knew there would be serious repercussions from that—a rip-off of my Godiva stash heading the list of possibilities. He'd been doing so well since the women left, and I didn't want to jar that. Still, I wasn't sure taking him back to his roots was such a good idea.

I arrived at a compromise.

"You can ride with me down to West King," I said. "But you can't get off the bike when I hand out the fliers. Are we clear?"

"What do I get if I'm good?" he said.

"You get me not ripping your nose hairs out with red-hot tweezers. And—we'll stop by and see your mom."

I watched his face as I put on my helmet. I'd been taking him to Sacrament House every other day to give Geneveve time with him, and so far he hadn't responded with anything other than a grunt or two. I didn't get much more than that now.

"They're making cookies over there," I said.

Desmond stopped with his own helmet halfway on. "She don't know nothin' 'bout cookin'."

"You've got a point there. But at least they're trying."

He gave another grunt and snapped his chinstrap.

"I'll take that as a 'good for them!'" I said. "Let's go deliver some fliers."

It was late afternoon, and now that we'd switched from Daylight Savings Time to Eastern Standard, the shadows were already making their ominous way across West King Street. It was still too early for the nightlife, so I didn't feel my usual uneasiness as we cruised in and stopped at the first still-viable place of business, C.A.R.S. Choice Auto Repair Service. I assumed—after I gave Desmond one last warning about staying on the bike and pushed through the smudgy glass door—that the ancient man behind the counter had come up with that clever acronym in his youth, some fifty years ago. The shop didn't appear to have been cleaned in that long, and for a moment after the bell on the door stopped half heartedly heralding my presence, I thought the old man had expired on his stool and no one had noticed yet.

But he adjusted thick glasses that had been polished about the same time the front windows were done and peered at me out of the tiniest eyes I had ever seen on a human being. With his gray hair slicked straight back from his forehead, he looked like an old mole.

"Hey there," I said. "Are you Mr. CARS?"

He remained grinless. "No. I'm Mr. Nelson."

The embroidery on his greasy shirt pocket said "Maharry," but I didn't argue with him. It would be easy to forget your name if nobody had said it in a while.

"I'm sorry, but we don't work on motorcycles," he said.

"Oh, I'm not here for a repair—although I do have a van that could use some work."

"We do vans."

I didn't ask who "we" were. So far there'd been no sign of another human being.

"I tell you what, if I promise to bring my van in next week, will you put this flier up for me?"

He eyed the paper in my hand. "What's it for?"

"We're feeding the homeless in the plaza on Saturday."

"Do I look homeless to you?"

I was almost startled into saying yes. "I'm sorry—I didn't make myself clear. I just hoped that as a businessman you'd be willing to post this in your window so your customers will know about it and come out and support the project."

"Support it how?"

I hadn't received this many questions anywhere else. Most of the shop owners had just told us to put it up there with the rest of the civic announcements.

"Um, sit down and share a bagel with them. Hear what they have to say. Find out how they can help them get off the streets."

"I'd like to get them off the streets." He wiped something wet from his weedy moustache with a slightly blackened rag. "Or at least out of my trash cans in the back. I call the cops, and sometimes they come, but they don't do anything about it."

"Then you should come to the plaza yourself, Mr. Nelson. Have a cup of coffee. Find out how they wound up without homes."

"I know how."

"Then you're a step ahead of the rest of us."

He narrowed the already minscule eyes at me until they all but disappeared into his head.

"It's Maharry," he said.

"I'm sorry?"

"Maharry Nelson. That's my name. And who are you?"

"Allison—just Allison."

"You with the city?"

"No."

"County?"

"No, sir."

"Some church?"

I stumbled, but shook my head.

"Then you must be all right. Give me the paper—give me a couple of them."

"You're a prince, Maharry," I said.

"You know why a lot of 'em's homeless, dontcha?"

I drew in a breath and wished I'd gotten out of there before we got into "because they're too lazy to work."

"They get in trouble once, and after that, nobody'll give them a chance again. I'd hire some of them, but nobody applies."

"Oh," I said. "Maybe you'll find an auto mechanic if you come."

"Is this some kinda job fair too?"

"It could be." I hadn't known it was going to be food for everyone and a chance to exchange ideas until I'd said it either. Chief was right. It was going to look like what it was going to look like.

"Well, I'll let you get back to work," I said.

And while we could both pretend he had work to get back to, I hurried out the front door. To find an empty Harley in the parking lot.

With visions of Geneveve thrown out with the garbage breaking their way into my head, I bolted for the driveway that ran beside C.A.R.S., already barking Desmond's name. The narrow passageway was empty, as was the stretch of parking lot on the other side of the building and the sidewalk beyond that cracked its way toward the hub of bars and street corner hangouts. *DearGoddearGoddearGod*—where was he?

I vacillated wildly between grabbing the phone to call Chief and taking off on the bike to find Desmond—which left me standing on the curb doing neither. *Okay—think like Desmond. What would he do if he got tired of sitting there waiting for me? Go across the street to Titus and try to finagle a tattoo? Slip down to the Magic Moment and beg for a beer? Go into a crack house and try to roll somebody?*

I couldn't picture any of that—because none of it was Desmond anymore, and I didn't know it until that moment. Which meant wherever he was, he hadn't gone there of his own will.

I groped for my phone in my bag, and then froze with my hand on it. A voice drifted from behind the building—a voice desperately trying to make "it's all good" sound convincing.

"I ain't playing with you, man," another voice said. Lower, like the growl of a Doberman on a chain. "You give her the message or I will find you and I will—"

"I don't live with her no more."

"You back with that white biker chick that tried to kill me with her—"

"They put me in foster care, dude. I don't know nothin' 'bout any of them."

I heard a long hiss as I made my way down the side of the building, my back to the wall. It was followed by a laugh that sounded more like a slap in the face.

"If you in foster care, what are you doin' down here?"

"I come down to see some ol' friends, bro."

The pause that followed was filled only with a sharp intake of breath I could hear from the corner of the building. I didn't dare peek around, but I knew it was Desmond, trying not to gasp out his fear.

"You don't got to grab me, bro," he said. His bravado was slipping away.

"I just want to make sure you hear me, 'cause next time it's gon' be Sultan hisself tellin' you—and you don't want that."

Before I could get my hand over my mouth to cover my own gasp, three things happened like rapid gunfire. A siren wailed into the alley behind the building, a hulking figure thundered past me and around the opposite corner into the darkness, and metal trash cans crashed to the beat of feet that were too big for somebody. Desmond ran headlong into me as he came around the corner. I clapped my hand over *his* mouth and half-dragged him up the driveway to the Harley.

"We'll walk it," I mouthed to him.

He nodded and helped me push the Classic silently out of the parking lot and a block up King before we got on and booked it all the way to Sacrament House.

I pulled up to the curb in front and let myself breathe. Desmond hadn't started to yet.

"I told you to stay on the bike," I said, still staring straight ahead.

"I did—till that jackal come up the street in his big ol' O'smobile, all lookin' out the window. I had to cut him off 'fore he saw the bike, 'cause he knows it."

"He could have killed you."

"Nah. He just wants me to be his little messenger nig—boy. And I ain't doin' it."

"So I heard. And just so you know, I didn't try to 'take him out' with my bike."

Desmond leaned back, head flopping. "Aw, man, I was hopin' he be tellin' the truth about that part."

"Okay, get off," I said.

He did. When I stood facing him, I put a hand on each shoulder and felt the tension in his bones.

"You need to tell me what the message was that Sultan wants you to give your mother."

Desmond's face darkened and he tried to squirm away but I tightened my grip.

"I have to know, Desmond. This person is threatening you—I can't just act like that's going to go away."

"He want her to come back, that's all I know."

"What's the deal with that? Does she have something of his? Does she owe him something? What's this hold that he has on her?"

"He owns her."

The hatred in his eyes transfigured the boy I tutored and nagged and made peanut butter sandwiches for into a thug every bit as intimidating as the bulky shadow I'd now encountered twice in an alley. It was all I could not to drop it right there and coax the boy out again.

"What do you mean he 'owns' her?" I said. "Nobody can 'own' another human being."

"You don't know. Somebody got enough power to make you turn into a animal—they own you."

I was chilled down to the sinew.

"I'm 'posed to tell her he said to come back 'cause she his property—and don't nobody steal his property."

"Was there a threat with it? Did he say what he'd do if she didn't?"

Desmond's eyes went into slits. "He don't have to say it. It's just there."

I let go of his shoulders and prayed, my hands against my lips. "Okay—so do I give her the message—"

"She already know the message," Desmond said.

But she didn't know that Desmond was now the one in danger if she didn't heed it. Would it do any good for her to know that? I was shaken by my own ignorance about things like this, things that kept coming up to grab me by the throat.

But Chief would know what to do. I'd managed to restrict our contact to phone calls all week, but I needed a face-to-face on this, and soon.

"Y'all comin' in?" Geneveve called from the front porch.

Desmond's eyes were still narrowed at me.

"We won't say anything for now," I whispered to him. "We'll just go in, maybe break a tooth on a cookie, and then we'll go home. Agreed?"

He all but dissolved into a relieved puddle on the sidewalk.

"We're coming," I called to Geneveve.

Desmond actually said hi to her and then blew by to follow the scent that actually did smell like warm peanut butter. It made me smile until I reached her and she latched onto my arm.

"Something wrong?" I said.

"I don't mean to criticize what you doin' with him," she said. "But why was he back in the neighborhood just now?"

"How did you—"

"I can smell it on him. Just like I can smell it on you."

I shoved my hands in my pockets so she wouldn't see them shaking. "We were just delivering some fliers, Gen."

"Maybe I don't got no right to say this, Miss Angel." I watched her swallow. "But I don't want him nowhere near that place."

"You have every right," I said. "You're his mother."

And for the first time, she was acting like one.

CHAPTER NINETEEN

The menu for our Thanksgiving dinner at my house would have impressed even my mother. The guest list, on the other hand, would have her rising from her coffin, waving the Confederate flag.

Jasmine, Mercedes, and Genevieve came over from Sacrament House, and Chief and Hank and the phantom husband, Joe, joined us. Desmond and I presided as host and hostess, although it was Hank and Joe who did most of the cooking. I'd never had spinach soufflé or pumpkin cheesecake, and they were divine.

"So have you always restricted your diet to junk food?" Hank asked me when we'd retired to the fireplace while Chief led the cleanup detail.

"No," I said. "My eating habits are another casualty of my upbringing. My parents were complete snobs about their cuts of meat and their imported cheeses, so naturally I went in the opposite direction."

"And cut off your nose to spite your face," Hank said. "I'd love to see you stop letting them limit your life—but that's just me. Personally I don't think there's a piece of bread on this earth that couldn't be improved by a pat of pure, organic butter and a little fresh garlic."

Food was also the order of the day on Saturday morning. Not long after the sun was up over the Bridge of Lions, we were in the plaza loading the tables in the pavilion at the far end of the park with piled-high platters of muffins and bagels and baskets overflowing with mangoes and bananas and Florida oranges. Hank barely had the cardboard carafes out of the back of her car when two men rolled out of the blankets in the gazebo and another crawled from under a pyracantha bush by the obelisk, eyes bloodshot but wide.

"Coffee, gentlemen?" she asked. "It's on the house this morning." She could have been Patrice the Hippie, ready to serve their table at the Galleon.

"That'd be nice," said the guy with the dog.

"And what do you take in that? Cream and sugar?"

"A little cream." He rubbed at his whiskers and smiled toothlessly. "Okay, a lotta cream."

"You got it."

By nine we'd served at least fifty people, not all of them from among the down-and-out. Several townies I recognized from the shops took part, as well as a handful of tourists. And Hank wasn't the only one who passed out the muffins and the java like she was waiting on St. Augustine's upper crust. Jasmine, Mercedes, Geneveve; Nita, Leighanne; Rex, for Pete's sake—their work put the team at the Café Alcazar to shame. But it was Desmond who enchanted me most.

He walked among the gathering crowd with a platter of bagels on his shoulder, stopping at the group gathered by the Civil War cannon, pausing on the steps of the gazebo, stepping over the pansy garden to get to a group seated on a blanket on the grass—all the while teasing out smiles with his running commentary.

"Bro, you just gonna eat one? You got to bulk up. It's cold out. Now that's what I'm talkin' about, see, she got one muffin to enjoy here and one to go. How 'bout you, Miss Thing, you too skinny now, you got to put some cream cheese on that."

He was audacious and charming and at times outrageous, particularly when he informed one man that he needed to put a lot of sugar in his coffee to sweeten himself up. I learned later that was his math teacher.

His interactions with the tattered, smelly, unshaven men showed him at his best. He sat next to each one and chatted about the dog or the guitar or whatever possession the man had managed to bring from his former life. He brought them seconds and thirds so they didn't have to go back to the table, and topped off their coffee without interrupting their conversations with each other.

"Look at him," I said to Chief. "I think he's actually having fun."

"Sure. He gets to be the one doing the handing out for a change."

"You really think that's it? Because you know, that would mean he doesn't have a personal agenda right now. I don't know if I've ever seen him without one."

That wasn't entirely true. There was the incident three days before, behind C.A.R.S., which, with all the Thanksgiving hoopla and today's deal, I hadn't had a chance to tell him about.

"We need to talk at some point," I said.

He was immediately eagle-eyeing me. "How about now?"

"Excuse me? Are you the one in charge of this?"

I turned from Chief to a fiftyish, white-haired woman whose maturing beauty was startling. Her well-matched man stood beside her with an Italian leather wallet in his hand. They had the aura of money.

"We are," I said, pointing to Chief, or at least where Chief had been seconds before.

"So if we wanted to donate to this, who would we make a check out to?" the woman said.

The man waited, Montblanc pen in hand.

"We aren't really an organization as such," I said. "I wouldn't know what to tell you."

"That's a shame," she said, "because this is the way it should be done."

"I mean, okay, it's a handout," the man said. "But you've got people counseling and talking about jobs."

"And that child—now he is darling."

The man clicked his pen. "Well, hey, let me just make a check out to you, and you can use it at your discretion. What's your name?"

"It's Allison Chamberlain, but—"

"Really." The woman's lovely eyebrows shot up. "Now it really impresses me that CE isn't linking their name with this for the PR."

"It shocks the *heck* out of me," the man said and added quickly, "I hope you don't take that the wrong way."

"There's only one way to take it," I said. "And just so you know, this project is in no way affiliated with Chamberlain Enterprises."

"Oh, is this where we give the money?" A large woman with a Mother Earth chest stuck a $10 bill between the couple. "I didn't see a place for donations."

"We aren't really taking any—"

"Then what's this about?"

That came from a thirty-ish guy with a sardonic mouth and a Bluetooth device in his ear. Middle management going for a CEO image.

"What's it about?" I shrugged. "It's about giving folks a chance to see that people who've had some bad breaks or made some bad choices are still people and could use a little food and a little support."

He lifted his chin in that I-know-and-you-don't way that always made me want to smack at it. "So this is just 'break a little bread with the homeless and feel better about yourself and go home.' I get that."

"No," I said, "you don't get it."

"So what's to get?"

"We're hoping somebody will step up to the plate and start something where people can be fed *and* helped to get back on their feet."

He actually rolled his eyes. "We've got social programs for that. These people aren't taking advantage of them because that would mean they'd actually have to do something with their lives besides stand around with their hands out."

With each supercilious syllable another hair rose on the back of my neck.

"What's your issue, dude?" somebody else said. "If you don't agree with what she's doing, go somewhere else. Here—I wanna give five bucks."

"Somebody give me a hat and we'll pass it—"

"Are you people serious? You don't know what's going to happen to that money. For all we know, this woman'll pocket it and run off to the Caymans."

"She's not even asking for money—"

"That's what she wants you to think—"

"Buddy, why don't you just take a bagel and—"

"Allison."

I turned gratefully to Hank, who had her lips to my ear.

"I think you should make a formal statement. From the gazebo—before this gets out of hand."

"I don't know what to say."

"When has that ever stopped you before?" she said.

We exchanged a long look that felt like a serious Nudge to me. I nodded.

"Chief," Hank said. "Allison needs everybody's attention."

He whistled and I was somehow ushered to the top step of the gazebo. When I looked down, the hundred or so people looking up to me merged in a blur of indecision. A few emerged with clarity. Bonner, fists pressed against his mouth, fighting me as if I were about to take a step too far. With him, India in huge sunglasses and a pashmina shawl over her head like she was going incognito.

"Preach it, sister," somebody said, and I knew, of course, that it was Ulysses.

"I'm not going to preach," I said, with a nod to him. "I just want to explain what we're about here."

I went over again what I'd said before, about offering food and support, about hoping someone would take what we had done and run with it.

"I already have a ministry with another segment of our population that needs to be heard and seen," I said. "We started with far less than this, so—"

"So this is a church thing," said the man who was becoming far more than a mere pain in the tail. His tone was belittling, the very set of his shoulders enough to make me pick up a bagel and hurl it at him. "That's what you religious types always do—act like you're just doing this out of the goodness of your hearts and then you sneak the Bible in there." He looked around with mock indignation. "What? No tracts to tell me what a sinner I am?"

"Who said anything about sinners?" I said. "We're not pointing a finger at anybody. We've all come up short—that's not the point."

"Then would you tell us what the point *is*?"

Why, oh why, was he still standing there heckling me?

Because he needs to hear what I have to say.

With the Pathetic Pleading Prayer barking from the back of my brain, I obeyed the Nudge.

"If you want a debate, you've come to the wrong place," I said to him. "God doesn't call me or any of us to 'debate' human suffering. We're called to relieve it." I found India and her pashima in the crowd. "If you want a sermon on what people have done to bring on their own poverty and homelessness, that's not what we're about, either. Look, we're just offering a blanket to somebody who's cold, water to someone who can't even speak because his throat's so parched, food to a man or woman whose pangs are more than hunger, but real pain." I looked at Bonner. "Maybe this sounds familiar to some of you. It's Jesus-talk—Jesus saying tend the sick, free those who are prisoners in their own minds—"

The Wannabe raised his arm and stabbed the air with his finger. "So take your salvation show down to West King Street. They're the ones to blame for the mess—"

"I told you—" I said. "I'm not going to argue over who's to blame. All I know is that what's happened on West King is a symptom of *all* of society's evils. You can go argue *why* with somebody else—but I'm telling you *we*"—I panned the smear of faces and saw a few more in high definition: Willie from the nursing home, Caroline in her Camelot Tours uniform—"can restore the neighborhood to its rightful owners. *We* can demand more police protection. *We* can run the evil out of there and make room for the good that's straining for life among *human* beings in community. And we can start with this—"

I closed my eyes and breathed in the words so I could breathe them out. "Every human being wants to be seen, really seen, by another human being, not as a statistic in some sociological study, not as a casualty of poverty, not as a victim of a corrupt social structure. We can start by seeing both what is and what can be. *That* is why we're in the plaza in the midst of the wealth and the history and the consumption. And if we don't start, I'm afraid for us all. For the safety of the sufferers, and the salvation of those who do nothing about it."

A sweet stillness hushed the crowd—broken by the slow, demeaning clapping of one man.

"Why are you still here?" the Mother Earth woman yelled at him.

"I've got as much right to speak out as she does."

"Y'all just don't pay any attention to him," someone else said. "Where's the hat? I didn't get to put anything in it."

Chief raised his motorcycle helmet over the crowd and several people reached for it, bills in hand. I leaned over the railing to Hank.

"What are we going to do with that money?" I said. "This is—"

"See? I told you this was a scam to raise money for—"

"You know what? I've had about enough of you...."

The voices rose to a pitch that rose further into somebody taking a swing at the heckler. The crowd swayed as if it were being knocked over as one. Women screamed, men shouted obscenities, and above it all I heard a whistle that didn't come from Chief.

Two city police officers cut through the crowd to the tangle on the ground, yelling for the fighters to break it up and the crowd to get back. I looked around wildly for Desmond and found him perched on a bench next to the guy with the dog, cheering like he had a front row seat at WrestleMania.

"Chief!" I said. "Can you get Desmond out of here?"

He handed me the overflowing helmet and headed across the park. By then the Sacrament women were huddled behind me with Hank, and the fight had been untangled. I took brief satisfaction in seeing that the troublemaker was dabbing a little blood from his upper lip. He wasn't going to make CEO if he showed up for work with a shiner.

I turned to my women. "Everybody okay?"

They only nodded, their gazes behind me and their faces deliberately blank. I'd seen that look before, so it didn't surprise me when I turned back around to see one of the police officers coming up to greet me.

"You Allison Chamberlain?" he said.

"Yes sir. Is everybody okay down there?"

"Yeah, listen, we're going to have to break up your meeting."

I glanced at my watch. "We have permission to be here until noon."

"That was before you went outside the boundaries of your permit, ma'am."

"What boundaries?"

"Your permit says you were going to give away food, that no money was to be exchanged."

"No money was."

He nodded at the money-stuffed helmet I was still clutching.

"This was collected by the people. I didn't ask for it."

"It's a separate permit to sell goods and services."

"I told you, I didn't 'sell' anything."

"Did you *promise* to sell anything? Some solicitation, maybe?"

I followed his gaze—to Jasmine and Mercedes and Geneveve.

"Hank," I said. "Go find Chief, would you?"

"If you're talking about Jack Ellington—ma'am, you don't need a lawyer. You're not under arrest. I'm just telling you that you have to break this up."

"And I'm just telling you that you are full of soup. I haven't breached any boundaries, and I certainly didn't bring these ladies here to 'solicit.' How dare you make that assumption? How *dare* you?"

"Allison, don't say another word."

Chief took the steps in one long lope and put his hand out to the cop, who had now been joined by his partner. They shook silently, as if a conversation were already going on.

"What's the problem?" Chief said.

"No problem. Y'all just need to knock off for the day."

"That *is* a problem!" I said. "We have a right to be here until noon and we're staying until noon—and I want an apology from you to these women or I am going to file a formal complaint against you. Then there really will be a problem."

The two officers gave each other the same look Heckler Boy had been giving me for the last hour.

"Girls," the first cop said, "my apologies. I didn't know you were off duty."

"Okay, that is *it.* Chief, do whatever you have to do to file a complaint for me. That is just unconscionable."

"Do what you gotta do," the cop said. "But right now you need to pack up and—"

"No," I said. "I'm not going anywhere." I sat down on the top step and stared across the park. What was left of the crowd had moved to the surrounding sidewalks. Traffic was almost at a standstill.

Chief leaned over me, mouth barely moving as he spoke. "You sure this is what you want to do? He can arrest you."

"Let him," I said.

"Ma'am, I'm going to ask you again—"

"Don't waste your breath," I said. "I'm staying until noon."

"All right then. You have the right to remain silent …"

"Good luck with that," I heard Chief mutter

While I was being Mirandized and handcuffed and looked at like a nutcase by the officer, Hank was having problems of her own. Geneveve was struggling to get past her, wrists out in a position that was disturbingly natural.

"If Miss Angel goin' to jail, I'm goin' with her!" she said.

"Geneveve, there is absolutely no point in that," Hank said.

Jasmine was, of course, crying. Mercedes brought her wrists together too.

"I ain't lettin' her go to no jail by herself," she said. "She don't know how to handle herself in there."

"I do," I said. "Don't you remember all that advice you gave me?"

I was trying to stay calm, which was hard with the officer's hard hand around my arm and the handcuffs cutting into my wrists. The one thing they hadn't told me was that those things hurt.

"I need you out here praying," I said to them. "You can't mess up everything you've started—this is my journey, okay?"

"I'll have her out in two hours," Chief said. "Hank, you want to see them back to the house?"

"What about Desmond?" I said as I was led down the steps.

"I've got the Desmond watch," Chief said. "He's right—"

The words died on his lips, and I saw a look cross his face that I could never have put there in my wildest imaginings. His color drained and his gaze darted from the cannon to the obelisk to the pavilion. I knew, because mine went with it.

"Where is he?" I said. "Where's Desmond?" I could hear the panic rising in my voice. "Okay, take these things off me. I'll leave the park. I have to find him."

"Too late, ma'am," the officer said. "You'll have to take it up with the judge now."

I tried to wrench my arm away but his grip was hard and frightening.

"Don't make it worse for yourself now," he said.

"Chief!"

He planted himself in front of us, hand up to the cop, who said, "One minute."

Chief put his face close to mine. "I'll find him—just go with them and keep your cool."

"I can't."

"Hey." His eyes grabbed mine and held on. "Do you trust me?"

DearGoddearGoddearGod, why did you let him ask me that question?

I didn't have time to wait for the answer. The officer was already motioning for Chief to step aside. I knew it anyway—it was the same answer I'd been given over and over for weeks. *You don't have a choice.*

"Yeah," I said. "I trust you."

Chief held my eyes for another second, before I was tugged away. It was long enough to see that I *had* had a choice. And that I'd made the right one.

But the rest of it, I thought, as they ducked my head into the back of the cruiser and closed me into a backseat I couldn't get out of—the rest of it I had blown somehow.

Otherwise why would I be going off to jail while Desmond was who knew where? I prayed *pleaseGodpleaseGodpleaseGod* until I couldn't pray anymore.

CHAPTER TWENTY

True to his word, Chief had me out within a few hours. I was never placed in a cell, though sitting in the sick-green hallway in handcuffs, on a bench with a drunk passed out on either side of me, I could hear the sounds of incarceration every time someone opened the metal door that led to them. Most were obscenities I hadn't heard even Desmond use, others were nonverbal expressions of mere frustration or just plain throwing up. Without ever seeing what was beyond that clanging door, I knew everything Jasmine and Mercedes and Geneveve had told me was true.

"Looks like I'll be able to handle this out of court," Chief said when we were safely out the front door of the police station. "You might have to eat a little crow."

"You didn't find Desmond."

Chief stopped, hand on one of two white columns. He didn't even have to shake his head. My fingers went straight to my temples.

"Hank checked your house," Chief said. "He didn't go to his mom's."

"Okay—will you take me to my bike so I can start looking? No—wait—we're only two blocks away. I'll just walk down there."

"Down where?"

I pointed west on King with one hand. The other one was covering my mouth—though *pleaseGodpleaseGodpleaseGod* was already moving my lips.

"I already did a drive-through while I was waiting for the paperwork," Chief said. "He's not anywhere obvious."

"Desmond's not going to *be* anywhere obvious! Okay. I'm just going—"

I bolted for the steps and ran into the arm Chief stuck in my path. He let me push it away, but the steam was seeping out of me.

"We've got to find him," I said.

"We will. It's still daylight."

"That doesn't make any difference. Last time it was four in the afternoon—"

"What last time?"

I hugged my arms around myself. "A couple of days ago—Wednesday, I guess it was ..."

I told him about the incident behind C.A.R.S. With each sentence his eyes grew harder and closer together.

"I was going to tell you—"

"Wish you had."

"All this stuff was going on ... but do you see why I'm freaking out here?"

He paused as a couple approached up the walkway, already looking at us as if there might be something to see here. "Come on," he said, "let's talk someplace else."

"We're wasting time!" I said.

The couple stared from the bottom step. Chief pressed his hand into the middle of my back and lowered his voice near my ear. "We're going to waste more if we don't have a plan. Let's go—I brought your helmet."

I got on the Road King behind him, and as we drove east, I wished my head could turn 360 degrees. I probed every parking lot and crosswalk and clump of tourists on the corners, searching for that pharaoh head atop a stick of a body, dying to hear "it's all good," praying for another chance to check his pockets for contraband candy

before I let him out of the house. When Chief pulled the bike up to a
bakery-coffee shop on Granada, I realized my fingers were curled into
the leather of his jacket

He turned his head, helmet tapping mine. "Classic," he said.

"Yeah?"

"It's not time to panic."

"And you're going to tell me when it is."

"You got it."

That was enough to get me seated at a table in a sunny corner
of the bakery with a cup of Earl Grey, but I was still scanning the
landscape through the window—the hedges around the museum, the
trails of visitors hurrying inside out of the wind that had picked up.

"I doubt he's hanging out at the Lightner," Chief said.

"What better place to scam a few tourists out of their money?"

"Do you really think that's what he's doing?"

"No. I don't know what to think."

"Try this." Chief cupped his big hands around his mug, smothering it from view. "He sees you get arrested; not a new scene for him,
except you're the one person who gives him stability, and if *you* can be
hauled off to jail, chances are he's next, so he splits."

"Is this supposed to be making me feel better?"

"Is it *about* you?"

I let my spoon fall onto the saucer. "I should have just done what
the cop said and gotten out of there. I wasn't even thinking about him
witnessing the whole thing."

"What did he witness?"

"Huh?"

"What did he see you do?"

"Why do I feel like I'm on the stand right now?"

"He saw you stand up for your rights, and his mother's rights. I don't think he's seen a lot of that in his life."

"It's not going to do him any good if he's dead in an alley."

"It doesn't sound like anybody's going to off Desmond. They're just trying to scare him into bringing Geneveve back. It wouldn't make any sense for them to take him out."

"You actually think any of this makes *sense*?"

"What people do almost always makes sense to them. It's my job to figure out how. It's what I do." He shook his head. "I'm not entirely convinced there's a connection between him running off today and what's happening with this Sultan character. Which is why it's not time to panic. I want to believe Desmond will get hungry and head for home—"

"Except that he doesn't know I'm not locked up. He thinks he's homeless again." My throat closed, and once more I put my hand over my mouth so I wouldn't wail.

"And where would he go if he needed a place to crash and score some food?" Chief said. "Not to his mother."

I shook my head. "In his mind it's all over. He'll think the whole safe-place-to-live thing was nice while it lasted and go looking for a drunk in a gutter to befriend."

"Or, come sundown, he'll go back to the safe place and wait."

"You think he has that much faith in it?"

"You're the expert on that."

"No. I'm not. And this is not the time to be pooh-poohing God when I need him the most, so just back off the cynicism."

I plunked my face into my hands, elbows on the table, which, of course, tilted, sending the tea cup sliding right into my lap. Lukewarm

Earl Grey splashed from my midriff to my knees and soaked miserably all the way to my skin. Face turned to the ceiling, I could feel the tears streaming into my ears—and I never cried. Ever.

Chief was on his feet, a wad of napkins in his hand. "Did it burn you?"

"No, it wasn't even hot. Look, I'm—"

"Come on. I'll take you home."

"We have to find Desmond."

"In wet clothes? You look like you didn't make it to the bathroom. Come on."

The temperature was a good sixty degrees, but between the wind and my damp lap and the wedge I'd just shoved between Chief and me, I was shivering when we got to Palm Row. I had to stop. My focus had to be on finding that kid.

"If you want to go in and get dried off, I'll put your helmet up," Chief said.

While he went toward the garage, I turned to the house, eyes sweeping the yard without a whole lot of hope. When a shadow crossed my path, I already had Desmond's name on my lips and my heart in my mouth, but it was Owen. It hadn't even occurred to me to call him—

"You lose somebody?" he said.

"Tell me he's with you," I said.

"He's not—"

My heart plummeted.

"I tried to get him to come over and wait with me, but he said he'd rather stay out there."

I pointed stupidly to the garage. He nodded.

"Owen," I said, "you are an angel from heaven."

I was still saying it as I tore back across the road and through the side door, where I skidded to a stop.

Before me stood Chief, taller than he'd been two minutes before, arms wrapped around a scrawny figure in a motorcycle helmet. Neither of them was saying a word as they rocked back and forth, Desmond's enormous feet dangling a foot from the ground. I wouldn't have spoken even if the lump in my throat had let me. I certainly didn't move, because the longer I watched Chief hug the boy, the more I felt him hugging me. This was as close as we were ever going to get to that, and I wanted it to last. For all of us.

When Chief finally set Desmond down, I rearranged my face and crossed to them.

"I knew the minute my back was turned you'd try to take off on my Harley," I said.

Desmond turned and grinned, though I could see him doing a little face-shifting of his own. If those were tears sparkling in his eyes, they weren't coming out if he could help it.

"I was just keepin' a eye on it for ya," he said.

"And a fine job you did."

He looked me over. "They didn't use no police brutality on you, did they?"

"Nah—it was a piece of cake. Speaking of which, anybody hungry?"

"No *doubt*," Desmond said. "You and me gotta talk about me havin' my own house key. I coulda starved to death out here."

"In your dreams, Clarence," I said. "Hey...." I heard my voice soften.

"You not gonna get all emo on me are ya?"

"Emo?"

"Yeah, all cryin' and huggin' my neck and sayin', 'Oh, my poor baby.'"

"Once again, in your dreams. I just wanted to say thanks for coming home."

Desmond pulled in his chin. "Where else I'm gonna go, Big Al?"

"Well, yeah," I said.

If I was ever going to "get all emo," that would've been the moment.

We called Hank to have her tell Geneveve her son had been found. I fed Desmond and hung out with him until he conked out on the couch in the den, while Chief went to the grocery and came back with everything Hank instructed him to buy so she could make some kind of amazing pasta thing that I shamelessly wolfed down. I was now wrapped in two blankets in the chair-and-a-half, listening to Chief's version of discovering Desmond in the garage.

"He was sitting there on the bike with his helmet on, just waiting for you."

"The kid's smart," Hank said. "He knows a die-hard biker will come back to her ride eventually."

"Either that or he was counting on me doing fifteen to twenty so he could take off with it."

Chief gave me an eagle look.

"No, I don't really think that. It's just hard for me to believe he trusts me."

"O ye of little faith," Hank said.

I made it a point not to look at Chief. After the way I spiritually mugged him in the bakery, I was surprised he was still here.

"Speaking of faith." Hank looked at Chief. "It might get a little religious here, just so you know."

"I'm good," he said.

She turned to me. "I know now what it is that's going on with you—the Nudges, the voice messages, the words coming out of your mouth that you didn't know were in your head."

"So I *am* crazy."

"Al, I'm serious."

I could see that she was, and my mouth went dry.

"It just hit me when you were standing up there in the park today. I've never heard you speak with that much passion before. I don't think you've heard yourself like that either."

"I haven't had time to think about it—what with being arrested and all." She frowned, and I shook my head. "Sorry. There's so much going on—it's hard for me not to run back to my shtick and hide."

"You can't hide from this," she said. "Allison, you are a prophet."

The room held its breath. Even Sylvia's German clock seemed to pause in its ticking, waiting for my response. In the pregnant stillness I could only shake my head again.

"I don't foresee things," I said.

"A prophet doesn't see the future. She sees the Word of God. She sees things exactly as they are now, and she knows what that's going to mean for the future."

"I see the obvious and that makes me a prophet?"

"It isn't obvious to everybody," Hank said, "although it should be."

"I don't think so." I shook my head again and felt my messy bun come undone. "You're talking Isaiah, Jeremiah—I'm not that caliber. I was falling all over myself up there today."

"What I heard was you speaking in the prophetic perfect tense."

"What?"

"You were speaking of things in the present tense as if they're already happening, but we heard it as the future tense."

I turned in desperation to Chief. "Okay, it's time for you to tell her this isn't making sense."

He shrugged. "What people say always makes sense to them."

"Hank—seriously—you don't know me that well. I am not prophet material. I'm not Isaiah going, 'Here I am. Use me.'"

"Really? Isn't that what you told me you prayed for seven years until God told you to buy a Harley?"

"But I was thinking he'd send me down to Ecuador real quick to do a little short-term mission trip or something. I'm not a good risk for something like this. I've never had a dream and followed it through. I've had no sense of direction. I've failed at just about everything I tried because I didn't really try."

Hank grinned. "I said you were a prophet, not a saint. Besides, I think those are all the very reasons God picked you. You're not all wrapped up in your own agenda, so you're free to adopt his. You don't know where you're going, so you might as well follow where he's taking you. You're afraid of success, so he gives you something that has nothing to do with succeeding." She held up both hands. "You're perfect for the job."

"'Prophet' is definitely not on my short list of possible careers."

Hank scooted to the edge of the couch and leaned toward me. "You *became* all the things you've said in the last two months before you ever said them. That's what a prophet does. You didn't choose this job—it chose you."

"And you're saying I don't have any choice but to keep doing it."

She sat back and said, "There you go."

"I don't know from prophets, obviously, but I do know this."

I looked at Chief, surprised he hadn't snuck out during that conversation just to get away from these two Jesus freaks.

"Speak to us, O Chief," Hank said, grinning.

He didn't grin back. "You made a lot of people uncomfortable in the park this morning. Five hundred dollars worth of uncomfortable." He pulled a bulky envelope out of his vest and dropped it on the coffee table trunk.

"That's what was in your helmet?" Hank said.

"Yep. Five big ones and change."

I pressed my palms together at my lips. "I need to pray about this."

"I'm going to leave you to it," Hank said. "Chief, don't feel like you have to run off just because I'm going."

I made a note to self: Knock Hank up the side of the head for that later.

She showed herself out, and Chief stood up.

"I'll leave the money for you," he said.

"I don't feel right doing anything with it," I said.

"Mind a suggestion?"

"Bring it."

He held his thumb and index finger close together. "You know we were this close to having to call the police if we hadn't found Desmond when we did."

"Yeah."

"And if *they* had found him, they would have either turned him over to his mother or put him in custody until they found a foster home. They wouldn't have given him to you—"

"Because I don't have legal guardianship," I finished for him.

"I think Geneveve would sign it over temporarily, and I'm happy to handle the paperwork for you, but there will still be court costs. If you want to go that route."

"I'll have to talk to her."

"Sure."

"Meanwhile—" I folded my arms uneasily across my chest— "could you put the money in an account or a fund or someplace until I can wrap my mind around this?"

"Around what?" he said. The twinkle was there in his eyes. "Being a mother?"

"Get out," I said cheerfully.

"Hey."

"What?"

"We did good today."

"Yeah, Chief," I said. "I guess at the end of the day, we did."

When he left, I leaned against the door and rolled the word *we* around in my head.

Chief called me early Monday morning to tell me he'd made an appointment for me with a woman I needed to see at FIP.

"Would her name be Elizabeth Doyle?" I said.

"Yeah, Liz Doyle. Do you know her?"

"Sort of."

"Is that problematic?"

No, it was just ironic. When Bonner had told me to go see her, I'd blown it off. Chief made the appointment for me and I had my lipstick on and my purse in my hand.

"I'll be there at ten," I said.

Whenever I ran into any of my former classmates, they usually remembered me first, making it necessary for me to rummage through the memories I'd purposely tossed into the mental recycle bin to find some tidbit I could mention so it didn't look like I didn't know who in the world they were. I had to do some serious rummaging on my way to the FIP office to come up with something—anything—about Elizabeth Doyle.

She was a year behind me.

She was the glasses, braces, hide-behind-a-book type. Prime target for the social bullies.

She'd told Bonner I had "rescued" her at some point, which—okay, she did have her gym locker near mine and was obviously and painfully embarrassed about having to undress in front of said bullies because the acne on her chest gave them such good humiliation material. I could remember telling them to back off the chick, which, after some, "Ooh, aren't you tough, rich girl?" they did. Money talks even when you try to shut it up.

With that little information I wouldn't have recognized the woman who greeted me in her cubicle at FIP as the Liz Doyle I went to high school with. She was slightly overweight but not bulgy in a deep olive suit. She now wore contact lenses that made her green eyes blink furiously, and her teeth seemed to have made the orthodontics worthwhile. Overall she wasn't unattractive, even with the weary look worn by most public servants. When she saw me, the weariness gave way to a delighted smile.

"Allison," she said as she gave my neck a brief squeeze. "Good to see you. It's been a long time. Come in—sit down if you can find a horizontal plane."

She removed a stack of files from a faded upholstered chair, and I was still sinking into it when I said, "Look—I'm sorry about standing you up last time. I can see you're swamped in here."

"Which is exactly why I was miffed about it for approximately—" Liz glanced at an oversized watch "—two minutes before I moved on to the next crisis." She let a sly smile pass through her eyes, something I *didn't* remember from high school. "I guess Jack Ellington is a little more persuasive than Bonner Bailey, huh?"

Good grief—was I blushing? *Blushing?* I was sure she didn't remember that about *me* from high school. It seemed to be amusing her to no end right now.

I managed to shake my head. "It's neither one of them. Another guy is persuading me."

"Desmond Sanborn."

I nodded.

"Good," she said. "That's what I wanted to hear." She somehow located a file on her desk. "From what Mr. Ellington tells me, it shouldn't be difficult to have Desmond's guardianship signed over to you as long as his mother is willing. And as long as you don't get yourself arrested again."

"He told you about that? I guess he had to."

"No, I read it in the paper."

I stared.

"Great piece about your homeless project. Don't tell anybody in this building I said this, but it sounds better than anything the county has going."

"And it mentioned my arrest?"

"In the most complimentary light." Liz gave a bright laugh I also didn't remember, since there hadn't been much for her to laugh at back when. "It didn't surprise me at all. I never told you this, but I always admired you for turning your back on what the Chamberlains stood for, including not marrying Troy."

I dug my fingernails into the chair arms.

She continued to talk as she filled in blanks on a form. "This wasn't mentioned in the article, of course, but I would be willing to bet that Chamberlain was behind the police breaking up your gathering. And you know yourself that Chamberlain means Troy Irwin."

Liz put the form aside and leaned toward me, eyes eager with the story. "For openers, I've heard he has these big plans for the West King Street neighborhood—four or five blocks in every direction. It just follows that the homeless people and drug dealers and prostitutes are in his way—so …"

"So he's trying to starve them out?"

"Somebody told me he actually said at some meeting that if they aren't fed here, they'll go somewhere else. I do know he has city council people, county commissioners, everybody in his pocket. So far he hasn't gotten his slimy tentacles into this office or I'd be tearing my hair out. It's bad enough as it is." She picked up the form again. "Your case is one of the easy ones, though. Now—I just need a little information and you can be on your way."

Yeah. On my way to Chamberlain Enterprises.

It was an encounter I'd been actively avoiding for over twenty years. I would rather meet that hulk in a West King Street alley any day. Chief said I was going to have to eat some crow in this, but he didn't say anything about swallowing the words, "I will never—ever—speak to you again as long as I live on this earth."

For Sacrament House, I was going to have to break out the spoon.

CHAPTER TWENTY-ONE

I was able to get an appointment with Troy Irwin on Tuesday, which was unexpected. From what little I *hadn't* been able to avoid seeing of him, I knew Mr. Irwin, Chamberlain Enterprises CEO, was a very busy man.

I'd seen his picture in the *St. Augustine Record* and even the Jacksonville paper dozens of times since he'd taken over the position once held by my father. It would sneak up on me when I was looking for a sale or at the comics—turning my stomach before I could rustle on to another page. Several times I'd seen him in parades, or at intersections with the top down on his BMW, or at the kinds of weddings I drove carriages for, funded by other corporate executives with princess daughters who didn't feel married without white horses. It was hard not to know that he owned acre upon acre of real estate, held seats on prestigious boards, and had a voice in every issue that affected the monetary life of the community. Or that his marriage to Trophy Wife Number Two had died from neglect.

Which was why when his secretary returned my call and said Mr. Irwin had made an opening for me the very next day, I was surprised. And then I was suspicious. I hadn't told her the nature of my business with him, and she hadn't asked. Why would he make time for me without even knowing what I wanted? Unless he somehow did know, which would be even creepier. If Frank Parker could have me watched, why couldn't Troy?

Okay—I was being paranoid, and I couldn't let that keep me from enjoying the part of this I was actually looking forward to. If what Liz said was true, it was going to be fun to let loose on him the way I'd been itching to go off on somebody ever since the park. I even admitted I relished seeing just how low he'd sunk—just so I could congratulate myself on having made the right decision so long ago.

Be that as it may, when I entered the First American Bank Building, I took the stairs, despite the lack of ventilation in the stairwell and the pinch of the closed-toe shoes I hadn't worn in a decade. It probably took me only five minutes longer to climb the five stories than it would have to use the elevator, but I had to indulge the avoidant side of my personality before it disappeared completely. I'd been dodging Troy Irwin for twenty-two years, four months, and five days. It seemed fitting that I should get it down to minutes, now that I was finally going to look him the eye. I just hoped I wouldn't spit when I did.

But the stairs were a mistake. While the rest of the building had been remodeled twice since 1985, the stairwell was exactly the same as it had been the summer Troy and I were both made to work as interns for my father. I shuddered now when I reached the landing between floors three and four—the dark secret spot where we used to meet during our coffee breaks to make out. The smell of cleaning compound brought with it every kiss, every wandering hand, every thrill that now rose up as acid from my stomach. I tried not to look at that corner where I couldn't get close enough to him, but my eyes went to it like I was passing a train wreck. Which was exactly what it had turned out to be.

By the time I entered the fifth-floor executive suite, I had a blister forming on my left heel and I could feel the bun I'd coaxed my hair into rebelling its way out of the clips. If the secretary had actually looked at me, she'd probably have called 911.

"I'll let Mr. Irwin know you're here," she said, as if it were all one word. "Can I get you a beverage while you wait?"

"I wasn't planning to wait that long," I said.

She gave me a non sequitur smile and returned to her desk, leaving me with my heels sinking into the carpet like I was standing in mud. I started a dialogue with myself to keep my mood from going down with them.

Of course being back here was physically affecting me. One of the worst scenes of my life was played out here.

But that didn't mean I hadn't healed emotionally.

Yeah. The fight I was ready for today had nothing to do with the one I walked away from back then.

Uh-huh.

And at least I had the advantage of knowing how a wealthy, unscrupulous, self-serving sleazeball of a businessman operated. Sickening as it was, I'd reviewed that most of the night. I still felt like I'd ingested poison.

By the time Secretary said, "Mr. Irwin is ready for you," I could say to myself in all honesty, "And I am so ready for him." Face carefully modulated, just as I'd practiced, I followed her.

Troy stood up the instant I crossed the threshold into his office. His chair rolled soundlessly out of his way as he stepped around a slick glass desk, hand outstretched. And trembling slightly.

There was no way the sight of me unnerved him. He must be hung over. Trying to quit smoking. Or, most likely, attempting to make me believe this was freaking him out.

I didn't refuse his offer of a silent handshake. I'd already wrestled with that at about three a.m. and arrived at the conclusion that making a big thing out of not touching him would only make him think I still cared enough to hate him. Still, when the second hand closed over mine, its cool smoothness was reptilian.

"Allison, I don't even know what to say."

Well, now there was a first.

"Please sit down." He finally let go. "Were you offered coffee?"

I looked at the woman still standing there invisibly waiting for orders. "I'm good," I said.

Then I took my time sitting down, finding a place to set my purse, deciding the best position for the arms that suddenly felt like they belonged on an ape. I didn't know why I was so startled at the change in his appearance. The only time I'd been within ten feet of him was at Sylvia's funeral, where I'd been flabbergasted that he had the nerve to show up to "pay his respects" when he'd never shown her any respect when she was alive—her or anybody else who mattered to me. I hadn't noticed that the pale blue eyes that had always reminded me of sailboats and sunshine were more reminiscent of yachts and paneled boardrooms. I couldn't imagine him on a surfboard now, laughing at whitecaps and lifeguards and rules. The gray-tinged temples, the neatly creased Armani suit, the crisp dismissal without eye contact to his secretary told me that now, he *was* the rules.

Hopefully those things were about to change. I found a place for my arms—folded tightly across my chest.

Troy took a seat on the short couch opposite mine and leaned slightly forward, hands on his knees, grinning like an eager young boy. I might have been convinced if he'd actually looked like that as a kid. He had been sensually and confidently a man since he was five years old.

"It's good to see you," he said. "I always hoped you'd show up here one day."

"You can skip the baloney slicing," I said. "Let's just get to why I'm here."

Troy sat back, still grinning. "I'm glad to see you haven't changed, Ally."

He was indeed shameless.

"I'm sure the shill you sent to the plaza Saturday has reported in by now," I said. "How's his lip, by the way?"

Troy raised the eyebrows I'd once thought were handsome. Before they were man-scaped.

"I'm thinking you've at least had lunch with the chief of police so he could fill you in on what went down when his henchmen came to break up our 'illegal gathering.'" I narrowed my eyes. "I'm not the only one who hasn't changed. That whole scene had your fingerprints all over it—although I have to admit I didn't suspect you at the time. Maybe because I didn't think even you would sink that low. But it made perfect sense once I put it beside Vivienne Harkness 'visiting' the house I rented."

Troy was staring. "I read about the plaza incident in the paper, but I had nothing to do with it."

"You can't deny Vivienne Harkness works for you."

"She's a colleague." The tiny lines under his eyes deepened. "Ally—really—I have no idea what you're talking about."

"I was told—"

"You got some bad information."

"I'd like to finish. I was told you're trying to develop the West King Street neighborhood."

"That part is true."

He leaned in more, hands poised to shape an image for me, and I recognized the pose. It was more polished now, but it still said, "I'm going to sell you this idea until you think you came up with it yourself." He obviously believed it would still work on me.

"You know I love this city as much as you do. And I'm sure you have the same reaction I do every time you have to pass through that neighborhood. I admit it: I've got the doors locked and the windows up and my phone set to call 911."

Troy waited, forehead also poised, like I was supposed to whole-heartedly agree. Which I partially did, but I just motioned for him to go on.

"All I want is for innocent people to be allowed to go anywhere in St. Augustine without fear." He shrugged, barely moving the shoulder pads on the Armani. "What's wrong with driving out the drugs and the prostitutes and the violent crime, and turning West King into a part of town where businesses can thrive and people can walk freely?"

"Is that the way you worded it in your business plan?" I said. "Because I bet that looks really good on paper."

"Of course I have a plan. So do you, from what I read in the *Record*." He was now just short of leaving the edge of the couch. "I hoped maybe you were coming in to ask for some financial backing for what you're doing."

I could feel my well-modulated facial expression unmodulating. "Are you *serious*?"

"Perfectly. But I'd want to take it one step further. I don't see why you and I can't work together to accomplish the same goal. You have the compassion. I have the wealth and the influence. When you think about that combination, what couldn't we do?"

"Do you really want me to answer that question?" I chopped a hand in the direction of his computer screen. "If you do, you'd better clear your calendar for the rest of the day."

"You're still looking down on wealth, aren't you, Ally?" His face softened. "I'm not your father, you know."

"We're not going there."

"Fine. I'm just saying money isn't all about greed and power. It can accomplish good things in the world—"

"Like food and shelter for those people we were trying to feed in the park before you—"

"Like the best private halfway house in the state for the women you have in that rental and private school for the boy. You let me buy out your lease on the house, and I'll provide enough for them to get on their feet and become productive members of society. It's a win-win."

I was too stunned to ask the obvious question—the one he answered before the chill got all the way through me.

"I've always kept up with what's going on in your life," he said. "I'm always looking for some way to reconnect. Maybe this thing we both have a passion for—maybe this is it."

He stayed very still—except for the eyes. They searched my face, not pleading—Troy Irwin never begged—yet not assured that he was going to get the answer he wanted. That was what kept me from clawing him with a tirade: He wasn't sure I'd say yes.

I wasn't sure I'd say no.

Not with stable options in front of me for Desmond and the women. And not with the faintest whisper of something genuine in his eyes. The only thing missing was the Nudge, saying yeah or nay.

"I want a week to think about it," I said.

"Fair enough." And then all assurance faded and he looked at me almost shyly. "Will it take you that long to think about going to dinner with me? Maybe put the past behind us?"

Reprobate. If he hadn't played that card, I might have bought the whole thing.

"Why now?" I said. "Because you want something from me?"

He looked down at his hands. "I deserved that once. I don't think I do now."

And then he waited, and so did I, until the space between us was clotted by our wills.

"Give me a week," I said. "For both."

As I left the building—using the elevator—I contemplated calling Hank and asking if we could meet at the Galleon even though it wasn't Friday. I stopped short of dialing her number when I remembered that the last time we talked, she called me a prophet. What had she said, that I saw things exactly as they are now and knew what that was going to mean for the future? This situation was about as clear as Matanzas Bay.

I was due at Sacrament House anyway, to take Geneveve to the dentist and Jasmine to Walmart to buy underwear because she was gaining enough weight to graduate from kids' sizes. And I was sure Mercedes would have some kind of beef she'd want to chew on with me. Her meltdowns had been replaced by marathon discussions that never quite got to the finish line.

I turned off the Harley's engine in front of the house and listened to her rumble fade. It was all so normal. The women were having cavities filled and buying lingerie and venting to each other in the kitchen. Maybe they were closer to being turned loose than I thought. It was that part of Troy's offer that made me say I'd think about the rest. What would it mean for them if I let go so they could have something better than what I had to offer?

I leaned the bike on its stand and shook my hair out of my helmet. I had a week. As I was learning all too well, a lot could happen in a week.

Going up the walkway, I saw that someone—probably Geneveve—had made a pine wreath and hung it on the door. The front window was festooned on the inside with red ribbon, framing the heads of the three women gathered in the living room.

I stopped, foot on the bottom step, and looked again. Make that four heads.

We'd never come to a complete conclusion about what to do if former associates from the neighborhood showed up again begging at the back door—which was why I knocked now like I always did instead of bursting in demanding to know what in the world they were thinking.

Jasmine came to the door, opened it without looking at me, and returned to the voices that stepped all over each other in the living room.

Mercedes's cigarette alto: "It ain't no good out there—it ain't gonna lead you nowhere—but don't be thinkin'—"

Geneveve's sweet lilt: "We know you tired, girl—you done the right thing comin' here—"

Jasmine's fragile half-whisper: "Miss Angel will take you in if—"

"I just don't want nobody crammin' no God down my throat."

That growl didn't belong to any of them. It came out of the mouth of a white woman who leaped from the couch like a feral cat when I walked in. Mercedes all but put her in a headlock and turned her to face me. The eyes that met mine were wild and unfocused. I'd now seen three other pairs of eyes like that, and the sight still unnerved me. Again, make that four. This was the same woman who had come here hungry once before, and I'd turned her away then. But there was something else familiar about her—

"Miss Angel," Geneveve said, "this is Sherry. She wants to come into Sacrament House."

I almost laughed out loud. The woman was struggling against Mercedes's arms, and I was sure she would have bitten her if she'd had sufficient teeth.

"We like our prospective residents to be a little more willing," I said. "Let her go, Mercedes."

"She gon' run if I do."

"Which means she doesn't want to stay. And if she doesn't want to stay—"

"Then she ain't ready to change," Geneveve concluded.

Mercedes let the woman loose. I could hear the whole room holding its breath as Sherry's long, yellowed body made up its mind whether to bolt or fold.

Geneveve took a step toward her but Sherry hiked up her shoulders, bare in a dirty green tube top, so Gen stopped, hands out. "We all been there. We all been so sure there ain't no way out, we turned on everybody wanted to help us."

"But ain't nobody can help you like somebody that's been there," Mercedes said.

My throat ached. But it was Jasmine who did me in.

"We can love you," she said.

Sherry crumpled. Three sets of arms reached out to catch her, but it was Geneveve who held her up and stroked her sparsely thatched hair.

"Jasmine, why don't you go run her a bath," she said. "Mercedes—"

"Food. I'm on it."

Mercedes hit the kitchen, muttering, "God love her, 'cause don't nobody else." Geneveve sat on the floor with Sherry in her lap, rocking and stroking. I stood and watched, until I could say, "I'll get another bed."

By Friday when I met Hank at the Galleon, I'd been Nudged to put Sherry in Geneveve's room and bring in Leighanne to talk to Sherry about NA. Mercedes didn't need any Nudging; she already had Sherry eating three meals a day.

"She's still sleeping eighteen hours out of twenty-four," I told Hank. "But that's normal for this stage. She's actually a little ahead of where Geneveve was at this point."

Hank put down her mocha and slowly shook her head at me.

"What?" I said.

"I'm listening to a woman who keeps telling me she has no idea what she's doing, while she's putting every drug rehab I've ever seen to shame."

"Even 'the best halfway house in the state'?"

"We're back to Troy Irwin now."

"I don't know what to do. I was standing there talking about 'our residents' like I have some kind of official program going over there. But how many more women can we take in? I'm already almost out of the money I use for running my own house." I pushed away the omelet I wasn't eating anyway. "They're too far along for a halfway house, but I don't know where else I could move them if I don't take him up on it. I thought you said I was a 'prophet.'"

"I did."

"Then why am I not feeling a Nudge about *this* decision?"

"If you're using that to prove you're not one, forget about it," Hank said. "What do you usually do when you don't hear a clear message—even recently?"

"I wait. But I can't this time. He wants an answer in a week."

"And then what happens?"

"There's no doubt in my mind. He'll get every house on that street, including mine."

"So make him an offer he can't refuse."

"I just don't want to deal with him. One minute I think he's changed—"

"You knew him before?"

I mentally smacked myself. "Everyone knows he's just a slimeball."

Hank squinted one eye. "You deal with slimeballs all the time. It's your new career."

I poked around in my purse for the Kleenex I knew wasn't in there, for the sniffles I didn't have. Hank was quiet. When I looked up, her mouth was in a straight line.

"You're under no obligation to tell me everything," she said. "Just make sure you're telling your*self* what you need to know."

So much for all that facial modulating. Hank could see through a concrete wall if it had feelings. Maybe I would have opened my mouth and told her why Troy Irwin was more than just a slimeball to me, if I hadn't smelled the faint but unmistakable odor of horse dung behind me.

"Hey, Allison," Lonnie said.

I twisted to look up into the brim of his cowboy hat. He removed his toothpick.

"Well, hey," I said. "How's business?"

"Okay."

"Bernard okay?"

"Yeah."

"You found him another driver, I'm sure."

Lonnie pushed his hat back with two fingers, revealing a sheepish face.

"It's okay," I said. "Look, my neck's about to twist off. Sit down—this is my friend, Hank—" who had slipped discreetly up to the counter and was already deep in conversation with Patrice.

"Join me," I said.

Lonnie looked like he'd rather stick a fork in his eye, but he perched on the edge of the third chair and struggled not to meet my gaze.

"For Pete's sake, Lonnie," I said. "I was a lousy employee, and you did what you had to do. I'm fine."

"I'm not."

I sat up straight. "What's wrong? Did you get canned too?"

"No."

"I feel like I'm pulling wisdom teeth here. Just spit it out, would you?"

He slumped in the chair and ran a hand across the beer belly that seemed to have expanded since the last time I saw him. Was that really almost two months ago?

"I saw you sitting in here, and I had to come in and tell you I wish I had your guts."

"Where in the world is *this* coming from?" If I'd had a toothpick in *my* mouth, I would have dropped it.

"You don't care what anybody thinks—you just do what you have to do." He stood up and pushed the chair back in one scraping motion. "That's all I'm allowed to say—"

"Allowed by whom?"

He stuck the toothpick back in, took it out, stared at it, until I reached up and snatched the thing out of his fingers. "Lonnie—dish, dude. You're making me crazy here."

"I didn't fire you because you were slacking off. I fired you because I had to, or I'd lose my job. I should've stood up for you—"

"Why did you 'have to'?"

He chewed at his lip as if the pick were still there. "You spoke the truth to the wrong people and it came back to bite you—but you just keep going on. I'd be like that in a heartbeat if I could."

He pulled the hat back over his forehead and hurried out. When Hank returned to the table, I was still staring at the toothpick.

"He didn't offer you your old job back, did he?" she said.

"No. He just told me why I lost it." I pressed against the table, my eyes boring into Hank. "Tell me once more you really believe this is all God."

"I don't have to, Al." Her wonderful mouth twisted. "I have a feeling he just did."

CHAPTER TWENTY-TWO

If Lonnie was right on both counts—one, that Troy Irwin was responsible for me losing my job, and two, that I had "guts," I had two phone calls to make while I sat in the van waiting for Desmond to come out of the school that afternoon. The first was to Bonner, who answered on the first ring. I tried not to feel guilty about that.

"I need your professional expertise," I said.

"I'm full of expertise," he said. "Whatcha need?"

There was only a faint trace of disappointment in his voice. I tried not to feel guilty about that either.

"Could you find out what the owner of Sacrament House would do if Troy Irwin offered to buy it?"

Bonner's silence was sharp.

"He hasn't," I said. "He just wants to buy me out of the lease."

"He approached you with that offer?"

"I approached him first about something else—"

"What 'something else'?"

I pushed aside the urge to say, "Would you get out of my grill-work and just answer my question?" and told him about Troy's hand in the park incident.

"So you went to his *office*?" Bonner said. "Nobody just goes to Troy Irwin and chews him out."

"I didn't 'chew him out.'"

"Is this Allison Chamberlain I'm speaking to? Because the Allison Chamberlain I know would've chewed him out."

"That was a little hard to do when he was offering me the moon for the women."

I could almost see him hitching at his necktie. "Let me tell you something about Troy Irwin: You can't trust him."

"I know that, Bonner, which is why I'm not taking him up on the offer. I just want to know what the owner would do if he offered to buy the place outright."

"You have a lease."

"And Troy Irwin's got more money than—"

"Doesn't matter. The owner won't go for it. Period."

"Okay." I could see myself blinking in the windshield. "Then I guess that's all I need to know."

"Allison."

"Yeah?"

"You're strong and you're stubborn and you're even right. But don't mess with Troy Irwin."

"I'm already messing with him. I'm not giving up the lease to him."

"Great. But swear to me you won't take it any further."

"Can't do it, Bonner," I said. "I'm not a swearing woman."

"I'm serious—"

"And speaking of swearing, here comes Desmond. Thanks—I owe you."

Bonner was still protesting when I turned off the phone. Through the reflection of my own face in the glass, I watched Desmond stroll across the school lawn, a pubescent female on either side. He was wearing the smile he told me he always used with "his women," the one he demonstrated for me just that morning at the breakfast table. He assured me that the cadlike grin and the eyes at half-mast were the very thing that kept them "right here."

The three stopped at the flagpole, and Desmond lounged against it and looked at his adoring harem as if to say, "Show me what you're workin' with." I was good for at least another five minutes.

Eyes still on him, I called Troy Irwin's office. The secretary launched into "Chamberlain-Enterprises-Mr.-Irwin's-office-how-may-I-help-you?" but I snipped her off midway.

"This is Allison Chamberlain. I'd like to make an appointment with Mr. Irwin as soon as possible."

"One moment please."

Why did they always say 'one moment' when they knew they were putting you on hold for at least five? I made sure Desmond was still staging auditions for the girl *du jour*. I really did need to have Chief talk to him—

"Ms. Chamberlain?"

"Ye—"

"Mr. Irwin would be happy to meet with you this evening at seven at the 95 Cordova. You're familiar with that restaurant?"

"No—"

"It's at ninety-five Cordova Street."

How she said that without guffawing into the phone I had no idea. "I meant, no, that doesn't work for me.'"

"That's the only opening Mr. Irwin has available unless you want to wait until next week."

I was sure if I'd said, "Then please tell Mr. Irwin I'll see him when Hades freezes over," she'd have said, "I'll see if he's available at that time." I would have loved to tell him that myself right over the phone, but I had to have one more face-to-face with the lowlife scum. And then the past could go back under the rock where I'd buried it under once and stay there.

"Shall I put you down for seven this evening?" said the secretary I'd forgotten was there.

"Do that little thing," I said. "And tell Mr. Irwin we're going dutch."

"I'll certainly pass on that information."

I was envisioning her jotting it on a sticky note when I saw Desmond strolling toward me. He'd obviously gotten one or both of his miniwomen "right there" and was making a leave-'em-wanting-more exit, still using the smile he reserved for them.

But when he found my gaze, his mouth split wide open, its corners reaching happily for his earlobes, and I knew something I didn't know before. That was the smile he reserved for me.

"We goin' for a ride on our Harley today, Big Al?" he said.

I glanced at my watch. "Actually I have to get ready to go out someplace."

"You got you a hot date with the Chief?"

I stalled the van.

"Yeah," he said, grin widening. "You do."

"I do not have a 'hot date' with Chief or anybody else."

"Uh-huh. Well how 'bout we swing by Hardee's and get me some fries and one of them big ol' burgers so I can have supper while you out not havin' a date."

"Do you seriously think I'm going to leave you home by yourself while I go out?" I cranked the starter until it whined to life and headed us toward Palm Row.

"If you not goin' out with Mr. Chief, then he can come stay with me. We ain't hung out in a while."

"Not since night before last. Chief's busy—probably."

I had no idea if he was or not. I would just prefer he didn't know I was having dinner with Troy. Not that it would matter to him. Not that it should matter to me. On any level.

"Then what else I'm gonna do but hang out here, watchin' the TV?" Desmond said.

"Call your women—eat me out of a week's groceries. Not gonna happen, Clarence. I'll figure something out."

"You ain't got time to figure nothin' out," he said, voice going falsetto. "You got to be all puttin' on makeup and puttin' on—"

I stopped at St. George and Bridge and gave him a mock glare. I could feel my lips twitching. "What's wrong with the way I look right now?"

"This ain't a goin'-out look you got on."

"What is it, then?"

"This is a mama pickin'-her-kid-up-from-school look."

Someone tapped a horn behind me, and I turned the corner, mind at a tilt.

"I know who," Desmond was saying. "Miss Hankenstein. She cool. She can come over and cook me something I don't know the name of. She says she givin' me a coronary education."

"Culinary," I said. "And no, it's not going to be Hank. I'm giving your mom a call."

I got the immediate silence I expected. It lasted while I drove on to Palm Row and parked on the driveway, where he broke it with, "Let me just tell you why I think that is not a good idea for me."

"Tell away," I said. "I'm calling her. You can spend the evening at Sacrament House."

I climbed out of the van to open the garage door, leaving him spewing out a list of reasons why that was going to be the boringest thing in life. I only had one reason for *my* case: I couldn't let him latch onto the idea that I was the mama.

No matter how good it felt.

Geneveve's voice went thin on the phone when I asked her, but there was no hemming and hawing; she just said yes. Perhaps the way a new mother says, yes, she's ready to take that baby home from the hospital, when in truth she has no idea what she's going to do with him when she gets there.

Which was precisely the point Desmond made from the time I hung up the phone until we climbed on the bike to leave. His main thrust was, "She don't know nothin' 'bout what I like to do. She ain't got the kinda food I like to eat," and the most telling part, "She just don't know nothin' about me."

"Then this is a good time for her to find out." I said. "And you, too. Now put your helmet on or we're taking the van."

He stuffed his fuzzy head into it, but not before I heard him mutter, "I know everything I *want* to know 'bout *her*."

I ached all the way to Sacrament House.

When we arrived, it was clear that Geneveve might not know a lot about her son, but in the two and a half hours since I'd called her, she'd knocked herself out preparing for his arrival. The windows gleamed light as I herded Desmond up the front walk, and I could hear the driving rhythm of one of my old Fleetwood Mac CDs. Mercedes flung the door open and let the light and the music and the aroma of baked sugar rush out to us. Somebody had finally learned to make cookies smell like cookies.

"Boy," she said to Desmond as she wrestled him into a hug. "It's about time you got your hind parts over here to see us. You think you too good for Sacrament House?"

I poked him in the back.

Mercedes hung her arm around his neck and pulled him inside, where Jasmine was setting a piled-high plate on the coffee table. She clapped her hands like a proud kindergartner.

"I hate that I have to go out," I said. "Looks like this is where the party's going to be." I elbowed the kid. "Right?"

But his eyes were on the skeletal figure sitting cross-legged in Geneveve's chair.

"Hey," Sherry said to him. "You remember me?"

"Maybe. Y'all got any milk to go with them cookies?"

"In the kitchen, honey," Mercedes said. "Your mama's in there—she'll pour you some."

I waited for him to get out of earshot before I whispered to Mercedes, "What was that about?"

"He never liked Sherry much," she whispered back. "But he never seen her when she wasn't loaded. It'll be all right."

I looked back at Sherry, who sat with her legs wrapped in a blanket, chugging a bottle of water and watching us hiss back and forth to each other like a pair of eighth-graders. She might be clean at the moment, but there was still something hostile about her. We had some work to do there.

Desmond emerged from the kitchen with a tumbler of milk, followed by Geneveve, who looked as if she'd just successfully bottle fed for the first time.

"Okay," I said, "let me just grab a cookie for the road and I'm out of here."

Jasmine was peering through the front window, a piece of the red ribbon trailing over her shoulder. "You goin' on a date on your motorcycle, Miss Angel?"

"It's not a date."

"I knew that," Mercedes said.

"No you did not," Jasmine said.

"Yes I did. Look at her face."

Geneveve studied me. "What I'm supposed to be seein'?"

"It's what you *not* seein'. What you *not* seein' is that glow she get every time she around Mr. Chief."

The "oohs" and "mmm-hmms" and "I know that, childs" drowned out even Stevie Nicks. My face flamed.

Mercedes pointed at my cheeks. "That's the one I'm talkin' about. All you got to do is mention his name and she go all pink."

"You guys are using again, aren't you?" I said. "You're seeing things. I'm calling every one of your sponsors."

"I ain't got no sponsor."

We turned to Sherry, the only female in the room besides me who wasn't holding her sides and cracking herself up.

"Do you want one?" I said.

She twitched. I took that as a shrug.

I crossed to her and rubbed my hands up and down her legs. I could feel the bones, even swathed in blankets. "When you're ready, we'll get you to an NA meeting. Meanwhile, we're just gonna love on you."

"I done tol' all y'all, I ain't about no higher power—"

She ended with a curse, and Mercedes stuck out a finger to check her, but I shook my head at her as I got up.

"You might not be about the higher power," I said, "but the higher power is about you."

She swore again, and again I held Mercedes back.

"Don't think I don't appreciate what y'all are doin' for me," Sherry said. "I wanna stay clean. But I told you when I come here— no pushin' God on me."

"I think we should leave her be for now." Geneveve sat on the arm of the chair and touched Sherry's hair, now washed and combed into a pitiful ponytail. "Miss Angel didn't never push nothin' on us, and we ain't gonna push on her. We got to let God do the pushin'.'"

Even as I stared at Geneveve, her eyes came up to me—wise and knowing. And Nudged.

"Gen's right," I said.

"Then let's get this party goin' again," Mercedes said. "'Cause this is about our Desmond. Get you a cookie, boy—get you two."

I left them woo-hooing and cranking up the music, and was halfway down the walk when I heard the door open behind me. I turned, fully expecting to see Desmond when I turned around, loaded up with five more reasons why he was going to die of boredom. But it was Geneveve, hurrying toward me.

"You okay?" I said.

She nodded and kept coming until she was flat up against me. I folded my arms around her.

"Thank you," she said into my jacket.

"For …"

"For trustin' me with Desmond. You don't know what that means to me, Miss Angel."

I held her out in front of me. "Genevieve, you're running this whole house. You just brought Sherry back from the dead, and I don't think I could have done that with her. Why wouldn't I think you could handle your own son for an evening?"

"I know. But he loves you—not me."

"Gen—"

"I know it's the truth, and it's my own fault." Her eyes were large and liquid. "But he gonna love me again—or maybe love me like he never done 'cause I never gave him nothin' of myself. It's gon' happen—I know that now. So thank you for showin' me I'm ready to start." A tear spilled over and she wiped it with the heel of her hand. "That's my son, Miss Angel. And I'm gon' have him someday."

A flicker of resentment chased through her eyes so quickly I was sure I hadn't seen it. She kissed my cheek and hurried back into the house. Back to her son.

As for me, I hurried the other way, to Troy Irwin, who owed me, big time, for the pain that was searing through me.

The 95 Cordova, tucked deep in the opulence of the Casa Monica Hotel, touted itself as being devoted to Old World Charm, and it did appear that way, especially amid the tiny white lights that had twinkled to life and draped themselves all over the historic district while I wasn't looking. The only thing not old-world charming about it was the price of the food. One of the last couples I'd squired around town in the carriage had raved about the special menu-for-two for only ninety-five dollars. I didn't spend that much on groceries in a month, before Desmond came. I was sure that tonight Troy intended to pay more for what he wanted.

Especially when the maitre d' told me Mr. Irwin was waiting for me, and led me through a showcase of antique tables and silk-covered chairs to a back alcove bathed in golden ambience. I'd grown up squirming in restaurants like this. Desmond had nothing on me when it came to childhood boredom.

Troy only got halfway up from his chair before I motioned for him to stay seated, but it was long enough for me to see that he was wearing silk blend gray trousers that probably cost more than my entire wardrobe. I was glad I'd opted for my leather Harley jacket and a black turtleneck. Surprise shot through his confident gaze.

He waited for the server to fluff my napkin onto my lap and leave before he spoke. It would never do to talk in front of the help. "Look at you," he said. "You dating somebody with a Harley?"

"The Harley's mine," I said. Too bad I was still operating in a Nudge-less state. I needed one right now to keep me from overturning my water glass into the lap of those silk pants. At least he hadn't known about the bike.

He looked at me for a long moment. When I didn't add anything, he moved his silverware a fraction of an inch.

"Thank you for meeting me here," he said. "I felt like we got off on the wrong foot the other day, and I know it was probably the venue. You can't have many happy memories in that office."

"I have none, actually."

"Then this was a better choice." He made another infinitesimal adjustment to the cutlery. "A place we never went to together."

I held in a breath and with it every snarky retort that fought to come out and end this. "Look," I said, "my wanting to meet with you again has nothing to do with what happened between you and me. This is about now."

"Is it?" His voice was husky and decidedly un-CEO.

"What is it that you think we can accomplish by dredging up the past?" I said.

"We can get it out of the way so we can sort this thing out."

"I got it out of the way a long time ago."

"Are you ready for your appetizers, sir?"

Troy nodded at the server, who wafted a gold-edged charger onto the table.

"I hope you still love fried green tomatoes," Troy said.

They didn't look like any greasy-diner fried green tomatoes I'd ever eaten with Troy. They seemed lost in their glazed, pretentious presentation.

I barely waited for the server to simper away. "Stop trying so hard, Troy. I forgave you, all right? I don't want to go over it. Any of it. I just came to tell you—"

"No, you didn't."

"Didn't what?"

"You didn't forgive me."

My chin came up before I could stop it. There was no point then in trying to hide the anger.

"You know absolutely nothing about my spiritual life," I said.

"I don't have to be a priest to see you're still carrying around everything I did to you."

Even as I squeezed the stem of my water glass, I felt the Nudge.

No. Come on, God. I bought a Harley. I took in prostitutes. I've gone to jail. Please, please, please, not this. Don't make me do this.

Troy's hands were flat on the tablecloth. "I want to help, Ally," he said. "But you're not going to let me unless we clear the air."

"And you chose a public place so I wouldn't scream at you the way you deserve to be screamed at."

"When did that ever stop you before?" His smile was hopeful. "If you really want to scream at me, we'll go someplace else."

I pressed into the table. "I don't want to scream at you. I don't want to talk about this at all."

"Because you haven't forgiven me. I wouldn't have forgiven me either. I should have come after you when you ran. Right? Isn't that what you're thinking?"

"You know what? I am not doing this."

I snatched my purse from the table and made my blind way back through the silk and the gilt and the filet mignons until I was out on the street where I could breathe.

DearGoddearGoddearGod, why are you making me do this? The Nudge was so strong it backed me against the front wall of the hotel. I couldn't move when Troy pushed the glass doors open, calling my name, and I couldn't resist when he closed his hand around my arm.

"I came after you this time," he said. "You want to keep running from it, I'll keep following, like I should have done before."

I used my other hand to peel his fingers away. "You did follow me when I ran," I said. "Coming after me was what did us in. Okay—we've talked about it. Are you satisfied?"

"I'm not talking about that time. I'm talking about when you left for good. I should have come after you when you left St. Augustine. I should have followed you and made it right."

I didn't need the Nudge to freeze me in place. He had just said the last words I ever expected to come out of his mouth. And his eyes begged me to believe him.

"I left too, after you did," he said. "Went to school. Tried to convince myself it was all your fault."

I found my voice. "You were already convinced of that before I ever left—which was *why* I left."

A black Lincoln pulled reverently up to the curb. Troy waved it on and once more took my arm.

"Please, let's walk," he said.

"Fine," I said. "We'll walk, and we'll talk. Just don't touch me."

He let go and slid his hands into the pockets of his slacks. I nodded and took off two steps ahead of him up Cordova.

"I'm not trying to clear my conscience, Ally," he said.

"And don't call me Ally. It's Allison." I quickened the pace to have an excuse for my ragged breathing.

"It was my fault. All of it. The accident—the argument in the hospital—your dad cutting you off. We could have had the life we dreamed of together if I had just come after you and told you that. If I'd just asked you to forgive me—like I'm doing now."

We'd reached the block of Cordova that ran along the college, deserted for the evening by the students. I stopped there, and I faced him, and I let myself be Nudged straight back to the past he'd just edited.

"Is that the way you remember it?" I said. "Or is that just the story you've told yourself so you can sleep at night?"

"What—"

"It has to be, or why else would you have come back from Harvard and gone to work for my father—with every intention of working your way straight up to where you are now? He groomed you for this from the time you were fifteen years old, even when you were telling me that the minute we graduated from high school, you wanted us to leave the life our parents had laid out for us and go chase our dreams. We both know what that was about, Troy. That was about you doing whatever it took to get in my pants. Is this the 'sorting this out' you wanted to do?"

"I wanted to marry you then."

I shoved my hair out of my face. "Aren't you leaving out a few of the finer points? The part where you *refused* to marry me? The part where you blackmailed me? The part where my father stood there in his office and said I was screwing up my life like Lincolnville trailer trash and he wasn't giving me another cent to screw it up anymore. Not then. Not ever. Because of you."

"And I'm sorry. You have to know that."

"No—I don't know that. I have been back here for almost twenty years and you never looked me up. I live two blocks from your office, but you never came to me with this—and I know why you're doing it now. It's because you want something from me. So let me just be clear: I met you tonight to tell you I'm not selling you the lease on that house so you can tear it down and extend your little dream world down West King Street. I'm not doing it. And if you continue to fight me, I'll fight back. Period. "

"One has nothing to do with the other. I just wanted you to do what you're doing right now, get this out, scream at me, hit me—"

"I'd love to belt you right in the mouth, but I'm not doing that, either."

Troy closed his eyes. When he opened them, they were swimming.

"Do you want to know something?" he said.

"No," I said.

"That was the thing I loved about you the most—that you never let me get away with anything."

"I let you get away with everything."

"I didn't get away with it, Ally," he said.

I looked away from him.

"I've just been waiting for a way to make it up to you."

"Oh, please—"

"These women—this cause of yours—it's something you have a passion for. And I can help."

"And it doesn't hurt that it helps you, too. How am I supposed to believe all this when you're going to gain from it? And at the expense of all those people?"

"What people?"

"The people who live on West King Street. Where are they supposed to go when you tear everything down and start over?"

"You can help me with that. I'll set up a fund for you, give you whatever you need to help them all relocate. This was the dream you had when we were kids."

"Don't you dare bring that up."

"You can't do this by yourself and you know it."

He pulled his hands from the pockets of the pricey pants, and I waited for the shaping in the air, the peak of the pitch. But he just let them fall at his sides.

"I don't know what else to say. I just want to help you."

I looked away again. "Right now you can help me by leaving me alone."

"Is that your answer?"

"No. I don't have an answer."

"Fair enough." He let out a long breath and reached for my arm again. "Let me walk you back."

"I'm fine. Go. Please."

I folded my arms against the sound of his wing tips receding down Cordova and fading into the city of walkers. I didn't join them, even after I knew he must be safely in his Lincoln. I just stood there, sagging under the weight of too much past. Funny how I'd carried it for so long and never known how heavy it was.

PleaseGodpleaseGodpleaseGod—please tell me where to drag it from here.

I was only Nudged to go back to my women.

CHAPTER TWENTY-THREE

No driving Fleetwood Mac greeted me when I got to Sacrament House, and no lights shone through the windows. I didn't even have to get inside the front door to know something had gone down in the hour and a half I'd been gone. I wiped my feet on the mat and tried to get the Troy Irwin angst off with the dirt.

I knocked and got "you might as well come on in" from a jagged-voiced Mercedes.

She, Jasmine, and Geneveve were sitting at the table in the dining alcove, where the only light on in the house framed them in a dismal circle. I didn't see Sherry anywhere, but my first instinct was to search the place for Desmond.

"He in the kitchen," Geneveve said. Her voice was tiny and flat.

I started to pull out a chair, but judging from the chill coming off of the three of them, I might be frozen if I actually sat down. I curled my fingers around the back of it.

"Is there a problem?"

Jasmine stared at the lazy Susan that held the saltshaker and the sugar bowl. Her eyes were tear-swollen. Mercedes glared at Geneveve and muttered under her breath.

"Did you two have a fight?" I said to Geneveve.

"Yeah," she said. "We did."

Mercedes whipped her head toward her. "But that ain't why—"

"Stop." Geneveve leveled a hand at her. "Just stop."

Jasmine bolted for the hallway, sobs more audible as she went.

Mercedes grunted. "That's gon' help a lot."

"Help what?" I said. "Somebody talk to me."

"It ain't gon' be me." Mercedes shoved the chair against the wall as she got up. Her eyes drilled through the top of Geneveve's head. "I got my orders. I'll tell Desmond you here."

I was pretty sure Desmond had heard the whole exchange. "Gen," I said, "let's go talk on the front porch."

She shrank from my touch on her shoulder as if I'd applied hot coals to it.

"No, ma'am," she said.

"I'm sorry?"

"I got nothin' to say."

I glanced toward the kitchen and lowered my voice. "Did something happen with Desmond?"

"No," she said. "Just please take him back to your house."

"Geneveve—"

She put both hands almost in my face and struggled out of the chair and down the hall. The door didn't slam—that wasn't Geneveve's style—but the hostility was palpable.

I headed for the kitchen but Desmond met me in the doorway with his backpack already on and his helmet under his arm. Behind him Mercedes stomped through the laundry room and out the back. She did give me a door slam.

"I told you this was a bad idea," Desmond said.

"We'll talk," I said. Right now I just wanted to get out of there before both of us got frostbite.

One thing was clear: I needed to calm down before I got Desmond home and interrogated him under a bare lightbulb.

"You didn't get a ride this afternoon," I said as we donned helmets. "So we better take one now."

He looked momentarily surprised, but he was on the bike and ready almost before I had the thing upright. I could feel him relax with every lean as we wove through the quiet streets behind the college and avoided the too-cheerful Christmas lights. We arched north of St. George Street and took the sweeping curve that led to the Bay Front. The salty chill should have been invigorating. Desmond's ease behind me should have been reassuring. But when we pulled into the garage on Palm Row, I was no closer to calm, and I knew it wasn't all about whatever Desmond had done.

"Are you going to get off?" I said. "Or were you planning to spend the night out here?"

"You gonna find out anyway," he said. "So I'ma just tell you."

I hung my helmet on the handlebar. "Can we get off first?"

"I don't know everything 'cause she sent me in the bathroom when she seen that lady comin'."

"What lady? Desmond, get off—now."

He took his time swinging his leg over, and he stood, still in his helmet, while I set the bike on its stand. His shoulders took on a curve I hadn't seen in weeks.

"Okay," I said. "I'm not going to yell at you, and I'm not going to take your helmet away. So just take it off and tell me what happened."

He pulled it off in slo-mo and hugged it against his side. Now I could see the war going on in his eyes. Desmond Sanborn never did battle with himself.

"What lady?" I said.

"I seen her before. You did too."

"Can you describe her?"

He let one hand leave the helmet and fished in his pocket. I thought he'd drawn a picture of her, but he pulled out a business card and handed it to me.

"I got it out the trash can when she left and they let me come out the bathroom."

I turned the card over. There was no time to stop my chin from dropping. *Vivienne Harkness, Real Estate,* it said.

"She that rich ... woman came to the house that one day in her espensive car," Desmond said.

The day the women moved in.

"She bad news, that woman. She come up on the porch like she already own the place."

"'Already' owned it?" I said. "Never mind—just tell me what she said. Did you hear any of it?"

The sly smile slipped halfway onto his face. "'Course I did. Them walls is thin as paper."

"What did she say?"

"I didn't get what she talkin' about at first. Something about you was gon' let go your leash on the house so she could buy it from the landlord. I do know 'bout landlords. They throw you out in the street so you don't got no home."

"You're sure she said *I* was giving up the 'leash.'"

"This exactly what she said." His voice went soprano. "'Allison Chamberling is gon' give up the leash on this house. She didn't tell you all?' And Mercedes and all them are goin', 'No, ma'am, she never said nothin' like that,' and that stuck-up lady, she's all goin' on 'bout buyin' it from the landlord and how she just come by to get a better look—see if she gon' fix it up or tear it down."

NANCY RUE

"She *said* that to them?"

Desmond nodded enthusiastically. He was enjoying the telling at this point. "I didn't see it, 'course, but Mercedes, she musta got all up in her face 'cause Jasmine's goin', 'No, Mercedes,' and Geneveve's sayin' 'That ain't no good.' Lady left after that—no, first she said …" He went into his female voice again. "'That was a wise choice. I'll leave my card in case Ms. Chamberling have any questions.'"

I had no doubt he was telling the truth. No way could he know Vivienne Harkness was after the house unless he'd heard exactly what he'd just told me. Fury charged up my spine but I prayed it down. I had to keep my cool at least until I got out of Desmond's hearing range. He was already watching me carefully.

"Okay," I said, "first of all, she was lying through her little bleached teeth."

"I know that," Desmond said, voice going even higher. "That's why when I heard Jasmine say to just throw that card away, I got it out the garbage first chance I got."

"You did good. Now, next thing. Do your mom and the others know you heard?"

"I don't know 'bout that Sherry woman—you can't trust her no way—but she was in her room the whole time. Everybody else whispered a while, and I didn't hear none of that, now."

He looked at me apologetically.

"That's okay," I said.

"And then when I come out, they tol' me whatever I heard, I better keep it to myself till they figured out what they was gonna do."

My heart sank. Everyone's past was wreaking havoc on their trust issues tonight.

"You were right to tell me," I said.

He loosened his grip on the helmet slightly.

"And just so you know, nobody's going anywhere."

"*I* know that. *They* don't."

"I'll fix that." I hoped. "I need to make some phone calls. Is your homework done?"

"You think I'ma get it done stuck in the bathroom all night?"

I nodded at the locker. "Put your stuff away and we'll go get you started."

"Tomorrow's Saturday."

"Then you won't have to worry about it Sunday night."

"You gon' feed me too?"

"The cookies weren't as good as they smelled?"

"I never even got onc. You weren't gone this long"—he snapped his fingers—"'fore that woman be knockin' at the door."

I pushed down the thought that Vivienne Harkness had been sitting around the corner in her white Lexus waiting for me to leave. "You can make yourself a sandwich. And you can have four Oreos."

"Man," he said happily, "that's cold."

I waited until he was well into his math sheet, cheeks stuffed with cookies and telling me he'd have that thing knocked out in five minutes because he flat tore math up now. Then I went upstairs, closed my bedroom door, and dialed the number on the card. I didn't care where Vivienne Harkness was or who she was bullying at the moment. She was getting an earful from me. I groaned when after three rings I realized I was about to get a voice message.

"You've reached Chamberlain Enterprises. Our business hours are eight thirty a.m. to—"

I couldn't stab the end-call button fast enough. I threw the phone on the bed and watched it bounce savagely onto the floor.

"Troy Irwin, you jackal," I said—out loud—to the room that was closing in. "You lying, thieving, blood-sucking jackal."

I had other words for myself—*naïve, gullible*, and *stupid* among them—as I crawled for the phone, ready to call Troy. But I sagged the minute I picked it up. I didn't have his personal contact information, and if I called CE, I'd get the same message. I was going to go crazy if I didn't talk to somebody about this, though. Hank? Chief?

Definitely not Chief.

Bonner. Duh. He'd told me not to "mess" with Troy Irwin—but I couldn't care about that. Fingers shaking, I punched his number.

And got a recording.

I tried to yank my bun tighter and the whole thing fell out, half of it in my face. Okay, I had to get a handle on this or I was going to have a Mercedes-style explosion.

"Oh for Pete's sake," I said. "Desmond! Get your jacket—we're going back over there."

I felt the reassuring Nudge all the way to Sacrament House, despite Desmond's protests every time we paused at a stop sign. But as I ushered him up the walkway at the house, I realized this time it wasn't a pushing forward while I kicked and screamed. It was a pulling back because I might. Before I knocked, I stood with my hands on the door and closed my eyes. *PleaseGodpleaseGodpleaseGod—don't let me mess this up.*

When I opened my eyes, Desmond said, "Amen."

I was still staring at him, emotions ready to cave in, when the door opened a crack and Geneveve's eye appeared.

"I need to talk to you," I said.

The eye disappeared, but the door didn't close. I had to let myself and Desmond in. He started for the kitchen, but I caught him by the back of his jacket.

"We all need to sit down together," I said.

Jasmine and Mercedes were on the couch, both wearing sweaters and shoes. I saw their purses waiting on the end tables.

"You told her didn't you, boy?" Mercedes gave Geneveve a look that would have withered a cactus.

Geneveve leaned against the wall, arms folded. "I wasn't the one told him to lie."

"We didn't tell him to lie. We told him to keep his mouth shut."

"It's the same thing—"

"Why didn't one of *you* tell me?" I said.

No one answered. I pushed Desmond into Geneveve's chair and sat on the arm. "Gen—sit down, please."

She blinked hard. "I'ma stand, thank you."

"All right. We're not going into why you didn't trust me. I think I get that."

"No you do not," Mercedes said.

"Why don't you just shut up for once and listen to somebody?" Jasmine's voice was so clogged I was surprised I understood her at all. Mercedes obviously did because she pressed her lips and fell sullenly silent.

"Vivienne Harkness—the woman who came here tonight—is not a real estate agent. She works for Chamberlain Enterprises, which is trying to buy up the entire West King neighborhood to turn it into— I don't know what—but it's going to make them a lot of money, and they'll do just about anything to make that happen."

"And you are 'Ms. Chamberlain,'" Mercedes said. So much for shutting up.

"That's my last name. But I don't have anything to do with them anymore. It would make me sick, actually. And what that woman told you was a complete lie."

No eyes softened. Nobody nodded. Only Mercedes was looking at me, hostility burning from every pore.

"I'm not going to sell the lease. Bonner Bailey has already assured me I don't have to. He's also told me the owner won't sell it."

"Little ol' Bonner Bailey with the sunglasses holders?" Jasmine said. "He a wuss."

"Not when it comes to real estate," I said.

Mercedes was shaking her head. "You just said them people do anything to get what they want."

"Which is why we have Chief," I said. It was another one of those I-didn't-know-it-until-I-said-it thoughts, but it was the first thing to lighten the tension since I walked in.

"Now he ain't a wuss," Jasmine said.

"No," I said—quickly, because Mercedes was rising to that one. "He's a good lawyer, and we'll take it to court if we have to. But I'm telling you, ladies, the house isn't going anywhere, and you can stay until you feel like you can make it on your own." I glanced toward the hall. "I know it's going to take longer for Sherry, but—"

"Sherry gone."

Those were Geneveve's first words since we sat down. Her voice quavered.

"*Gone* gone?" I said. "Or just out?"

Jasmine glowered at Mercedes. "Somebody told her what was goin' down, and she freaked out and left."

"What happened?" I said to Geneveve.

Her eyes filled. "She said we was stupid to ever trust 'do-gooders,' and she just left. She ain't gonna make it."

Vivienne Harkness was so lucky I didn't have her number.

"She always run before she gets throwed out," Jasmine said.

"And you all understand that nobody's getting thrown out," I said. "Yes?"

Jasmine looked at Mercedes and sank back into the couch. Mercedes grunted. Geneveve was a statue at the wall. Only Desmond, mute until now, reached up to slap my hand.

"All right," I said. "The Lord be with you."

Heads turned to me.

"Look, if you won't believe me, you can at least believe God. I think we should ask him. Now, the Lord be with you."

"And also with you," Geneveve whispered.

No one offered to join hands, but they bowed their heads, and that had to be enough. It was for me. I was Nudged into words I didn't form—words of trust and safety and shelter from harm. Before I said amen, I half believed that Hank might be right about me.

When I lifted my head, Jasmine was crying, head on Mercedes's shoulder.

"We ain't got no choice," Mercedes said. "We got to believe you."

"I do believe you," Jasmine said.

Desmond gave me a thumbs-up. What would I do without that kid?

I turned abruptly to his mother. "What about you, Gen?"

She hugged her arms around herself. "I don't know why I ever stopped," she said. "I don't even know why I lied—and not tellin' you was a lie."

"A lie I understand."

"I don't!" She pulled her gaze down to me. "Sherry—she said ain't none of us changed all the way. She said Mercedes still have her temper and Jasmine still cryin' over everything." Geneveve jabbed her thumb at her chest. "I still hold things back when I should tell the truth."

"And yet here you are," I said. "You didn't run off with Sherry."

Mercedes gave her signature grunt. "We was about to."

"You got the opposite problem," Jasmine said to her. "Geneveve hold back too much, and you don't hold back nothin'."

"If anybody would let me finish." Mercedes homed in on me. "Me and Jasmine was ready to go. Geneveve—she the one sittin' here talkin' us out of it when you come." She looked at Geneveve. "You coulda run, but you didn't. You told us this was *our* home and we need to stay and fight for it."

I didn't need a Nudge to tell me she was speaking the truth.

I was on the phone to Chief the next morning before Desmond was out of bed. The grog in Chief's voice indicated he hadn't been out of his for long. He came awake by the time I finished telling him about Vivienne Harkness's visit to Sacrament House.

"Let me make sure I'm hearing you," he said. "She deliberately led them to believe she was an independent realtor."

"Right. There must be a law against impersonating a real estate agent."

"If that were the case, half the ones with licenses would be in jail." He paused. "I'm not putting down your boy Bonner."

"He's not—okay, forget that. Is there anything we can do about this?"

"We might be looking at fraud. She did gain entry into their home under false pretenses. You still have the card, right?"

"Yeah."

"That's evidence, although the chain's a little dubious."

"Chain?"

"Her to one of the women to the trash can to Desmond to you."

"I'm not seeing Desmond on a witness stand."

"That would take the judicial system back about a hundred years. We'll cross that bridge if we get to it. I hope it won't come to that, but it might if we prove the Chamberlain connection. You ready to play hardball?"

"Whatever it takes."

"I just wish we had more to go on to implicate Chamberlain. I'd love to put it to Troy Irwin."

I chewed at my fingernail.

"What aren't you saying?" Chief said.

Could I not get away from Troy Irwin to save my *soul*?

"Come on, Classic, if you've got something I can work with …"

"Liz Doyle told me Troy's planning to buy up the whole neigh-borhood for development. You could check with her."

"Good. And?"

"And … he admitted it to me. He asked me to let him buy me out of the lease so he could recreate West King. He basically offered me a job relocating everybody he's going to turn out on the street."

"When?"

"I don't know—and I told him I wasn't interested—"

"No, when did he tell you this?"

Aw, man. "Last night," I said.

"Last night."

"Yeah. While Vivienne Harkness was freaking out the women of Sacrament House, he was trying to wine and dine me—"

"Did he try anything?" Chief's voice hardened. "If he did any-thing even remotely sexual, we can get him on—"

"No! It wasn't like that."

"I'm not getting this."

"Okay—I've known him since we were kids. I haven't seen him in years, but I thought since I knew him, I could go to him—"

"You invited *him* to dinner."

"No. This was earlier in the week. When I went to his office."

His pause was so long I checked to see if he'd hung up. When he did speak, his tone was leaden.

"Do you want me to represent you?"

"Yes—"

"Then you're going to have to tell me you'll never do something like that without consulting me first, or we can't work together."

"I consulted Bonner," I said. "I thought it was just a real-estate thing until last night."

"And when you found out it wasn't, did you call me right away?"

"No." I squeezed my eyes shut. Was I blowing this, or was I blowing it?

"I thought we had a trust thing," he said.

"We do."

"Do we? Because a friend who trusted me would've called me when she was in trouble."

Yeah. I was blowing it.

"I'm sorry," I said.

"Yeah," he said. "Me, too. All right—" His voice shifted. "I'll come by and get that card."

Thank you, God.

"And I'll probably have some more questions."

"I'll think about anything I left out—not on purpose—"

"That'd be good," he said.

When we hung up, I banged the phone against my forehead.

CHAPTER TWENTY-FOUR

Chief did come by briefly, and except for his required head-butting with Desmond, he was uber-professional. I took my cue from that. If I blurted out, "I'm sorry I was an idiot, and I only kept it from you because I didn't want you to know I went out with another guy even though I despise him and even though you only think of me as a daughter or a sister or a buddy, and I think of you—" anyway, I was afraid he'd freeze-dry me.

"There's not much I can do until Monday when Liz Doyle's back in her office," he said as he was putting on his helmet. "In the meantime I suggest you cancel any appointments you have set up with Troy Irwin." He snapped the catch on the strap. "Personal or professional."

"I don't *have* any."

"Good. See you tomorrow."

"Oh?"

"I told Desmond I'd take him for a ride."

"Oh. Right. Yeah."

I watched through the kitchen window as he pulled out of Palm Row a little faster than he had to on the Road King. Longing. That was what I felt. For what—that I didn't know. And it was probably pointless anyway, because spiritually Chief and I weren't even in the same realm. It felt like we were at times—but that brought me right back to where I started. Since when could I count on my feelings?

"Trouble with your man, Big Al?" Desmond said behind me.

"He's not my—"

I stopped and turned to him. His eyes were big and almost sad. "Yeah, I've got trouble with my man, Desmond," I said.

"You gon' fix it?"

"I don't know."

"I could talk to him if you want. I know all about this stuff."

I tried to smile and tapped my palm. "You gonna show me how to get him 'right there'?"

Desmond shook his head. "He already there. Just don't nobody know it.'"

I pulled his ball cap over his eyes so he wouldn't see mine.

"You are a nut bar," I said. "Let's go for a ride."

Sunday was the longest day on record. When Chief came by to take Desmond on a HOG ride, he politely asked me if I wanted to come with, but I begged off, saying I was wiped out. I couldn't tell if he was disappointed, and I was afraid to find out.

My house was like a cave when they left, so I took some Christmas decorations to the women. Nobody had heard from Sherry, but it seemed their relief over *their* house was enough to carry them through for the time being. Genevieve was wistful, though she smiled gamely when I said we'd go get a tree this next week.

"I know you're worried about Sherry," I said. "But what if we focus on giving Desmond a nice Christmas?"

She just nodded and stretched the corners of her eyes with her fingers. I realized as I left that it was a lot easier on her back when she didn't care if he loved her. I knew the feeling.

With no place else to go, I went home and put a grocery-store log in the fireplace. The sky was threatening one of those dismal early December rains that belies everything you believe about winter in Florida. Between that and my mood, Desmond was going to need something cheerful when he got back. I was considering opening a roll of cookie dough and baking what I didn't eat when someone knocked on the front door. I wiped my sooty hands on the seat of my jeans as I hurried to answer it, but when I spotted the car through the window, I slowed to a crawl. It was the Reverend Garry Howard's gray Buick.

God? What are you doing to me?

Unfortunately no adamant Nudge told me to duck into the coat closet, so I opened the door. He stood, hands folded against his thighs, face drawn and older than I remembered. Funny. Even after not seeing him for two and a half months, I expected him to look just as he had then—smile in place, wings extended for the ministerial hug.

"I apologize for not calling first," he said. "I was afraid you'd keep avoiding me."

What was I supposed to say to that?

"Do you have a few minutes to talk?" he said.

I knew even less what to say to that, but it was starting to drizzle, and I couldn't leave him standing in it while I made up my mind. "Sure," I said.

It wasn't until I was taking his jacket that I saw he was shivering slightly. It was enough to make me offer him some tea.

"That would be nice," he said.

"You sit, and I'll go fix us some," I said.

I planned to use the time it took for water to boil to figure out a way to tell him why I wasn't coming back to his church. But he followed me into the kitchen and sat at the bistro table. The chair didn't fit him at all.

"I hear you've been doing some very good things," he said. "Bonner has told me about your Sacrament House."

"Really?" I said. I took my time filling the kettle and getting it on the stove.

"It's a fine thing you're doing, Allison. A godly thing."

Hitching myself up onto the other bistro chair, I looked at him warily.

"I like to think it's godly," I said. "It's what I'm hearing from God to do, anyway."

He nodded. If he'd just come to tell me I was wonderful, the lines on his face wouldn't be etching a scolding into my near future.

"Bonner also tells me you're seeing to their Christian education."

"Whose?" I said.

"The, uh, the women you're taking care of."

"The former prostitutes and recovering drug addicts, you mean."

"Well, yes." I'd never seen a grown man squirm before. "You've led them to the Lord—is that what I'm to understand?"

"Led them to the Lord," I said. "You know—I've come to wonder exactly what that means."

The Reverend Howard's head tilted back, and he looked at me through the bottoms of his bifocals. "You know what it means. You introduce them to a life with Jesus Christ as their Lord and Savior."

"And what does that look like, exactly?" I pulled my feet up onto the seat. I knew my voice was teetering on the edge of sarcasm, and I tried to pull it back. "See, that's where I was getting confused. I'm sure Bonner told you that, too."

His eyebrows came together in a tangle of white over his nose. "Bonner had nothing but praise for you. The others in your small group were a little more concerned."

"I bet they were. But I'm fine."

"And these—women?"

"What about them?"

"Are they—"

"They're turning their lives around, step by step."

"Following the plan for salvation, then."

"The plan for salvation." I ran my hand down the back of my neck to make sure the hair wasn't literally standing up like hackles. "That's another catchy little phrase I'm not sure I know the meaning of. Our plan is to take it day by day, praying our way through, going with what God tells us."

Garry put his hands on the table as if he were about to slice bread and fixed his gaze between them. "It is one thing to feed and clothe and shelter in the name of the Lord," he said. "But not everything that is warm and fuzzy is Jesus." He looked at me, eyes bordering on stern. "I just want to encourage you to make sure that what you're teaching is solid Christianity. You may not be attending my church right now, Allison, but you are still my daughter in Christ."

"So let me get this straight."

"Of course." He nodded and encouraged me with his hands to go on.

"No one at Flagler Community Church is willing to help me with Sacrament House, with the exception of Bonner. But you're all willing to tell me how to run it—ready to jump on what I might be doing wrong 'in the name of Jesus.'"

"I just don't want to see you water down the gospel. We can't call someone a Christian just because she's stopped using drugs."

"O-oh," I said. "See, there's our communication problem, Reverend—the one you told me we had that day you did my friend's father's funeral."

He looked puzzled, but he nodded again.

"Our trouble is that we're not talking about the same gospel. The gospel I know is the one where Jesus preached and lived the unconditional love of salvation. You know—the one where he ate at the same table with the hookers and the drug addicts and the victims of injustice and poverty—that one. The one you're talking about is the one I haven't read—where only the right kind of people get into the closed club and get saved." I shook my head. "It is such a relief to finally have that cleared up."

The Reverend Howard drew himself up in the bistro chair, hands on the table like he was gripping the pulpit. "I don't appreciate your sarcasm, Allison."

I didn't either, but it was the only way I could keep myself from snatching out a handful of his wavy white pastoral hair.

"We can't communicate at all if you're going to be that way." He looked at me through the bifocals again until he seemed satisfied that I was in my place, even though I hadn't moved so much as an eyebrow. "I have a responsibility to make sure this is a truly Christian endeavor before I offer our help."

It was my turn to tilt my head back—so he wouldn't see my eyes narrowing. "What kind of help?" I said.

"Since you haven't been with us for several weeks, you don't know that the church has received a generous donation, most of which will be used to build a Christian school here in the city proper. I would like to propose to the elders that we use some of the money to support your ministry of turning these misguided people into upstanding members of the church, provided it operates under the same belief statement. You can certainly understand why that would be necessary."

The Nudge was uneasy. I unfolded my legs and tilted toward him.

"Where are you building the school?" I said. "I don't know of any vacant property in the city proper."

"Again, you're a bit out of the loop. We've been told that most of what is currently the West King Street neighborhood is going to be torn down. We're being given a prime piece of real estate just off the main road."

"By whom?" I said.

But I could have mouthed it with him when he answered, "By the Chamberlain Foundation."

"Then thanks but no thanks." I leaned back. "I won't touch a dime of Troy Irwin's money."

"He's not a member of our church, but he has always been there for all the churches in the city when they've been in need."

"Oh yeah—we've all got beautiful buildings. I'm sure your school will be state of the art. But every kid that goes there is going to come out believing what you're sitting here telling me."

"Well, yes."

"You *want* them to find it easier to say no to the real Jesus than to say no to the Jesus they've made up?"

He shook his head, but I went on.

"This money you're offering isn't about compassion for my women. It's about shaping them up so they're fit for a club that I personally no longer want to belong to."

"What are you saying, Allison?"

"I'm saying yes to Jesus, and no to you."

The kettle whistled as he let himself out the door. We never did have tea.

According to our agreement about all things Troy Irwin, I repeated my conversation with Garry Howard verbatim to Chief when he brought Desmond home. He remained stoic, even through the Jesus parts.

"Irwin's not breaking a law by making a donation to the church," he said.

"I know, but it still makes me want to vomit."

"Just don't go vomit on him. I'll call you tomorrow when I've talked to Liz Doyle."

He left with a still somewhat businesslike good-bye. Desmond hung in the doorway to the den, looking from me to the door and back again, and then seemed to decide I wouldn't benefit from his advice this time and headed for the pantry. If he'd opened up the conversation, I might have said, "I don't want him to just be my lawyer, Desmond. I at least want him for my friend."

But Chief's voice on the phone the next day didn't sound like a lawyer. I pressed the phone to my ear to make sure the softened tone was coming from the Chief I'd been hearing for the past two days.

"You free this morning, Classic?" he said.

"After I take Desmond to school."

"Mind if I swing by?"

"I'll have the coffee on."

I didn't know whether to be relieved or scared, so I settled for cautiously optimistic. When I missed the school driveway and had to make a U-turn, Desmond saw it as Big Al freaking out.

"You got to get yourself together," he told me when he got out of the van.

He had no idea.

I made coffee and the cookies I'd planned to bake the day before, and then stuck the latter in the cabinet because I didn't want to look too eager. I would have told myself I was behaving like a silly teenager, except that I'd never been one until now.

Chief's sober face in my back-door window erased any possibility that the conversation was going to be about us. When I motioned him in, he went straight to the coffee pot.

"I hope you made this strong," he said.

"Why?"

"Because you're going to need it."

I sagged against the sink. "This can't be good."

"The first part is. I talked to Liz Doyle."

"Yeah?"

"She confirmed what you said about the West King development plans—and she showed me all the emails that are going through the city channels. Irwin hasn't made a public statement yet—I'm sure he'll make some big deal out of that—but he's pulling out all the stops to get approval."

"And in the meantime he's got his investors lined up," I said. "I took them all on a carriage tour one day."

Chief's face darkened. "When was that?"

"Relax. It was months ago, before I even rented Sacrament House." I folded my arms. "I made my opinions about Chamberlain and Troy Irwin known on that tour. I just found out the other day that was why I was 'terminated.'"

He scrubbed his face with his hand. "Do you see why I don't want you within a hundred yards of the guy?"

"Trust me. I don't want to *be* within a hundred yards of him. Make that five hundred."

In the moment he paused I was afraid he was going to take me further in that direction, but he carried his coffee to the bistro table and eased into a chair. He looked so natural in it, I had to look away. Wiping out the sink made a good excuse.

"While I was talking to Liz, she brought up the guardianship papers."

"Good," I said. "Geneveve wants to be able to take care of Desmond again, but they still have a long way to go before that happens. I want to be legal in the meantime. Do I need to go sign them?"

"They're not ready." I turned in time to see him grimace at the mug. "She hit a couple of snags."

I tossed the sponge aside. "Define 'snags.'"

"You're not gainfully employed—although you do have enough in the bank for them to overlook that."

"They've looked at my bank account?"

"You also have a court case pending against you."

"What—oh, you mean the noise thing?"

"I'm working on the Vernell woman's lawyer to get her to drop that. Once I do, Liz says they won't hold that against you."

"So what's the real snag?"

He held up two fingers.

"There's more than one? For Pete's sake, it's not like I have a rap sheet!"

"Your arrest in the park is one. We go to court next week. Again, depending on the judge, I think we'll get that dismissed."

I scratched at my scalp with both hands and realized too late that they were still wet. "I don't get what else there could possibly be."

"Vehicular assault doesn't ring a bell?"

"Vehicular …" My voice trailed off into a vision of an arm hitting the windshield of my motorcycle in a West King alley. But nobody knew about that except Jasmine. Even the creep who jumped in front of me didn't know who I was.

"Back in 1986?" Chief said.

Everything in me went heavy. I grabbed the counter so I wouldn't thud to the floor.

"Hey—you okay?"

"No. I don't believe this." I turned to the sink and held on, head toward the drain I wished I could put myself into.

"Classic."

Only because he called me that did I answer with a feeble, "What?"

"Liz wouldn't give me details because there's still some question about whether you were considered an adult at the time of the—"

"I was just before turning eighteen. And it wasn't vehicular assault. It was an accident."

"Were you formally charged?"

I shook my head at the sink. "There were no lawyers—nothing like that. I was told it was settled."

"And no one's brought it up in all this time."

"No." There was no need to. I'd done what I was asked to do and I thought it went away. I stood up, my back still to Chief. "I suppose you have to know what happened."

"Not unless you want to tell me."

I did turn around then. He wasn't using the eagle eyes to watch me.

"Why aren't you reaming me for not telling you everything you could possibly need to know as my lawyer?"

"Because in the first place, everybody's youth has a dark spot in it. As your lawyer it doesn't matter until something like this comes up—and the way it sounds—" he shrugged his big shoulders—"it won't matter now."

"And in the second place?"

"I know how much it means to you to be able to take care of that kid. You don't need me reaming you when you feel bad enough that all this stuff is blocking your way." His face flinched. "As your friend I feel bad *for* you."

I put my hands to my mouth and closed my eyes. The chair scraped on the floor.

"I have to get to the office," Chief said. "Try to hang in there. This will probably all go through. Like I said, we've just hit a few snags. In the meantime nobody is going to come take Desmond. His mother hasn't lost custody of him, so unless you have to get medical treatment for him or he gets in trouble with the law, you're just babysitting, and you don't need legal guardianship to do that."

"Okay," I said.

And I let him leave thinking my fear of losing Desmond was the only thing that made me smother my mouth with my hands until it was too late to call him back. If I hadn't, I would have told him the whole horrible story. And then he might never call me friend again.

I was never good at putting a good spin on an inner disaster, so I was glad only Geneveve was there when Desmond and I took the van to Sacrament House that night so that we could go out and buy a Christmas tree. Mercedes and Jasmine were at an NA meeting, and Sherry was still MIA. Mercedes would have picked up on my mood in a glance and been on me like the proverbial white on rice. It was bad enough that Desmond kept offering to talk to Chief for me, even though I didn't say a word about the man.

But I underestimated Geneveve. Deep in the Christmas tree lot, while Desmond was trying to charm the woman at the counter out of a free wreath, she caught shyly at my sleeve and said, "You got you some troubles, Miss Angel?"

"It's not about the house," I said quickly. "I told you—nobody's going anywhere."

"I know it's not about the house." She pressed her hand against her chest. "It's about somethin' in here."

"You can thank me now, or you can thank me later." We turned to look at Desmond, who emerged amid the packed-in trees with a fluffy circle of evergreen over each shoulder like a pair of epaulets. "I scored us not one, but two, of these bad boys."

I opened my mouth, but Geneveve inserted herself neatly between us.

"Did you steal those, boy?"

Desmond blinked, but he recovered. "No, I did not. That lady up there give 'em to me."

"Why?"

"'Cause I told her we wasn't gon' have no Christmas this year on accounta—"

"On accounta nothin'. You take those right back up to that counter, and you tell her you were mistaken. We don't lie at Sacrament House."

"I don't live at Sacrament House."

Geneveve took a step forward and took her voice to a menacing low. "You live at Miss Angel house, and that is part of the Sacrament family. Now you go on and give them wreaths back."

Desmond's eyes narrowed into resentful slits, but he headed through the trees, dragging the wreaths at his sides. Some small part of my core turned to jelly. Maybe I wasn't going to need those papers after all.

But even after we got back to Sacrament House and put up the tree and started Desmond on the decorating, I felt so low I was sure I'd have to scrape myself off the floor any minute. Unwilling to suck out any of the poorly concealed joy on Desmond's face as he hung Harley ornaments on the tree, I slipped out to the front step. I had my head on my knees when Geneveve joined me.

"Am I interruptin' your prayin', Miss Angel?" she asked.

"It's okay," I said. "It wasn't doing that much good anyway."

She stretched her legs down the steps and rubbed her thighs against the slight chill. "I feel that way sometime."

"I can only imagine."

"When I don't feel like God's listenin' to me, I usually talk to you."

I tried to laugh. "I am definitely no substitute for God, Geneveve."

"No, but you know him pretty good. Lotta times you say what he want me to hear. I *know* that thing, now."

"Well, I'm glad."

She seemed to ponder her feet for a minute before she said, "I ain't no Miss Angel, but I listen pretty good. We might could figure out his answer, the two of us."

"What's the question?" I said.

"Whatever it is makin' your eyes so scared."

I turned my head to look at her, to deny that I was quietly terrified, but I couldn't. I wasn't looking at the woman I carried on the back of my motorcycle a hundred years ago in September. This was a woman I wanted to know and trust. If I hadn't seen her lying in an alley in her own vomit or pushed her into a shower to wash away the stench of her life, I would have confided in her.

And then because of all those things, I wanted to.

"You're not the only one with a past, Gen," I said.

"Everybody got a story. I heard things in them NA meetings make me feel like I been Cinderella."

"Did any of them throw their lives away over—" I rolled my eyes. "I guess they all did or they wouldn't be there."

"They have just as hard of a time tellin' it as you," Geneveve said. "Most times they just start at the beginning."

"Okay," I said. I moved the mental rock and dragged out the first phrase. "I grew up a rich kid."

"I knew that. You got that kinda class. Ain't nothin' wrong with bein' rich."

"There can be a lot wrong with it, and I think I was born knowing what that was. And when I was sixteen or so, I fell in love with somebody who knew it too. Or so I thought."

"He was a rich kid."

"Yeah. His daddy and my daddy had it all planned out over their golf games that the two of us were going to get married someday."

Genevieve shrugged. "You was in love anyway."

"Love when you're sixteen isn't the same as love when you're— anyway, I was infatuated. He was just hormonal."

She squinted.

"He just wanted to get me into bed."

"What man don't?"

"He was pretty sly about it, though, y'know?"

"Mmm-hmm."

"He had me convinced that he shared my dream of leaving all our privileges behind right after high-school graduation and traveling around the country with just our backpacks and a few bucks, doing good for people. He never said, 'Come on, baby, you know you want to.' He said, 'I just want us to share everything—our dreams, our souls, our bodies.'"

"You went to bed with him."

"Yeah."

Genevieve dropped her head against my arm and laughed. The deep, throaty sound of it soothed off my edge.

"It was the most incredibly stupid thing I've ever done," I said. "Two months later I found out I was pregnant."

"Oh."

"It was just before my eighteenth birthday, and about two weeks before we graduated from high school. I was scared, right?"

"I hear that."

"But I thought since we were so close to being 'adults' and we already had a plan, it would be all right."

I could hear my voice getting thick.

"But it wasn't all right," Geneveve said.

"Not even a little bit. I went to Tr—the guy—and told him, and I said we would just strap the baby on my back and take him with us on our dream. I was talking about how differently our child was going to grow up from the way we did, and I watched his eyes just turn to—I don't know—"

"Stones."

"What?"

"They look like stones. When a man show you he don't love you like you thought, his eyes always look like stones in his head."

Geneveve demonstrated, eyes hard and cold.

"Yeah," I said. "That's it exactly. I just stood there and watched him turn into some other person while he was telling me that the whole dream thing was ridiculous and he never planned to do it to begin with. He said he thought I'd see how unrealistic it was when the time came to actually leave." I could hear Troy's incredulous tone as I repeated his exact words to Geneveve: "Did you really think we were going to go live like hippies? You're insane."

"And I *know* he never talked to you like before that."

"No—I was talking to somebody I didn't even know. Somebody I didn't *want* to know. I remember feeling like if I didn't get out of there, he was going to haul me away too, to wherever he'd taken the Troy Irwin I loved and killed him off."

"Troy? That was his name?"

"Yeah."

Geneveve waited. I was sure she could see me swallowing.

"So you ran," she said.

"It was the first time in my life I ever ran away from anything. I've pretty much been doing it ever since."

"You didn't run away from us."

"No. I guess I didn't."

"Ain't no guessin' to it." She curled her fingers around my sleeve. "You coulda turned us out anytime, and you never did."

"That's all God's doing, Gen."

She gave the sleeve a shake. "But you do what he tells you. Back then you just wasn't listenin'."

"You got that right."

Geneveve moved from the step to the space in front of me and, on her knees, took both of my hands. Hers were hot, as if she'd been warming them by a fire.

"You know what I'm thinkin' every time Miss Hank give me the communion bread?"

"What?" I said.

"I'm thinkin' it's a good thing Jesus' body keep feedin' me, 'cause all the bad things I done in my life was eatin' me up before I come here. I just keep thinkin' pretty soon, the feedin' gon' get ahead of the eatin', and I'ma be able to live like I never done before."

I put my hands on her face and pulled it to my forehead. I could barely breathe.

"What happened when you ran, Miss Angel?" she whispered.

"I can't," I said. "Really."

"It ain't gon' hurt this time like it done before."

I couldn't imagine that. The rock I'd moved was now pressing on my chest, forcing the words out. "I was crying too hard to drive, but I got in my car anyway and took off. I didn't see him run ahead of me in the driveway until it was too late to stop...."

"You need to say it."

I couldn't. And then I did—in a voice strangled by years of holding it back. "I ran over him, Geneveve."

For twenty-four years I'd kept the image out of my head by never speaking it except to Sylvia in those last weeks. Even then it was just to be reassured that the part I'd asked her to play in covering it up didn't go to her grave with her. I'd never fooled her for a moment. She'd known all along. When I finally confessed it to her all those years later, she said, "I'm just sorry I never had the satisfaction of running him over myself."

Somehow that had given me permission to bury it again, in a place I'd thought it would stay. Until those words came out of my mouth now—and with them the image of Troy, tossed to the edge of the gravel driveway of our secret hideaway.

"I was screaming when I got to him," I said, "but he wasn't making a sound. He was just sitting there, clutching at his leg. When he reached up and grabbed my arm—it's a blur but I know his blood soaked right into my skin. I may have screamed that I was sorry or that I would get help or that if he wouldn't die I would do whatever he wanted me to do. I'm still not sure what I said."

"You was in shock, Miss Angel. Don't nobody know what they sayin' when they get like that."

"I do remember one thing, though. He put his hand on my lips to stop me, and I could taste his blood. And then he did this weird thing."

"What he do?"

I closed my eyes and saw it again. "He smiled."

"No he didn't."

"He did. And he said, 'It's okay. I'll make it okay.' I just kept shaking my head. I had all this long hair and it just kept getting in the blood. It was like being in a horror movie." I pressed my thumbs to my temples and closed my eyes again to see. "He told me to go to a phone and call for help, and I tried to get up and go, but he pulled me back and he said, 'Don't give them your name. And when you're done, go home and don't let anybody see you until you're cleaned up.' It was like he'd had an hour to plan, y'know? He said to tell my nanny that I hit a tree and to make her get the car fixed before my dad saw it. He said she'd do it—he said it like I was going to ask her to get me a glass of juice."

"That one of them things you said was wrong with bein' rich?"

I shoved the back of my hand against my mouth, but it all continued to shove its way out. "I told him *I* couldn't do that, but he said I had to. He said they'd never believe it was an accident and I would go to jail. 'I'll make up a story'—that's what he said. 'You never saw me today.'"

I opened my eyes, but I could still see it. His face was gray, and his body seized every time he tried to touch his leg. But it was as if he had to, as if he were trying to keep it from dying.

"So I did it." I looked at Geneveve, whose eyes held every word I'd just let free. "I've only told one other person this, and she's gone now."

"And ain't nobody gon' hear it from me." She rocked back on her heels and watched me rub my hand up and down on my chest.

"It hurts rememberin', don't it?" she said. "Not as bad as when it happened—but it hurts."

"Yeah, which is why I managed not to do it for two decades."

"The pain'll stop when you got it all out."

I put my hand up. "That's all I can handle right now."

"What happened to your baby, Miss Angel?"

If Nita's car hadn't nosed up to the curb, I might have told her. I might not. The only thing I knew for sure was that the last piece of the pain I'd buried had survived the grave I made for it.

Mercedes and Jasmine climbed out of Nita's Hyundai, but she didn't pull away.

"She said she need to talk to you, Miss Angel," Jasmine said.

I virtually ran down the walkway, readjusting my face as I went. At least it was dark, because no amount of faking was going to account for the mascara that was surely collected under my eyes by now.

"Everything okay?" I said when I got to Nita.

She turned down the Trini Lopez version of "Feliz Navidad." "Oh, yeah. Those two are a trip, aren't they?"

"They're a whole journey."

She started the nodding that always preceded her sentences. "Well, listen, I just wanted to let you know that I am going to be out of town for the holidays. I leave tomorrow."

I got up enough wherewithal to ask her where she was going, but I didn't hear the answer.

"Anyway, I will be back in a week. They can call Leighanne or anybody else in the group if they have trouble. The holidays can be hard when you're in recovery." She patted my hand on the car door. "And of course they have you. You have saved their lives, you know."

"I think they've saved mine."

Nita squeezed my hand. "Then everybody lives," she said. "Have a merry Christmas."

I was relieved to see that Mercedes and Jasmine were still on the porch with Geneveve. I really couldn't talk anymore tonight. I needed to get to my red chair and muck through what I'd turned loose, because it was now in a bog at my feet. *God, please be there waiting. Please.*

"You got to just put her out your mind, Geneveve," Mercedes was saying when I got to the porch.

"Could you put *Jasmine* out your mind if she was back there on the street without nobody carin' what happened to her?"

"I known Jasmine a long time. We like sisters now—same with you. You don't even hardly know Sherry."

"Don't matter. I just feel like the Lord is callin' me to care. That's all." Geneveve looked at me and her eyes jumped, as if she'd just realized I was standing there. "I'ma go get Desmond for you," she said. "He needs to get to bed—it's a school night."

I was still watching her go when Jasmine grabbed my hand. "I know she heard the Lord and all that—I'm not sayin' she lyin'."

"But the Lord ain't the only reason she worried 'bout Sherry bein' on the street." Mercedes looked at the door and then back at me. "She afraid of Sherry usin', 'cause when Sherry usin', she do anything Sultan tell her to do. And that is a fact now."

"Mmm-hmm—"

"Sultan?" I said. "Has he tried to get in touch with Geneveve? Why don't you *tell* me this stuff?"

"No—you don't need to be gettin' all worked up. We just know that about Sherry."

Jasmine nodded. "Long as Sherry was here, Geneveve didn't have to worry 'bout Sultan findin' her 'cause he didn't have his spy."

"Is that why she came here, do you think?"

They both shrugged.

I pressed my whole head with my hands. "Ladies, how am I supposed to protect you if I don't know what it is I'm protecting you from?"

Mercedes closed her face. Jasmine crossed me out with her arms. A wall went up that I was not going to knock down tonight.

"All right," I said. "Promise me that you will *not* let Geneveve go out looking for Sherry. And if you can't stop her, you call me. Immediately. Am I clear?"

Mercedes grunted.

"Not good enough, Mercedes. The future of this house depends on it being a safe place. We don't play by street rules here. You got that?"

"We got it," Jasmine said. She looked hard at Mercedes. "Both of us."

"All right—I'm going to go talk to Geneveve."

"She done went to bed," Desmond said from the doorway. "After she give me a hour lecture 'bout not givin' you no trouble tonight 'cause you got a lot on your mind." He hit his soprano range. "Like I don't know that."

A lot on my mind didn't even begin to cover it. It was on my heart, my soul.…

It was even on the air. I breathed hard against a sudden heaviness and cranked the van to reluctant life. In the rearview mirror, Sacrament House sank into the shadows.

"Go on in, and I'll meet you in a minute," I said to Desmond when we pulled into the garage.

"I don't got a—"

I tossed him the house key from my ring. He only gazed at it for two seconds before he bolted with it as if I might change my mind. When the door slammed, I called Chief.

He picked up with, "You okay?"

"No," I said. "Can you … do you have time—"

"I can be there in ten."

"Okay," I said. "I'm ready to tell you what happened."

CHAPTER TWENTY-FIVE

Porches, it seemed, were good places for telling. Chief propped his feet next to mine on my side porch railing as he listened. I could only see his face clearly when the chilly night almost-wind brushed the Spanish moss away from the stream of light from Miz Vernell's and gave me a wispy glimpse of his eyes or his mouth. They were pieces of compassion that kept me talking until I reached the place where I'd left off with Geneveve.

"It was an accident," Chief said. "Troy Irwin was as full of it then as he is now."

I surprised myself with a laugh. I was much closer to tears.

"So what was his 'story'?"

The chortle died in my throat. "I had no idea until Clive Irwin called my parents three hours later and said Troy had been the victim of a hit-and-run."

"Longest three hours of your life."

"Ya think? I still kept waiting for the police to come question me, take me off to jail. Between the fear and being pregnant, I threw up for two days. The more information my mother got from Troy's mother, the worse it got. His leg was broken in three places. He had to have surgery. He got an infection. By the time his mother called to say he was ready to see me, I expected him to be half-dead."

"I take it he wasn't."

"Not even close."

"Too bad," Chief said.

I wanted to hug him. But then I always wanted to hug him.

"It actually seemed like he was enjoying the attention—like nothing serious had happened and I wasn't pregnant and we didn't have some major decisions to make." I swallowed, but none of the ache went down. "There was no 'we' about it. He'd already made the decision—which I didn't know when I started in about how I was willing to give up the 'unrealistic' idea of traveling like hippies, but that because of the baby, we should get married right away instead of waiting."

I looked down at my hands, which sparkled with sweat even in the wet chill.

"Stop if you want," Chief said.

"No—you need to hear this part because it—well—let me just—"

"Sure. Take your time."

I huffed. "I've taken twenty-four years. That ought to be long enough."

"It takes what it takes."

"Troy didn't even let me get that out of my mouth before he was …" I squeezed my hands into fists. "Laughing at me. That derisive hissing kind of thing men do—well, not all men—"

"We all have it in us."

"No," I said. "Not all of you." I stared at my feet on the rail. "Troy told me what he saw happening. He was going to pay for an abortion, and then we were going to go off and do the whole college thing and come back to St. Augustine after graduation and get married then."

"You must be a completely different person now than you were then," Chief said.

"One would hope."

"Now you'd tell him where to take his 'plan.'"

"Oh, I did."

I saw the twinkle I hadn't seen in days.

"I told him I was having the baby with or without him." The breath I drew in was ragged. "I guess he saw that coming because he didn't even hesitate. He said if I didn't get the abortion, he'd go straight to the police and tell them I'd run over him on purpose. He said they'd break Sylvia down, make her confess to the coverup. He had it all figured out."

"You weren't insisting that he marry you and support the baby."

"No. He just didn't want there to *be* a baby."

"What am I not seeing here?"

"What you're not seeing is my father."

Chief tucked in his chin. "What—your old man would go after him with a shotgun?"

"Hardly. Troy said my father had told him the summer before—so we're talking almost nine months back—that he wanted Troy to come home after he got his business degree and let him groom Troy to run Chamberlain Enterprises someday—since I obviously wasn't CEO material."

"And if you came up pregnant with Troy's kid, all bets were off."

"That's why they pay you the big bucks, Chief. That is it on the nose."

It was all out, almost all of it. And Geneveve was wrong. It ripped me apart even more in the telling than it had the day I walked out of Troy's hospital room into a world that had crumbled into fragments too tiny to piece back together. Maybe it hurt more tonight, because that day I didn't know that I would never even try.

"So—" I said. "I never spoke to Troy Irwin again until I went to his office the other day."

"Good."

I twisted to face Chief.

"I'm an idiot," he said.

"I'm sorry?"

"I'm an idiot."

He jerked his legs from the railing and moved so far to the edge of the canvas chair its back legs left the ground. He rubbed at his thighs with the heels of his hands. I had the unexplainable urge to put him out of whatever misery he was suddenly in.

"Okay—so why are you an idiot?" I said.

"Because I thought Troy Irwin was some old flame of yours that you wanted to rekindle."

"You have *got* to be *kid*din' me. I'd rather be burned at the stake."

"I should've seen that—even without what you just told me. Knowing you—like I think I do—like I said, I'm an idiot."

"No doubt." I knew I was pulling out the old cover of wit, but I couldn't help it. He was headed where I wanted to go, and I was terrified.

"So no Troy Irwin in your life," he said. "What about Bonner Bailey?"

"Bonner Bailey. You're not serious."

"I'm thinking he's like an annoying little brother to you, but I could be an idiot about that, too. Am I?"

"If you think we are or have ever been romantically involved, then, yes, you're an idiot, and you ought to be on heavy medication."

He nodded. The eagle eyes were at close range, where they clearly weren't used to being, where they were vulnerable. I couldn't pull mine away.

"Then you're free," he said. "Except for that one guy."

I couldn't breathe. I didn't know how I was able to say, "Desmond?"

Maybe I didn't. Maybe my cell phone rang before I even got the word out.

Chief rocked back and the moment was gone. I pulled the phone out with the words, "This better be important" already formed on my lips.

Mercedes swept them away. Her voice was so shrill I barely made out, "Geneveve just left. She gone to the street lookin' for Sherry."

"Okay, Mercedes. Slow down...."

I held out the phone so Chief could hear but there was no need. She was screaming at that point, as was Jasmine in the background.

"Sherry called here, beggin' Geneveve to come help her. We tol' her to call you and let you handle it but she said for *us* to call, 'cause she goin' on ahead. I tried to stop her, Miss Angel. I threw myself over the door, and she just bust right past me."

"All right. It'll be fine—"

"I don't think so. After you left tonight, Geneveve was all walkin' around, jumpin' at her own shadow—she kept sayin', 'Somethin' goin' down. Somethin' goin' down—I can feel it.'"

I'd felt it myself, and I should've gone back.

"Whatchoo want us to do?" Her voice was calmer, but I knew that was only a momentary lull.

"Okay, you stay there, you and Jasmine, and you call me the minute you hear from Geneveve or Sherry. Lock all the doors, and don't open them to anybody but them or me or Chief."

"He with you?"

"Yes."

"Then maybe we *will* be okay."

"We will." I put my hand over the phone to whisper to Chief. "Will you—?"

"I'm gone. You stay with Desmond."

"Chief's on his way over to West King now," I said to Mercedes. "Call me the minute you hear anything."

She was breathing hard, but she managed to get in an "okay."

"You and Jasmine pray," I said. "I'll see if I can find Hank— maybe she'll come over and be with you."

"We need all the Jesus people we can get," she said.

The minute I ended the call, I got Hank on the phone.

"You know what," she said when I filled her in, "I'm coming to you first."

I didn't ask her why. I could hear my own voice unraveling.

It wasn't hard to imagine Geneveve pacing around the house, wringing her hands. I did the same thing now, praying "pleaseGod-pleaseGodpleaseGod" with more fervor than I'd ever chanted Allison's Pathetic Pleading Prayer. The Allison of Then couldn't hold a candle to me now. I finally landed in Desmond's doorway, watching his back rise and fall in an even rhythm, begging for a Nudge that would show me whether to go or stay or wait some more.

Think.

Think. I dragged my hand through my hair. Think. What a concept.

Cell phone clutched in my hand, I went back to the side porch and sank into the canvas chair again. Think—where would Geneveve go on West King? She'd go where she knew Sherry would hide. Or where Sultan would hold her until she drew Geneveve out. That thought left me cold, but I had to chase it. I still knew nothing about the man—except that he didn't do his dirty work himself. He was the Troy Irwin of the underworld. Troy had his Vivienne Harkness. Sultan had his—who?

For the second time that day the image of the hulking figure in the alley flickered onto my screen. One of the women had spoken of him by name—Opie? Otis? I shook my head and stood up to pace again. Didn't matter. He was the same guy who had accosted Desmond behind C.A.R.S. He had to be Sultan's lackey.

And I knew how he operated.

I clawed my phone out of my pocket and hurtled through the kitchen to check on Desmond again, begging, "Please answer, Hank, please, please."

She did, voice breathless. "I'm almost there—I'm two blocks away."

"Okay—I'm going down there. Will you stay with Desmond?"

"Down where?"

"West King. I think I know where Geneveve went to find Sherry—only she's not going to find her, she's going to find—"

"Where is Chief?"

"He's down there, but he doesn't know to look behind the car place. Hank, I have to go. Will you stay here?"

"Is it going to do me any good to try to talk you out of it?"

"No. If you don't hear from me in an hour, call the police."

"I think you should call them right now."

"No crime's been committed. Yet."

"I don't like this, Al," she said.

"I don't either," I said.

I hung up and ran for the door and grabbed the keys from the hook. The sense of *déjà vu* was almost overwhelming as I tore across the lane and got the garage door open. I fought against the image of

Geneveve lying in a pile of squalor, but one part shouldered its way through: Chief carrying her to the van I'd had to come back for the last time we rescued her.

I hoisted myself into it now and fumbled the key into the ignition. The engine cranked once, twice. By the third try, I could taste the noxious gas fumes.

"Come *on*—not tonight—" I pumped, panicked, at the accelerator and tried the ignition again, but the motor only groaned halfheartedly. I abandoned the van and scrambled for the locker. Geneveve would be riding back with me—that was all there was to it—that was the way it had to be.

I crammed my helmet on and fired up the bike. She came to life with an alarmed rumble.

"I know," I said. "I'm freaked out too."

I rolled the throttle and took off out of the garage. Out of the corner of my eye, I saw a flashlight beam zigzag across the road. I slowed to look, heart in my throat, but it was Owen running toward me, his other hand pointing frantically toward Miz Vernell's.

She was just going to have to deal with the noise tonight. I'd see her in court. I shot through the flashlight's beam and left Owen yelling behind me.

🛵

The ride to West King was endless. I was sure it must be midnight by the time I lurched to a stop across the street from C.A.R.S. and strained to see through the uneven splotches from the few streetlights that still worked. The block was eerily quiet, as if holding its breath could delay some inevitable evil. I held mine, too, but there was no rumble of a Road King. I thought of trying Chief on his cell phone but discarded that idea. He'd never hear me on the bike. Aloneness began a slow, cold curl around me.

Keeping my eyes on C.A.R.S., I cut the engine and leaned the Classic on her stand. If I took her back there, I'd broadcast my presence to every thug in the neighborhood. I hung my helmet on the handlebars, begging to be stolen, and broke into a run across the street.

Every footfall slapped the wet asphalt of the parking lot, every breath announced me. By the time I flattened myself against the side of the building, I was sure I could be heard all the way down the alley. I sucked in cold air and peered down into the darkness. Seeing nothing, I started to make my way into it, back plastered to the damp brick, but the sudden hurried flap of footsteps froze me to the wall.

The sound kept on, not in the alley, but on the other side of the building, as if they were making their way upstairs. An image of a woman trudging the steps with her laundry flashed on.

I took one more anxious look down the alley and returned to the front of the building. The footsteps were fading on the far side. What I was going to ask their owner, I had no idea. *Have you seen Geneveve?* It was ridiculous, but I kept going, faster and more frantically, until I rounded the corner and saw the yellowed legs ascending above me. Legs I'd wrapped in a blanket and rubbed with my hands and my love. This was where I'd seen her before.

"Sherry!"

The steps paused for only an instant before they quickened and stumbled and disappeared.

"Sherry!"

"Shhh, Big Al! Shhh!"

I peered once again into the darkness, this time under the stairs. Desmond reached out a lanky arm and pulled me by the sleeve. I grazed my head on a step as I staggered into him.

"What are you *doing* here?"

Desmond found my mouth with a clammy hand and tried to cover it. I grabbed his wrist and pulled him close to me. My words died in my throat when I saw his eyes, glistening with fear.

"She not up there," he whispered.

"Your mama?"

He nodded.

I took his head in my hands and put my lips next to his ear. "Do you know where she is?"

"Maybe. Where she always hide."

"She's not hiding, Desmond—" I started to say.

But he wriggled from my grasp and into the cement gutter along the building. I followed him, hands scraping the raw concrete as I clawed at it to keep my balance. Above me, a female cry rose and just as suddenly fell. I couldn't stop for it—Desmond was already around the corner and into the back alley—so I stumbled forward to the end of the gutter. It dropped off sharply, and I flung my arm out to catch myself, but the wall had ended too. I sprawled onto the brick and slid until my head hit something soft. Desmond grabbed at my shoulder.

"I'm okay," I said.

He hauled me up by my sleeve and pointed to the trash cans lined up next to the back door. The ones Maharry Nelson said the homeless couldn't stay out of. *No—please no—not again.*

Desmond took off toward them, and I was still trying to get vertical as I went after him. If this truly was *déjà vu*, I couldn't let him find his mother lying amid the garbage.

Before I could get there, he had already flung one can aside and sent it bouncing on its battered sides against the far wall. He kicked the second one over and went to his hands and knees.

"Desmond—*what?*"

My cry was useless. He was disappearing through a low opening in the wall. I dropped to my own knees and put my head inside, but Desmond's turban of hair collided with my face and pushed me backward onto my rear. He crouched before me, taking in air through his nose in frenzied gasps.

"What? What's in there?" I said.

He tried to get to his feet, but I caught his hands. He froze and looked down at them. We stared at the blood, smeared on both of us.

I took him by the shoulders and moved his body aside. "Wait," I said. "Wait right here."

He nodded, but I knew he didn't hear a word I said.

Heart throbbing in my ears, I got to my knees again and pushed my head and shoulders into the crawl space. It was tar black, but as I felt my way forward, I knew what I wasn't seeing. My hand fell at once onto a tiny form that moaned under my touch.

"Geneveve? *Gen?*"

She moaned again.

With no idea what I was grabbing, I took hold of whatever I could get my hands around and crawled backward, dragging her with me.

"Desmond! Get my phone out of my pocket—call 911."

He didn't answer.

"Do it, Desmond!"

I gave Geneveve a final pull and fell back with her in my arms. I twisted to call to Desmond once more, but he was gone. Panic seized me.

"Okay, okay, Geneveve. Hang on. I'm calling for help."

One arm holding her head against me, I groped in my pocket and yanked out the phone. It shot from my bloody hand like a bar of soap and skipped down the alley, out of my reach.

"Miss Angel?"

"Dear God, Geneveve …" I slid my other arm under her and cradled her. "Desmond went for help—your son went for help, okay? Just hang in there."

Her lips parted, but I couldn't hear the words she was trying to form. I pulled her face up to mine, and felt only a faint breath on my cheek.

"Don't talk," I said. "I've got you—"

A siren wailed from too far away.

"See? Help's coming. Please, Geneveve, please, just hang on a little longer."

But she was already going limp, and we were soaked in more blood than she could afford to lose. Her eyes began to stare.

I pulled her face into my neck so I couldn't look into those eyes without the life in them. But I could feel her—feel her last breath against my skin, feel her slip away. I held on, to her and to the piece of myself she was taking with her. I held onto us both until I felt a pair of arms go around us.

"Chief," I said. "Oh, dear God, Chief. He's killed her."

CHAPTER TWENTY-SIX

It was my turn in the red chair-and-a-half. My pain matched that of every woman I had tucked there before me, swaddled in blankets that couldn't stop the shivering.

My sweet Geneveve was dead.

Mercedes and Jasmine and Sherry were nowhere to be found.

And Desmond. Desmond was even now on his way to FIP custody.

I'd made Chief explain that to me no less than ten times during the night.

"When the police found him, he was covered in blood. Once they saw that he wasn't hurt, they assumed he'd been involved in a crime."

"He was going for help," I said, over and over. "Why didn't they believe him when he told them what happened?"

Chief gave me the same answer every time. "He didn't tell them. He was barely coherent."

And I gave him the same response every time. "He's so scared. I have to be with him—he's so scared."

That was the deepest pain of all, the part I didn't make Chief repeat because it sent me over the edge. They wouldn't release Desmond to me because I wasn't his legal guardian. I was more his mother than any woman had ever been, but I didn't have the piece of paper to prove it.

By five a.m. my voice was no more than a thread. Chief sat on the edge of the trunk coffee table, his face white with fatigue. "I'll be in Liz Doyle's office the minute it opens. I've already left a message on her voice mail."

"It's not going to do any good, is it?" I could feel my face crumpling. "Nothing changes except to get worse."

"Isn't this where your faith is supposed to kick in?" he said.

I couldn't answer. I'd been waiting for that all night, from the moment they took Geneveve from me in the alley, but all I could feel was the ache in my arms from trying to hold onto her life. The longer I sat here, doing nothing, the more frightening the empty pain became.

I shoved the blankets from my shoulders and swung my still-swathed legs over the side of the ottoman.

"What can I get you?" Chief said.

"Nothing. I'm going to go look for them. Mercedes and Jasmine—"

"Not a good plan, Classic."

"Do you have a better one?"

I kicked the blankets away and started blindly for the front door.

"Hey, Allison—no."

"I have to bring them home—"

"We'll find them at daylight."

I whirled to face him, everything flailing—arms, hair, words. "Dead? Will we find them dead?"

"I don't know. But if you go out that door now, I'm liable to find *you* dead."

"I don't care!"

"I do."

I smothered my face in my hands. I didn't know Chief was holding me until I smelled the leather.

"We're going to see this through together, Classic," he said. "One road at a time."

I didn't know how long I sobbed, or when Hank rose from the couch where she'd fallen asleep at three, or which one of them got me back into the chair. When I woke up, the sun was slanting through the blinds, and Chief was gone.

"He'll be back," Hank said before I even asked. "He went home to shower and shave so he won't look like one of the Hell's Angels when he goes to see the social worker."

She handed me a cup of coffee and sat on the ottoman facing me.

"I'm going to fix you some breakfast as soon as you get that down."

"I'm not hungry."

"I knew you'd say that, which is why I'll spoon feed you if I have to. You have to keep up your strength for what you've got ahead of you."

I looked bleakly into the mug. "What have I got ahead of me?"

"We don't know. That's why you need the strength. And the faith."

"I'm not feeling it, Hank. There's no Nudge. I feel like Geneveve took God with her. That's so stupid, but …" I shook my head and handed her the mug. "All this time I've felt so led and now I think I've ended up nowhere after all."

Hank set the mug on the trunk and folded her hands in the tidy way I'd seen her do so many times.

"You have an answer for me," I said. "Tell me you have one."

But she shook her head. "You're dealing with things that, frankly, I don't even think make sense to God himself."

"Then what am I supposed to do?"

"What you always do, my precious prophet. Pray. Wait for an answer. And eat."

"I don't always eat."

"That's where I come in. What do you want? Anything sound good?"

"Eggs Dominic," I said.

I wept in Hank's arms until I fell asleep again.

Hank talked me into a shower at mid-morning, which woke me up too much. I checked my phone every ten minutes to make sure I hadn't missed a call from Chief, and imagined every scenario from him bringing Desmond home with him to taking me to see him in some dank, smelly cell where there were no Oreos.

I was grateful I even had the phone, since the last time I'd seen it, it was skidding away from me down the alley. The police had given it to Chief when they decided it wasn't evidence in the murder. As for my Harley, Rex had brought it home around midnight, at Chief's request. The helmet was gone, but I didn't care. If I got Desmond back, I'd buy a new one, and six for him. If he didn't come home, I would never ride the bike again anyway.

When the phone finally rang at eleven o'clock, I was saying, "Hello? Chief?" before I even got it to my ear. But it was Bonner.

"Allison," he said. "I am so, so sorry."

"How did you know?" I said.

"Chief called me. What can I do for you? Anything you need— just ask."

"There's nothing. Not unless you can bring Desmond home or find Mercedes and Jasmine. Or Sherry."

"I wish I could. You know I'd do it in a heartbeat. There must be something else—"

"Pray. Pray double. Because I'm having a hard time doing it myself."

"I'm on it," he said.

Hank poked her head out of the kitchen. "Chief's back."

I didn't even say good-bye to Bonner, and I was out on the side porch before Chief could get up the steps. His face showed nothing—which was bad news in itself. The fact that he didn't have Desmond with him was worse.

"Tell me," I said.

He sank into the swing and patted the seat next to him.

"I can't sit. Just tell me straight out. I'm dying here."

"He's not going to Juvie. The police are satisfied that he had nothing to do with his mother's death."

"Well *I* could have told them that!"

"And I got the judge to dismiss the charges against you for that deal in the park."

He rubbed at his cheek and avoided my eyes.

"That's the end of the good news, isn't it?"

"Yeah. Well, no—Liz Doyle is working on the vehicular assault thing. Evidently the charge was brought after you left here in eighty-six, but by the time you came back, the statute of limitations had run out on it, and no one pursued it."

"That jackal."

"Liz says if that were the only strike you had against you, you'd have Desmond with you right now. We've got the noise violation—I'm on that. And the fact that we don't have Geneveve's signature on this."

"How could we get her signature when we didn't even have the paperwork?" I made circles on my temples with my fingers but they continued to throb. "She was so close to being able to be his mom again—I was seeing it more all the time. Just last night I was even thinking that I wouldn't need guardianship."

"Parents die all the time without making arrangements for their kids and people who want them get custody of them. FIP's biggest concern is that you left Desmond here unsupervised last night."

"He wasn't unsupervised! Hank was here—she'll testify to that."

"He was already gone when she got here," Chief said. "She told me that this morning."

"Then how did he get to the alley before I did?"

"He must have left before you."

"When I was talking to her on the phone? Didn't I check him again when I hung up? I can't even remember—"

"Don't tell the judge that."

"What judge?"

"Liz is setting it up an interview with him."

"And what happens to Desmond in the meantime?"

"He's in a group home—right here in town—"

"He just found his mother murdered and stuffed in a hole! He needs to be with people who love him—not some bureaucratic … I can't stand this, Chief. I can't."

He caught my hand and pulled me onto the swing. I folded in half beside him.

"What did we agree on?" he said. "One road at a time."

"Which road are we on now?"

"We're on the road to the police station."

I straightened up. "Why?"

"Because there's nothing you can do about Desmond until we see him this afternoon—"

"I'm going to see him?"

"Liz set that up for us too. Good call sticking up for her in high school, Classic. I think she'd give you a kidney if you needed one."

"Okay, okay, good. I need to get some Oreos to take to him—and his drawing stuff—and his helmet. That'll make him feel better."

Chief's eyes held a hint of the twinkle. "I'll find out what we're allowed to bring. But that's not until three, and you're going to freak out on me if I don't find you something to do between now and then. I thought we'd tell the police everything you know about Sultan and his, what do you always call him, his 'henchman'?"

"Opus," I said. "I just remembered—his name is Opus Behr."

"Good. We'll take all of that to the police. And then we can take a cruise around and look for Sherry."

"Won't they look for her once we tell them all that?"

Chief's face softened. He reached over and brushed a strand of hair away from my eyes.

"What?" I said.

"The cops aren't going to look very hard for Geneveve's killer. To them she was just another hooker." He put his finger to my lips before I could open them. "I know. It's going to take every bit of self-control you have not to rip into the first person who even implies it. But Desmond doesn't need you locked up right now—again." He twitched a smile. "And neither do I. You've already been enough trouble."

"Don't leave me, Chief," I said. "Please—just walk me through this, okay?"

"That's the plan, Classic. That's the plan."

It was a good thing Chief prepared me for the indifference we expe-rienced at the police station, or I definitely would have plucked out a few nose hairs and ripped off a few lips. I did correct the detective every time he referred to Geneveve as "the victim."

"Geneveve Sanborn," I said, teeth gritted. "She was a mother and a sister and a friend, and she didn't deserve to die like that."

Nobody put handcuffs on me, and Chief told me I did okay.

The only encouraging thing we got out of the meeting was the detective's nod when I mentioned Sultan.

"You know him?" Chief asked.

"Know *of* him. His real name is Jude Lowery. Big time dealer. Pimp. He's been in and out of here, but we've never been able to make anything stick."

"Then here's your chance," I said. "If you get him for murder, he's gone for good."

"Well, there's that," the detective said.

Chief squeezed my shoulder and I shut up, but only until we got outside the building.

"What does that mean—'there's that'?" I said. "They really don't care, do they?"

"I don't know," Chief said. "It's hard to care after you've been in that business for a while. Which is why we have to." He glanced at his watch. "That took longer than I thought. Let's grab some lunch and head on over to see Desmond."

Needless to say, I couldn't eat.

The group home I'd imagined was a cinder-block house among many, a village overgrown with kudzu and the grass worn down into sandy paths. The actual home was worse. I was right about the cinder block, but the whole thing was one big dormitory with multi-locked doors and common areas that had as much personality as a shower stall. I clutched my bag of Oreos and drawing paper and bit my lip to keep from screaming, "These are kids! It's not their fault they're in here!"

Liz Doyle led us to the east wing and got us settled in a common room identical to all the others. When she went to get Desmond, I stared at the endless list of rules that hung over the television and sucked in the odor of bleach and dirty tennis shoes.

"Desmond isn't used to living like this," I said. "He'll die in here."

Chief nodded. "Ironic, isn't it?"

"What?"

"Three months ago this would've been a huge improvement over what he was used to."

The bolt slid on the door to the hallway, and suddenly Desmond was there. I started toward him, but he flung himself across the room and into my chest. The long, lanky arms circled me and hung on, so tight I could feel his rickety ribs against mine. Coarse sobs ripped from his throat and cut straight into me. They went on and on, and I didn't care. He could cry all he wanted, as long as I didn't have to let go.

"I think y'all will be all right," Liz whispered. "I'll be back there in the office if you need me."

When Desmond finally pulled away, he saw Chief and hurled himself at him. Chief covered the back of Desmond's head with his hand and pressed the boy's face into his neck. It was an uncommon moment to realize that, for the first time, I was in love.

Chief let him go, and Desmond smeared his sleeve across his eyes. He was wearing a T-shirt I didn't recognize and jeans that drooped from his waist and fell in limp folds over the tops of his shoes. I'd never seen those before either.

"They told you about your mama?" I said.

"They didn't have to tell me."

"I'm sorry, Desmond. She loved you. She was trying to get her life together so she could take care of you."

If he heard me, he gave no indication, but pointed to the bag over my arm. "Whatcha got in there?"

"Oh, I brought you some things. Oreos—of course—can't live without those, right? And a sketchpad so you can draw. They said they'd give you pencils, chalk, whatever."

I didn't tell him I wasn't allowed to provide him with sharp instruments, or that they said the helmet would probably get stolen or trashed by some angry adolescent if I brought it in.

"I'll bring you some clothes next time," I said. "You want a couple of your Harley shirts?"

Desmond took a step back. His shoulders were already curving into his chest. "I ain't goin' home with you?"

My own chest caved. "Not today," I said. "But we're working on it."

"We'll get you home as soon as we can, buddy," Chief said. "We have to talk to the judge, get some papers signed."

"Why you gotta talk to a judge? I didn't do nothin' wrong—I swear."

His eyes went wild, and I grabbed his sleeve.

"No, Desmond—you didn't. They just have to make sure I'm the best person to take care of you now that your mom's gone."

"Whatchoo mean, now that she gone? Ain't nobody *ever* took care of me but you."

He backed away again until his spine hit the wall. He took a dog-eared poster down with him as he slid to the floor. Liz Doyle put her head out of the office door, but Chief waved her off. I knelt in front of Desmond.

"It doesn't make any sense to me either," I said. "If I could I'd stick you on the back of that Harley right now and we'd ride forever. But we have to wait—and we will—and we'll trust, okay? We'll trust in God."

Desmond let out a low hiss.

"What's with that?" I said. "God brought you to me in the first place. He's been there through everything. He's got your mama in his arms. Come on, Desmond—we can't give up on him." I put my palm to his. "It's all good."

They were the words I myself had needed to hear all morning. I sat back on my heels and watched Desmond and hoped they would seep into him, too. But no outrageous retort played at the lips where a tiny hardness formed. No charming reply danced through the dull haze in his eyes. There was no smile reserved for me that put me "right there." He was already edging away from the boy who lived at my house. I had to get him out of there. Soon. Or I wasn't going to be able to save him.

Chief had to go to his office from there. After practically signing a sworn statement that I would take every precaution driving my bike home alone, he agreed to go on without me. I fully intended to go straight to Palm Row, but as I drove down Ponce de Leon Boulevard, I thought I felt the faintest of Nudges moving me toward Sacrament House. I really should go over and secure the place. Chances were that in their state of panic, Mercedes and Jasmine hadn't even locked it up. As I got closer, though, I had to doubt the Nudge a little. If word had gotten out on West King that they'd split, the house could be filled with crack addicts by now.

I had to swallow hard. Two days ago I would have welcomed any woman who came there tired enough of herself to surrender to our love. Geneveve's wasn't the only life that had been cut off by the brutal stabs of that knife.

Sacrament House looked the same when I shut down the Harley in front of it. No windows had been smashed, no graffiti had been scrawled on the paint. But it wasn't the same. The hope was gone. Everything we'd worked for had gone down its drains and seeped out of the cracks around its windows. Despite the wreath still hanging bravely on the door, it was as empty as every other house on the bleak street.

There was really no point in holding back the sobs as I made my way up the walk, so I let them go. That made it hard to locate my key when I found the front door locked, and to get it into the lock once I did. Still weeping from the pit of my soul, I stumbled into the living room, where my cries rose with those of two figures huddled on the couch. Mercedes pulled her arms from Jasmine's back and held them up to me.

CHAPTER TWENTY-SEVEN

We untangled a few things—they'd heard about the sirens and run to the scene—watching with the gawking crowd in the side alley as the paramedics loaded Geneveve's lifeless body into the ambulance. Terrified, they'd spent the night in an abandoned car and returned to the house at daylight. There was no crime tape to keep them out, so they'd come inside to wait for me. I didn't tell them I never thought I'd find them there.

I could tell they still had more to say but couldn't yet, so I called Hank and Leighanne and was about to dial Nita's number when I remembered she was out of town.

"She love Geneveve," Mercedes said. "This gon' tear her up."

"She was a good sponsor to her," I said.

Jasmine's hand crept into mine. "But weren't nobody as good to her as you, Miss Angel."

Maybe. But a lot of good that was doing me now. I tried not to think of Desmond—tried to focus on them. We gathered in the dining alcove, hands grasping at hands on the table.

"I know it isn't going to bring Geneveve back," I said, "but I think it would help us all if we could see her killer put away."

Mercedes's eyes flashed. "They ain't gon' catch Sultan—I know that."

"Do we know for sure it was Sultan?"

"That's what Sherry told us," Jasmine said.

Mercedes started to pull her hand away, but I grabbed her wrist.

"When did you see Sherry?" I said. "You saw her since she called Geneveve last night?"

Jasmine shook her head at Mercedes. "We through hidin' things from Miss Angel. She got to know this."

Mercedes got her hand away and hooked it onto her neck. Of all the women, trust came hardest to her. As much as I wanted to shake the words from her, I waited.

"We was lookin' for a place to be after they took Geneveve away," she said finally. "And she come out of nowhere, all shakin' and all blue around her mouth."

"Sherry," I said.

"Yeah. We was so scared but she worse—and we tol' her, come with us. Maybe we goin' home in the mornin'—and this her home too."

"She wouldn't," Jasmine said. "She don't want us involved in none of this trouble."

"She said it was all her fault, which—" Mercedes took in both of us with wide eyes. "I ain't never heard her take responsibility for nothin' before."

"That was huge," I said.

"Mmm hmm."

The rhythm was coming back. I nodded her on.

"She said she want to come back here and start her steps and have what we got—even God. But she said you gon' hate her now, 'cause she the reason Geneveve is dead."

"She's not the reason," I said. "She was just used."

"That don't make it okay," Jasmine said.

"No. But it doesn't mean she has to let it ruin the rest of her life, either." I grabbed both of their hands. "I don't want you going to West King—"

"We ain't never goin' there again," Jasmine said.

"But if Sherry comes here, bring her in, lock the doors, and call me."

"She ain't comin' here."

I looked closely at Mercedes as she worked her hand away from mine.

"What do you know?" I said. "Come on—everything on the table."

"She hidin' at C. A .R. S."

"In the apartment upstairs? Isn't that where she lived before she came here?"

"Before Opus kicked her out."

"Opus lives there?"

"Yeah—but she not up there with him. He beat her up one too many times. One thing she did learn from Geneveve—you ain't got to put up with that now."

"So what are you saying—she's hiding out in the store?"

"That old man runs it?"

"Yeah."

"That's her daddy."

"Daddy as in father—or daddy as in keeper."

Mercedes grunted. "He can't hardly keep hisself. No—he Sherry's father. He rents that apartment to her and Opus, only he don't know Opus work for Sultan. He just take the money 'cause he ain't makin' none on that shop now. He ain't got no idea what go on up there."

"He must know now if Sherry's hiding out with him."

Jasmine shook her head. "He don't even know she there."

I didn't even ask how that could possibly be. I just hugged them both and thanked them for trusting me, and the minute Hank and Leighanne arrived, I was outside on the phone to Chief.

"Can you meet me at C.A.R.S.?" I said. "I think we've found Sherry."

I agreed to wait for Chief in front of the police station so we could ride to the car shop together. When he pulled up beside me, he drew his hand across his throat and I cut the engine.

"We need to be clear on how we're going to do this," he said. "You say she's hiding in there someplace and the old man doesn't know it?"

"Yeah, but I've been thinking about this—and I think I know a way to distract him so you can look around."

"I'm not exactly unobtrusive, Classic."

"You haven't met this guy. Trust me. You could probably walk off with a crate of motor oil and he'd never know it."

Maharry Nelson looked like he hadn't moved from the stool since I was there three weeks ago. He didn't even stir when the bell on the door rang halfheartedly to herald our arrival.

I was at the counter before the old man raised his head and peered at me through his greasy glasses. I'd forgotten how tiny his eyes were.

"Hey, Mr. Nelson," I said. "I'm sure you don't remember me—"

"I'm not senile," he said. "You're the one who was gonna bring that van in, and you never did."

"You have a mind like a steel trap, sir," I said. "So—can I get on the schedule to get it in here? I know the starter's shot, and we may be looking at a new alternator."

In my peripheral vision I could see Chief moving toward the back shelves on my right. I pointed at a stack of tires to the left. "You do tires, too?"

"We do it all," he said.

"Can we take a look?"

"Go ahead."

"I meant you and me. I have no idea what I'm looking at."

Maharry started to turn his head toward Chief, but I laughed. "He's no help. He doesn't know a steel radial from a bicycle tire." I jerked my head toward the tires. "I need your expertise."

It took him an eternity to shuffle out from behind the counter, which gave Chief time to disappear through a swinging door marked EMPL ONL. I had a sudden attack of guilt for invading a life that was already half-gone.

I positioned myself at the tires so that Maharry had to turn his back to the other side of the store. I didn't know if I knew enough questions to ask about tread and rubber quality for Chief to be able to locate Sherry and get her out the back door.

I started with, "I'm not sure what size."

"I saw your feed-the-homeless thing didn't turn out so well."

I felt my eyes bulge.

"I seen it in the paper," he said. "Too bad."

"We fed a lot of people," I managed to say. "Raised some awareness."

"You got arrested."

"Well, yeah, I did."

"Was it worth it?"

I opened my mouth to answer, but I didn't know what to say. Was it worth it, or was I any closer today to a solution than I was then?

"Well, good for you for tryin', is what I say."

"Thanks," I said. There was still no sign of Chief, and my mouth was going dry. "So—what about these?"

"You didn't come in here for tires."

"Excuse me?"

"She's in the storage room."

"Who?"

"Sherry Lynn. That's who you're looking for, right?"

All the air went out of me. "Sherry Lynn, your daughter."

"Only one I got. I hope you can help her, because I've never been able to." His tiny eyes all but disappeared behind the smears on his glasses. "Like I said, good for you for tryin'."

I nodded. "Chief," I called out. "Did you find her? It's okay—you can bring her out."

He appeared within seconds, holding Sherry up with one arm. She looked worse than I had ever seen her, perhaps because of the sadness in her eyes when she looked at her father.

"You knew I was here?"

"'Course I knew you were here. You think I'm senile?"

He pulled a familiar blackened rag out of his back pocket and shuffled through the door they'd just come out of. I could hear him blowing his nose.

"I screwed up everybody's life," Sherry said. "Including his."

"Come on," I said. "Let's unscrew yours."

Somehow we convinced her to go the police with us. She said, over and over, that nobody had ever stood up for her like Geneveve did, until I finally latched on to that and told her this was her chance to stand up for Geneveve.

Even then she shook her head. "The police aint' gonna believe a stinkin' thing I say."

"We'll be there with you," Chief said. "I'll make sure they treat you right."

Like every other woman who knew him, Sherry succumbed to that uncanny energy and gave in.

At first the detective insisted on interviewing Sherry alone, so Chief had to pull the lawyer card. Resigned to that with a roll of his eyes, he let me sit in too.

"I'm Detective Kylie," he droned to Sherry. "I'm just going to ask you a few questions. Contrary to what your attorney thinks, you are not a suspect."

Sherry nodded, eyes leaking. I wasn't sure she understood a word of that.

"Just tell me what you know."

She looked at me. When I nodded, she told him why she left Sacrament House and returned to the boyfriend who beat her—Opus Behr. He waved her through the explanation that she didn't intend to let Opus bully her anymore, that she just needed a place to be until she could make another plan. His eyes had no interest at all, even when she said Opus threatened to kill her if she didn't lure Geneveve to their apartment. Clearly he'd heard far worse.

"I thought I could warn her when she got there," Sherry said, head bowed over the table. "And I thought we could both run together—someplace far from here. I always got away from Opus before, and I thought I could do it again. Only this time ..."

"This time what?" I said.

Kylie shot me a look. "What happened this time?" he said to Sherry. So far he'd written nothing on the pad in front of him.

"I told Opus I was gonna meet Geneveve under the steps—that I needed to talk her into comin' upstairs. And he said okay. I thought we could run from there."

"We got that part," Kylie said.

Chief put his hand over mine—like he knew I wanted to smack the man.

"I shoulda known when he let me go so easy—but I was just so scared. When I saw Geneveve coming around the corner from the alley, I ran to her. But then Sultan was there, right behind her. He grabbed her around the neck and pulled her back, and I heard her scream."

Detective Kylie picked up his pencil. "How could you see if it was Sultan? Isn't it dark back there?"

Sherry squinted at him. "It ain't hard to tell Sultan from every other man on West King Street. He's the only white man down there besides my father. He struts around like a big ol' white crane. I *know* Sultan."

I tried not to look startled. I'd always pictured Sultan as a black man.

"Did you actually see him stab her?" the detective said.

"No. I waited there until she stopped screamin' and I was gonna go help her, but I heard him coming back around the corner, so I ran. I knew he'd kill me, too, just for standing there." She jerked in the chair, toward Chief and me. "He'll kill me now if he finds out I told this."

"I want police protection for my client," Chief said.

"We can put her in protective custody—"

"No," I said. "She'll stay with me. You can protect her there."

I avoided the black look Chief lowered on me.

"We can have your house patrolled regularly," Kylie said, "but we can't guarantee her safety outside of this building."

"You don't care if your key witness is—" I stopped and looked at Sherry. I could see the terror pulsing through the vein in her forehead. "She'll be safe at my place until this Jude Lowery person is caught. And he'd better be."

"I think we're done here," Chief said to Kylie. To me he murmured, "But I'm not done with you."

I knew what he was going to say when he had the chance. But even Chief couldn't convince me to ignore a Nudge.

He waited until we had Sherry home and fed and tucked into bed before he started in. He was only halfway through the first, "What were you thinking?" when the doorbell rang. I didn't care who it was—I blessed their hearts all the way to the door.

When I opened it, Mary Alice and India were standing there, arms full of bags.

"Bonner called us," India said. "We brought you some things. If you'd be more comfortable, we can just leave them with you."

Mary Alice bobbed the chins as if she were hoping I'd lean that way, but I shook my head.

"No, please," I said. "Come in."

I introduced them to Chief, who sat on the hearth and glowered at me. He clearly wasn't going anywhere until he'd officially chastised me.

"This should go in the refrigerator," Mary Alice said. Her voice was like a thin china saucer.

"You brought me food?" I said.

"It's what we do when there's a loss, isn't it?"

I closed my eyes. Behind them was the image of Mary Alice humming a hymn and feeding tapioca pudding to Sylvia.

"Thank you," I said.

They followed me to the kitchen, where Mary Alice opened the refrigerator and made room for at least three casseroles. India set her bags on the bistro table.

"I don't know what you have to wear to the funeral," she said, "but I brought several choices for you and—the women."

"India, I can't afford—"

"Allison, why don't you just slap me in the face, girl."

I looked at her, stunned.

"These are a gift from me. You know I wouldn't come in here hawking my wares at a time like this."

The tears on the edge of her voice made me nod.

"I do know that," I said. "I don't know what I was thinking."

"You were obviously thinking we aren't sisters anymore, and you're wrong." India put her hands on my shoulders. Her fingers were anxious-chilly. "I still don't get what you're doing, Allison, but I know it's good because it's you that's doing it. I'm sorry I ever thought anything else."

She blurred in front of me.

"I'm not planning to join the take-in-a-homeless-person program, but I can sure make you look good while you're doing it."

I fell into the arms she held out to me. Beside us Mary Alice pulled a fresh Kleenex from her bosom.

When they left, Chief was still sitting on the hearth, waiting to go for my jugular. Or so I thought. I came back from showing them out, ready with my first argument, but he said, "At least that wreck of a van is good for something."

I felt my eyebrows rise. "I didn't really need it with Maharry Nelson. He knew why we were there the minute we walked in the door."

"No. It's going to be my sleeping quarters until they book Jude Lowery."

"What?"

"We're going to be lucky to see the cops cruise by here once a night, two at the most. I'm not leaving you here unguarded. This'll be the first place they look."

"They didn't look in her own father's place," I said. "I don't think they're going to look for her at all. From what Mercedes and Jasmine told me, Sultan has an ego the size of Alaska. I don't think he'll ever believe she'd turn him in."

Chief gave me a slow nod.

"You're agreeing with me?" I said.

"Not entirely. But I get the feeling you know this character somehow."

"He's a jackal. I know jackals."

"I'll give you that," he said. "But I'm still sleeping in your driveway."

"Miz Vernell is going to have a field day with that. And don't tell me one road at a time. I feel like I'm on about three at once."

"I have that one covered. Now—you have an air mattress around here?"

I actually slept that night, between wake-ups to cry for Geneveve and to wonder if Desmond had enough blankets. The five total hours I managed were enough to get me through the next day's planning of Geneveve's funeral—which the HOGs had taken up a collection to pay for. Hank, Mercedes, Jasmine, and I worked in my dining room while Sherry slept fitfully upstairs, with Leighanne at her bedside.

"I really think she'll do better with Nita," Leighanne told me at one point. "Who, by the way, hates that she's going to miss the memorial service, but she's on a cruise. I'm surprised she hasn't jumped ship to get here."

I left most of the planning to Hank, because I was fine as long as I was doing something active, but the minute I started to think too much, I folded. The few contributions I did make were adamant. I didn't want the service at Bates and Hockley, and wherever we did it, I wanted Hank to be in charge.

"As if I would let anybody else do it," she said. "Trinity Church says we can use their small chapel if you'd like that."

I did.

"And I think you should give the eulogy."

"I can't," I said.

"You talkin' about sayin' somethin' over Geneveve?" Mercedes said.

"That's it," Hank said.

"You got to do that, Miss Angel."

"I can't," I said again. "I'll fall apart. You have more experience, Hank. You do it."

Hank nodded, but her eyes stayed on me, even after Mercedes went on to say she wanted communion at the service and Jasmine said there should be a Christmas tree instead of flowers. I knew she saw the real reason—it was probably as plain as the tears I was pushing away with my knuckles. I couldn't speak of faith and comfort when I wasn't feeling it myself. God was coming to me in fits and starts that I couldn't hold onto.

"We got to have a tree there," Jasmine was saying, "'cause Geneveve was wantin' to make Christmas special for Desmond."

I agreed, though I didn't see how it was going to be special for any of us, especially Desmond. Every time Chief called or came in the side door, I held my breath for the words, "Desmond's coming home." By the morning of the funeral, I still hadn't heard them.

If nothing else, Mercedes, Jasmine, Sherry, and I looked fabulous in our dresses from India's shop. Geneveve's eyes would be sparkling at the sight of it. She had grown to love pretty. The magnitude of the things that were just falling within her grasp when she died pressed down on me.

The only thing that lifted me up when we entered the chapel was the fact that every shiny pew was filled. As the three women and Chief and I filed up the tiny center aisle, I saw that Bonner was there, and India, and Mary Alice, as well as all the HOGs who'd helped with the house. Leighanne filled up a whole row with people I assumed were from NA. Two of the biggest surprises were Owen Schatz and Maharry Nelson. Sherry went to sit with him and clung to his arm.

But no one surprised me more than Desmond.

Liz Doyle brought him to me just as Hank stood up to begin the service.

"I have to take him back when it's over," she whispered. "I'll be in the back if you need me."

Hank waited while Desmond inserted himself between Chief and me. He didn't look like my Desmond in faded, too-big black slacks and a wrinkled white dress shirt. Someone had done a bad job of tying the necktie that appeared to have belonged to someone's grandfather. Even after Chief removed it from his neck, Desmond was still another boy—stiff and wary, with nothing of the old wit and charm. I fought back the thought that he was as dead as Geneveve.

But he was there. I looped my arm through his and nodded for Hank to start.

The service was everything Edwin Sanborn's funeral had not been. Hank made it a true celebration of the life his daughter had lived in the last three and a half months—her sweet love as we exchanged the peace, her deep longing to be whole as we shared communion— "Greater love has no one than this, that he lay down his life for his friends"—her sacrifice of herself as Hank read from the Scripture. It was all true, all good, and I knew Geneveve would be glowing in her quiet way. But I was still flat and unmoved. Until Hank called for the women of Sacrament House.

This part I didn't know about. Mercedes, Jasmine, and Sherry all went forward and each took something from Hank. One by one they turned to the simple casket.

Sherry covered it with the blanket Geneveve had wrapped her in the night she arrived, hiding her terror behind hostile eyes. Jasmine added the ribbon Geneveve had hung in the window to welcome Desmond. Mercedes left Geneveve's key to Sacrament House, the one I tucked into her hand the day it became their home. None of them said a word, but their message called to me and shaped a vision in my head.

Sacrament House—the light at the center of a block of homes all filled with women praying and healing and reaching for their lives. Mercedes and Jasmine and Sherry, standing in the several doorways, opening their arms, drying the tears, speaking the truths in the rhythm only they could sing to. I could see it. I could feel it. I yearned for it. And I was Nudged toward it.

"Hank," I said. "I'd like to say something."

She folded her hands as only she could do and smiled the Hank smile. "Good," she said, "because nobody was leaving until you did."

I found a place in the aisle and looked at the unlikely collection of people who had come together. They looked back at me, some with faces puffed with tears, others with cheeks drawn in sorrow they couldn't express, and I loved them. All of them.

Then speak to them. Tell them this.

"The complete Christian needs two conversions," I said. "The first is to Jesus as our personal Savior. Geneveve Sanborn had such a conversion. She realized that through Jesus, God was loving her and saving her, and she said, 'Yes, I want to be loved that way.' When she died, she was on her way to a life of discipleship.'"

"Amen," someone said. I was sure it was Mary Alice.

"A second conversion comes when we discover that God is concerned not only about us as individuals, or even about our tiny group of fellow disciples, but about every person. Geneveve had that conversion, too. She loved Jasmine and Mercedes and Sherry and Desmond and me the way Jesus loved her. She laid down her life for Sherry, just the way Jesus laid down his life for her."

I saw Sherry bury her face in her father's shoulder. "By doing that," I said, "she didn't just save her friend. She made a statement to her entire community that love is a huge and powerful thing, that it is a force to be reckoned with in a world that assumes evil is stronger than good, and that in order to survive, we need to pull into our fortress churches and our safe-houses and hunker down."

The chapel was silent. "Geneveve lost her life, but she set the rest of us free in our hearts, in our souls, where we now know how bold love is, how courageous, and how dependable. She has converted us from believers who know God has saved us individually, into doers who will bring the world to him one NA meeting, one warm blanket, one middle-of-the-night phone call at a time." My tears came, but I didn't stop. "We will grieve the loss of our sister, but at the same time, we have to continue what she taught us with her life, not just for ourselves individually, but for the community she died for. We must be converted once more, so we can let ourselves be drawn into new places, new hopes, new changes."

I turned to the blanket-draped casket behind me. "And we will, sister. I promise you, we will."

The women and I had decided beforehand that we didn't want to go to the cemetery and watch Geneveve be lowered into the ground. Hank and the NA people went alone, and Hank promised to meet us at Sacrament House, where Mary Alice and India had prepared a feast. Before she left, Hank reached up and hooked a sturdy arm around my neck.

"That wasn't a eulogy, my friend," she said. "That was a prophecy. There's no turning back now."

I knew that. There was just still so much I didn't know about how God was going to move me forward.

The biggest piece of that was Desmond. Liz Doyle brought him to the house and kept a discreet distance while Mercedes pulled him

down the walk, one arm around his rigid shoulders, the other punc-
tuating the air.

"Look at that."

I turned in my seat on the porch steps and gave Bonner what
I knew was a pale smile. He deserved more, but I didn't have the
energy.

"What are we looking at?" I said as he sat beside me.

"Desmond. Right now he looks like any twelve- year-old boy
who's just lost his mother and needs somebody to tell him who to
be now."

I stared at him.

"He's a great kid, Allison. I hope it works out for him to stay with
you."

"I—wow, Bonner—thank you." I sighed into my knees. "There
are a lot of things that are going to have to work out."

"Such as?"

"Such as finding a way to keep paying the lease on this house. I
know you said the owner won't sell to Troy Irwin—"

"He won't."

I shook my head ruefully. "I'm finding out that everybody has
his price."

"Not me. Not when it comes to this."

"We're not talking about you. I wish we were."

"We are." Bonner tilted his head at me. "I'm the owner, Allison.
Until you form a nonprofit, and then I'm donating it. Meanwhile,
don't worry about the lease. You have enough—"

"Bonner—are you *serious*?"

"I am."

"Okay—but, wait. You're messing with Troy Irwin by doing this. You're the one who told me not to do that."

"If you don't listen to me, why should I?"

I stared at him, long and hard. "All right—who are you and what have you done with Bonner Bailey?"

"No," he said. "What have *you* done with him?" He touched my chin with his fingertips. "I'm doing this for you, Allison—but I have no expectations. I know where your heart is."

He dropped his hand and looked over my head. When he stood up and extended his hand, I knew Chief was behind me.

"Take care of her out there, will you?" Bonner said.

Before Chief could answer, Bonner hurried down the steps and down the walkway to Sylvia's Jaguar. Not until he pulled away did I see the black Lincoln parked across the street.

"No, he did not," I said.

"What's that, Classic?" Chief said.

But I was already marching down the walkway myself, toward the man climbing out of the Lincoln with an armful of roses.

"Allison!" Chief barked behind me.

I didn't stop. Not until I was face to face with Troy Irwin in the middle of the street.

"I just heard this morning," he said. "I've been out of town—"

"Get back in your car."

"I'm not here to intrude. I just wanted you to have these."

"Take them with you."

"Come on, Allison, I'm trying to—"

"I know exactly what you're trying to do—what you've never stopped trying to do."

"Which is?"

"Whatever you want. And what you want is not what I want. At all. So stop trying."

Troy dropped the arm that held the roses. Genevieve was right. His eyes did turn to stones.

"I won't stop—you know that," he said.

"Then it's on," I said.

"Don't think you still have enough Chamberlain in you to pull this off," he said.

"I don't need Chamberlain," I said. "I have enough God."

I didn't move as he dropped the flowers at my feet and thrust himself into the backseat of the Lincoln. I waited until the driver turned the corner before I leaned over and pulled off the card.

"'I'm so sorry for your loss, Ally,' it said. "We can stop these tragedies together. My offer still stands."

As I tore it into confetti and ground it with my heel, it came to me that he saw it as a generous gesture. That was the most disturbing piece of the whole thing.

"Good choice, Classic," Chief said.

I turned and went toward him at the curb. "Did you really think I was going to do something stupid?"

"Something stupid, no. Something justifiable, yes. Either one would've landed you in the back of a police car. Again."

"Are you ever going to let me live that down?"

"Not a chance. Desmond had to go."

My face froze. "He's gone?"

"Liz took him back to the home."

"I didn't get to say good-bye—"

"He didn't want to say good-bye," Chief said. "But he said to give you this."

He handed me a sheet of paper, curled at the edges and smudged with pencil. I knew before I turned it over that it was a Desmond original.

"Did you see this?" I said.

"Yeah."

"It's you."

It was in fact an almost perfect likeness of Chief, astride an exaggerated Road King, dressed in full leathers, and complete with ponytail. The details were off here and there—Chief's biceps were not in actuality that large—but the mystical intensity of the man was there in the whole. Desmond saw Chief exactly the way I did.

"I can't give this one up, Chief," I said.

"This one?" he said.

I hugged my arms around myself. "I didn't have that abortion. I gave my baby up for adoption. But this one—"

"We won't lose him, Classic," he said.

I hung onto the "we."

CHAPTER TWENTY-EIGHT

I fell into an exhausted sleep around midnight, only to be awakened an hour later by Sherry beside my bed, clawing at my arm.

"It's okay," I said. I made an opening with the covers. "Come on, just climb in with me."

"I saw Opus. He's here."

I was immediately awake and reaching for the bedside lamp. Sherry grabbed my wrist and dumped a glass of water across the nightstand.

"Don't turn that on!" she said. "He'll know I seen him,"

"Where?"

"In the street. The motorcycle woke me up, and I looked out, and I thought I seen him by one of them palm trees."

"Chief's motorcycle?"

"I knew Sultan was gonna send him for me. I gotta get outta here—"

Sherry started for the door, but I caught her by the hood of her sweatshirt and scrambled out of the bed to wrap my arms around her from behind, as I'd seen Mercedes do. Her toughness was all verbal. She collapsed against me, sobbing once more.

"I have to go—please—he's gonna kill me—"

"No one's going to kill you. Come on, get in the bed—"

"They killed Geneveve—"

"Get in there—*now*."

It worked better on her than it ever had on Desmond. She let me half-carry her to the bed without further struggle. She clutched one of the pillows to her chest. I went to the window and tilted the plantation shutter just enough to get a narrow view of the street below.

"Don't let him see you," Sherry whispered hoarsely. "He'll kill us both."

"I don't even see *him*." I wiped my already clammy palms on the sides of my pajama pants. "There's a shadow from my trash can—could that be what you saw?"

"No, I don't know—"

"Come here and look. Come on, babe, it's okay."

Sherry crawled across the bed like a cornered cat and came into the circle of my arm. I pointed through the slats of the shutter.

"See? That shadow right there? Was that what you saw?"

"Maybe. I don't know—I'm just so scared."

"Understandable. All right—I'm going to call Chief on his cell and get him to look around. Remember? He's sleeping in the van?"

I waited, hoping she'd forget she'd just heard a motorcycle pull away. She did.

"Okay," she said. "Okay."

"You get back in my bed, and I'll join you, and we'll let him handle it."

"Okay."

She was slipping into shock, but it was easier to deal with than hysteria. Her body still shook even after I coaxed her under the comforter, fully clad as if she'd already been halfway out the door. I shook too when I reached for my phone on the bedside table and found it in a puddle of water. I didn't even have to pick it up to know it was now useless.

"I'm going to take this downstairs and call him," I said. "The signal's better."

She whimpered from a fetal position.

I grabbed my sweatpants from the back of the chair and my tennis shoes from underneath and closed the bedroom door behind me. Anxiety seethed under my skin. What Sherry saw probably wasn't Opus, but I was more concerned with what she'd heard. It was hard to confuse the sound of a Harley with anything else.

I managed to get the sweatpants and shoes on before I got downstairs and opened the side door. The air nipped at me, so I snatched up my Harley jacket from the back of a bistro chair and thanked God I was a slob.

The night was moonless as I hurried down the porch steps. All the outside lights on Palm Row had been turned out hours ago. I should've grabbed a flashlight, but I was afraid if I went back in the house one more time, Sherry was going to suspect I was doing more than making a phone call. As I crossed the lane, I glanced up at my bedroom window; the shutters were still closed. She'd probably gone back to sleep, and I was going to feel like an idiot waking Chief up if he hadn't actually ridden away.

The dead van sat dark and still in the driveway, waiting for its inevitable haul to the junkyard. With one more wary glance toward the shadow of the trash can, I rapped my knuckles on the passenger side window.

Nothing stirred. If he was as wiped out as the rest of us, that wasn't going to do it.

"Chief?" I hissed, and then rolled my eyes. Why was I whispering, for Pete's sake? "Chief!"

Still no answer. Hoping the man didn't sleep in his boxers, I opened the door and peered in. We'd taken out the seats, so I could see all the way to the back even without a dome light. The only thing in there was a rumpled sleeping bag and a tossed-aside pillow.

I tried to talk myself out of a cold sweat. Okay—nature had called and he'd gone to take a pee behind the garage. That's who Sherry had seen. That was it.

But I didn't call his name as I backed out of the van and raised the garage door. I already knew the Road King would be gone.

"Chief," I said out loud, "where did you *go?*"

"He gone lookin' for me."

A gasp caught in my chest.

"He gone lookin' for me so I could look for you."

I whipped around in time to be shoved back by two enormous black hands. I had to grasp behind me at my bike to keep from crashing it to the floor and taking myself with it. It rocked, startled, on the kickstand but remained upright. I clung to the handlebar with one hand and dug with the other into my pocket for something, anything to scratch into the dark face that forced itself toward me. All I found was my Harley key, but I worked it between my fingers, jagged side out. It wasn't going to do me much good against this beast. All I could think of was Desmond, backed against the wall in the alley, relying on his faltering wit.

PleaseGodpleaseGodpleaseGod.

"So," I said, "you must be Opus. I've heard so much about you."

He pulled his arm across his chest and came at my face with the back of his hand. I twisted away so that he caught me on the shoulder. The bulky glove muffled the blow.

"Yeah," I said, "that's one of the things I heard about you: You love to hit women. Now that's the sign of a real man."

He swore at me.

"So's that."

His eyes were like two poke-holes in the mud, but I could see the flicker of surprise I'd hoped for.

"What else did she tell you?" Opus said.

"Who?"

"You know who."

He swore at me again, and I shook my head. "Actually the name's Allison. Not whatever that was you just called me."

My hands were sliding on the handlebars, covering them with sweat, but his forehead furrowed. No wonder Desmond used this technique. If I could just keep it up until Chief came back.

"So I don't get it," I said. "You sent Chief off to find you, only you're here. How did you manage that?"

"Called him. Told him I had the kid over at C.A.R.S. if he wanted him."

"What kid?"

"Geneveve's kid." Opus smirked. "I don't—but he don't know that."

I swallowed and forced a smirk of my own. "Now just how did you get Chief's cell phone number? Just out of curiosity."

"Sultan give it to me."

"Smart man, that Sultan. That must be why you work for him."

Opus pulled off his right glove and wiggled his fingers, flashing several obnoxiously gold rings. "*This* is why I work for him."

"Yeah, money talks, doesn't it?"

"Sure do. But I'm done talkin'. You 'bout to take me to Sherry."

"And that would be because …"

"Because Sultan wants to see her."

I folded my arms and hoped I looked casual. "Interesting. See, I thought Sherry was *your* girlfriend. I can't keep up with y'all."

"I'm done with that—"

"So now Sultan wants her."

"No—he wants to make sure she don't open her big mouth—and you either."

"About?"

The poke-hole eyes squeezed in. "That's enough. You just shut up and take me to Sherry."

He reached for my shoulder but I tilted away. The Harley rocked, and Opus took a startled step backward. My heart was racing, but I clutched at that moment like a lifeline. Opus was afraid of my motorcycle.

"Looks like I don't have much choice, do I?" I said.

"No, you don't." He recovered the smirk. "She in your house, right? I know she weren't stupid enough to stay in that other house."

"Y'know, that Sherry, she's pretty stupid. That's probably exactly where she is—man, we can't pull anything over on you."

He seemed to struggle with that, which assured me he hadn't been to Sacrament House looking for her. At least there was that.

"I tell you what," I said. "My van's dead, but I'd be happy to take you by there on the bike to check. Jump on."

Opus pulled back as if I'd just offered him a boa constrictor.

"Unless you have your own wheels," I said. In which case I would call the police and the women and the National Guard—if I had a working cell phone. If I hadn't taken out my landline.

"I ain't ridin' on that thing," he said. "I got my car around the corner."

"The Oldsmobile?" I said. At least I thought that was what Desmond said it was.

Opus gave a caught-off-guard nod.

"Those women will call the cops if they see that coming," I said. "Now, if they hear my Harley pull up, they'll get up and put the coffee on. You can waltz right in and take Sherry—on one condition."

"I ain't lettin' you go, if that's what you're thinkin'. You got a bigger mouth than Sherry do."

"I get that—it was only a matter of time before you got to me. Don't let my calm exterior fool you—I'm terrified right now."

The line between his eyebrows twisted into his thick forehead.

"I just have to know—that night I ran you down in the alley—"

His eyes darted to the bike I was still clinging to.

"Was it you who beat up Geneveve and left her to die in the garbage—or was that Sultan? I mean, I know you get off on beating your girlfriends—"

"She wasn't my girlfriend. She belong to Sultan. She always belong to Sultan."

"So he came here and took her to the alley and beat her up because he loved her. Y'all have a whole other mating ritual going on."

"*I* come here and took her—"

"And my DVD player and my laptop. Am I ever going to get those back?"

"I done that to make it look like she ripped you off."

"So did you shoot her up too?"

"I didn't shoot nobody."

"I'm sorry—I don't know the lingo. With drugs."

"Yeah, I done that. But I didn't beat her. Sultan done that, warnin' her."

"About what?"

"About leavin' him. He tol' her next time she try to get away from him, he gon' take the kid—"

"The kid." I heard the cover slip off of my voice, but I didn't care. "He was going to take Desmond? Why?"

His eyes sank into the incredulous folds of his face. "Because that's *his* kid," he said.

Scattered pieces lifted in my mind and frantically put themselves together. Sultan's hold on Geneveve was Desmond. She didn't die for Sherry—she died for her son. And it wasn't Sherry who Sultan was looking for.

"You're not as stupid as I thought you were, Opus," I said.

"Whatchoo mean?"

"Sultan doesn't just want Sherry so he can shut her up. He wants me so I can tell him where Desmond is. Right?"

He didn't have to answer.

"Hey, he's not my kid," I forced myself to say, "And he's sure not worth my life. Get on—I'll take you straight to him, and you'll be the man in Sultan's eyes."

His face worked.

"Fine—I'll get the kid and take him to Sultan myself."

I dug the key out of my pocket and straddled the bike. "You coming or not? Look, you're safer on it with me than in front of me when I'm driving it. We've established that."

He licked his lips and nodded.

"Good. Let me walk it out of the garage, and you can get on. I don't want to wake up the neighbors."

He nodded again and kept a frightened three-foot margin between the Classic and me as I power walked beyond the garage door and past the van.

"Okay," I said over my shoulder. "Come on."

He took a step toward me, and I rolled the throttle—once, twice, three times, and screamed out of the driveway and down Palm Row. Before I rounded the corner onto St. George, Miz Vernell's porch lights startled on. I didn't have to look back to know that Opus was left standing in their accusing glare in the middle of the road.

My hair snapped its stinging ends at my eyes, but I couldn't slow down. The Nudge was more than a Nudge—it was an uncontrollable slam that hurtled the bike through the night as if someone else was driving her. I didn't have to think where to go. I shot straight down St. George to King, barely rolling back on the throttle before I leaned into the turn and gunned it again, past the plaza, the college, the police station. Two blocks and I'd be at Ponce de Leon Boulevard—a few more to the right and I'd be at the boys' home, with Desmond—and I wasn't leaving there without him.

The light at the intersection was red. I slowed down only enough to see if I could make the turn without having to stop. Two tractor-trailer rigs barreled toward me, side-by-side, horns blaring. If I turned the wheel and braked, I was going down. I kept the handlebars straight and downshifted, but it wasn't enough. The force of both trucks sucked me in as they blew by. I had no choice but to hang on to the straightened handlebars and shoot across the highway to the other side.

DearGoddearGoddearGod. The engine was screaming a protest against the low gear. Insides turning to jelly, I clicked into third and swerved into the C.A.R.S. parking lot to make a wide U-turn. A tall figure took the space between me and the corner of the building in two strides. I swerved to miss him and did. But something long and hard smashed into my windshield. The bike jerked to a tilt and slid on her side. Asphalt bit into my face until we careened into the rotting fence that bordered the property. The engine died on top of me, and I heard footsteps striding toward me, as if their owner were sure there was no need to hurry.

I wrenched my left leg free and clawed at the weeds to crawl away.

"Stop right there."

I didn't. I got to my feet and stumbled forward. Something zinged past, close to my ear and stabbed into the fence, sending shards of wood flying. I froze, until the footsteps once again approached. Jolted by that unseen slam, I took the last few feet to the fence and grabbed for the handle of the knife. The man's hand got to me first and wrapped its white iron fingers around my wrist.

"I think we're about done with this game."

It wasn't the painful clench of his hand that took away my breath. It was the voice. Low and rich. And oozing charm. When he pulled me up to his face, I knew I was going to see a smile designed to manipulate. A twisted version of my Desmond's grin.

"It's time to make a deal," he said. "You tell me where my son is, and I won't kill you. How does that sound?"

"It sounds like I'm going to die," I said.

He was a colder, quicker man than Opus Behr. I never saw the hand that slammed into my face and snapped my head back.

"Where's my son?" he said. The charm had drained from his voice, leaving nothing. Not even anger. The absence of emotion was frightening.

"I don't have him," I said. "They won't let me have him, and they sure aren't going to let you have him."

"Who?"

"You're the man, Sultan. You can figure that out for yourself—or have Opus do it. Now there's a winner right there."

My bitterness was no longer a cover for fear. I'd gone beyond that, all the way to the hard edge of nothing left to lose—except Desmond. I was going to my grave knowing he would never learn to be what this man had become.

"I told you, I'm done with this game."

Sultan closed both of my wrists in one hand and yanked me toward the parking lot. I tried to dig my heels in, but pain shot up my left leg and I stumbled. He pulled my arms over my head and shook me, and I kicked at him with my good leg. He was unfazed.

"You can make this hard, or I can make it easy. Your choice. But it's going down either way." He pulled me within inches of his face. "What's it going to be?"

"This way," I said. And I spit.

Something cracked. Sultan's hand jerked and released my wrists. For the first time I saw surprise in his eyes, as if at last he'd encountered the unexpected. Then he teetered sideways and dropped to the ground.

My first impulse was to run, until I saw the blood. Disbelief pulsing through me, I knelt and pressed my hand to his throat. If there was a beat, it was too faint for trembling fingers to feel. I didn't check for breath—I was sure I wasn't going to find it.

Footsteps brought my head up, but they were fading off in the other direction. The thought finally formed: This man had been shot, inches away from me, by someone who was now fleeing down the alley behind C.A.R.S. Again.

Terror finally took hold and pulled me from my knees. I limped to the Harley, but I couldn't lift it, even with adrenalin coursing through my veins. I patted all my pockets, all the while knowing my dead cell phone was lying on the bistro table. The police—okay—run to the station.

I abandoned my fallen bike and hurled myself forward, but my left leg buckled, and I met the ground with a jar so hard I could barely breathe. My hand hit a tuft of weed, and I used it to pull myself forward. Hand over hand, and weed after clump of weed, I crawled to the curb and clawed my way up the front of the wood fence. Leaning and sliding, I kept going toward the highway until I ran out of fence. Then all I could do was lower myself and pray *Ican'tdoitIcan'tdoitplease GodpleaseGod*. Until I heard the Road King, growling for me.

CHAPTER TWENTY-NINE

My leg wasn't broken. Neither was my nose. Except for the road rash down the side of my face and the strained ligaments in my knee, the consensus in the emergency room was that I was the luckiest woman on the planet.

"I hope this means you'll wear a helmet from now on," the fuzzy-faced young ER doctor said.

My Harley did not get off as easy. Chief said it had suffered some serious cosmetic damage, but as soon as the police determined it hadn't been used in the commission of a crime, he'd make sure it got to the Harley dealership for full assessment and repair. I couldn't even think about that as I sat propped up on a gurney with my knee packed in ice, waiting for somebody to let me out of there so I could go throw up or weep or both.

"You're sure Desmond's okay," I said for the fifteenth time.

For the fifteenth time Chief said, "Yes. I called the home. He's zonked out."

"Did they shake out the covers, make sure it isn't a dummy in the bed?"

"I woke Liz Doyle up and had her go over there personally." Chief squeezed the hand he hadn't let go of for an hour. "I told you she'd give you a kidney."

"What about Sherry?"

"She's at Sacrament House. Evidently she went over there as soon as Opus left. Walked, I guess. Hank's there with all of them now."

"I owe her big time."

"She's got help. Leighanne's there, and Nita's flying back ASAP."

"What about her cruise? What time is it, anyway?"

"She cut it short, and it's four a.m."

"What about Opus?"

"Miz Vernell called the cops on him, but he was gone by the time they got there. They'll put a warrant out on him after they take your statement."

"Then Sherry's not safe!"

"With a cruiser parked out in front of Sacrament House, I think she'll be all right." Chief's eyes showed their first hint of twinkle. "Detective Kylie's got some egg to wipe off his face right now."

"When's he coming for my statement? I still won't be satisfied until Opus is picked up."

Chief let go of my hand so he could use both of his to push me back against the lone pillow. That was how Detective Kylie found us when the nurse pushed the curtain aside to let him in.

"So you're in one piece," he said.

"Yeah," I said. "Do you have your notepad? I'm ready to talk."

He pulled up a stool and perched at its edge. Bags hung under his eyes. "You don't even want to hear that you've been eliminated as a suspect?"

"I didn't know I ever was one."

"You left the scene of the crime. That's always a red flag."

"I didn't want to be next," I said.

"I called 911 when I found her," Chief said—his don't-mess-with-me-man-I'm-a-lawyer voice firmly in gear. "The ambulance got there before the police. Enough said?"

Kylie put up a hand. "Like I said, your client's not a suspect."

"Hello," I said. "Sitting right here."

"You lucked out," he said. "The old man who owns the auto repair shop has video cameras trained on the parking lot."

"You're not serious."

"He had them put in after the last murder was committed on his property. We got the whole thing on film—minus the perpetrator who, from what we can tell, shot our guy from the landing of the steps on the side of the building. Unfortunately, that put the shooter off camera."

His shrug told me it really wasn't all that unfortunate in his opinion.

"So Sultan's dead," I said. "Jude Lowery's dead."

"We assume so."

"You 'assume'?" Chief said.

"Yeah," Kylie crossed one leg over the other knee as if he were cozying up to the conversation. "The camera also caught three people in black—hoods, the whole bit—cleaning up the crime scene. By the time our people got there, there was nothing left but your motorcycle and a pool of blood."

"They took the body?" I said.

"They did. We don't actually know that it was Jude Lowery who got shot. You've never seen him before, isn't that right?"

"Right."

"Did he tell you he was Sultan'?"

"I called him that, and he didn't deny it." I didn't add that he'd claimed to be Desmond's father. Chief and I had agreed to keep that information to ourselves unless we needed to use it.

"You've got the blood," Chief said. "A DNA test would clear it up."

"If we had anything to compare it to. We take fingerprints when we arrest people—not hair samples. This isn't *CSI: Miami*." He pulled the pad out of his jacket and flipped it open. "I assume you want to give us a statement about Opus Behr's alleged attack on you."

I ignored the word *alleged* and sat up on the table. "Yeah. I want him off the streets. He's dangerous."

"One thing before we go there," Chief said. "I'm just curious. Why would these guys steal the dead body?"

Kylie gave his pen an impatient click. "Sultan was the Mack Daddy of his cell. They don't want any of the other drug cells to know that he's dead and they're in a weakened state."

"Cells?" I said. "Aren't you talking about gangs?"

He looked at me with the first sign of humor I'd seen teasing at his mouth. "We don't have 'gangs' in St. Augustine, Ms. Chamberlain. What would that do to our image?"

The hospital finally released me at dawn with two ice packs and a prescription for Lortab.

"I'm not taking any of those until I talk to the women," I told Chief. "Will you take me to Sacrament House?"

"Not on my bike," he said. "I'll call us a cab."

"I don't care if we have to walk. I have to know if they're all right. And then I want to go see Desmond."

"You're a pain, you know that?"

"Yeah," I said. "I think it's my career."

Mercedes, Jasmine, and Sherry were in a knot on the couch when we arrived. I knew the minute I walked in that they were sitting on a pact. I could see it in the set of their chins. I wasn't sure I wanted to know what it was.

But when Hank and Chief went into the kitchen to get breakfast going, I sat on the coffee table facing them and said, "It's just us now. Anything you want to tell me?"

Their heads shook in unison.

"Anything you *should* tell me?"

"No," Sherry said. "Somethin' I want to ask you, though."

I was surprised at the calm in her voice. Last time I saw her, she was curled up like an embryo in my bed.

"Anything," I said.

"Where is Opus?"

"Hopefully in the back of a police car by now. He'll go to jail—there's no doubt about that."

Mercedes grunted, but just as the others' did, her shoulders relaxed.

"And Sultan's dead?" Sherry said.

"The last time I saw him, he looked pretty dead to me," I said.

Mercedes narrowed her eyes. "What are *you* not tellin' *us*?"

"Somebody took his body," I said.

"Now that is disgusting," Jasmine said.

"No," Sherry said. "That is *good*. Maybe now his stink is gone forever." She squeezed out from between the two of them and stood up to look down at me. "I want to move back here if y'all will let me. I can move on now, and the only place I can do it is here."

I looked at Mercedes, then at Jasmine. "What do you think, ladies? This is as much your decision as it is mine."

"Unh-uh," Jasmine said. "This *her* decision. Can't nobody make it for her, and can't nobody talk her into it like we done before."

"Mmm-hmm," Mercedes said.

The rhythm was clear. "All right," I said to Sherry. "I'll have somebody bring your things over. Maybe Leighanne can. Did she go home?"

"She done gone to Jacksonville to pick up Nita," Jasmine said. "She gon' get her a earful when she come off that plane."

Mercedes was looking at me, eyes narrowed.

"What?" I said.

"You lookin' like you been run over, Miss Angel."

"That's basically true."

"Chief better get you home before you fall out right here."

"I'm okay," I said. But as the couch suddenly rose up to meet me, I realized I wasn't.

Sherry caught me on the way down. While Mercedes was yelling for Chief to come in there and take care of his woman, Sherry put her lips close to my ear.

"Time to let it be, Miss Angel," she whispered.

I moved my head to look in her eyes. They'd lost their haze in the burn of purpose.

"Okay," I said. "We'll let it be."

Chief borrowed Hank's car to drive me home. All the way I insisted that I was going to see Desmond, but when he carried me into the foyer and made me look in the mirror, I agreed that the boy didn't need to see me looking like I'd been in a street brawl.

He set me up in the chair and made tea and sat on the coffee table trunk.

"Here we are again," I said.

"Alone at last," he said.

We exchanged a look we didn't know what to do with. Chief rested his forearms on his thighs—a posture I loved the way I loved his eagle eyes and the twinkle he brought out so rarely. It ached—not being able to tell him. It ached with my leg and my face and my torn-apart heart.

"So what's going to happen, Classic?" he said.

"I'm sorry?"

"Hank says you're a prophet. "

"Do you really want to debate that right now? Because I don't."

"Neither do I. Because I accept it."

"You accept it."

"Probably more than you do." He rubbed his palms together, the only unsure gesture I'd ever seen him make. "There's no question you've got some kind of power. The business I'm in, I see a lot of people with power using it in every wrong way imaginable. You've imagined a good way. Call it being a 'prophet' if you want to, but it is what it is, and you can do something with it."

He straightened his back and looked everywhere in the room except at me. But all *I* could look at was him. He was suddenly vulnerable—but I had never felt safer in his presence. Safe enough to say what might chase him away.

"It's all God," I said. "All of it."

"I know you believe that."

"But do you?"

He brought his gaze back to me from the corners of the room. "Two months ago—maybe even two weeks ago—I would have said no without hesitating."

"And now?"

"Now—I don't know. That's the best I can do."

"Then for now," I said, "that's good enough."

"How good?" he said.

I stopped breathing. He kept his eyes on me, even when his phone rang—and rang—stopped—and began again.

"Somebody wants you bad," I said. I didn't say that somebody was me.

He answered it with a terse "Jack Ellington," but as he listened, his face changed—pensive lines to smoothing brow to a smile I'd never seen before—a smile of unguarded joy.

"Can you meet us at FIP?" he said finally.

"FIP?" I said.

"See you in ten."

"Chief—*what?*" I said. "What's going on?"

"I'll tell you on the way."

"I'm dying here—give me the headline."

He scooped me up in his big arms. "I think Desmond's coming home."

I had it memorized by the time we got to Liz Doyle's office, but I made Nita repeat it twice, three times until I believed it was real. And then I read the letter—over and over, until the edges of the paper were damp from my clammy palms and my tears. The first happy tears I may ever have cried.

"I, Geneveve Sanborn, being of sound mind," it began.

I could hear her soft voice, dictating to Nita in some private middle of the night, telling the world that in the event of her death, Allison Chamberlain was to have legal custody of her son, Desmond Sanborn, father unknown.

I loved that Geneveve hadn't quite forgotten how to lie.

"Are you sure this is legal?" I said every time I finished reading it.

"It's notarized," Nita said. "I'm a notary—we have to be in the mortgage business." She looked apologetically at Chief, nodding agreement from him. "I wanted her to go through you, but she wanted to keep this as far away from 'Miss Angel' as she could. And that wasn't anything against you, Allison," she added quickly.

"I know," I said. "She wanted to be his mother so bad."

"And she never thought she was going to be able to be the kind of mother you were."

"It turns out she was after all." We turned to Liz, who was speaking through tears. "She made sure her son was going to be taken care of. By the best." She reached over and squeezed my good knee. "I'll finish the paperwork. You can take him home as soon as they're done."

"Define done," I said.

"Day after tomorrow?"

"That's Christmas Day," Chief said.

Liz beamed at me. "I can't think of a better gift."

Nita stayed to get a copy of the letter. Chief held my elbow all the way down the hall, but he didn't speak until he'd steered me out to the sidewalk.

"Merry Christmas, Classic," he said. He took my face in his hands and kissed me. Not like a brother. Not like a buddy. Not like a father. Like the man who loved me. The man I kissed back.

GodpleaseGodpleaseGodplease. Please. Let this be okay with you.

Chief and Hank let me go on my newly repaired Classic to pick up Desmond, as long as they could both ride behind us in case I got wobbly. Everything inside me was wobbly, but I was sure the unmistakable Nudge wasn't going to let me fall.

I waited outside, astride the Harley, helmet in hand until they brought him out. He looked taller, paler, thinner, maybe a little harder at the edges. But when he gave me the smile he reserved only for me, I knew he was the same. And that he had me right there. Right there.

"You ready to go for a ride?" I said.

"Can I drive?" he said.

"In your dreams, Clarence."

It was our best ride. We leaned as one and laughed at the cold and waved to Chief and Hank as they peeled off at the end of Palm Row. I realized somewhere along the way that I wasn't just in love with Desmond and Chief and God. I was in love with this bike, this thing I had so resisted at first—just as I'd learned to love so many things that had seemed like such a bad idea, until I was Nudged straight into them.

When we walked in the house, I expected Desmond to head straight for the snack drawer that I had stuffed with Oreos. But as soon as we were inside the door, he turned to me and said, "I want to see it."

"See what?" I said.

"That letter she wrote. The one says she give me to you."

"Okay," I said. "It's here."

He followed me into the den and watched me pull my copy from the desk drawer. When I handed it to him, he read it silently, lips moving. When his eyes reached the bottom, he whispered, "Thank you, Mama."

Then he handed it back to me and *then* he headed for the Oreos.

I tucked that moment away for later. "I want to show you something else," I said.

"My Christmas presents?" he said, wiggling his eyebrows. But he sobered. "This all the present I need, Big Al. Bein' here."

"Yeah, but you aren't going to turn down the leathers I got ya, are you?"

"No way!"

"Way. But I want to talk to you about this first." I went to the bulletin board by the door and took down the picture he'd drawn for me.

"Pretty good, huh?" he said.

"Yeah," I said. "Mr. Schatz liked it too. So did Miz Vernell."

Desmond pointed east. "The old lady?"

"Yeah, they saw it when they came over to tell me I don't have to go to court."

"Huh?"

"Never mind. Long story. I need to warn you, though, that Schatzie is going to be all over you about not coming back when he yelled at you that night you snuck out of here. I thought he was yelling at me."

"What about you?" Desmond said. "You gonna yell at me?"

"Not today. Okay—this picture." I spread it on the table and looked in my mind for the lines I'd prepared. "I know you think Chief is cool and all that—and I do too."

Desmond patted his palm. "I know you do."

"I just want to make sure you know that Chief and I … it may or may not end up … it depends on some things.…" So much for the prepared speech. "It depends on God, just like everything else does."

Desmond wrinkled his brow over the picture. "I don't think it's that good now."

"Why not?"

"'Cause you don't even know what it is."

"It's Chief, isn't it?"

Desmond rolled his eyes completely up into his head. "No. This ain't Chief. This God—least the way I see him. I don't know 'bout how you see Hhim, but me—I got him on a Harley anytime."

I pressed my hands to my lips.

"You ain't gon' cry, are you, Big Al?" he said. 'Cause I don't see us cryin' on Christmas."

"No, kid," I said. "In fact I don't see us crying for a long time. A *long* time."

Desmond loved his leathers. He put them on immediately and we rode, all Christmas Day until our hands were claws even inside our gloves. Hot chocolate was definitely in order, although I couldn't resist telling him that there would be no marshmallows, seeing how he kept eating them by the bag.

I was in the kitchen heating up milk when the doorbell rang. I ignored my irritation—I'd asked everybody to leave us alone this first day—and told Desmond to answer it and use his considerable charms to get rid of whoever it was. But a minute later he was back, jerking his head toward the door.

"You better get this," he said.

"Who is it?" I whispered.

"You jus' better get it."

Every vision possible flashed through my head, all of them some version of somebody there to take Desmond away. I opened the door the rest of the way, another prepared speech on my lips. But it wasn't a county official or a cop who looked back at me.

It was a painfully thin woman of indeterminate age, who even from the edge of the porch smelled like putrid neglect of self. She didn't say anything. She didn't have to. I read the familiar words in her eyes: "I've had it. I'm tired. I'm ready for help."

"Desmond," I said.

"I know," he said. "Go run her a bath."

I nodded and held out my hand. "Come on in," I said. "You're home."

I was Nudged, of course. But I might have done it anyway. Because I found Jesus seven years ago. And now I knew what to do with him.

... a little more ...

When a delightful concert comes to an end,

the orchestra might offer an encore.

When a fine meal comes to an end,

it's always nice to savor a bit of dessert.

When a great story comes to an end,

we think you may want to linger.

And so, we offer ...

AfterWords—just a little something more after you

have finished a David C. Cook novel.

We invite you to stay awhile in the story.

Thanks for reading!

Turn the page for ...

- **Discussion Questions**
- **About Magdalene**

Discussion Questions

A few thoughts to spur discussion. Should your conversation lead to questions for me, I would love to hear from you: nnrue@att.net.

- Before I begin to write a novel, I always form the question I hope to answer in the course of the story. The question for *The Reluctant Prophet* was: What would happen if you truly did "the Jesus thing" and obeyed God—whether you wanted to or not? After reading the book, what do you think is the answer to that question?

- I never write a piece of fiction that doesn't have to do with transformation into one's authentic self. The guiding Scripture verse for my ministry is, in fact, John 1:12–13, as translated in *The Message*. How do you think this applies to each of the characters?

> *Whoever did want him,*
> *who believed he was who he claimed*
> *and would do what he said,*
>
> *He made to be their true selves,*
> *their child-of-God selves.*

- As I allow the characters to tell me about themselves and direct the action, I always find that their past is as much a part of the story as what takes place in the present. After you chat about what events in Allison's history have shaped her into who she is—and any other characters who pique your interest—consider yourself. Are there specific turning points in your story that changed your direction, for better or for worse? How much of that effect is due to the events themselves and how much to our attitudes and reactions to them?

¤ Point of view is essential in a novel too. Consider these POV issues:

- Allison takes some pretty radical steps to obey the God who's finally telling her what to do with Jesus. Be one of the Wednesday Night Watchdogs for a few minutes and talk about whether everybody's called to that kind of drastic commitment. If not, how far could you go outside the pew?

- Can you see Troy Irwin's point at all? How about The Reverend Garry Howard's?

- Do you think Allison was right to basically leave the church? Do you think she'll go back? Does she need to?

¤ I like to think about what readers will think about after they close the book for the last time.

- It looks like Allison has fallen in love with Chief. What kinds of problems might that create for her? Does this lead you to wonder what really makes a person a Christian?

- I don't think any of us knows what we'd be willing to sacrifice for God if he Nudged us the way he did Allison. After you discuss what she gave up and risked (and gained) you might want to ponder what you

personally have sacrificed to follow Christ, or what
you've refused to for really good reasons, or what you
might have to if …

- Do you want to ride a Harley now?

About Magdalene

My inspiration for Allison's Sacrament House comes from a real
ministry in Nashville, Tennessee, called Magdalene. Founded in
1997, Magdalene is a two-year residential community for women
with a history of prostitution and drug addiction. As the women say
in their mission statement, "We stand in solidarity with women who
are recovering from sexual abuse, violence, and life on the streets."

At no cost to them, Magdalene offers women a safe, disciplined,
and compassionate community paid for by gifts from individuals and
private grants. The ministry is also supported by Thistle Farms, a nonprofit business operated by the women who create handmade natural
bath and body products. "Our dream," they say, "is that people will
come to see Thistle Farms as a humble but powerful business synony-
mous with women's freedom."

While the fictional Sacrament House in *The Reluctant Prophet*
is not precisely patterned after this living, breathing ministry, I hope
that it sends the same message: the message of Christ Jesus.

To learn more about Magdalene, including how you can help
financially support it, visit www.thistlefarms.org/donate.html.

WANT MORE TIME WITH NANCY RUE?

 **NANCY RUE**, author of over one hundred titles for teens, tweens, and adults, has sold over one million books. But she is also in demand as a speaker, workshop teacher, and retreat leader for all three age groups. For more information on booking Nancy for events, and for a more in-depth study of *The Reluctant Prophet* and her other novels, visit www.NancyRue.com or email her at nnrue@att.net.